A HAND FOR AN EYE

ISBNs:
979-8-9902205-2-2 (eBook)
979-8-9902205-3-9 (paperback)

A HAND FOR AN EYE

Haydn Boyce

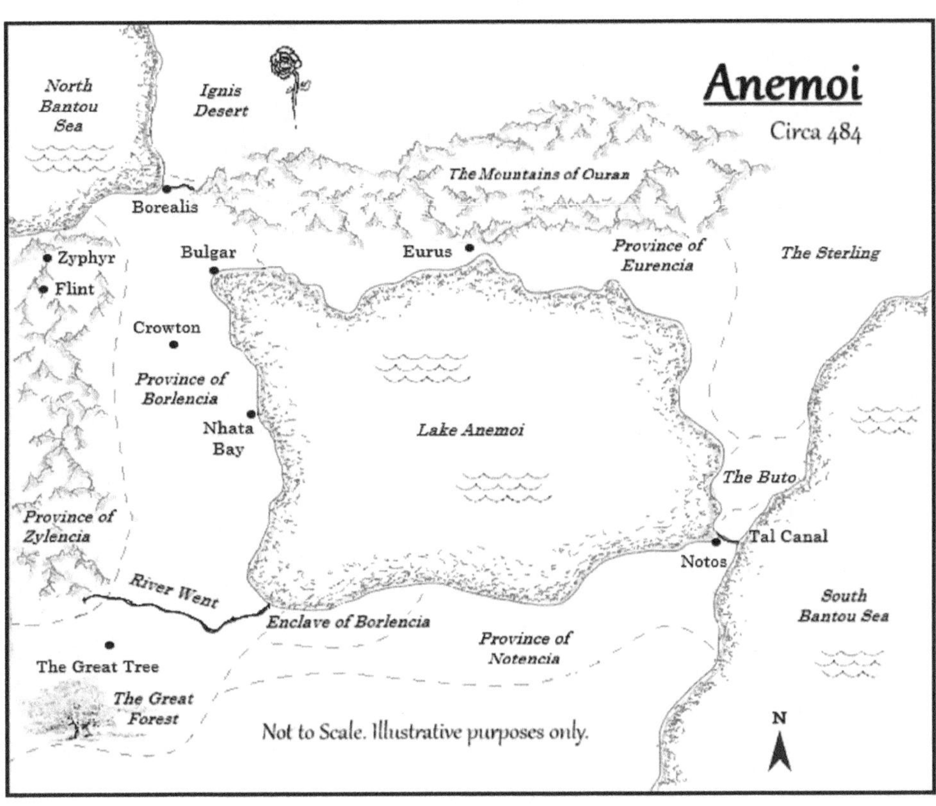

North Bantou Sea
Ignis Desert
Anemoi
Circa 484
The Mountains of Ouran
Borealis
Zyphyr
Bulgar
Eurus
Province of Eurencia
The Sterling
Flint
Crowton
Province of Borlencia
Lake Anemoi
Nhata Bay
The Buto
Province of Zylencia
Tal Canal
Notos
River Went
South Bantou Sea
Enclave of Borlencia
Province of Notencia
The Great Tree
The Great Forest
Not to Scale. Illustrative purposes only.
N

CHAPTER 1

Xander stopped scratching her right hand and clenched both fists in frustration at the gnawing itch seemingly clawing through her flesh. Dead skin marked the fingernails on her left hand, and raw scratches traced across her right like lightning from the clouds above.

Desperate for reprieve, she peered across the quaint field of wheat she had happened across in search of a river or well. Forest enveloped the acreage along three of its edges, and a stone wall bordered the fourth, which overlooked a rolling landscape of hills covered in trees and fields. The morning sun had already begun to poke its head over this serene horizon, warming the air and the ground and relieving the frigid winter night of its biting chill.

To one corner of the farm stood a cute cottage that she couldn't recall being there only moments before. A transgression common in sleepy minds preoccupied with pain or irritation. She trudged over to it at a clumsy stroll, careful not to trip on the frozen divots and clumps of hard ground underfoot.

The itch had grown into a blistering pain by the time she reached the cottage, so much so that all semblance of courtesy or wariness had become absent from thought. Like a blundering fool, she practically slammed the door open and barged inside, forgetting to announce her presence or take her shoes off as she scrambled into the building's tidy kitchen. She immediately made for the countertop where a bucket stood beside a tray of clean dishes. Inside the bucket was water, much to her relief.

About to thrust her hand into the cool transparent liquid, a light aromatic scent tickled her nose, sending a shiver down her back. Her gaze craned towards the pantry in the corner of the room, and she shuffled over and stepped into the spacious affair. Eyes scouring the shelves lined with vegetables, herbs, and spices, she locked on to a bundle of wrinkly green leaves.

"Peppermint," she uttered through gritted teeth and grabbed the bundle with her left hand.

She bounded back to the countertop and thrust her right hand into the water for temporary relief of the invisible burn that had seemingly enveloped her entire forearm. Even with her hand submerged in the cool liquid, it wasn't enough to fully subdue the unbearable pain that had arisen from nowhere.

With her right hand submerged, she grabbed a spoon from the tray using her left and began the arduous process of mincing the leaves to release the plant's valuable oil. Minutes passed, and she could see the sun already eager to ascend the height of the cottage window. Finally, content with the quantity of oil recovered, she withdrew her right hand, dried it, and then rubbed the soothing substance over her skin. The cooling effect was instantaneous, and though not completely effective at ridding her of the irritation, it was enough to calm her nerves.

She breathed relief and slumped onto the cold kitchen tiles in a tired heap. Head resting against the countertop, her heavy eyelids began to slide down, massaging the bloodshot membrane underneath. But just as sleep seemed all but certain in that awkward position, a young girl's voice pierced the silent void of the cottage.

Whoever it was, they sang without regard for rhythm or pitch, blaring away with the uncontained joy of those that had not yet tasted the bitterness of reality. Curious to seek out this disturber of the peace, Xander pulled herself up and peered through the cottage window towards the rolling landscape.

It was a girl in a dress dancing on the stone wall with her back to the cottage—a strange dance under the glowing stare of the sun. Left leg up, right leg up, marching back and then forth, all the while screaming at the top of her lungs. Xander left the cottage through the door she had entered and began towards the oblivious girl dancing for the fiery ball climbing from the carpet of trees.

An involuntary smile took Xander as she approached, the painful irritation in her arm almost forgotten. The girl on the stone wall moved with exaggerated silliness, a recital at one with the unintelligible words spilling from her mouth.

Metres from the wall, Xander stopped, but before she could greet or speak, the girl also stopped. The girl didn't turn around as a string of quietly muttered words crept from her hidden mouth.

"I'm—" Xander began, but again the girl spoke, cutting her off. "I can't hear you," she said, edging closer. Again, the girl spoke. "Sorry, what? Let me come up," Xander said, and she reached a hand to the wall.

"An eye for a hand, a hand for an eye."

Xander stopped as a tingle shot down her spine, and a wave of goosebumps enveloped her right arm. "What does that mean?" she said, both confused and unnerved.

"An eye for a hand, a hand for an eye."

"I...I don't know—"

The girl slowly turned around and revealed her face. Xander gaped in horror at the fleshy canvas deprived of its eyes. Breath caught in her throat, Xander stumbled backwards, and landed on the hard, frosty ground with a thud, crushing her hand in the process.

▲ ▲ ▲

Decembrix 19, 484; western fringe of the River Went, where the Great Forest meets the Hunter's Passage; present day—"Dreaming again, kiddo?"

Xander opened a groggy eye, only to be greeted by the thick, luscious canopy of the Great Forest's northern frontier. "More like a nightmare," she said, stretching her arms and back.

Suddenly recalling her dream, she reached for her right arm and breathed relief at the untainted skin and absence of searing pain. Though her arm was still a tad sore from her encounter with the vine lurking at the bottom of the Great Tree, her strength and flexibility had returned in full. She was wearing her mother's green jacket and a scarf for warmth, and her green eyes and light-brown cheeks carried a healthy glow despite the rough sleeping.

Ricard was on the other side of their small camp, rolling up his bed, and Aes was sitting beside the last glowing embers of their midnight fire. Unlike Xander, Ricard's ruffled hair and unkept beard had left him with a slightly haggard appearance.

Even though the forest was temperate and a tad humid, Xander could feel the wisps of the cool air eager to penetrate the tree line from the north. "Where's Aika?" she asked.

Ricard stopped what he was doing and stood straight. He nodded his head in the direction of the tree line.

"Still?" Xander said worriedly.

"Since before sunup."

"I'll go and speak to her."

"Good luck."

Xander trudged through the colourful weeds and bramble of the forest floor towards the tree line, where the frigid tundra of the Hunter's Passage stared bleakly from the other side. She could see Aika perched on the very edge of the River Went, peering into the distance.

"You okay?" Xander asked as she came up beside her friend.

"Define okay," Aika retorted and turned to her with a nervous grin. In the morning light, Aika's pale skin and wild, dark hair greatly accentuated the mystery of her deep-blue eyes. "I can't remember the last time I stepped out of the forest."

"Not much different to staring up from a clearing into the sky, don't you think? Just a bit vaster."

Aika lifted an unamused eyebrow. "Slightly different, don't you think?"

Xander chuckled. "Maybe a bit. But you'll be okay. Just got to remember you're not going to be picked off by a giant eagle or sucked up into the sky."

"Xander…" She laughed and turned towards the camp. "Come on, let's finish packing before Ricard has a fit. Who would've thought a man so prone to having a good time could be so—"

"Punctual?"

"You said it, not me."

CHAPTER 2

Augustx 27, 484; Nhata Bay, province of Borlencia; sixteen and a half weeks earlier—Joseph pulled back from the window of Evia's cottage. The humidity was heavy that afternoon, and swarms of insects ravaged the uncovered skin. Both were the uncomfortable product of the late-summer thunderstorms drifting from the south over the prior fortnight, and to the locals the irritable sensation was more nuisance than the Zylencians occupying the town.

"We must leave tonight." A thin film of grease covered Joseph's tanned skin, and his black hair was sleeked back with sweat.

"Evia's not ready," Dogner said. His nose and cheeks were flustered by the heat, and watery beads clung to his barren scalp. "I'm not ready. My wife, my brats. I'll not just leave them, lad."

Joseph looked at the big man and the prone woman who had slipped back into darkness several days earlier.

"It's now or never, Dogner. You can do more for your family without the shackles and with your life intact."

"Aye, and you said—"

"Forget what I said. The situation's changed. My contact told me the forces north of here, not more than an hour's ride, have begun to slaughter any that could pose a threat and relocate the rest to Zyphyr."

"My family!" the big man shouted.

"Not just your family. Etlinga will follow soon after Nhata, and we don't have the time or the means to get them out, let alone your family, Dogner. Now's not the time."

Dogner wrestled with indecision, both guilt and distress written across his demeanour. It was only by chance that Joseph had been able to convince the captain of the guard—an old acquaintance of his—that the big man was not only harmless but also a sorely needed helping hand for the ailing woman. Still, Joseph didn't doubt that Dogner would be top of the list if and when it came to the executions. Neither he nor the captain could change that after the men he had bloodied.

Dogner grimaced. "When do we leave?"

"Two after midnight."

"We can't move her."

"And yet we're without choice. I doubt it's by chance that they watch her health and whereabouts so closely. They must know her history."

"How, then, do you s'pose we'll get her out?"

"Distraction, a favour, and maybe a bit of blood." Joseph pulled a wicked-looking war hammer from a sack under the bed. He tossed it to Dogner, and an equally wicked grin took the man.

"You shouldn't have."

"Heard you have a soft spot for them, so why not reacquaint you with one I hold dear?"

"She's a beauty. Never thought I'd hold one again, mind you."

"No?"

"For a while I thought maybe, even after the hype of Borealis and the appearance of the girl, I'd pass of old age and boredom with the brats fighting over the scraps." He admired the weapon of yesteryear. "How I dreaded it! And yet, how much I have to lose now…and you, Joseph. You have no obligation to Evia. Why risk the limb?"

"She's a convincing woman and…"

"You care for her and the girl. Ha! I get it, lad. They grow on ya. Come on, then. What's this plan of yours?"

▲ ▲ ▲

That evening—"They're late," Dogner said nervously from the door.

"They'll come," Joseph responded, though he failed to hide his worry.

Gunshots rang out from the north of the village, followed by the eruption of alarmed commotion as the occupying soldiers came to. More explosions emanated from the south and then voices from just outside the cottage.

"How many guys you got working this job, lad?" Dogner asked sternly.

"Just the two, plus the captain. And they're boys, not men."

"You'd risk the lives of wee boys for this?"

"They're in no danger."

The door opened. On the floor lay one guard, battered and bruised, and the captain stood beside him, apprehension etched into his brow. "The road to the west's alright. You've only got a couple minutes though, so better get moving."

Joseph shook the man's hand. "Appreciate it."

"Least I can do. Who would've thought we'd meet again under such circumstances? Sorry I can't do more, but I've got my own skin to think about."

Dogner hefted Evia's slumped form and then strode past the captain, absent the same gratefulness Joseph had shown.

"You'd better make it look convincing," the captain said hesitantly.

"You sure you don't want me to help?" Dogner asked mischievously.

"I'm sure," Joseph said and then knocked the captain unconscious with two swings of his fist.

"Should've let me do it. He would've been out with one," the big man said as they passed the garden.

Except for a single guard on the road west to Etlinga, their departure from the village was without confrontation. Still, resigned to animal trails and the bush, and wary of the lone rustle or whisper that could carry on the wind and alert others to their presence, their progress was slow and largely devoid of conversation. It was only when the purple sky overhead opened to release the torrent of pent-up humidity that more than a mumble was uttered between them.

"This way," Joseph said as the downpour started to matt their hair and wet their clothes. They were in the thick of the woods somewhere between Nhata and Etlinga, but he knew the area well. Cautiously, he led them to a nearby oak to shelter from the rain.

A wooded giant birthed long before his childhood, he was well acquainted with the ancient resident and felt a sliver of peace under its canopy as Dogner rested Evia against its rough bark. Resigned that she was as comfortable as could be, the pair slumped down, one on each side of her. Gently, Dogner rested Evia's head against his shoulder and began to dry her cheeks with a patch of his sleeve not completely sodden.

Taking in the heavy rain as it pelted the forest around them, Joseph exhaled a prolonged breath of sadness. "It'll not be the same after this."

Dogner looked at him. "It's not been the same since that army sacked Borealis a decade ago."

Joseph's gaze remained distant as Dogner stopped drying Evia and let his hands rest. "There was still some semblance of normality down here, even after the attack. We were just far enough removed to have not lost it all in the wake of Borealis's destruction. But now even that's gone."

"Aye, but we also knew that'd be the case as soon as you learned of the recent movements on the walls of Borealis and of the plights facing the provinces in the east."

Joseph turned to Dogner. His concern was visible through the dark. "Will it be too much?"

"If it was just the Zylencians sacking our towns, then I'd rest easy. But the movement on the walls of Borealis is something else altogether. And this new, unknown enemy on Eurencia's eastern border that your network's informed you of—you really think the Eurencians will be in any position to intervene here? And what of the corruption that's apparently taken the government in Notencia to the point of dysfunction? Can't imagine they'll be in any shape to help if it's as bad as you're hearing."

Joseph softly knocked the back of his head against the trunk as he peered back into the forest. He had considered the same, as had Evia, and it had been frightening enough to rip the sanctity of sleep from his routine.

"Evia was right in what she told you," Dogner continued. "This is an existential threat. We'll need every tool we can get our hands on." He took in the man that had become a close friend, and Joseph returned the gaze. "Do I think Anemoi will come out the other side? I reckon yes, but I don't think there's much chance of that happening with everything intact. I'd have to be a fool to think otherwise."

But for the patter of the rain, there was a sullen silence as both men took in the weary fatigue in each other's features. Even with their ordinary minds, they could feel each other's angst. Their fear of loss was palpable.

Dogner grunted, disturbing the stillness. "And yet, that doesn't mean we won't try."

Joseph nodded and slowly peered back into the dark. He desperately hoped those dear to them would make it through the approaching storm dry and unharmed. But deep down, he felt it unlikely.

They sat quietly under the tree for another hour until the rain subsided, leaving the earthy scent of damp plants and soil to permeate through the undergrowth. Traversing the soggy ground at no greater pace than before the storm, it wasn't until the morning sun touched mid-mast that they reached the boundary of Etlinga. It was about this time that Evia regained consciousness, but what should have been a moment of rejoice was unsurprisingly marred by sadness, regret, and anger for those left behind as the pair answered Evia's questions. Despite the days spent in slumber, her mind was sharp and absent the fog synonymous with prolonged sleep. And naturally, she wanted to know what had happened in her absence.

Questions answered, Joseph left Dogner and Evia resting a little way off from the village's line of sight, and he crept as close to the boundary as daylight would permit him. Through the tree line, he could narrowly make out the small village that was his home. It was eerily quiet but not empty. A dozen Zylencian soldiers patrolled the quaint streets and the boundary, and another dozen sat in the village centre sifting through stolen wares. If his family was in there, he wouldn't be able to reach them without serious risk to himself and the others. With a lump in his throat, he crept back into the woods.

"Leave me be," Evia demanded as Dogner attempted to steady her against a sturdy tree. "It won't do us any good if I'm confined to your arms." Her face was gaunt and her skin pale, but she had managed to stand unaided. "Plus, I'm sure you could do with the break."

"Nonsense, woman," Dogner protested. "I've barely broken a sweat since we left."

"Not from what I've seen," Joseph said, torn between Evia's fragility and the need to keep the big man strong. "Maybe we should pay Evia some heed."

"Well, ya need your sight checked, lad. Nothing but endurance and strength glowing from these arms."

"When you're quite done," Evia said weakly, her posture one of exhaustion. "What of Etlinga, Joseph? What did you see?"

"We'll not be getting any closer than the tree line, not without discovery."

"That's unfortunate. But we will get your family to safety. And yours, Dogner. Every person along the lakeshore that still lives, we'll make it our priority to rescue as many of them as we can." She spoke with a confidence that could only come from someone that had seen it all and then some.

Joseph nodded, though the inspired hope was short-lived. "Are you sure you don't want to rest some more?"

She pushed herself from the tree and stabilised herself. Dogner and

Joseph instinctively reached out their hands to steady her, but she stayed them with a flash of her palm. "I've rested enough. This is the only way I'm going to rebuild my strength," she said and began to amble along.

CHAPTER 3

Augustx 30, 484; the countryside of Borlencia—"Our chances?" Joseph asked the scruffy farmer leaning on his shovel at the edge of one of his fields.

"Slim if you ask me, but then, what do I know? I'm just a farmer. Perhaps you should look for yourself."

"Thanks for your time, and best of luck with the crop if I don't return."

The man nodded, and Joseph disappeared into the woods.

"A dozen women and children and five guards," Joseph said to Dogner, who had been watching from the bushes.

"That's an easy handle."

"Two on horseback," he added. "There's a risk one of those two will be gone before we can get them all."

"Then we'll hit them first."

"And what then?" Joseph asked. "Can't take the prisoners with us, and if we leave them, they'll probably be recaptured in no time. Not to mention we'll bring a storm down on our heads."

"Can't leave them, lad. Next lot could be our own. And this isn't Nhata with the hangman's noose running against us. We have the chance to do something here."

Joseph stared into the bush, lost in contemplation. "We need to find a way to get them to one of the other provinces, away from the province of Zylencia and Erzse's armies, maybe even out of Anemoi."

"It's a sound idea and one we can use again when it's our own kin we're saving."

"It won't be without its risks."

"Aye, but better than leaving them helpless to the whims of the witch and her unnatural...*yearning* for young girls."

"The whispers of Erzse's tastes certainly don't leave much room for comfort."

"It's been more than just the odd whispering over the years, Joseph. Not a chance I'll let any from Nhata come to the same fate. I'd rather they went at my own hands than hers, my own lot included."

Joseph nodded. "Come, let's talk to my farmer friend and then suss the soldiers' positioning out. Can then return to Evia. We've left her long enough."

The farmer was where Joseph had left him, leaning on his shovel, admiring his crop. Their exchange was far from fleeting, but it was highly productive. Content with the conclusion, Joseph and Dogner crept into the settlement to watch the soldiers and their movements. For two hours they spied and learned, returning to the abandoned shed where Evia rested only once they were comfortable that they had enough information to go on. A mile from the road, the shed was blanketed by overgrown weeds and a thick layer of moss, and it provided much-needed shelter from the coming storm.

"They're not from Nhata, but neither of us think it fair to leave them to this fate," Joseph said, taking a seat in the corner.

"What do you suggest?" Evia asked. She was sitting on a thick blanket, and her face was still gaunt.

"There're five guards, two on horseback, but it looks like they've decided to hole up at the local inn for the night, presumably with the prisoners in the cellar."

"There's barely half a dozen houses, and they have an inn?" she said, surprised.

"Aye, quaint little one with beer," Dogner said longingly.

"Either way, they'll put up for the night with maybe one on guard," Joseph said. "That'll be our opportunity."

"Then what?" she asked sternly.

"Well, whilst I'd prefer not to cut their throats, I'd much prefer not to have five irate soldiers on the hunt for their escaped charge, if that's quite alright."

"Some things can't be helped," she said with regret. "But that was only part of my question. What will we do once we've released a dozen fugitives from their shackles? Not so easy to just disappear into the forest with that many mouths, and I fear no place west of the lake can be considered safe with Erzse's sights intent on dominion."

"With a bit of convincing, our farmer friend agreed to take them on as farmhands for a fortnight, working several fields in the next town over. 'Imported' labour from a farming community in the northeast. It'll give us the guise to move them along when the time is right."

"How much?" she asked.

"Goodness of his heart."

"Very well."

"When we reach Crowton, I'll arrange the transport," Joseph added.

"And you don't think the vermin will just apprehend the lot on the road east?" Dogner frowned, still somewhat doubtful.

"Unlikely. Erzse's focus hasn't extended beyond the borders of eastern Borlencia. She probably doesn't wish to drag the two eastern provinces into the fray at this point. Providing the group sticks to their story, they'll be okay. Plus, I'll have them attached to the appropriate trade group. Even see if I can hook them up with residency papers from one of the towns not on Erzse's bad books."

CHAPTER 4

Decembrix 19, 484; ten kilometres north of the Great Forest, the Hunter's Passage, province of Zylencia—Xander tightened her jacket to protect from the chill as she craned her head up from the rocky flats underfoot to the clear sky overhead. A single eagle hovered alone, caught on an unseen airstream, a tiny speck amidst the vast ocean of light with no bottom. It was a somewhat refreshing contrast to the dense woodlands that perpetually fought to block light and sight.

"Beautiful, isn't it?" Ricard said of the bird. Happy for the rest, he was leaning against Aes as they waited for Aika to return from her reconnaissance mission. Unsurprisingly, the hefty stag was wholly unbothered by the man's weight. "Of course, doubt it's as magnificent as the one that gifted you your blade."

Xander peered to the west where a mountain range blocked the horizon for as far north as the eye could see and then back to the eagle that likely called the mountains home. "What do you suppose it's hunting?"

"Mice. Rabbits, maybe. The vegetation's sparse. Not going to be much around here, but then, a few small meals like that would suffice for the creature." He lifted his arm and stretched it, an awkward affair with his axe and kit bound to him.

"How is it?"

"Stiff. The stiches may have come out, but it still hurts like nobody's business. Truth be told, I'm a tad worried Gladis's mushrooms will run out before the pain's fully gone."

Aes looked at Xander, and she chuckled.

Ricard laughed. "Not you too? I've not got a problem."

"I didn't say anything."

"No, but clearly the stag did. Anyway, Aika's said enough for the lot of you. You know, not all of us are—how old did you say you were again?"

"Hey! You know I'm seventeen."

"Right, which means you've got the healing powers of a goddess."

The three of them abruptly turned around to see Aika appear from behind a wall of scraggly, thorned bushes.

"The road ahead is blocked," she panted.

"How many?" Ricard queried.

"Lots! And it's not just the one blockade. I skirted around and counted another three along the stretch of road I could see. Plus, patrols rummage the surrounding shrub. We'll have to continue off the road."

"Still risky. We're no longer in the forest, so there's just not the same cover."

"And if we wait for night?" Xander asked.

"It'll be hard going, I reckon," Ricard replied. "But I don't see what choice we have."

"I saw a path nearby," Aika added. "It's hidden but veers off towards the mountains. No blockades and no patrols."

Xander peered west across the expanse of rocky ground to the horizon and then took out the map. "It's marked. And there are settlements up there. One of the other bearers must've taken the route."

"The Black Mountains," Ricard began. "Though some would rather liken them to hills when you consider the ragged mountains in the north. Still, full of miners and mountain folk. A rough lot, but I'm sure friendly enough."

"We can get to Zyphyr if we follow the trails, but—" Xander looked at Aes. "To take the mountains will take us even farther from where you felt Evia when we connected with her in the Great Forest."

"That was nearly two months ago." Aika spoke up. "She could be halfway across Anemoi by now."

"Agreed. And it'll probably be easier to avoid prying eyes up there, kiddo," Ricard said.

Xander stared at the map, then at the horizon. She swallowed her anxiety.

The path they took was little more than an animal trail as it weaved in and out of the sparse shrubbery and rocky crags of the steppe. The air was somewhat drier than the humidity and warmth of the forest, and Aika seemed perpetually ill at ease without the cover of the trees.

"How you managing, Princess?" Ricard grinned as they set up for the night within a shallow depression that was provided additional cover by an unwieldy bush to the rear and several boulders to the sides.

"I'll survive, old man. And you? You're looking a bit flustered after the exertion. Not sure how you'll manage once we hit the slopes."

"Hadn't realised the Great Forest afforded you much opportunity to experience little more than the odd slope. I, on the other hand, am from sturdy mountain stock and will get my mountain legs and lungs back in no time."

Aika didn't retort. She was too tired to jest and set back to unrolling her mat.

His jibe wasn't wrong, though. Xander could tell Aika felt exposed under the bare twilight sky, the weight of the cosmos seemingly on her shoulders without much possibility of refuge on the barren plains.

"My father didn't tell me much about when you met," Xander said to Ricard as she snuggled against the warmth of Aes. "Only that you met by chance in the mountains you called home."

"Yep, that much is true. Your father was a runaway, same as I would become, though I didn't know it at the time, and we first butted heads in the cosy mountain village I called home. A place where the grass always grew true, goats and chickens and dogs littered the grounds, and the seasons seemed content to split between mild winter and brisk springs. It was a village of little superstition, unlike what one might expect in remote backcountry, and instead was characterized by punctuality and hard work. And oh, how I loathed it."

"What was it called?"

"I forget," Ricard said, expression lost in recollection.

"Was it in Anemoi?"

"Not even close."

"He said you were a mischievous bugger, and you got him into trouble after you'd barely met."

He chortled. "Is that so? Well, it's not quite how I recall, but then, it was a very long time ago, neither of us much older than you two are now."

"You're right. That's not a few summers ago," Aika said, and he laughed.

"Right you are. Anyway, your father had it in mind to be an adventurer and a mender of wrongs, which was beyond laughable at the time, given he looked the half-starved runt of the litter when I first met him. Nonetheless, he coaxed me into our first quest, as he liked to put it, and we sought out a legendary bandit by the name of Threit. A scoundrel and fiend who had terrorized the mountain villages for years."

"How so? I would've thought bandits common in the backcountry," Xander said.

"Well, true to form, he thieved our animals and grains and, on the odd occasion, hijacked our routes…but that's not why we thought him a fiend, no. It was the fact that he also robbed our graveyards."

"What?" Aika spat in disgust.

"Exactly. It was not uncommon to find deceased villagers robbed of their final possessions or even the odd limb gnawed to the bone."

Xander grimaced. "That's revolting. So not just a thief but a cannibal also."

"Though that was the consensus, I think the last part is open to debate," Ricard said. "There's a lot of scavengers in the mountain territories—wolves and vultures and other beasts that wouldn't blink twice at the opportunity to feast on a half-decomposed corpse."

"Still, how disrespectful."

"Without a doubt."

"I assume you found the bandit?" Xander asked.

"We did…"

"And?"

"We killed him."

Xander's expression dropped, shocked and baffled as she was by the uncharacteristic action of her father. "No trial?"

"If you'd seen what we had, I don't doubt you'd have done the same. I suspect it was those early years and the contradictory nature of our actions in the guise of noble causes that influenced your father's policies and arguments in favour of fair trials when he entered politics. The burden of unplaced guilt grew too great."

"Do you think that was part of the reason why he let Damain live?" she asked solemnly, recalling the havoc Damain—the Dragon King—and the bugs unleashed on the Great Forest.

"Part of it, maybe. But killing Damain's brat certainly left its mark. Whichever way you look at it, Threit's death, and Damain's survival for that matter, were defining moments in both our lives. Both were villains deserving of death. One summarily executed and the other left to live."

Silence abounded but for the chirp of the crickets and the rustle of the shrubs.

"So then, are you going to tell us how you got him into trouble?" Xander asked, still eager for more.

"Like I said, not how I recall it. I used to enjoy trapping. Meat was scarce at times, for we couldn't always rely on the caravans nor eat our livestock without depriving ourselves down the road. So I used to set traps to catch wild mountain goats, hares, and other game. Funnily enough, that's how I met your father. He was thieving one of my traps."

"And you apprehended him?"

"I wanted to, but the man was so damn skinny I let him have the catch on the condition that he help with some chores. Anyway, during those chores it came up about Threit and how he was a nuisance and a fiend, and your father suggested we catch him using one of my traps."

"Let me guess—caught the wrong person?"

"That we did. The chief's son, in fact. Left quite the bruising on the boy, and even though we rid the community of the fiend not too long afterwards, the chief couldn't forgive me, and he certainly had it in for Carolus. Made a point of making both our lives miserable."

"So you decided to leave?"

"Yep, pretty much. And I haven't looked back since."

Several howls echoed across the plain, and both Aes and Aika started up.

"Nothing to worry about. They're a way off," Ricard said nonchalantly.

"What is it?" Aika asked nervously.

"Coyotes probably. Anyway, you two get some shut-eye. I'll take first watch. Don't want no bandits getting the best of us whilst we're asleep now, do we?"

"Bandits? Here? Can't imagine why anybody would want to linger in a place too cold for life to grow," Aika muttered.

▲ ▲ ▲

Xander woke with a start. From where she lay, she took in a sliver of the barren landscape below that carried a purple tinge under the early-morning light. The air was cool, but she found warmth from Aes on one side and Aika on the other, the girl having quietly sought heat and comfort during the brisk night.

24

She carefully climbed from between them and walked to the invisible edge of the camp. Not far from Aes and Aika lay Ricard on the hard rock, snoring a storm. Clearly the fatigue of the hike had been too much for him.

Not a cloud blessed the glimmer of the morning sky, and from her vantage point, she could just make out the frontier of the Great Forest where the western fringe of the River Went abruptly collided with the purple glow of the Hunter's Passage, a thin strip of steppe that hugged the shoulder of the Black Mountains in the west and ran parallel to the rich plains and woodlands of Lake Anemoi and the valley to the east. To the passage's south sat the Great Forest and, at its northern peak, Borealis and the vast desert plains. But the steppe was not completely contained, for it and the plains curved with the lake and stretched across the northern edge of Anemoi from Borealis in the northwest to Eurus in the east, and on its shoulders to the north, the Ouran Mountains. No known climber had ever defeated their fearsome snowy peaks, but legend told a contradictory tale of an ancient kingdom that once adorned the most dangerous looking of the cloud-makers, as some referred to the loftiest of the lofty peaks.

"Xander."

She turned, startled, to the voice she did not recognise and the tall silhouette whose clothes and features she could not make out.

"Who are you?" she stammered, aware she was without her blade.

"You must not continue down this path. It'll be the death of you and your friends. You must turn back," the man behind the shroud warned.

"Who are you, and what do you mean, 'turn back'? From the Black Mountains?"

"The mountains that take you to Erzse and beyond. It's a battle that cannot be won by you alone."

She held her surprise in check—or at least she thought she did—from this stranger in the steppe. "But I'm not alone."

"Please, Xander, I implore you."

"How do you know who I am and where I go?"

But for Ricard's continued snore, the air was silent, and still she could not make out the figure.

"You've grown into a finer woman than I could ever have imagined, and yet I still see the young girl I once knew," the figure said after several moments.

Confusion took her at the remark. "Hemish?" she uttered her friend's name. For who else, other than the dead, could make such an observation?

Before she could reach out and grab it, the silhouette turned and vanished, stirring in her the same empty loss she had felt in the wake of her friend's departure from Nhata Bay nearly two years prior.

"Who are you calling Hemish?" Ricard said, half asleep. "You didn't forget my name again, did you? Told you to keep away from the violet ones with yellow dots," he muttered and slumped back to the ground, leaving her unsure if he ever really woke.

"What in Anemoi just happened?" she spoke softly. She peered past where the figure had stood and to the steep slopes of the mountains still more than two days' walk away.

Fatigue began to worm its way into her, an unnatural cloud of exhaustion, but just as she sought to lay her head and find slumber, a rustle from the bush to the rear of the camp drew her gaze. She stared at it for a brief moment, expecting to see a rabbit or a mouse emerge from its shadow, but nothing appeared. She shrugged and looked to her bed, its allure too much. About to make for it, she stopped and peered back to the bush.

An uncomfortable feeling suddenly washed over her. Cautious of her movements, she leant forward ever so slightly, her eyes piercing into the obscured shrub. An unnerving shiver traversed her spine, and she inadvertently glanced to the others just as Aes stirred from sleep. Without hesitation, Aes subtly peered across the bush and the boulders, then whispered into Xander's mind.

Her eyes widened as a single word involuntarily escaped her breath. "Wolves."

Another rustle came from the shrub, but neither Xander nor Aes waited in idle anticipation.

"Wolves!" Xander screamed as she rushed to her bed and pulled out her blade.

She turned to see three of the hefty grey-and-blue beasts emerge from cover as Aika and Ricard scrambled to their feet, weapons drawn. The creatures were half the size of Aes, their eyes were dark yellow, and their fur was long and shaggy. Aes, determined to keep the massive predators in sight, backed up to the others with his lopsided antlers lowered.

"Blue wolves," Ricard muttered warily. "Thought they'd been driven from Anemoi centuries ago."

"It's just the three, if we—" Aika had begun when Aes abruptly turned to the side of the camp facing downslope.

"What is it?" Ricard asked nervously, unwilling to turn and look for himself.

Xander glanced over and tensed at the sight of two more of the beasts stalking towards them. None growled or bared their fangs, but the intent was clear.

"Well? Don't keep me waiting!" the big man spluttered.

"Five," Xander said.

"What?"

"There's five in total."

"Five," he uttered. "Aika, how many do you reckon you can fell before they reach us?"

"Their hides look thick," she responded.

"Which means?"

"We'll be lucky if I can down one before they get to us."

A series of howls erupted from a short distance off to the north, putting them all on edge.

"Damn it!" Ricard spat. "We've no choice. We've got to make the first move, or there'll be more of the bastards on top of—"

Aes pounced into a sprint and rushed past the two newly emerged wolves and then down the rocky slope. Not a moment later, spurred by nature's instinct, the pack of five bolted after him, determined to catch the largest of their prey. Aika launched two arrows into the one on the rear as it disappeared over the crest of the depression, causing it to yowl in pain as it raced on.

"Aes!" Xander shouted.

Ricard grabbed her arm. "He's buying us time. Pack your kit, and let's get a move on before those others catch up."

All three of them fumbled as they hastily packed the camp, the danger of the situation not lost on them. And though instinct begged for them to just run, it wasn't an option to leave without their gear, for the harsh elements of the steppe were lethal to those unprepared.

With their sacks packed, Ricard pointed southwest, where the steep gradient was marked by large, round boulders and sporadic tufts of coarse grass. "We need to stay downwind."

The other two nodded, and the trio quickly left the path, with Ricard in the lead and Xander on the rear. Wary of the slightest sounds and deviations in wind direction, they pushed on through the burn of their calves and their worry for Aes. But it wasn't just the exertion of the climb taking its toll.

The same mental fatigue that had enveloped Xander in the moments after her visitor disappeared had returned with a vengeance, dulling her senses and interrupting her thoughts. Thirty minutes along, she abruptly dropped to a knee and put her palm to her aching forehead. She looked up through fuzzy eyes to the other two as they continued on, unaware she had stopped.

Xander shook her head of its growing dizziness and opened her mouth to call to them. A weak croak was all she could manage, not enough to catch their attention even with the aid of the wind. Again, she shook her head of its grogginess, but this time, when she looked up, she was greeted only by the bare terrain of the slope.

"Oh no!"

She forced herself up and pushed one leg in front of the other, determined to wave them down before they lost her. With much effort, she stumbled past the boulder they had disappeared behind, only to be greeted by an empty continuation of the difficult slope.

"Aika! Ricard!" she called again through hoarse breaths, though every attempt at raising her voice only worsened the sharp pain in her head.

Again she dropped to her knees, just as a chorus of piercing howls carried on the wind from behind her. Panic reared through her, and she frantically clutched a tuft of grass and tried to pull herself up. The grass ripped and she fell backwards, landing with a thump on a boulder. She gritted her teeth and held the impulse to cry out.

Another howl emanated from behind, this time much closer. She swore under her breath and grabbed her blade, determined to fight off the impeding offensive for as long as her friends needed in order to find her. But as she awkwardly positioned herself to counter the onslaught, she locked on to a small burrow dug under the boulder to her side.

There was no telling how deep it was, or where it led, but it was surely narrow enough to keep her hunters at bay. With the last of her dissipating energy, she crawled up to it, got onto her belly, and threw her kit and blade in. Leaving her shield behind, with much regret, she then pushed herself into the hole's muddy entrance. Accompanied by the strong earthy odour of its narrow walls, she clambered into the dark, pushing and pulling down the perfectly straight hole.

Moments later, the muffled yaps of the wolves at the burrow's entrance reached her. She could sense their hesitation to pursue, no doubt the fit of the tunnel too tight for their bulky frames. Still, unwilling to linger, she burrowed deeper into the abyss until she came upon a bend illuminated by faint natural light.

She rounded it and gasped at the massive cavern adjoined to the tunnel. Breaching near to the cavern's ceiling, she had a view of the entire chamber whose light source was a single, sizeable opening in the rocky roof overhead. At the mouth of the tunnel was a shallow slope of soft earth leading all the way down to the cavern floor. And at its base, an unkept garden surrounded a stone temple with stained glass windows and a spire decorating its V-shaped roof. The far end of the building backed right up onto the cavern wall, and the near end was positioned directly in the centre of the chamber where a stone fountain stood at its entrance.

Carefully, with her kit secured, she reached forward and placed her hands on the soft dirt of the slope. Confident she could hold her weight, she pulled her lower body out and then let herself slide gently down until she found the hard bottom.

She tried to stand but keeled over, still unable to best the exhaustion that had taken her. She peered back up towards the tunnel. There was no movement, and she couldn't hear any attempt by the carnivorous beasts to make the tight journey.

But rather than sit up or take account of her surroundings, she sighed in relief. No longer able to keep slumber at bay, she closed her eyes and let it take her.

CHAPTER 5

Septembrix 3, 484; the town of Crowton, Borlencia; fifteen and a half weeks earlier—Evia knelt down and peeled off a lump of mud stuck to her shin. The roads in Crowton were a bumpy mess of mud and puddles, courtesy of that morning's downpour, but with the exhausted horses secured at an inn on the edge of town, along with two rescued women from the day prior, Evia, Joseph, and Dogner had been left to brave the muck on foot. A slow but necessary trudge to the centre of the town.

Standing on a busy street outside a noisy tavern, Evia turned to Dogner as a grunt of disapproval escaped his lips. The big man bent over and picked up a soiled rag someone had just tossed onto his foot. Dogner traced the rag's trajectory and locked on to a bald merchant sitting atop his cart as it continued down the road.

"Dogner—" Evia began, but it was too late.

The big man threw the dirty rag and hit the merchant in the back of the head with a wet slap. The merchant turned around, his cheeks red, but immediately cowered under the big man's dangerous glare. There was a brief moment of indecision before the merchant decided to carry on rather than risk probable harm.

"The lad's been a while," Dogner said nonchalantly as he wiped his hand on his trousers.

"Joseph said it could take some time to find his contact," Evia responded calmly. Her features had regained some of their youth, and the fatigue of the prior weeks had been replaced by a sharp alertness.

"Still, no reason why we couldn't have joined him in the tavern and taken another table."

The tavern door creaked open, and the pair turned to see a group of drunks stumble out onto the street. The door closed behind them, though not before a whiff of the establishment's ale caught Dogner's nose. He sighed.

Evia chuckled. "Soon enough, my friend."

"It's been too long, but then—" He peered at the three Zylencian soldiers rounding onto the street. "Better to keep the wits about than find fault with the likes of this lot."

The armed men walked by without haste and seemed wholly unbothered by the hostile stares directed at them by the drunkards and townsfolk going about their business.

"You're not wrong," Evia agreed. Her expression glazed over for a second before relaxing.

"Anything to worry about?" Dogner asked.

"They're harmless. It's obvious that Crowton, along with every other town in central Borlencia, has been spared the violent blight of the towns on the lakeshore. Still, I'll not be able to relax until we've got those women and children on a ship or cart headed to the provinces of Eurencia or Notencia."

"No doubt we've got our work cut out for us. And speak of the man himself," Dogner said as Joseph rounded the corner from the adjacent street. "Could've sworn you were in the tavern," he said when Joseph reached them.

"I was, but my contact's contact asked that I follow him through the back. Had to trek a couple of streets over."

"And how did you know he wasn't going to cut your throat? Bit foolish, don't you think?"

Joseph grinned. "I've been doing this a long time, Dogner. I know what I'm doing."

"And what's the verdict?" Evia asked.

"He'll help us. We've got a lot of details to nail out, though."

"And for all those we have yet to rescue?"

"He's on board. He also knows the man you speak of."

"Admiral Grendal?" she said. Grendal was a long-time confidant of Evia's, and he was Hemish's uncle—it was he who Hemish had joined in Notencia after leaving Nhata Bay.

"Of Anemoi's merchant navy—yes," Joseph replied. "He'll send a messenger this afternoon once he's had a chance to meet you."

"What time?" Dogner asked.

"Five. Why, got somewhere to be?"

"No, but could do with a bite and a clean." He looked Joseph up and down. All of them were equally filthy. "As could you."

Joseph chortled. "Can't argue your point."

"Shall we go back to the inn, then?"

"Not just yet. My contact mentioned another name that piqued my interest. A man that's hard as steel and who's got the ear of the mayor. A man willing to get dirty for a good cause."

"Oh yeah?"

"Does the name Santos ring a bell?"

"Xander's friend from the Ranclet?" Evia queried.

"Yes," Joseph said. "It so happens that he works in the mayor's office."

"And where can we find him?"

"My contact said he'd likely be at a pub a short walk from here. The Wispy—"

"Tavern."

"You know it?"

"You could say that."

Dogner laughed. "Didn't take you for the type!"

"It's not what they sell but who they serve," she retorted. "And I know where it is from here. Shall we?"

"Of course!" Joseph said. "But before we do, isn't there that little issue of you toying with his memory when he left Nhata? Is he going to remember us?"

"Us, yes. Xander, now that'll take a little while, but it'll come back to him as he joins the dots. With a little encouragement from me, of course."

She began down the muddy street, and the others quickly followed. Navigating the busy town centre with ease, it took them all of ten minutes to arrive at their destination.

"The Wispy Tavern." Joseph read the sign atop the green door.

A yellow-and-white cottage with two stories, it carried none of the grime or rowdiness of the last one. The same could be said of the street, which was carpeted in cobblestone and absent of the crowds and muck.

"Well, I could definitely see myself having a bevvy here," Dogner said with an excited grin. "Not enough to lose the senses, just enough to—"

"Wet the tongue," Evia interjected.

"Exactly! I'll do the honours," he said, opening the door.

The interior was cool and without the stench of stale beer some establishments were prone to. The tables and chairs were neatly arranged and the patrons an assortment of well-dressed politicians, wealthy merchants, and military officers.

A man wearing the tavern's uniform approached them, and though he appeared slightly offended by their dirty garments, he continued with his pleasantries. "Where would you like to sit, ma'am, gentlemen?"

Evia looked around the room and then smiled. "In the corner, please. The table next to that gentleman."

The waiter followed her gaze to the man whose brown skin and scarred face stood out from the rest of the clientele. Engrossed in a book, the man did not notice Evia and the others as they took the table next to him.

"I'll be back over shortly," the waiter said and left to the bar.

With the waiter gone, Evia turned to the others. "It's him."

Joseph snuck a peek at the man who was still deep in his book. "It'll be a bit obvious we've sought him out, don't you think?"

"I should hope so; otherwise we should be asking ourselves if we really want to rely on someone without their wits." She turned to the man and leant over. "Santos?"

The man's expression perked, and he looked over at them. There was a moment's hesitation. "Now why do you look so familiar? You and your friends?"

"We met some time ago down in Nhata."

His eyes lit up. "The Ranclet?"

Evia smiled. "Yes! You raced alongside my niece."

"I…hmm…I must admit I don't really recall your niece or any female contestant for that matter. Not this last one, anyway. Not to say there couldn't have been, but…well, talk about being disrespectful. My apologies."

"That's quite alright. Tell you what, would you like to join us? We're about ready to order a round of drinks after being on the road so long and could do with a friendly chat with someone that knows the area. It's our treat."

He looked at his book, clearly wanting to re-enter its world, and then back at them. He shrugged. "Not every day you cross paths with old acquaintances. Yes, I think I'll join you for that drink." With book in hand, he hopped over and took the empty seat.

"This is Joseph and Dogner," she introduced. "And I'm Evia."

"It's a pleasure. And what brings the lot of you to Crowton?"

Evia's eyes lost focus for the briefest of seconds before locking back on to the man. To the others, it was clear she had just taken a quick peek into Santos's mind as he was engaging with them.

"Nothing good, unfortunately," Evia said, comfortable with what she had seen. "I don't suppose you've heard about what's happened to some of the towns to the east?"

Santos's features hardened. "Nhata, too, then?"

"Unfortunately, yes."

"I'm sorry to hear that," he said softly. "Nhata's always held a spot in my heart. Much of the lakeshore has. I guess Erzse's greed and need for retribution know no bounds."

"You're familiar with the situation, then?" Joseph asked.

"It doesn't take a crony to know that Erzse isn't occupying Borlencia to quell an insurrection."

"Insurrection?"

"Yes. It's the advertised reason for her occupation." Santos leant forward. "That Borlencia is in the midst of a grab for power, an insurrection if you will, led by a small group of Borlencians that have illegitimately placed themselves into positions of note. A group that seeks dominion not just over Borlencia but the whole of western Anemoi. Complete fabrication, of course, but it's her justification. We've figured it's largely why the eastern provinces haven't intervened. That they think the Zylencian actions are acceptable. And if you think about it, because the occupying force has taken most of the major towns, it gives the impression that the Zylencians are making headway without the need for reinforcements."

"They think Zylencia's actions are to Anemoi's benefit," Evia murmured. "This isn't good. The other provinces also have problems of their own that'll prevent them from committing to any real investigation or intervention, if they so decide."

About to continue, curiosity took Santos. "You're referring to this new enemy that's appeared on the eastern border of Eurencia?"

The concern in Evia's expression matched Joseph's and Dogner's. They knew as much as Joseph had been able to discern several weeks prior when they were still situated in Nhata, and that was that the Eurencians had already engaged with this unknown foe in a handful of pitched battles. Beyond that, however, they were still frustratingly in the dark.

"In part, yes," Evia said. "But we're still working on the details. How much have you heard?"

"Just the odd comment from one or two Eurencian traders. Rumour has it that the Eurencians have had to borrow a large sum from the Zylencians to fund their campaign." He took in the immediate discomfort of the others. "And judging by the synchronised drop in your mouths, this is a new, somewhat alarming development for you."

"No understatement there, lad," Dogner remarked with a scoff.

Santos chortled lightly at the big man's gruffness. "Well, as with any news, a little time and digestion help build perspective."

"Do tell?" Evia said, intrigued.

"The Eurencians have managed to hold this new enemy on the fringes of their territory for some months now. Their military's strong. Arguably the strongest in Anemoi. And they've got the funding. It tells me that the situation might not be quite as dire as initial impressions suggest. It's also not unusual for nations to borrow in wartime to build a capital buffer. You know, to get ahead of the possible crunch."

Evia breathed through pursed lips as she considered his words. "You might be right about the severity of their specific predicament, but it does still add to the complexity of the overall situation."

"Hard to argue against the complexities," Santos said. "Three hostile armies converging on Anemoi and one of them is our own. Already mighty complex without the intricacies of who owes who what. Especially when one considers that the lender in this instance is the same controlling the traitorous army."

"That's certainly one of my worries."

"I gathered. Speaking of the Zylencians, most of Crowton's heard the news now that Erzse has forced the towns on the lakeshore into lockdown for resisting her troops. I think a couple were also pillaged. Shameful as it is to say, the towns in the east should never have shown their fangs. Not without unity. Now even those that didn't are paying the price of provoking the woman's wrath."

"No lockdown here," Dogner spoke. "Think it's safe to say the town didn't put up any resistance or qualm?"

"We've got a decent garrison, but there wasn't much that could be done by the time we realised what was happening. Given the Zylencians are meant to be our allies and all. And there certainly wasn't enough political cohesion across the larger towns to put up a front after the deed. Each is looking out for their own."

"Tell me, Santos," Joseph said, "is it also common knowledge that Zylencian soldiers are transporting many of the women and children from the lakeshore to Zylencia in chains? In small groups to avoid arousing suspicion. All likely to be sold off or used for other…unpleasant means."

"Or that she's completely razed dozens of towns on the lakeshore along with any man that can put up a front?" Dogner added. "Regardless of if they resisted or not."

Santos's shock was evident. "I wasn't aware of the extent of the Zylencians' destruction. It would seem some of the news is slow to reach us here."

"Or it's been carefully curated, much like her reason for occupation," Evia said sternly.

He looked at them curiously. "I think it's time to let on. Are you here as refugees? Or should I assume this meeting is more than coincidence?"

"You wouldn't be wrong to assume the latter," Evia said, pleased he'd caught on quickly.

"Thought as much. And you need my help?"

She nodded.

He leant back against his chair as he eyed them. "And which of my services?"

"You're a soldier, no?" Dogner queried, eager to confirm his suspicions from the first time they had all met.

"I was."

"I figured! You've got the walk. When and where did you serve?"

"Borealis. Right up until it fell. And then the back and forth in the aftermath."

"You were there the day it fell?" Joseph said in awe.

"One of the last regiments out. Along with my commander and what was left of our men. But there are many soldiers in these parts, and I'm just one man. I doubt that's the only reason you're here for me."

"You can never have too many friends for a venture like the one we have planned. But it's also who you know that could perhaps be of use."

Santos glanced around the room to see who was within earshot and then leant forward. About to speak, he stopped as the waiter appeared back at the table with three menus in hand. The waiter handed them to Evia, Joseph, and Dogner, then turned to Santos.

"The usual?" he asked.

Santos considered for a moment. "Please."

The waiter hung around for another minute as the other three gave their orders and then left back to the bar.

With the waiter gone, Santos continued. "The mayor?"

"Aye," Dogner said. "The mayor."

"You'll need to let me in on your plan before I do that. Not so easy to rebuild favour once you use it. And no offence meant by this, but I do get dozens of propositions a week, the majority of which aren't going to happen."

Evia smiled. "Naturally."

▲ ▲ ▲

Santos took a polite sip of his drink as he pushed his empty plate away. Unlike the others, he had chosen a light lunch. Of course, unlike the others, he wasn't fresh off the road and in dire need of nourishment.

"It's risky," he said. "We can arrange papers legitimising the residency of some of the women and children in Crowton, and maybe even the other big towns in central Borlencia with their blessing, but that opens the mayor's office up to accusations of fraud. All it would take is a single glance at the books, and Erzse and her administrators would see that we've been supplying wanted 'insurrectionists' with false papers, leaving the mayor in an awkward position. Nobody wants to owe a Zylencian, especially not this one."

"Our other option, and one that we also pursue," Evia began, "is to provide some of the groups with residency papers from the provinces of Eurencia and Notencia. But these papers will take a bit longer to acquire. So far, Erzse hasn't shown the same kind of hostilities to the people of Crowton and the other large towns in central and western Borlencia as she has to the ones along the lakeshore, and she likely won't, providing they stay in line—"

"These towns are also much larger," Dogner interjected, his mouth full. "I don't know the woman, but she'll understand the problems entailed in trying to keep half a dozen enraged Crowtons from rising up at the same time."

"Point is," Evia continued, "the papers will provide the groups a degree of security as we resituate them. Either in the other provinces or elsewhere in Borlencia."

"Perhaps, but no telling how long this security will hold up," Santos said with a shrug. "Especially if this other plan of yours gains traction."

"An election?"

He nodded.

"You think Erzse would stand in the way of a legitimate election by using violence?" Joseph asked.

"You don't?" Santos responded.

"We think there's risk. But I'd be curious to hear your thoughts given your position."

"Why would she accept an election to re-establish Borlencia's Lower House? Like I said, the advertised reason for her occupation is that Borlencia's in the midst of an insurrection led by an illegitimate group of radicals. A freshly elected Lower House, if done legitimately, and with the backing of all the major towns and their garrisons, means no more illegal grab for power. It'd be a legal parliament with the strength of a reassembled provincial garrison ensuring the stability of the province, thus contesting her need to keep occupying troops on the ground. Heck, she'll know the chances of us taking her to court for illegally marching troops into Borlencia. I reckon she'll just claim any election is unlawful and install her own people. Not only undoing all your work, but putting us, the perpetrators, in an even-more-dangerous situation. Like I said, risky."

Evia bit her cheek. "The other option is we leave Erzse with free rein in a fractured Borlencia. I doubt the other provinces will be in a position to aid us to the extent we'd like, even if Erzse's lie came to light. Not yet anyway. And certainly not as long as her followers continue to spread lies as to why she is here. So, with free rein, how long before she replicates the atrocities in the east across the rest of the province?"

"Not saying I disagree with you, and I'm definitely not saying I won't help you." Santos spoke up. "I'm just saying you might not get the reception you want. Public election. Secret election. Both carry risks, especially to those looking to be elected."

"It's a risk any serious candidate will surely understand. Nevertheless, you'll arrange a meeting with your boss for us?"

"I'll arrange it. And I'll also join your meetings with Joseph's contact. I'm familiar with the area and have my own resources. I think I can be of use. Even if the elections come to nothing, I'd very much like to help blunt Erzse's cruel reach. No man, woman, or child should have their home razed and their freedom taken because they stood up to an oppressor."

Evia beamed. "Thank you, really."

▲ ▲ ▲

The afternoon was irritatingly damp, and the small shed in which they congregated was unbearably stuffy. Evia, Joseph, and Dogner sat on creaky little stools to one side of a large wooden table marked with scribbles and stains. On the other side sat Joseph's contact. The scrawny man, despite his handsome features, was unusually hairy and seemed to have ginger fur growing out of every visible orifice. Seated on an equally flimsy stool with his elbows rested on the table, he stared at the trio in quiet contemplation.

"Fredrick, if—" Joseph began when the man raised his finger.

"If we avoid the main roads, it'll add weeks on to the journeys," the hairy man said quietly.

"Depending on where we pick them up and where we send them."

"I get that, but my point's valid. And the longer it takes us to move some of these groups, the less resources we'll have to help others. I've only got so many hands I can lend ya. Hope you understand."

"It's not that we don't," Joseph said. "But taking the main roads increases the risk."

"Says you. And how'd you go about explaining to a Zylencian simpleton with a sword why you're braving a trodden path in a cart rather than the surety of a paved road?"

"They can't all take the main roads, lad," Dogner countered. "It'd be too obvious to the checkpoints if they suddenly see an increase in migrating farmhands and traders in those groups pretty much the same time as they start receiving news of ambushes and prisoners being freed in the droves. Especially if those groups are laden with teenage girls and children. The longer it takes them to catch on, the more we can rescue with less risk to ourselves and our charges."

Fredrick stroked the excessively long hair on his arm. "Something to think about. Either way, the lot tomorrow, the ones you've got holed up in the inn on the edge of town, I'll have them on the first cart out in the morning along the main road. The ones at the farmstead will take a little longer, but they, too, will be on the main road. They're the first of many, so no harm, I don't think."

"Both groups to Bulgar?" Joseph asked.

"Both groups to Bulgar. Already got their papers ready." Fredrick looked at Evia. "My merchant will use the opportunity to deliver your message to Admiral Grendal."

"Your merchant's due for Notencia, then?" Evia said.

"No, but there's always half a fleet of Notencian trade ships moored at Bulgar. If Grendal isn't about, one of his officers certainly will be."

"And you can—"

"Yes, I wouldn't use him if he weren't trustworthy. Have you got the letter?"

Evia nodded and withdrew an envelope from her robe.

"Encrypted?" Fredrick asked, reaching out his hand.

Evia passed him the envelope. "Yes."

"Good, good. Not that I'd charge you anything for the service, but it's something I'd have to insist on, just in case."

They tensed as a rap came from the door and a head popped through. It was one of Fredrick's grunts.

"Yep?" Fredrick asked impatiently.

"Santos is here with the mayor."

"Alright then, let them in."

The four of them stood up as the door opened.

"Evia, gentlemen," Santos greeted them as he entered.

He shuffled to the side, giving his guest room to enter. The mayor was a neat man in his fifties with a thin moustache and a wrinkled forehead. Eagerly, he clasped Fredrick's hand and then turned to the rest of them.

"The name's Ronal. And you must be the ones with a plan," he said with a fascinated grin.

"We are," Evia responded with a curt bow as the mayor and Santos sat down on the opposite side of the table. Same as had happened many times in the preceding weeks, her eyes glazed over for the briefest of seconds as she scanned the mayor's mind for even the slightest hint of deceit. There was none. She continued, "Though a plan without buy-in from those best positioned is a—"

"Plan likely to fail."

"Exactly. I'm Evia." She reached her hand across the table and shook his. "This is Dogner, and this is—"

"Joseph. Yes, I've heard all about the three of you and your intentions. Can't say I'm disappointed, given your reputation, Evia. Surprised I've heard of you?"

"Somewhat, yes. I haven't been active in these parts for years."

"Reputations don't wither away the moment you let go of them. And I've been active in this town's politics since I was yay high. Not a name or face I can't recall. And yours has barely aged from the little glimpse I remember! Anyway, to the point, I'm in."

"You're in?" Joseph asked with a raised eyebrow.

"Yes, on both accounts," the mayor responded. "Santos filled me in. The residency papers won't be a problem. We can start issuing them as soon as you need them. I'd just be cautious when and where you send these groups and to make sure that they're rehearsed on their new backgrounds. We can also issue Crowton trade permits. They hold a certain degree of protection. For now, anyway."

"Thank you, Ronal. That's very generous," Evia said.

He waved his hand, dismissive of her praise. "And then there's the election. I've got to tell you, when Santos told me what you had in mind, I nearly tripped. I've tried numerous times to unite the towns to rebuild parliament, but I've always come up against the same blocks. Who's going to host parliament? Who's going to oversee the election? Who can be trusted? It always comes down to the same two things, trust and ego. But with you, Evia, with your reputation, I'm confident we can get them on the same page."

"Like I said, it's been some time since I've been active in the area. Not everybody will have the same familiarity."

"And all they need to do is pick up a book. It can work. Of course, how exactly you convince them is something we'll need to work out, especially as we've now got external parties to factor in."

Evia nodded. "I guess the first step would be for me to ask you this:

Would you be open to the proposition of alternating the meeting hall between the big towns? As you've already made clear, with Borealis not an option, the host town has been a major hurdle in getting everybody on the same page. And we know it's been the case long before the Zylencians' involvement."

He thought for a moment, not betraying any emotion, not even to Evia. "That's a sensible solution. Hopefully a sentiment that'll be universal. That's not to say it's all fairies and dandelions from here on out, though, even if the other towns get on board. There's still the practical matter of whether the Zylencians would even permit an election."

"Could do a secret ballot," Fredrick spoke up, keen to help write history.

"We could, but where's the legitimacy?"

"There would be none," Evia agreed. "A secret ballot may do more harm than good. Not to mention, how do we keep something like this from getting back to Erzse, when you've got half the population of Borlencia voting on it?"

"Then a public ballot?" Dogner asked, surprised by the woman's revelation. "Have to agree with Santos on this one. Can't see Erzse allowing it. We'd be inviting her to come down on us."

"She might not have much choice but to allow it."

"Do tell?"

Again, Evia glanced into the unfamiliar minds in the room in search of something, anything, that could suggest she shouldn't trust her company. But there was none. All were eager and sincere in their desire to help, and all held some revulsion towards Erzse. Still, not wanting to divulge more than necessary, she spoke with measure: "Ronal, Santos, can you organise a meeting with the mayors and any other political offices of note for me? I'd like the chance to speak with what's left of Borlencia's government."

"Absolutely!" Ronal said. "Do you have a date in mind?"

"As soon as feasible. And please keep the message simple and unrelated to talk of an election. We wouldn't want to initiate dangerous gossip, not that it isn't something that's been openly broached before."

"Use the movement on the northern border," Joseph said. "The army walled within Borealis is a legitimate reason to call a meeting. And let it be known. I doubt Erzse would see through the facade, unless, of course, anybody in this room was to make it known otherwise. After all, nobody besides us knows what's been discussed this day."

They all nodded, aware of Joseph's veiled threat.

"Fantastic!" Ronal said, clapping his hands. "I think that's a good start and a cause for celebration, wouldn't you agree?"

"Lot of work to be done before a celebration, don't you think?" Dogner grunted.

"Sure, but a single drink's unlikely to harm. We can work out the rest of the logistics over a beer. Or wine, if you fancy."

The others shrugged, not seeing any reason not to.

"Great!" he said excitedly. "So, to the Wispy Tavern?"

▲ ▲ ▲

Joseph collapsed onto his bed and used the ledge at its base to pull his shoes off. The candlelit room was quaint with its three beds, copper bowl, and mirror.

"That beer hits hard." He groaned, rubbing his temple. "Didn't even drink that much."

"Old age, I presume," Evia said as she mixed him and herself a little concoction to take the sting of the alcohol away.

"So much for keeping our wits about us."

They both peered to the corner bed as Dogner began snoring heavily.

"Going to be a long night if he doesn't shut up," Joseph muttered.

Evia chuckled. "Leave the poor man."

"Poor man!" he said, sitting up. "What about us? I ought to smother him."

"Maybe another night, when we don't need him."

"Hmm! For you, Evia, I shall let him live a little longer."

"Thank you, dearly."

"Don't mention it." He drained the glass of water on his bedside table. "So, Evia, now that we have the room, what's your plan?"

"Plan?"

"Yes, the one that you correctly decided not to announce to the group earlier. Though it must be said, I do think you're a tad careless mentioning the election to any of that lot so soon into the game."

"We were going to have to bring people in at some point."

"Of course! And Fredrick I would trust with my life. But Santos and the mayor? We don't know them."

"I didn't sense anything untrustworthy in them."

"And have you ever been wrong?"

"Seldom."

"This is dangerous, Evia."

"How many times have the Borlencians tried to set up a functioning provincial government in the past decade?" she asked. "A dozen times? Maybe more? It's not unheard of."

"Not the point. This time it's different. This time you've got the Zylencians occupying the province. Either way, the plan?"

"I've had a chance to think on it. If we can get the Eurencian ministers on board as organisers, I think they can seal the election's legitimacy and provide the oversight we need."

"They have problems of their own. Maybe you've heard?"

"No need for the sarcasm," she rebutted playfully. "We're not asking them to send their garrison or to take the Zylencians to court—we're simply asking them to recognise the election for what it is."

"To do that, I think we'll need to convince them that there's no insurrection. That what's left of Borlencia's existing government can be trusted, seeing as many of those in it will likely run for the vacant ministerial and council positions."

"Something I'll work on. I imagine it'll take me a little while to get the Eurencians to agree, but it will happen. But until they're on board, I'd like to keep that hand close to my chest."

"And until we have them on board?"

"We proceed with organising the election."

"And yet, there's still that little issue of Erzse retaliating," he retorted.

"That's why we get her to sanction it."

Joseph opened his mouth to speak but instead stared at her, dumbfounded.

"All this takes time we just don't have," she continued. "Let's be honest. Erzse will suspect the reason for the election once it comes to light. She'll see the danger. But rather than let her nip it in the bud before it has a chance to fester, we sell it to her."

"How, might I ask?"

"I think this is where Ronal will come in."

"Ronal?"

"Yes, Ronal. And maybe one or two others that hold weight amongst their peers. Ones that can be trusted."

"You intend to spend time with them? Have a bevvy or two and get to know them?" he jibed.

"Yes, and when you're quite done!" she said, shaking her head with amusement. "We get them to approach Erzse. To be 'traitors' per se. If she thinks, from the onset, that she can manipulate the election and have her own people installed, Ronal being one of them, then why wouldn't she let it run its course? She might also see it as a win for her narrative with the other provinces—that she's helping to subdue this group of rogue Borlencians by allowing it."

"Subdue this group of rogue Borlencians," he repeated slowly, unconvinced. "Isn't there a risk that all this turns the Borlencian people against their existing officials? From what Santos told us, even with the dislike for the Zylencians, it sounds like nobody's sure of who or what to believe at this point, with all the lies that've been spread. And because the only Borlencians with any actual power are the existing ones, who else is there to be accused?"

"Erzse's accusations have been very general. She hasn't called anybody out in particular. Who's to say if those running are implicated or not. Still, if she's bright, she'll understand the need for unblemished candidates that already hold power. She'll want people that have established roots and a following. Those that know the game and that can bring value. An unknown Borlencian with no political experience or mercantile ties won't be ideal. At the local level, it's in her best interest to quell any gossip concerning rogue politicians, soldiers, and merchants, so to avoid clouding judgment on those that'll support her."

"Providing Ronal and whoever else can convince her?"

"Yes."

"And the other provinces?" he asked. "Her boast won't exactly help us in convincing them she was lying from the onset."

"I don't think it'll make a difference either way. It'll all come back to 'he said, she said.' The onus is on me to convince the Eurencians otherwise, and Erzse's endorsement simply buys me the time to do that."

He scratched his chin. "What if Ronal and these other 'traitors' don't win? What if, with her army of spies and miscreants, Erzse comes to realise that she's being played and that this path could, in all likelihood, lead to an elected Lower House eager to kick her out and take her to court?"

"As soon as we have the Eurencians on board, it won't matter. If she comes to realise by then that Ronal and the others are in fact duping her—"

"There won't be anything she can do about it."

"Exactly. Once the Eurencians are monitoring, Ronal and whoever else will be able to run with considerably less fear of retaliation stemming from discovery or even just a word out of place. Of course, sensibility suggests they should still refrain from rhetoric attacking Erzse and the Zylencians—for why antagonise the lunatic holding a knife to your throat—but they'd have much greater peace of mind than otherwise."

He grunted, his expression pensive. "And what of the Notencians? Worth getting their input? Word on the street is they're not to be trusted."

"Notencia's government has many problems of its own. I'm not so sure we can rely on timely intervention from them. Still, we do have the ear of Admiral Grendal, who in turn has the written backing of the province's government. Besides being our means of attaining the Notencian residency papers, maybe he can put his support behind the election also."

Joseph tapped his fingers against the empty glass. "Maybe it could work. Once all this is in play, it would be very difficult for Erzse to insist every single one of the candidates she permitted to run in fact make up the entire rogue group that was trying to seize power illegally. And it certainly wouldn't do her any good to suddenly shut down a sanctioned vote of the people to elect their new government when it's a direct solution to her fabrication."

"No, it wouldn't. Still, it all rides on the Eurencians' willingness to help. Otherwise, she can, and probably will, go back on any result unfavourable to her. With the Eurencians on board, an officially recognised Lower House can then label the Zylencian occupation unnecessary and have their troops removed."

"And then we can take her and that whole bloody province to court," Dogner said with a grunt, having woken up in the middle of the conversation.

"Exactly," Evia said.

"And when will you reach out to these Eurencian ministers?" Joseph asked.

"The letter's already been sent."

"The one to Grendal?"

She nodded. "It contained a separate instruction in there that he's to redirect via ship to Eurus, home of the Eurencian parliament."

"Always a step ahead."

"And would you expect any less, lad?" Dogner said as he shuffled onto his side and closed his eyes.

"I think Dogner has the right idea," Evia spoke. "Time we get some rest. We have a very busy few weeks ahead of us."

"Can't argue that," Joseph said.

Exhausted, they slumped onto their respective beds, and Joseph blew out the lone candle.

CHAPTER 6

Septembrix 8, 484; Crowton, Borlencia; fifteen weeks earlier—"That's a lot to ask, Evia," Ronal said, his expression transitioning from one of calm and tipsiness to one of worry.

He took a nervous sip of his beer and peered around the Wispy Tavern with all its measured raucous as Crowton's elite stuck into dinner. Despite the humidity outside and the candles inside, the room was refreshingly cool.

"I wouldn't ask if I didn't think it was necessary," Evia responded.

The two of them had spent the best part of the evening simply chatting, getting to know each other, and whilst Evia suspected that Ronal may not be the most honest of men when it came to money, his dislike of Erzse was clear as day.

"The woman's unpredictable," he said. "And the layman may not know it, but I'm fully aware of what she's done on the lakeshore and what she continues to do."

"If we get her buy-in, we get our election. She'll only fall for it if you, and others with your chance of success, put your hands up and bargain with her."

"An election in return for our traitorous obedience," he muttered and took another sip. "And what of our morals?"

"This is one of those instances where you need to turn a blind eye. At least until we've succeeded in getting the Lower House elected."

"And do you think the people will go for it?" he said, unsure. "Am I really likely to be elected when running in support of the Zylencians?"

"You don't need to publicly show your support for them. And Erzse will understand that. Your goal is to get elected with the secret promise that you can pander to her whims. Not to mention, it may hurt all our chances to run on a platform against her. I think the candidates will know that. And any that don't, we can have a word with them."

He sucked on his lip and then took another nervous swig of his beer. "You may not know it, but the Zylencian ministers are somewhat difficult to get a hold of. If I'm to do this, I'll need to arrange it through the commander of the occupying force."

"Do you know him?"

"I've met with him on occasion. Out of necessity, not desire." He downed the last of his beer. "And to think I was quite enjoying my rendezvous with a woman of legend." He chuckled. "If I had known you were grooming me to do your bidding…well, I probably would've still gone along with it. A chance to do some good." He waved over the waiter, the same that had greeted Evia and the others the day they arrived in Crowton. As the man began towards them, Ronal continued, "I know of a couple others that can help with this. I'm sure Erzse will need the guarantee of more than one man."

"Thank you, Ronal."

He nodded acceptance and turned to the waiter who had arrived at the table. "On my tab. Both of us."

"Sir," the waiter said and walked off.

Ronal stood up, and Evia followed suit.

"I'll walk you home," he said, offering his arm out.

She smiled and took it in hers.

CHAPTER 7

Decembrix 21, 484; the Hunter's Passage, Zylencia—Xander stirred groggily. Her head was throbbing and her eyelids heavy. She pulled her face from the ground and wiped away the dirt plastered to her cheek. Through tired eyes, she took in the floor beneath her. Old, weathered tiles adorned with faded colour carpeted the perimeter of the chamber and flowed like gentle streams through the garden up to the temple's entrance.

She craned her head up to the tunnel from which she had emerged and then across the surprisingly warm cavern to the hole in the rocky ceiling. Taking in the sun's angle of entry, she determined it to be afternoon.

"Then why does it feel like I've been asleep an age?" she muttered as she stood up with jelly-like legs, unaware she had slept right through the prior day and into the current.

She took a gulp of water from her flask, reached her arms overhead, and stretched a long, therapeutic stretch. Then, with minimal caution, she began towards the temple. The overgrown trees and plants that decorated the garden were fairly ordinary compared to the likes of Gladis's or Evia's, but the ambience was tranquil nonetheless. As she approached the stone fountain that had long ago dried up, she noticed an unfamiliar marking on the centrepiece. Three triangles of equal size in a column. She made a mental note of the design and continued on to the temple door, which was not much taller than herself. With a bit of effort, she pushed it open and stepped inside.

The air was dry and smelled of plants. Modest in size, the interior was similar in almost every aspect to the temples back in central Borlencia. There were dozens of rows of pews facing the far end, with large stained glass windows along the walls. However, unlike those she had entered into before, at the far end of this temple, directly above the altar, clear windows had been built into the roof, right below the natural hole in the cavern's ceiling. And on both sides of the altar there stood stone statues of a man holding an axe. Amidst the pews and altar and along the walls, plants and grasses and vines had found life, making it seem as if the temple itself had risen from the weeds.

Curious to explore the structure's mystery, she began down the central aisle towards the front. The benches were worn. Not one had remained untarnished by some unknown's backside. It was a surprising observation, given she was in the wilds of Zylencia.

The armour worn by the statues had the same marking of three triangles etched into the breastplates. She brushed a finger over the marking carved into the stone man in front of her and then glanced to the altar. A thick book rested in its centre. Eager to glimpse its purpose, she walked over and opened it. The pages were discoloured but legible, and in the bottom right corner of each page, the column of triangles was printed in ink. The book's language was her own, though clearly from another time. She flicked through the pages to the one divided by a bronze bookmark and laid her eyes on a single paragraph underlined in red ink.

"And so shall it be, that the kingdoms of the godless shall rise, vanquishing and assimilating those of the ordained. Those blessed by the God, the gods, and the witch doctor shall fall prey to the might of the heathens, rightfully left to rot and wither under the heathen's name. A future set in stone until one bearing the mark of the witch doctor can rise from the earth and set in such stone thy

control in an unending reign of oppression."

Multiple scratches obscured the next sentence. She pulled in close and read it aloud:

"A reign that will endure a hundred generations, unless they, too, can be cut down and driven back into the earth at the hand of a heathen marked by both worlds."

The scurry of little feet, presumably a rodent of sorts, drew her attention from the scripture to the rear of the temple where a narrow door hid behind a dusty curtain. She approached it and put her hand to the doorknob but quickly jerked her hand away. A shudder traversed her spine, and painful goosebumps erupted up and down her legs. Taking a step back, she drew her blade, unsure of whether to run or give in to her compounding desire to know what exactly lay behind it.

Slowly, she reached out and turned the strangely icy knob. The door abruptly flung open as a strong breeze tore through the temple into the hidden room, forcing a cloud of dust into the air. No greenery decorated the room, and it was only sparsely illuminated by a small window out of view. Cautiously she stepped through the opening and then immediately stopped, mouth agape.

Dozens of skeletons littered the floor to the side. All wore tattered robes. All carried shattered bones and skulls from some horrendous attack many years ago. And now she had disturbed their tomb. Suddenly desperate to be out of there, away from the vacant stares of those clearly murdered, she backed out and slammed the door shut.

The peace of the cavern was wholly absent of its prior allure in that moment. She marched back to the book as if she could find a justification for what she had just witnessed, but a niggle somewhere deep inside of her spoke against it. She hesitated. The red ink under that passage. The scratched-out sentence. Surely they meant something. She reached back for the book but again stopped short of touching it. Evia had always taught her to never disregard a niggle. A warning perhaps heeded in such a situation.

Decided, she shook her head and exited the temple.

Eager to escape the cavern, she jogged around the perimeter in search of another tunnel or door but found none. Her only escape was the way she had come. Back into the teeth of the wolves, if they still waited. She swore. What choice did she have? There was no way in Anemoi she would willingly spend a night down there. Resigned to her only choice, she gritted her teeth and climbed back up the hill with greater haste than that with which she had explored the tomb.

The tunnel seemed shorter than when she had entered, but she was also without the lethargy that had plagued her previously. Metres from the end of the tunnel, the afternoon sunlight clear, she stopped and waited. For a good twenty minutes she lay there, hand cupped to her ear, listening for the slightest of noises. But there were none. About to crawl forward, she stopped again and this time reached out for Aes with her mind. Her expression brightened. He was near. It was safe.

She made quick work of the last of the tunnel and breached into the open air, thankful to be out of the eerie space.

"My shield," she said louder than she had meant and swiftly picked it up from where she had left it. Worry took her at the implication, however. "It means Ricard and Aika didn't come back this way."

She turned around just as Aes came into sight and immediately rushed up to him and hugged him.

"You're safe!" She took a step back and frowned at the bite marks on his hind legs. "But not without cost. Thank you, my friend. You saved our lives. Mine, at least. Have you seen the others? Oh no," she uttered, dismayed. "The last time I saw them, they were headed that—"

A streak of lightning pierced the sky, and a second later a thunderous roar shook the ground beneath them.

Aes knelt down slightly, beckoning her to climb up. He spoke into her mind as she did.

"Where's this hut?" she responded aloud. "Okay, then. Best we get to it before the sky opens up on us."

But barely had they made it a couple of minutes up the hill when the storm started to pelt the pair with everything it had. Sodden and frightfully cold, they pulled up to a round wooden hut draped in carpet. Situated on a small patch of flat ground nestled into the mountainside, it stood next to a large boulder that had a crooked, wiry length of metal poking from the top. Wary of stumbling on its owners unannounced, Xander knocked on the door. No response. Cautiously she opened the door and peeked inside. Nobody was home.

The interior was chilly and dimly lit by a couple of small windows. In the centre of the round room was a big, round firepit and an empty cauldron in the heart of it all. The edges of the hut weren't particularly tidy, but despite the miserable chill, it exuded an almost irresistible ambience of cosiness with an army of blankets and pillows strewn about.

"I guess we're without choice," she said, picking up a blanket to wipe herself down with. Removing her clothes, she dried herself off and then got to lighting the firepit.

It didn't take long for the fire to find life, and within moments the hut had warmed to a much more comfortable temperature. She slumped onto one of the many piles of pillows and peered to Aes, who had taken a position right next to the flame in a bid to dry off.

"You know, Aes, I could just use the blanket to dry you off." She chuckled. "Ah! Didn't realise you were so particular about ruffled fur. Okay then, suit yourself." She yawned. "To think, it was just this morning we were being heckled by wolves. And now—"

She sat upright and locked eyes with Aes.

"I…I don't understand. I couldn't have woken up more than an hour or two before I found you, and that was this afternoon. There's no way I slept through the night and then some down in that…" She squirmed, the thought of sleeping so close to the mass grave terrifying.

Without a word, she put her head back down and stared into the roof of the hut. Unable to shake the eerie feeling of having passed out amidst a group of tormented spirits, she lay on the soft heap for a number of hours, replaying the scene in her head and repeating the sentence that had been purposefully scratched out.

"Unless they, too, can be cut down and driven back into the earth at the hand of a heathen marked by both worlds."

CHAPTER 8

Octobrix 23, 484; small town five kilometres east of Crowton, Borlencia; eight and a half weeks earlier—Evia shifted on her saddle in search of reprieve from the dull pain that had gnawed its way into her right buttock. The early-afternoon air was muggy, an unusuality for that time of year, and the gnats were brave. Coupled with the hours already spent on the uncomfortable saddle throughout the morning, she was in an irritable mood.

She looked to her right just in time to see Fredrick stroke the long hairs on his arm with something bordering pleasure. He caught her glance and stopped short of seductively caressing his arm like she had seen him do in the past. It was a habit of his usually beckoned when they were stationary and in wait.

"They've been gone some time," he croaked, clearly eager to change the unspoken topic.

Then, evidently desperate to avoid Evia's gaze, he peered back to the three men also sitting in wait with seven empty mounts tied to them. Ex-soldiers turned merchants, they had heeded his and Santos's call once made aware of Erzse's atrocities. One of them acknowledged Fredrick with a nod, whilst the other two busied themselves with the army of gnats determined to leave no exposed skin unblemished.

"They'll be back soon," Evia said, turning back to the forest path that Dogner and Santos had left down.

"Your magic?" Fredrick spoke.

She looked at him with a quizzical stare.

"Sorry, didn't mean anything by it," he stammered. "Just mean, you can tell where they are, can't you?"

She chuckled. "Don't need magic for that, my dear. They said forty to fifty minutes. We're coming up on forty now."

"Like I said, magic. A woman that can tell the time without a clock. A difficult one to fathom."

"And if I was a man?"

He laughed nervously. "Didn't mean it like that. Woman, man, doesn't matter. Only said it because—"

"They're here." Her face hardened. "Something's not right."

A worried look took Fredrick and the others, and they quickly readied themselves for a possible confrontation.

"I don't see them," Fredrick said, eyes intent on the forest ahead. "Are they being chased? Are they injured? What's happened?"

She didn't respond, though the sudden hurt etched into her expression was enough to unsettle Fredrick. Moments later, Santos and Dogner appeared from the woods. Their faces were stern and their backs rigid. They rode with obvious anger and were silent as they merged with the group.

"What happened?" Fredrick asked nervously. "What did you see?"

Santos's eyes were red, though not from the dust of the road. He opened his mouth to respond but struggled for words.

"How many?" Evia asked solemnly.

"The four men local to the hamlet, along with the two mothers and three sons we had rescued," Dogner spoke angrily. "Hanged, but not before having their limbs cut off."

Fredrick's eyes widened, and the three other men shifted uncomfortably.

"And the rescued daughters?" Evia spoke, her voice starting to crack.

Dogner sighed. "All five were taken. The two elderly women native to the hamlet were left, but not before being tied up and made to watch."

"Watch what?" one of the men blurted. "The amputations? The hangings? What?"

"All the above and then some," Dogner said. "An example was made of every single one of them. That enough to go on or do I need to spell it out?"

The man nodded, both embarrassed by his own questioning and saddened by the revelation.

"Where does the trail lead?" Evia asked.

"Doesn't matter," Dogner said, shaking his head. "Happened two days ago. They'll be long gone by now."

"Damn it!" Santos seethed through gritted teeth. "That's—"

"Not our fault," Dogner said, swiftly cutting him off. "You heard it yourself. Like the old woman said, one of the Zylencians just happened to recognise one of the women. It was poor luck, nothing more."

"We should've come sooner."

"We didn't have the men," Fredrick said defensively.

"Then we need to get more!" Santos raged.

"You know—"

Evia cleared her throat. "Have the men, women, and children been buried?"

"It's why we came back," Dogner said. "We need the hands."

"Then let's go. It won't do to leave those two poor women to watch the horror any longer."

Dogner nodded and waved to the others. "Let's get this done."

At that, the seven of them began silently down the path, every glance at the empty saddles in their wake a brutal reminder of their failed deed.

That evening—Joseph handed a letter to Evia. "Delivered by one of Grendal's traders," he said, watching as she opened it.

They were alone in the room at the inn and had arrived at the same time from their respective errands along with Dogner. Though Dogner, keen to rid himself of the dirt from the hamlet, had been quick to leave to the local baths without more than a rushed greeting to Joseph. A small glimmer of hope took Evia's weary eyes as she finished reading it, and Joseph relaxed too.

"Good news?" he asked.

"You've not read it?"

"Why the surprise?"

She shrugged. "It's good news. Senior Minister Wiston of the Eurencians is coming to Crowton with Senior Minster Robyn. They've got the approval of the Eurencian parliament to help organise the election of Borlencia's Lower House. They arrive three weeks from now."

"Then you did it! And all from a single letter. They must really trust your word to drop it all in light of what they face at home."

"They understand the danger."

"All that gathered from your lone letter?"

She handed him the parchment. "They've got their own resources. They know, or at least suspect, Erzse isn't telling the whole truth in her justification for occupation. They're eager to meet with what's left of Borlencia's government and to publicly announce the legitimate election under their own supervision. It'll be under the pretence of heeding Erzse's own concerns about insurrection."

"So no intention to condemn Erzse's actions?"

She frowned. "I think that has yet to be seen. The letter's brief, but to garner the support of their peers, they had to convince them of the need to rebuild the Borlencian Lower House if they, the Eurencians, are to have any hope of overcoming their own issues. That a legal government in Borlencia could spare Zylencia's necessary military intervention in the region and free up troops to march east to face this new, unknown enemy that's appeared on the Eurencian border."

"Better than nothing. And I guess if we're looking at the facts, they need irrefutable proof of the witch's intentions if they're to act against her and the Zylencians. Without evidence, it makes little sense to accuse them outright."

"True, but I'm hopeful their sentiment will change once they see the situation for themselves. They have to cross through half of Borlencia to get to Crowton. They'll see the destruction with their own eyes. It'll not just be the unsure word of a couple of traders and spies contending with Erzse's army of professional liars. And then when they meet with the Borlencians, those that can attend of their own free will, they'll see that the insurrection Erzse speaks of is of her own making. I think, at that point, they'll not only support the election but throw their weight behind taking the Zylencians to court."

"Could be quite the platform to run on. Opposing Zylencian occupation. Even calling out Erzse for her crimes."

"Like I've said before, as tempting as it may be, I think it best the candidates keep the personal attacks against Erzse and the Zylencians to a minimum until we've got surer footing."

"Less likely to act volatile?"

She shrugged. "Riling up a woman as unpredictable as her with direct threats probably isn't sensible, even with the Eurencians watching. There are subtler ways of calling to light the illegality of Zylencian occupation. Once the Lower House is elected and the occupying force removed, then we should consider the next phase. Taking not just Erzse but the whole Zylencian parliament to court."

She walked over to her bed and sat down with a heavy thump.

"Everything alright?" Joseph asked.

"I wish it were. There was an incident today."

"Oh?"

"The group at the hamlet was discovered. The men, boys, and two of the women were killed. And the young girls taken."

Glumness took the man. "And here I was hoping to brighten your day with good news. I'm sorry, Evia. Sorry you had to witness that. And Dogner? I assume that was his reason for leaving with barely a word?"

She nodded. "Santos and the others are pretty shaken too." She pondered for a moment. "I should go see him. Santos, that is. See if he's okay. Won't do us any good to lose him."

"Bit late to wander the streets, Evia, and I can't accompany you. Not tonight."

"No need. I'll wait for Dogner. I think it would be good for those that were there to find some consolation in each other."

"So be it."

▲ ▲ ▲

Dogner looked up and down the quiet, dimly lit street, whilst Evia did a quick scan with her mind. Confident they hadn't been followed, he knocked four times on the heavy wooden door in front of them. Several moments later, it opened, and a hand waved them in. Evia entered first into the temperate room decorated by a simple stove and a round wooden table with four chairs.

She turned to her welcomer as he closed the door behind Dogner. "Santos."

His eyes were tired, but a weak smile arose as he hugged her. "Evia. Dogner. Come sit down. I'll pour us some tea."

"That's alright," Evia said, staying by the door with Dogner at her side. "We won't keep you long."

"Must be important if it couldn't wait until tomorrow."

"We don't bring news. We just wanted to check on you."

"She means to ask, are you okay, lad?" Dogner said.

Santos stood there silently. He had seen much in the weeks preceding. A shocking truth completely at odds with the stories being told by Erzse's paid stooges. What had been even more surprising, though, was the public's stubborn unwillingness to accept that the Zylencians—their brethren by nationality—could commit such unspeakable acts. And all despite the population's general dislike for the occupiers. The handful of stories concerning the atrocities that had managed to do the rounds were swiftly, and somewhat easily, condemned as falsehoods and the perpetrators imprisoned as insurrectionists. It was a treacherous game that had physically and mentally drained the group and all those involved in the rescues.

He looked at them, his tired eyes desperate for rest. "Are you sure you don't want a drink?"

"We're sure," Evia said. "It's dangerous for us to linger. Best we don't risk running into the wrong crowd at such an hour, when the streets are quiet and the witnesses few."

"Right, foolish of me to forget." He sighed. "I'll survive. What we saw earlier—it's only strengthened my resolve to do what's right. But…you need to know. That hamlet today, it's not the only incident. There was a similar occurrence some distance south of here, with the young girls taken and the rest left for dead. Coincidence again, it seems, but still—there's too many rescues, Evia. We've not got enough resources or caravans. And every day we make these people wait in some hideout until we can get to them is a day they risk discovery. It's almost safer just to let them get taken to Zylencia, rather than leave them in hiding without papers and a believable cover story in the face of Zylencian retribution if they're found. We should be more selective with those we can help and those we can't."

"Thought we already were," Dogner said. "Those groups with teenage girls and children, when it's not making it too bloody obvious who we're targeting, have to remain the priority."

"Yes, but unless there's a clear path with a time limit, I don't think we should even attempt the groups that fit our criteria. Our venture's also raising alarm from what I've heard. The number of Zylencian groups being attacked and their prisoners released hasn't gone unnoticed. Not sure what their next move will be, but I reckon it'll be only a matter of time before we happen upon a group overly ready for us."

"It's bound to happen sooner or later. Erzse's desire for discreetness can last only as long as those groups can defend themselves."

"Still, the riskier it gets, the more difficult it'll be for us to keep the hands we have. Especially when word gets around of what happened today."

"What solution do you have in mind?" Evia asked.

"I'd say rope in more towns or parties that can help, but I already know what your answer will be."

"It increases the risk of discovery. More people that can talk. More incidence of attack."

"I know," Santos said tiredly. "But we're too small an operation at the moment to be sustainable. We need to spread the burden and reduce the risk for those involved; otherwise, difficult choices will have to be made."

Evia sighed. "I'm making the choice for us. We continue as we are. If the network becomes too big, the chance for discovery of our origins or infiltration of our people becomes too great."

"Then it means we're condemning a lot of people when it's within our power to help them," Santos said, his exasperation evident.

"It's only within our power if we expand."

"What if," Dogner spoke up, "we create cells in some of the towns to the west. No more than four or five men, and their only contact will be with Santos or one of his trusted captains. Most of our activity's been concentrated in the wilds of eastern and central Borlencia, with the appearance of being random in location. So, we let a few through the net here and let them get picked up out west. It'll make it even harder to pinpoint us and it gives us a breather here. And if we keep up with the appearance of random selection, it'll continue to give the impression we're leaderless. Plus, if any of those cells are captured, they'll have minimal information to work with."

"It could work," Santos said. "Though I don't think it'll do anything to dissuade the Zylencians from beefing up their units."

"No, but that can't be helped. It was just a question of when, not if."

Evia bit her lip. The last thing she wanted was to give Erzse ammo and the Eurencians the wrong impression. "It's a good idea, but we still don't want to play into Erzse's narrative any more than we have."

"You don't think we've fully crossed that river already?" Santos asked.

"We've not made enough of a dent. Yes, the Zylencians will likely start using more troops to transport the prisoners, but our actions still don't give that obvious whiff of a grab for power by some unseen outfit. As if there's a sinister army in wait. An army that needs putting down. At most, we probably look like a small, semi-organised outfit just trying to rescue a few poor prisoners."

"Dogner's suggestion doesn't necessarily entail increasing the number of rescues. Simply the number of rescuers and the area in which we operate."

"I know, but to the Zylencians it'll make sense that there's a few fires to put out in central and eastern Borlencia, given what's happened. But if we start doing it in the west, then it could give the impression that the issue is a bit more widespread than they originally thought. Our priority now should be the election. Let's not upset that."

"Right, the election," Santos muttered as he rubbed his eyes and forehead. "There's more to why the teenage girls take priority than you've let on, isn't there? To have discarded the women, men, and boys like that today. It's the girls' value to Erzse, not to protect them from the soldiers?"

She nodded. "It's a hunch I can't be sure of. Even now, we can't prove it. But one I'd rather not disregard."

"But now that we know where the value lies, is that still not enough to convince you of the need to expand?" Santos asked.

Evia's fatigue was clear. "Perhaps something to discuss once we've slept on it."

"I think that might be a good idea," Dogner said, gripping Santos's shoulder. "We'll do what needs doing, lad. Don't you worry."

About to speak, Santos simply nodded.

"See you in the morning?" Evia asked sympathetically.

"Not tomorrow, no," Santos responded. "We've still not received responses from two of the mayors in the northwest. I'm riding out to see what the issue is. I'll not be back for a couple of days."

"And the meeting on the twenty-eighth?" Evia asked.

"Still set, unless you're having second thoughts?"

"No, it still works."

"Good. Ronal would have me killed if you wanted to change it. Every day he comes back to me saying that'll be the day that Erzse goes back on her word and has him and the others hung. He can't wait until we make it public." He yawned and then walked over to the door and opened it. "I'll see you three days from now."

"Good luck."

"And you."

"We'll see you soon, lad," Dogner said, and he and Evia exited onto the street.

CHAPTER 9

Decembrix 22, 484; the Hunter's Passage, Zylencia—"No, no, no, Malum. It's like I told you before, the sky is a big blue bubble that rests on the peak of Crassus."

"I have to respectfully disagree with you there, Gemin. If it was a big blue bubble balanced atop Crassus, then surely the peak would pop it, pop it into many little bubbles."

"Well, it's impervious to sharp objects."

"I don't know. What about the clouds and the stars? How do you explain them?"

"Well, Malum, it's like this. The clouds are simply discolourations of the bubble, and the stars are refractions of light."

"Refractions from where?"

"Huh?"

"Well, where does the light refract from?"

"How do I know? What a silly question. Does it look like I've got wings? All I know is the sky's a bubble, and unless you can prove otherwise, that's what we'll believe. Oh! Look, she's awake."

The two stout, rotund men, clad in blue and identical except for the wonkiness of their noses and the faintest speck of a mole on the ever-so-portlier one's upper lip, looked down to where Xander lay dazedly. Behind them, the cauldron bubbled atop the fire, exuding a delicious aroma of spiced meat and vegetables.

"Who are you?" she said, sitting up, her head light. "Where's Aes?"

"A lot of questions for someone we barely know, right, Malum?" the one with the whisper of a mole said.

"Certainly is, Gemin. Very rude if you ask me."

"Very rude, indeed. Not to mention, she's a bit strange making herself at home in a home that doesn't belong to her."

"A bit strange, indeed. But I guess, when a situation can't be helped, sometimes there's little choice but to do that which makes you seem a little bit strange."

"I'm sorry," she said, embarrassed. "Look, I don't know who you are, and I would very much like to know where my friend is." She felt no danger from the pair, though she was a tad perplexed by their oddness.

"Well, ha, well, missy, my name's Malum and his is Gemin, and you're now, apparently, a guest in our—"

"Hush, Malum. We still don't know who she is."

They looked at her expectantly.

"I'm Xander. And where's my friend?"

"Friend? We didn't see any friends when we found you," Malum responded.

"No friends, just you and the stag with a broken crown," Gemin added.

Xander's face brightened. "His name's Aes, and he *is* my friend."

"Oh! He has a name. Who would've thought?" Malum said with genuine surprise.

Gemin grunted as he rubbed his chin. "Indeed, who would've thought? Very odd."

Her brow creased, and she could feel a dull ache worming its way into her forehead. "I don't understand. Where is he? What've you done with him?"

"That's certainly a very good question, isn't it, Gemin?"

"Very good, indeed."

"And one better left answered by showing you. Are you able to walk?"

She stood with some difficulty, her eyes fuzzy, but she soon found herself, and they walked out of the wooden hut into the evening haze.

"Aes, what a relief!" She smiled and placed her hand to his neck, though her eyes quickly widened. "I slept right through the night and day! Oh no!" she said, dread gripping her innards.

"And we found you both this morning. You, asleep and snoring inside, and the stag, just there," Gemin said, pointing a metre to Xander's left. "But that's beside the case. What a remarkable gift," he said with curiosity etched across his chubby cheeks.

"Very remarkable, indeed," Malum added.

She looked at them quizzically.

Gemin chortled. "Isn't it obvious? You're both sky-whisperers."

"A rare occurrence. Who would've thought!" Malum added.

"Indeed, who would've thought."

"A sky-whisperer?" Xander repeated, puzzled.

"A man, woman, or critter," Gemin began, "that is capable of hearing and communicating with others without a spoken word."

Xander thought back to what her aunt had told her when she was younger, and though she felt a little tingle of hope and excitement at the thought of being a sky-whisperer, she also recalled her aunt's inability to find any spark within her. "I think you're mistaken. I haven't got the spark. I know I can communicate with Aes—when he lets me—but that's because we're bonded. He's the one with the ability to talk to other sky-whisperers, not me. None of this makes me a sky-whisperer."

"Ah, maybe not then. Silly us."

"Silly indeed," Malum said. "After all, Gemin, it's common knowledge amongst us sky-whisperers that a single connection to another's mind—one born from a unique bonding event such as theirs—does not signify the mind of one of our own."

"Yes, yes. It's an easy one to misconstrue, and if you really think about it, Malum, slim chance of meeting one sky-whisperer, let alone two."

"There, there, it can't always be helped. At least you got to meet the one, however quiet," Malum added, peering at Aes.

"So, now that we've solved the riddle of the missing friend—"

"Friends," Xander interrupted.

"Friends?" Gemin remarked, surprised.

"We're traveling as a party of four, and we got separated. You said you found us here this morning, which means you must've been on the road. Did you by chance see a middle-aged man and a young woman? They were headed southwest, up the slope. They were off the path, but that was two days ago. Anything could've happened since then."

The twins glanced at each other.

"You've seen them, haven't you?" she said excitedly. "When? Where were they headed? Were they on the path?"

"A path of sorts," Malum said awkwardly.

"A path of sorts?"

"They passed not far from here two days ago. They were in quite the hurry, if I recall."

"Understandable when you consider what was chasing them," Gemin added. "They didn't stop to say hello, though we did try to wave them down."

"Must not have seen us, right, Gemin?"

"Right! Anyway, as it happened, we thought we'd give them a helping hand and so took it upon ourselves to show them a path."

"Though, perhaps not the path you're referring to," Malum said.

She raised an eyebrow. "What did you do?"

Gemin looked at Malum. "That was two days ago. Likely they'll be gone a couple more days. Does that sound about right?"

Malum scratched his chin pensively. "Sounds about right, Gemin."

"Where are they?" she said with growing impatience.

"The path takes them on a big loop around the nearest peaks before they'll find themselves ascending the little path you came along to reach here. Nothing to worry about, all quite harmless."

"A couple more days? I think they'll figure it out long before then that it's bringing them back here," she scoffed.

"Oh! Is that so?" Gemin said, surprised. "You might be right. Silly me, I shouldn't be so quick to assume."

"Silly indeed," Malum said. "It's never a perfect science with the paths we built when you take into account the navigator's abilities."

"Wait—you built them?" she asked.

"Yes, we built them. All fun and games, really, though some have been known to get hurt," Gemin said regretfully. "Usually a sprained ankle or delirium. Nothing fatal," he quickly added.

"Still, I'm sure her friends will be fine," Malum chimed in. "She seems to think so."

"Indeed, you're right. Nothing to worry about. So, dinner?"

"Wait, hold on," Xander said, increasingly annoyed by their nonchalant demeanour. "I need to find my friends. You built the paths. Point me in the right direction."

"Would be more than happy to," Gemin began, "but at this point it would be faster for all if they were left to their own devices."

"Right he is," Malum said. "So dinner it is, then." At that, the pair turned towards the hut.

Xander stepped after them. "Wait—what do you mean, 'dinner'? What about my friends?"

"Dinner. It should be ready right about now," Malum replied, looking up at the overcast sky as if judging the position of the sun.

She gave them an exasperated look—it was a strained stare born from her growing frustration and confusion with the fast-paced, tipsy tit-for-tat coming from the two brothers practically indiscernible in appearance and voice.

Gemin beamed. "We like to simmer it, you see."

"Helps release the flavours—" Malum began.

"Please, my friends," Xander interjected. "Malum, Gemin, please. We can't spare the time. We must get—"

"To Zyphyr. Right she is, Malum. Silly us."

"Silly indeed," Malum responded. "But at this point it really would be—"

She rubbed her tired eyes. "I didn't mention Zyphyr…"

Malum's brow creased with shock. "Did you not? Maybe it was the stag, then."

"Right! Must've been," Gemin exclaimed. "As we were saying, Xander, it really would be much faster…"

But she wasn't listening and half stumbled into the hut in search of her kit. When she emerged, the two odd fellows hadn't moved and continued to stare with keen interest at the agitated girl.

"Come on, Aes. We'll take our chances." But he didn't budge once she mounted. "Come on. Let's go," she whispered, shifting uncomfortably under the duo's stare, but still he refused to move.

"You sure you don't want some dinner?" Gemin asked softly. "Won't do you any good riding on an empty stomach." On cue, Xander's stomach cramped, and hunger gnawed. "Plus, it's getting a tad late, and I'd certainly feel guilty letting you ride off in the dark."

"Come on, Aes…You want us to stay…but the others? You really think they'll be fine? And us with these two…" She glanced back and then slumped in defeat at his silent insistence.

"It's settled, then. You're staying for dinner," Gemin said joyously.

"Indeed," Malum chimed in. "Come on, you'll love how we tenderize and marinate the meat."

"And the tea—it really is very special," Gemin added. "Will put hairs on your lip."

The comfortable warmth of the hut and the delicious meaty scent it carried were like an elixir to Xander's tired body, and she couldn't help but beam with joy as the four of them splayed themselves around the hearth amidst a jungle of cushions and blankets. The twins were sitting atop lofty throw cushions on opposite sides of the firepit, a mere metre from the flames, and Xander and Aes were lounging in between, albeit with more distance between them and the scorch of the fire.

Gemin snorted as he laughed. "That's the silliest theory I've heard yet. A rock within a bubble—that's nonsensical. Isn't it, Malum?"

"Well, respectfully, Gemin, I think it holds weight. Xander, how big is this bubble?"

"Difficult to tell," she replied. "Though one of my old teachers, Putantis, always used to say, 'Bigger than you could possibly imagine.'"

"Well, that's just ridiculous!" Gemin scoffed. "Surely it depends on the imagination, then. And how does the rock just float there in the centre of this bubble? And what of the sun and the stars? Too many flaws for my comfort. Refraction of light is the only logical theory." He grumbled something under his breath before taking a sip of his tea.

"The sun is a star, and all stars are contained within the bubble," Xander continued.

"Preposterous. Again, what nonsense."

"Hold on, Gemin," Malum said. "Don't be so rash to dismiss. The science may be logical."

"Indeed, it might be, but I don't see how, and what is this bubble inside…"

Xander stifled a laugh as they continued arguing about the stars and the planets and people and their actions and everything, really. The stew and tea, as delicious and hearty as they were, had dissolved her stress and fatigue, and though she wrestled with the impatience of her friends' arrival, she marvelled at the crafty genius of the twins, as she had come to think of them. The paths they had built were what some would call smoke and mirrors. They weren't real but somehow dreamt up in what they described as "blatant disregard of reality's governing laws and a nod to the corruption of its boundaries." In this realm, no real harm could come to Ricard and Aika, as all provisions were attainable and the route not so dangerous, but there was also no way back but to complete the path before them.

"An opportunity to relax and reflect," as Malum, or maybe it was Gemin, had put it. She had chuckled, knowing full well Ricard would not think the same.

"Why's there a wire sticking out of the boulder outside your home?" Xander interrupted, her curiosity sudden in its approach.

They stopped mid-argument and looked at her, as did Aes, who had to that point been quietly vegetating in his little nook of cosiness.

"Why the stare?" she said defensively.

"Well, that's a good question and a fair observation, isn't it, Malum?" Gemin said.

"Indeed. We were wondering when you were going to ask us that."

"We were. Shall I, or would you like to enlighten her?"

"You know how I like to tell a story—"

"Hold on, Malum. Let's try an experiment," Gemin said with a cheeky smile.

Malum matched Gemin's grin. "I like your thought process."

Outside, the air was frigid, borderline undesirable.

"Climb the boulder?" Xander asked, confused.

"Need I repeat myself thrice?" Gemin said.

She nodded and then climbed the cold, rough surface. Only about three metres in height, it felt much higher from the top, and she gaped at the moonlit steppe that held up the bountiful cluster of stars that seemed otherworldly in their shine and quantity.

"Now what?"

"Hold the wire," Gemin called up. "How exciting this is."

"Very exciting!" Malum agreed. "Now, Xander, close your eyes."

She closed her eyes. "What now?"

"Just wait. You'll know when the time is right."

She gripped the icy metal in her hand and stood in silence, with the sound of her breath and the wind and the steppe below all that filled her ears. Calm befell her, as did clarity, and she heard the faintest rustle at the back of her mind, though what it was, she could not decipher.

Again the rustle sounded, though fainter than the first, and she strained to find the source before it again disappeared. This time, the faintest glimmer of happiness and laughter rang through, and she smiled at the warmth it brought.

"I felt something," she called excitedly.

The laughter grew, as did the feeling of joy, so much so that she could both sense and hear the euphoria that drove to overwhelm her.

"It…it's bizarre but surreal." She giggled. "Does the same happen to you?" she called with her eyes still closed.

The laughter grew, but it was rowdier and more mischievous than in its inception, and she opened her eyes to see the empty ground where the three had stood, near hysterics emanating from inside.

"Cretins!" She laughed and climbed down and into the hut to the cheers and claps of the twins and the evident amusement of Aes.

"Congratulations, Xander. What a success," Gemin chuckled.

"Indeed it was," Malum said, patting her back.

CHAPTER 10

Octobrix 27, 484; Crowton, Borlencia; eight weeks earlier—Desperate for reprieve from the muggy afternoon heat that was so unusual for that time of year, Evia stood by the open bedroom window with wet hair and a damp cloth on her neck. To her dismay, however, it seemed no amount of cool liquid could work to lessen the effects of the discomfort, and she now found herself nursing a growing headache. She puffed her cheeks and blew with exaggerated exasperation.

"It'll do me little good going into that meeting if I can't even think—"

She turned abruptly from the window to the bedroom door as it slammed open, and Dogner charged through with Joseph immediately behind, the little man's obvious attempt at calming the larger man futile.

"It's my family, lad," Dogner said angrily, his cheeks crimson. "The bastards have them in damn chains and you—you'd ask me not to go?"

Dread took Evia. "The group you scouted this morning?"

"Aye. It's my brats."

"And your wife?"

"Not with them. But that matters not." He looked at Joseph. "I'll not sit back and leave it to the fates, as you'd so desire."

"It's not that I desire that," Joseph retorted. "But if you turn up and lose—"

"Lose what? My composure? You think I'm some untrained squirt—"

"Doesn't matter how well trained you are, Dogner. I could feel your rage today. You were a hair's breadth from losing it and charging in headfirst."

Dogner slammed his fist into the wall, causing the plaster to crumble. "I'm going with ya, and that's all there is to it!"

Joseph peered pleadingly to Evia.

She sighed. "We can't stop him, Joseph."

"But—" Joseph began.

"I know. But we couldn't even if we tried."

"Evia?"

She ignored the appeal. "Did you also scout where you'll set up the ambush?"

Resigned, Joseph nodded. "Afterwards, yes. A town six kilometres southeast of here."

"A town?" she said, raising a quizzical eyebrow. "Thought the Zylencians tried to avoid anything larger than a small village?"

"Not this one. It's the only route over a river for a number of kilometres. They've no choice but to ride through it."

"And the locals?"

"Keep to themselves," Dogner said. "They pose no harm to us and give no cares about the Zylencians, providing they're left to their own devices."

"This group's moving slow," Joseph continued. "They'll not reach it until tomorrow afternoon at the earliest. But we'll be ready."

Evia glanced back at Dogner, and he shuffled awkwardly under her gaze. "Will you take some advice?" she asked him.

"Depends on the advice," he responded.

"Rashness—"

Dogner lifted his hand to stop her. "I'm no fool, Evia. A rash decision on my part will get my family killed. I'll not let that happen. Don't you worry."

"Okay, then. So when do you leave?"

"We'll set up shop tomorrow morning," Joseph said, taking a seat on his bed. "I'll rendezvous with Fredrick tonight to get some men. He said he was able to get his hands on a couple of rifles and some gunpowder, so that'll be helpful."

Surprise took Evia. "They've been in short supply since Borealis's fall."

"Rarer than untampered Zylencian shillings, that's for sure. What's wrong?"

"You'll not be here for the meeting."

"No, we won't," Dogner spoke up. "And for that, I'm sorry, but in this instance—"

"You needn't say anymore, my friend," she said. "Your family comes first in every way. I understand."

"You'll have Santos by your side, though," Joseph added. "He'll not let any harm come to you. And he's trusted by the mayors."

"Yes, yes, I'll be alright." She looked at the pair, and a little niggle of worry wormed its way into her. "For preparation's sake, why don't you show me a layout of what you've got planned? That way we can even out any wrinkles."

Despite the seriousness, Joseph chortled at Evia's tendency for overprotectiveness. "If it'll make you feel better."

"It would."

He got up and pulled a map from his sack. Unrolling it onto his bed, the three of them huddled closer, and together they ran through the motions of the setup until the dim of the early evening made reading hard and forced them to run their final errands and seek out dinner.

CHAPTER 11

Decembrix 23, 484; the Hunter's Passage, Zylencia—"Who were they?" Xander asked as the twins examined her sketch of the three triangles stacked in a column.

They had just finished breakfast, a delightful blend of goat cheese and bread, and whilst Aes dozed off to the side, Xander and her new friends sat around the centre conversing.

Gemin looked up at her. "Part of a non-religious sect. The group was common throughout the Black Mountains before Anemoi became a non-religious state."

"Even after they had accomplished their goal of removing religion from government, many of them remained intact," Malum added, handing the sketch back to Xander. "Squabbling and often fighting with the religious fanatics behind the scenes."

"We know the temple you speak of, though we've never been down there."

"And although it's been some sixty-odd years since we've come across any of the members, we'd simply assumed that they'd grown bored and returned to their villages. Of course, now we know it was likely a rival sect that—"

"Sixty!" she said belatedly, nearly spilling her tea. "You both barely look a day over forty."

They chuckled.

"We're quite a bit older than sixty," Gemin said.

"Probably closer to one hundred and sixty," Malum added.

"What?" she said in disbelief. "And what do you mean, 'probably'?"

"Those first years were a bit of a blur."

"And recordkeeping back then wasn't the most reliable this far out in the sticks," Gemin said.

"Which means no telling exactly when we popped out, so to say."

They threw each other a glance and nodded. They looked back to her, keen to continue.

"Our father died before we were born and our mother when we were no older than seven or eight," Gemin said.

"The village tried to provide for us after we were orphaned," Malum continued, "but times were hard. Around our twelfth, or maybe it was our thirteenth, birthday, it was determined we were too much of a burden on the village, and thus we were left to fend for ourselves."

"Of course, the villagers never drove us out. They just refused to feed us with what little supplies they had."

"What did you do?" Xander asked.

"Scavenged," Gemin replied.

"And stole," Malum added. "It was also about this time that we learned we weren't your ordinary village folk."

"You realised you were sky-whisperers?" she said with an eager smile.

"Oh! We knew we were sky-whisperers from the moment we could communicate with each other in our mother's womb," Malum said excitedly. "Though we didn't have a name for it until much later."

"Correct! In fact, it was about this time that we realised we were sky-whisperers with a fantastic ability to…" Gemin held out his hand to the side, and an image of Aika and Ricard appeared at the end of his fingertips.

It was as if the pair were a mere thirty metres away, visible through a borderless window in the middle of the hut. Walking along a path together with nothing but the rock and grass of the steppe on the horizon, the two of them were covered in the filth of the road and looked knackered.

"Over here!" Xander shouted, startling Aes out of his stupor, but neither looked up. "Ricard! Aika!" Still nothing. "They can't hear me?" she asked the twins.

"Not through this, no," Malum said. "They're still some distance away, unfortunately."

"As we said before, nothing we can do but let them finish this leg of the journey," Gemin added.

At that, the image disappeared.

"Can't imagine they'll be too happy when they find out what you've done to them," Xander said.

Aes grunted his agreement.

"Some things can't be helped, right, Gemin?" Malum said.

"Indeed, Malum!"

"Anyhow, back to the story. Left to fend for ourselves in the wilds with nobody to show us right from wrong, it was about this time that we ran into your aunt Evia."

"Evia?" Xander asked, confused.

"You did say that your aunt, the sky-whisperer, is Evia of Nhata Bay, did you not?" Malum said.

"I don't recall mentioning her name to you," she said, confused, though not quite sure if she had or hadn't, given the blur of the preceding days.

"Well, maybe it was the stag, then," Gemin said, scratching his cheek. "Either way, yes, your aunt Evia."

"But if what you say is true, that would mean—she never told me how old she was."

"And yet, she's got a few years on us."

Malum tittered. "Though she'll likely tell you otherwise."

"She became the guardian our village couldn't provide," Gemin continued. "And it's a mantle she still holds, when she's got the time to speak."

"Though it has been some time since we've spoken, hasn't it, Gemin?"

"Indeed it has. A seldom occurrence these days."

"She never mentioned you," Xander said somewhat guiltily. "I wish she had. I'm sure she has many stories to tell, but she raised you. Made you into the men you are. A wholesome story and truly fascinating."

Gemin shrugged. "Evia has lived more lifetimes than most, and that's irrespective of her age."

"She's a trove of tales and adventures and encounters," Malum continued. "And we, we are but a pair of devious divots on her long and winding road. We slowed her cart and left an impression but possessed only a fraction of her time."

"Indeed. Couldn't have put it better myself."

She quietly stared at them, taking in the roundness of their cheeks, the shallow wrinkles that decorated their mischievous expressions, and the oval gems that stared back. She was in complete awe at the revelation. A chance in a billion that she would stumble upon their hut in the wilds, she figured.

"There are so many questions I want to ask you," she said finally. "And I don't know where to start."

Malum smiled and raised a finger. "How about whether or not you really are a sky-whisperer?"

"Oh yes! That sounds like a fun experiment," Gemin said joyfully.

▲ ▲ ▲

Morning of the 24th—Xander opened an eye and peeked at Malum and Gemin, both of whom had theirs closed. Sitting cross-legged on the floor of the hut, the three of them had the warmth of the hearth and the spicy aromas of that morning's breakfast to keep them company.

She closed her eye and took a deep breath, reaching her mind out to them the same way she could with Aes. But there was nothing. No thoughts or semblance of a presence. She huffed and opened her eyes. About to speak,

Malum, with his eyes still closed, interrupted her:

"A student of patience, I see."

"Indeed! And a strong one at that," Gemin added.

"We've been trying this for hours," she said in frustration. "My legs are numb. My back is sore. And poor Aes is freezing his nose off out there just so we can do this without 'disturbance.' I can't hear anything other than your heavy breathing and the crackle of the fire. And you clearly can't hear my attempts to speak to you using my…" She tapped her head. "I told you I'm not a sky-whisperer. You're mistaken, like you originally said."

"A jest taken to heart," Malum murmured.

"Who would've thought we'd be held to words spoken in jest," Gemin said, shaking his head.

"If I were a sky-whisperer, don't you think I would know it by now?" Xander asked.

They both laughed, eyelids still closed.

"It was my aunt—the woman that helped raise you—who said she couldn't find a spark," Xander rebutted.

"It wouldn't be the first time Evia's been wrong," Gemin said, though he meant no malice. "Remember, how can someone that isn't a sky-whisperer converse with someone that is, all without speaking a word?"

Xander puffed her cheeks. She was still weak, and the worry of falling into another deep sleep lingered. It was a feeling somewhat at odds with the embarrassment of repeatedly and unsuccessfully trying to communicate with them using her mind.

"I understand the logic," she said. "A sky-whisperer isn't specifically listening to another sky-whisperer's thoughts when they're communicating; they're *intentionally* communicating back and forth using the vibrations of their minds. Therefore, if there's no special bond to enable the communication—like mine and Aes's—the only other way I could've communicated with that person on the steppe was if we were both sky-whisperers. I get that part. I do. But…"

The twins opened their eyes and looked at her.

"You're still nervous?" Gemin asked rhetorically.

"Yes, I am," she admitted. "I'm still worried I'll slip back into another deep sleep."

"The prolonged sleep was solely the product of your visitor's projection," Malum said, referring to the silhouetted man that had appeared to her as a vision on the night she and the others were attacked by wolves.

"I know. You told me. But isn't what we're trying to do now kind of the same?"

"It isn't. A projection not only consumes more energy but we've since determined that your visitor wasn't able to find the energy to project themself to you, so they used a portion of your energy. Therein lies the difference."

Xander stared at them quizzically. "You didn't mention that second part before."

"We only determined it about thirty minutes ago," Malum said.

"Whilst you were sitting there not doing much," Gemin teased. The twins looked at each other and then back at Xander. "It did raise another interesting point, however. One which we were reluctant to reveal for fear of upsetting your training."

She raised an eyebrow. "So you're still playing your tricks?"

Malum sat back, hands clasped. "Depends on who you ask, but it's not for no reason. We've arrived at another conclusion concerning your interaction with that mystery person."

"Not only are you a sky-whisperer," Gemin said, "but you're also bonded to them."

"Wait…what?" Xander stammered, unsure she had heard correctly.

Gemin continued, "Some strong sky-whisperers are fully capable of projecting an image of themselves into the mind of another, regardless of the recipient's abilities. But this particular encounter suggests there's a connection similar to the one you have with the stag. The assumed distance. The significant energy usage and their ability to requisition some of yours.

The fact that your mystery person was not strong enough to do it of their own accord. And the fact that there was two-way communication without the help of Aes."

"It's impossible. I have no idea who this person is."

"*Impossible* is a strong word," Malum replied. "And on the contrary, it's your ability as a sky-whisperer, coupled with your connection to this mysterious person, that allowed you both—two sky-whisperers with still-questionable strength—to communicate as you did. You and this person have a potentially powerful combination not unlike mine and Malum's."

Shock and uncertainty tore into Xander's expression.

"It's all very exciting," Malum said enthusiastically. "But back to the original point—the chance of experiencing the same exhaustion from these simple exercises is remote at best."

"Adding to that," Gemin said, "if your visitor does reappear, you'll be better able to handle the stresses after some training."

Xander chewed her cheek as she digested the information, having barely registered the last comment meant to reassure.

"Still, a distracted mind isn't always a productive mind, Malum," Gemin said. "Perhaps we should take a break."

"Putting it like that, I think a break would be sensible," Malum agreed.

"Fancy a walk?" they asked Xander, her mind caught on the two theories.

She wanted to explore whatever it was they had seen in her that Evia hadn't—to understand who it was that had visited her that night—but she couldn't deny the fact that she was tired, irritable, and still a tad nervous about falling back into a deep sleep, despite their assurances. "I think a walk would do me good."

Wrapped for warmth, they stepped into the cold outdoors where their steamy breath carried on the air. Aes was immediately excited for the company, and the four of them began along a path Xander hadn't noticed the day before.

"How do you do that?" she asked curiously.

"Do what?" Gemin responded.

"This path wasn't here yesterday. I'm sure of it. And now we walk along it as if it were always here."

"And how do you know it wasn't here, and you didn't just miss it?" Malum said.

Her mouth twisted as she considered the question. "I guess I can't say I'm absolutely certain. But I'm pretty sure."

"Pretty sure and absolute certainty are two very different outlooks," Gemin remarked. "Down here." He pointed to a path deviating from the one they were on that appeared from nothing.

"Now that one definitely wasn't there a second ago!"

"And you're certain?"

She rubbed her palm against her forehead. "You're playing with me."

"Us?" Malum said with feigned shock. "Would we do such a thing, Gemin?"

"Absolutely not! What an accusation."

They peered at her with mischievous grins, and then both pointed to the left where another path appeared from nowhere. This one was much steeper and had them all clambering up awkwardly until their legs ached and the way down seemed a sheer drop. Still, the climb was all but a matter of minutes, and soon enough they rounded onto the flat ground at the top of the climb. To Xander and Aes's shock, the four of them were met with an unimpeded view of the mountains to the south and north of their position, as if they stood in the clouds above.

"How…how's this possible?" Xander stammered. "We couldn't have been climbing for more than a few minutes."

Gemin chuckled. "Whatever could you mean?"

"Tricksters! So is this view even real?"

"Define real."

She looked at them and then laughed. "I guess even if it isn't, it really is quite beautiful."

"A beautiful view from which to clear your mind—" Gemin began.

"Through peace of mind," Malum finished.

Suddenly the image shuffled, and they found themselves looking down on a vast rolling landscape of farms, towns, and villages.

"Central Borlencia," Gemin said, sensing Xander's question.

"You see that large settlement in the middle? That's Crowton," Malum said. "And it's currently where your aunt stays."

"Evia!" Xander blurted. "Is she okay?"

"Yes."

"And you can speak to her?"

"Not right now, no. She's busy," Gemin responded.

"When she's less busy, we'll reach out and let her know we have you," Malum said.

"Maybe you can even try yourself, once you've figured out how."

She bit her lip, knowing it wasn't an easy ask.

The twins abruptly turned to her, making her jump. "Afternoon tea?"

CHAPTER 12

Octobrix 28, 484; Crowton, Zylencia; eight weeks earlier—Evia shifted on her chair as the Wispy Tavern continued to fill with men and women, some young but the majority middle-aged, from all over Borlencia. None wore the robes or marks of their political, military, or mercantile positions, and all carried a cautious air and a film of sweat from the afternoon's humidity.

Sitting at the back of the room with Santos on one side and Fredrick on the other, she fiddled with the cutlery laid before her. To her discomfort, the nervous niggle of the prior night had compounded into a hot flush content to ravage her bowels. She knew the niggle had nothing to do with the crowd gathering before her and everything to do with Dogner and Joseph. But she couldn't figure out why. Intent to dwell as she watched the success of Santos's call to gather, she jumped as Santos leant over and spoke into her ear:

"You lied to me."

She turned to him to see that he was smiling. "Do tell?"

"Maybe *lied* is not the right word. You misled me. My mind, that is. I remember your niece now, as clear as light—Xander. It came to me this morning. It's definitely not a face or an encounter I could forget. And yet I did. You did something, didn't you?"

"It's a long story, perhaps one for another time."

He sat back. "It'll be an interesting story, I'm sure. Don't worry. I don't doubt you wouldn't have done such a thing if not out of necessity."

Fredrick leant forward and looked at them. "Even the mayor of Bulgar's here. You've done well, Santos."

Santos's expression hardened. "We'll still be a few short, I'm sorry to say. Most of the towns on the lakeshore north of Nhata were, well, let's just say, there were none left to requisition. Couple of mayors from the northwest were also missing."

"It'll have to do," Evia said as she peered around the room. She locked eyes with Ronal, and the man raised his glass with eager anticipation. Evia nodded and subtly began to scan the room with her mind. Other than the nervous chatter and joyous greetings that one would expect from such a gathering, the room was silent of anything malicious.

Once the audience was settled, Ronal stood and urged for quiet with his hands. "Now that the lot of you are here as guests in my town, time we got down to business."

"This better not be another one of your tricks, Ronal," a man with a nondescript face said to quiet chuckles.

"Nope, not today. I mean, that's not to say I won't indulge later. But for now, I'd like to pass you over to Evia," he said and sat back down.

The room erupted with whispers and mumbles as everybody present strained to see the woman they'd heard and read so much about, not just in the preceding weeks but through their learned history.

Not wanting to waste a moment, Evia stood. "Thank you for coming. I know it was a long journey for a lot of you. Long and dangerous."

Grumblings abounded.

"But I wouldn't have called you here if not out of necessity."

"The shadow warriors?" A woman with long grey hair spoke up, parroting Santos's reason for calling the meeting.

"Are just one part of the problem."

"Then the Zylencians?"

Nervous chatter did the rounds, forcing Evia to raise her hand for quiet.

"Another part of the problem, I won't lie," Evia said. "Both are problems that have forced your hand, whether you realise it or not. As it is, Borlencia is more akin to a rabble of warring city-states than a united province of Anemoi. There's little unity—"

"And what would you expect?" a big man roared. "What would you expect after those masked bastards ripped the heart from our province and ravaged our countryside for two years?"

"That was a decade ago, Percy," Ronal said, irritated, without looking at the man.

"Don't matter. Without Borealis, we're nothing. And no amount of plotting from the likes of that bastard"—he pointed at Ronal—"will do anything to change it."

"Just let the woman finish," the lady with long grey hair said.

Though keen to protest further, the man sat down with a disapproving grunt.

"Thank you," Evia said with a gentle nod to the woman. "There's little unity between the towns, and as a result we've been left with a group of semi-functioning local governments. This dysfunction is directly responsible for the Zylencian aggression." She raised her hands, stemming the expected protest before it could start. "I am not saying you are insurrectionists eager to seize power across western Anemoi. Far from it. What I am saying is Erzse and her allies saw an opportunity in your dysfunction, and they took it. And unfortunately for us, the other provinces aren't in a state to come to our aid. That means, for now, we are on our own."

"So you would have us unify?" the woman with grey hair asked.

"She would have us call an election and re-establish the Lower House," Ronal said. "Elect the senior and common ministerial positions, as well as the council positions."

The woman looked at Evia, cunning in her eyes. "And you know why we haven't, right?"

"I do," Evia spoke. "Before the Zylencians, it was disagreement on location—"

The woman scoffed. "Not just the location. Some of the cretins in this room wanted to bypass the election altogether, claiming war and time of need. They felt their precious mayoral position or military rank should give them a guaranteed path to becoming a minister or councilman. I should know; I was a member of the bloody Lower House before—"

"Alright, we know the story," Ronal said with an agitation Evia hadn't seen before.

"All I'm saying," the woman continued, "is maybe Erzse isn't too far off the point. Not everybody's as honest as you think they are."

Evia's expression remained straight. "Well, a legitimate election would go some way to fixing that then, wouldn't it? Every ministerial and council position would be voted on and the hosting town alternated every year." She raised her hand before anybody from the crowd could favour or object aloud. "With the town to be drawn at random from a hat by me this year and through random selection in future years."

"And what of Erzse?" a wiry man with a scar across his face asked. "The witch'll have us all hanged before the first ballot's dropped."

"You think she would stand in the way of a legitimate election of Borlencia and risk the ire of the other provinces?" Evia said with feigned surprise.

"I think you're playing with fire. That's what I think. And I don't think I want any part of it. And I highly doubt any from my town—heck, my county—will go for this."

The woman with grey hair stood up. "Then you, your town, and your county can go without representation. Evia, you'll have the support of Bulgar."

"And that's because you've not been soiled by the damn witch," the wiry man hissed. "Only town on the northwest lakeshore not to have faced the witch's wrath. What does that tell ya?"

"What are you insinuating, you dense bastard?"

Evia cleared her throat in an attempt to interrupt the bickering but to little avail.

"You know what I'm saying," the wiry man spat. "And even if it ain't true, what will ya tell your kin if Erzse does decide to run a rake through their backsides, huh?"

"Evia's right," the woman with grey hair said. "It's the only way. And why would Erzse stand in the way of a—"

"Don't give me that nonsense. You know why. She'll label any involved as insurrectionists and have them hung."

Loud wrangling abounded but swiftly died down as Santos stood up with a threatening glare.

"I think you underestimate the power we have as a group," he said. "Picking off towns to the east was an easy feat for the Zylencians because we lacked unity. It was also an attempt to subdue the rest of us by taking out the smallest and weakest of us with a show of force. And look, it's worked. You've shrivelled up like little—"

"I'll not have some marauder from the desert question my backbone!" the wiry man growled.

"Please," Evia said, voice raised. The onlookers went quiet and immediately settled themselves. "A public election shows transparency on our part. And puts Erzse in a position where interference could be seen as not giving the people an opportunity to build a government that can face the army in the north and also counter the rogue group she speaks of. But the question of whether she'll allow it matters not. Ronal has convinced her to sanction the vote, and she's agreed."

There was silence, with none sure how to respond.

Finally, the woman with grey hair stood. "This is the same Erzse that occupies our province and indirectly calls the people in this room insurrectionists?"

Evia nodded. "The same that's razed a dozen towns in the east and executed thousands of Borlencian men. The same that's now shipping the women and children to Zylencia to be used for, and as, who knows what."

"Those are just rumours," one of the men in the room scoffed. "A couple groups of rogue Zylencian soldiers with their Borlencian whores isn't enough—"

"Get your head out your arse and wake up," the woman with grey hair muttered. She looked at Evia. "And we can be sure she won't go back on her word?"

"She won't," Ronal spoke.

"And what's in it for you?" the man called Percy asked suspiciously.

"You mean, what's in it for us? An election sanctioned by the Zylencians, that's what. Seems Erzse believes her accusations as much as the next person. That's why she's given us her blessing."

It was a statement only a handful of them knew was not entirely true. It had taken much persuasion by Ronal and several others brought in by him and Evia to convince Erzse that they supported the Zylencians and would play kind to her side if given the chance to run and be elected to positions of power.

Evia spoke loud and clear for all to hear. "Speak far and wide that an election will be held in the new year to elect the new functioning Lower House for Borlencia. Advertise that it's a necessity to face the shadow army in the north and ensure a legitimate government that can restore Borlencia's voice in Anemoi. Get the people on your side. Get them excited so that they're campaigning in the streets in the thousands, across all the major towns. Once the Zylencians see the appetite for an election, and what they could be up against if they were to try and stop it, it'll be difficult for them to go back on their word. Especially as an election is a solution to their advertised reason for aggression."

"And once the Lower House is established? I take it we're to keep quiet about Erzse's transgressions as the price for the election?" the woman with grey hair asked, catching on to Evia's lack of mention.

Not knowing who could be trusted and who couldn't be, Evia was careful with her response. "Run on the need to legitimise the province's Lower House. Run on the danger to the north. Run on whatever you think is a necessity that the people can vote on. But avoid direct talk of rogue elites, as this may work only to sow distrust in yourselves. And please, do not run on a platform that directly threatens the Zylencians with legal action. Once the Lower House is established, it'll then be up to those ministers and councilmen to do what's in the interest of their people."

"The Zylencians should answer for their crimes."

Nobody protested the woman's retort, not even the man that had called into question the extent of the Zylencian destruction. To Evia, this was a good sign—but one that needed tact.

"Without the Zylencians' backing, there can be no election. Remember that when you proceed with this opportunity."

▲ ▲ ▲

"That went well," Santos said to Evia once alone outside. "They want Erzse and the Zylencians to pay. You can tell."

"A decision they can make of their own accord once they're elected."

"I'm still surprised Ronal was actually able to convince Erzse. It'll be a tricky affair for him to maintain loyalty to her right up until when it counts."

"He only needs to pander behind closed doors. In public, he can and should do what's necessary to win a seat, short of calling her out for her crimes."

Evia wiped the beads of sweat from her forehead and pinched the dull pain in her gut.

"Are you okay?" he asked.

She nodded. "Go back inside and see to it that nothing upsets our win. There's something I must attend."

"Are you sure? You don't look too good."

"I'm okay," she said with forced calmness. "I'll see you tonight." At that, she hopped into a brisk walk in the direction of the stables without glancing back, her niggle no longer ignorable.

CHAPTER 13

Decembrix 25, 484; the Hunter's Passage, Zylencia—Ricard took another clumsy swig of the beer Gemin had handed him and then returned to glaring at the twins. His cheeks were dirtied and his beard untidy, and he was sprawled on a thick cushion on the side of the firepit opposite the mischievous brothers. Aika was wrapped in a towel beside Xander and Aes, and she, too, wore a frown of indignation.

"Now that we have that out the way—" Gemin began, but Ricard raised a threatening finger into the air.

He wiped his mouth of the beer's frothy residue. "You really couldn't see fit to just let us be?" he said sternly. "Let us try our luck with the wolves, rather than have us wandering in the wilds with the growing thought that we'd gone mad?" Malum opened his mouth, but Ricard cut him off. "Four days. Four days! We knew something wasn't right, you damn rascals, but every time we tried to right ourselves, we ended up back on that damn path." He shook his head and peered into the empty beer mug.

"Another?" Malum asked softly.

"Damn right, I'll take another," Ricard scolded. "The stuff's never tasted so damn good." He turned to Xander. "And you—"

"I tried," she spoke up before he could finish. "Multiple times. And always I was met with the same response—"

"It'd be faster to let them continue the course," the twins said in unison as Malum refilled Ricard's mug.

Aika put down the tea she had been nursing and rubbed her tired eyes. "I need to sleep."

"Of course!" Gemin said. He got up and scurried over to a bundle of pillows, then draped a sheet and duvet over them. "Your bed's ready."

"I'd also like to bathe."

"Right, right!" Gemin grabbed a towel and hurried over to the door. "With me."

Aika raised a quizzical eyebrow and peered to Xander.

"There's a small cave with a hot spring not far off," Xander said. "He means you no harm."

"Could've fooled us," Aika muttered as she stood. With a tired gait, she followed Gemin out of the hut.

"And you?" Malum asked Ricard. "Would you also—"

"When the girl's done," he interjected coldly.

"Indeed, when the girl's done."

Ricard sighed loudly and shook his head again. "That was a lot of time wasted, kiddo."

Xander bit her cheek guiltily, though she knew it wasn't her doing. "I'm sorry."

He shrugged. "It's done. Just a matter of figuring out the next step. And good to see Aes is fine for the most part."

Aes dipped his head in acknowledgment.

"We'll rest up tonight and get back on the road tomorrow," he continued. "The real road this time."

"About that," Xander said hesitantly.

"What now?"

"I need a couple of days."

Ricard's forehead creased and he glanced at Malum, who looked on eagerly. "Why?"

"The twins…they're trying to help me—"

"With what?"

"Strengthening her abilities," Malum answered.

"A useful toolkit for the road," Gemin added from the door. He entered the hut and took a seat next to Malum.

"You mean this thing you do with Aes?" Ricard asked.

Xander nodded.

There was a moment's silence before Ricard spoke again. "So be it. Like the cretin said, can't hurt our chances. And what's a couple more days at this point after keeping us in the wilds for four days." He stood up, downed his beer, and then stretched his back.

This time Malum didn't ask. He got up, grabbed the jug of beer, and poured Ricard another.

Ricard stared at the little man, but then, despite his obvious anger, he grinned. "If it's going to be like this, I'll forgive." The twins' faces brightened. "Just no more tricks. Not against us at least."

"Our word!" they blurted excitedly.

▲ ▲ ▲

To some, our dreams are a glimpse into one of any infinite number of futures and thus should not be ignored—Xander rubbed her finger along the rear pew as she rounded into the central aisle. It was covered in dust, and she pulled her finger from the wood with a thin film of the stuff on her fingertip. She wiped the residue on her jacket as she took in the stained glass windows of the arid temple.

Though not extravagant, they told a story. One she may have been keen to dive into, if not for the glare of the two stone men watching her from the front. Their axes cruel, their charge none other than the book of non-religious riddles. She could feel its draw, or perhaps it was the draw of the stone men watching over it.

She peered back to the windows, keen to escape the feeling of being watched. Slowly, she edged forward, avoiding direct eye contact with the altar right up until it became all but impossible to curiously glance its way. Her heart thumped in her chest. About to turn and run, as caution instructed her to do, she impulsively pushed forward until the book atop the altar stared up from under her nose.

It was open, and in the bottom right corner of the two pages, there were the familiar triangles. A prolonged breath escaped her lips as she guided her eyes up to the now-familiar words:

"But they too will be cut down by the heathen and driven back into the earth to rot."

A knock came from the door to the rear of the temple, and she immediately shuddered. She knew what she would find if she were to answer the noise. A horror she could do without revisiting. She looked back to the book, the source of her novel curiosity, and jerked backwards as something was viciously scratched onto the page.

The thump of her heart was now audible and the tension in her neck painful. Cautiously, and oh so nervously, she leant back over the book and read the words that had moments ago been scratched onto it:

"Beware the—"

The last words were illegible. She reached a thumb to the page to see if she could smooth them out, but as she did, another sound emanated from the room to the rear. This time much louder and more violent than before. Gaze locked on the eerie wooden door, she could hear shuffling and murmurs on the other side. The fear was too much. She swiftly turned around and began for the main entrance.

"Xander! Xander!"

A shudder traversed her spine as she abruptly swivelled in the direction of the room.

"Xander, help us! Please, help us!"

She swore under her breath and tightened her fist until her nails pierced the skin underneath.

"Xander, please!"

"Damn it!" she hissed after several seconds, and then, summoning all the bravado she could, she raced to the door and opened it, ready to face the haunting display of cruelty.

She clambered in and turned to the corner where she expected the slaughtered congregation to lay untidily. But what faced her wasn't the torn remains of those unknown victims but the clearly recognisable faces of her friends. Slashed and broken and bloodied. Evia, Joseph, and Dogner slumped in a huddle. To their side, Ricard, Aes, and Hemish, their limbs hacked off and their torsos mutilated. And to the back, mangled nearly beyond recognition, Aika's once-beautiful face. Her eyes scratched out and her lips sawn off.

Xander wretched violently as she staggered backwards and then screamed as a hand gripped her shoulder from behind.

"That must've been quite the dream," Ricard said, looking over from the firepit. He had a beer in one hand and a chicken wing in the other.

Still struggling for breath, Xander peered from him to Aika, who nursed a bowl of soup on a bed of pillows.

"I…" Xander began and then shook her head of the vivid images still imprinted in her recent memory. She breathed out a long breath of relief and then rubbed at her eyes. "That was…not a pleasant dream. Wow!"

"Care to enlighten?" he asked.

She looked at the man, his innocent expression comforting, but decided against worrying him or the others with something that was likely just the conjuring of her imagination. "No, it was only an old memory. Nothing to dwell on."

"If you say so, kiddo. Want some breakfast? Can certainly give the rascals this; it's quite delicious."

They turned to the door as the twins entered. Both carried fat smiles and walked with a skip in their step.

"What's got you two prancing around like that?" Ricard asked.

Though he seemed more cheerful, Xander could tell he was still a bit sore about the twins' trickery.

"We've got news for Xander," Malum said.

"Indeed, very good news," Gemin added.

"We spoke to Evia."

"You did?" she said, elated. "But without me! Why?"

"You were asleep and seemed too peaceful to wake," Gemin responded.

She shrugged off the comment, knowing if anybody could have felt her dreamworld angst, it would have been the two of them. "Well, how is she?"

"Fine," Malum said.

Xander waited to see if there would be more, but the brothers just stood there staring. "Just fine?" she finally asked.

"Just fine."

"Why does it feel like you're hiding something?"

"We're not."

"But our words can only convey so much emotion," Gemin said.

"Better you speak to her yourself when you're ready to find and communicate with her," Malum added.

"But that could take me an age. I'm still learning."

"Is that so? I guess we've overestimated you, then. Right, Gemin?"

"Right!"

She puffed her cheeks in frustration. "Well, can you at least tell me about my friends? You know it's something I wanted to ask her."

"Friends?"

"Yes! Joseph and Dogner. Are they okay?"

"Ah yes! She told us everything."

"So?"

CHAPTER 14

Octobrix 28, 484; small town six kilometres from Crowton, Borlencia; eight weeks earlier—Evia breathed relief as she spotted the town in the distance. Through the rough movements of her mount's gallop across the uneven ground beneath, and the niggle that had some time ago seen fit to scream for her to make haste, she quietened her mind. Calmly, but with no less urgency, she reached out in search of her friends' presence, scanning and scanning until familiarity flared up.

She gasped as her eyes widened, and she abruptly pushed her mount to go faster with little care for the damage that would ensue if she were to fall.

▲ ▲ ▲

Joseph wiped the sweat and rain from his eyes—it was a temporary reprieve from the torrent that hadn't let up since morning. Cold, but no less sharp, he lay with Dogner beneath a pile of discarded boxes situated on the narrowest part of the street where they had set their ambush.

Twenty metres ahead, a dozen guards walked the narrow, muddied road with little to no shelter from the elements. Three out in front and the remainder on the rear, the guards were vigilant and wary of the choke point, but their options through the town were limited. Joseph scanned the prisoners in the centre of the group, half of them Dogner's children. The forced march had taken its toll.

"Don't take this the wrong way, but I'm amazed by your restraint," Joseph remarked quietly to Dogner, both of their gazes still intent on the approaching group.

"Is that so? Well, as I've said a dozen times, wouldn't do them much good if their father foiled his own plan."

"Right you are…okay, they're at the mark. Let's do this."

"Aye."

With their rifles aimed through tiny gaps in the sodden boxes, they fired their single shots into two of the soldiers on the front line. The echo deafened as it roared from wall to wall in the narrow passage, and the remaining guards crouched instinctively for fear of a second volley. It didn't come, not from the rear or from above—as had been intended—and instead a splattered thud sounded from in front of the boxes, followed by the sounds of struggle from the roofs above.

"Damn it! They've made us," Joseph spat after identifying the source of the thud—two of their comrades originally perched on the roof had fallen the two stories onto the ground, their throats slit.

The pair sprang to their feet, shields up and wary of the danger to the front and still veiled above. Another half a dozen soldiers on horseback appeared at the rear of the group. Led by a wily officer, the horsemen pushed to the front, their swords tinged red and their grins bloodthirsty.

"They got the others by the looks of it," Dogner muttered as the duo backstepped, unwilling to turn and expose their backs.

The officer sneered arrogantly, his crooked face all the part. "Your turn," he spat, and he and the other riders charged in a scatter, but barely had they made a brisk pace when Dogner launched his war hammer at the grunt riding alongside the officer.

Even with the distance, the blow was ferocious and nearly split the man's chest as it threw him into those behind, instantly weakening the group's resolve. The brief impediment in the charge further goaded Dogner, and seemingly oblivious to the still-existent danger overhead, he threw himself into the fray with his sword drawn. In rapid succession, he dispatched the next with a cut to the neck of the man's horse and then a lunge into the rider's now-exposed flank. The others instantly turned their sights on the shockingly agile man of another generation, his style both methodical and measured, even if a tad wild to the untrained eye.

Using the lapse in the enemy's attention, Joseph sprinted and jumped at one from the side with a rapid slash of his blade to the man's throat. But his contribution was short-lived, for as he landed, he received a face full of iron from a foot solider just joining the melee. On the ground and amidst the dozen flailing feet of Dogner's fearsome commotion, Joseph glimpsed the new foes that had emerged above—three men leaning over the roof of the nearest house, pointing the guns of the previous owners down at the pair.

"Dogner!" Joseph hissed. "Calm yourself!"

Like a dog called to attention, Dogner froze and slowly withdrew a blade from the original owner's stomach, while Joseph cautiously climbed to his feet.

"Thought you'd set another trap and kill some more of my men," the officer snarled, wiping the splattered blood of a colleague from his cheek. He jumped to the ground and walloped the now-restrained Dogner across the mouth. The officer smiled at the pain inflicted, though Joseph suspected it hurt him more than it did the big man.

Dogner looked at the officer. "Well, it goes like this: We were just out for a stroll when we saw you and the strays looking a bit worse for wear. It was at that point that I thought I'd help—"

The officer lashed out again.

"Like I was saying," Dogner continued with a bloodied grin, "I thought I'd help put some of you out of your misery."

The officer kicked Dogner in the stomach, and a whimper sounded from the prisoners. He had been about to go in for a second, but the whimper had been enough to stay him. Slowly but surely, a smug grin etched onto his face. "Very interesting."

Still on his knees, Dogner straightened his back and expertly hid the nervousness he felt for the source of the whimper. He forced calmness into his voice as he spoke. "It's what happens when you don't take care of your charges. They get the sniffles."

"That's unfortunate. It really is," the officer said and drew his blade, to Dogner's concealed horror. "Bring whichever whelp bears this one's name. I want to see the scum beg before I cut his throat."

Dogner tried to wrestle free, as did Joseph, but their captors were too many. A soldier dragged one of Dogner's little ones through the muck, the screams of his other children fuel to the officer's gloating. Despite the child's scrawniness, he was spritely in his ineffective swings at the soldier, and it quickly landed him a welt on the cheek.

"I presume this one's yours?" the officer asked Dogner.

"Never seen the lass. Anyway, bit too weedy to be one of mine. Maybe she's one of yours." The boy pouted, embarrassed by his father's jibe, though he sensibly kept his mouth shut.

"Quite the humour on you. Still, I'm getting bored. Kill the boy and then—" Blankness stole the officer's expression and concern the rest. After a few moments of what seemed an internal struggle, he spoke again. "Let the kid go and…and the two men."

Bewilderment erupted across the armed group.

"You lost your mind?" one guard shouted.

"He's bewitched, I bet," another spat fearfully as he and the others peered around uneasily.

"What's that?" The boy pointed.

They all followed his dirtied finger to the thick mist flowing in from the other side of the alley, which was about to swallow the prisoners. In a panic, the soldiers nearest the approaching obscurity clumsily clambered away towards the cluster of men surrounding Joseph and Dogner.

"We ain't paid enough for this," one of them moaned.

"We should let 'em go and get the heck outta here," another said, cowering.

Dogner's brat looked on fearfully, and even Dogner and Joseph themselves were a little taken aback, though they suspected the origin.

Gurgled cries sounded from above, and two of the soldiers on the roof fell into the group below, knocking one soldier on the ground unconscious and spooking the horses into a gallop down the street with two riders clinging for dear life.

The mist continued towards the group, and all the soldiers drew away, bar the entranced officer still fraught with internal strife and another also quite suddenly inflicted by the same vacant gaze. Still wary of the prize, the group dragged the two men and the boy with them but abruptly let go the instant the officer and the other stationary soldier began screaming in agony as the mist swallowed them. Tails tucked and ready to flee, the guards clambered backwards in horror.

The two unrestrained men righted themselves, and Dogner walked into the mist and back out with his war hammer pulled from the first victim, much to the terror of those watching.

"Get back with the others, lad," Dogner ordered his son, his eyes locked on the threat.

"Into that mist? You must be mad!" the little one spoke squeakily.

Dogner shot him a look. "Not the time. Didn't ya just see me go in?"

"Alright, alright, don't lose your last hair over it. Looks like the fog's thinning anyway," he said as cries of struggle emanated from the roof.

"And looks like your luck's dried up," one of the soldiers sniggered, suddenly surer of himself. "Come on, you lot. Let's wipe the smirks before they try any more of that magic." He started cautiously towards the pair with the others following.

"Shouldn't be too difficult without the riders," Dogner said, rolling his war hammer in his grip, clearly eager for the scuffle.

"Old fool," Joseph muttered less enthusiastically, readying himself for the melee to come.

▲ ▲ ▲

Evia reeled from a punch to her mouth and collapsed onto the rough material carpeting the roof. The brute that had hit her was triple her weight and carried fists the size of hefty potatoes.

"I'll teach you for messin' with my head, old bag, and do to you the same I've done to all the other rats that've crossed me."

"I should've thrown you over with the others," she said, struggling to stand.

"You should've," he growled and smacked her across the head and back onto the ground before landing another hit. "This should be fun," he snarled, but as he leaned in to punish her, a bang rang out, and his cruel smile twisted into one of agony.

He reached a hand to his back and withdrew it bloodied.

"Damned witch!" He coughed and fell to the ground.

But the fault was misplaced, for it was one of Joseph's men, slumped on the floor by the roof's ledge and slowly passing from life, who had fired the fatal shot into the assailant's back.

Evia breathed a heavy sigh of relief and peered at the dying commotion on the street below. Nine children and as many years away from full-on combat had done nothing to diminish Dogner's prowess in battle. And Joseph, a merchant, smuggler, and spy, wasn't without his uses in a tight spot, she observed, as he launched a knife skilfully into the neck of one who charged him.

Shock and elation rapidly gave way to a dull pain in her jaw and neck. "Better get this over with." She frowned and picked up a loaded rifle.

▲ ▲ ▲

Novembrix 1, 484; Crowton, Borlencia—Joseph turned from the window of the bedroom and peered across the clutter to Evia. She was sitting up on her bed, and her face was bruised and cut.

"You spoke to Xander?" he asked her, shocked.

"Yes, briefly."

"That's the first we've heard from her since she left Nhata. Where's she now?"

"Deep in the Great Forest, from what I could tell. She's with an old friend—Aes."

"The stag?"

"Yes."

"Did you let on to our plight?"

"I couldn't. The communication cut out. But even so, I wouldn't have done. If she came to know of the ordeal we face, she would return without hesitation. And if we fail in what we must do and she learns the truth about Nhata, she will forever hold herself responsible. No, she must get the shard from the Great Tree, and we must save as many as we can without her knowing."

"And you don't think she'll come for you?" Joseph said as he peeked out the crack in the window to the busy street, the muggy evening air outside little reprieve from the heat of the room.

"She may, but I think deep down she trusts that I'm safe. She was also unable to query my whereabouts, though I am sorry I missed the opportunity to mention your well-being—and Dogner's. She won't take that lightly, nor will it do us any favours."

"Agreed, might've been for the best if she knew rather than fret over your being alone. We can't risk her returning without the shard. Not now, not after all that's happened."

"No," Evia said and tried to readjust herself.

"Need a hand?"

"I'm okay. My body is worn, and the pain seeps into my bones, but the bruises heal, albeit slowly."

"How I'd like to lay my hands on the miscreant that did you so bad."

"Calm yourself, Joseph. He got his. It's how the world works. You can't commit that many wrongs and pass unscathed."

"You say that, but I've seen many a man that has lied, cheated, and thieved his way through life without a blemish to his body and mind. The world doesn't operate according to fairness but according to those who have no qualm about doing others wrong to benefit themselves. That's the world we live in."

"You've seen much during your life, Joseph. You've dealt with all sorts of men, women, and cretin. If you say it is so, then perhaps I am naive in my views."

"Or maybe you find comfort in the knowledge that evil can't go unpunished."

"Or maybe I think that if you're not punished in this life, then you surely will be in the next."

"Careful, Evia," he said in jest. "You talk of religion. You mustn't forget, Anemoi's no longer a religious state. Of course, you wouldn't think it walking around some of these towns. Seems someone, somewhere, forgot to tell the peasant on the street."

"Just because a state isn't religious doesn't mean its people can't keep their faith."

"I don't disagree."

"Anyway, it's not religion I refer to but the energy that lies within all living things. The energy that embodies us—that is what and who we are and what we pass on to our children, and them to their children, and so on. It doesn't simply vanish upon our death. It retains form in our offspring, if we're lucky enough to procreate. And it can occasionally linger on through some semblance of our consciousness after death, a perpetual state of being—a shadow, if you will."

"And let me guess, this energy that we're born with and that we mould through experience, it becomes corrupted or tainted through natural as well as nurtured means?"

Evia smiled. "You've done your reading."

"Wouldn't be any good at my job if I didn't keep abreast of superstitions."

"Some superstitions are born from truth. It therefore remains feasible that an individual's energy that has soured, be it through disease or ill-intentioned actions, can just as easily sour that of their offspring, who may not in turn remain unscathed from the workings of the universe."

"Right," Joseph remarked. "And if there's continued consciousness after death, the poor blight that wronged so many could spend an eternity as an impure apparition deserved to witness the inherited destruction of those he or she brought into this world." He looked at her quietly as he pondered her words. "It's quite a mouthful, isn't it? And certainly another way of looking at it. At least if eternal consciousness as a tainted spirit doesn't get them, our knowledge that their children may not fare as well in life is of some comfort, although vindictive."

Someone tried to open the locked door, causing Joseph to draw his dagger.

"Who goes there?" he called.

"Well, who else might it be, lad?" Dogner responded cheerfully. "Come on, open up. Got some fine meats here that aren't going to eat themselves."

The big man barely fit through the crooked entrance, his bulky frame and the large bags filled with goodies a hinderance to easy access, and all in spite of the weight he had dropped since Nhata.

"A bit busy out there, certainly not like our good old village." Dogner frowned and handed wrapped meats and cheeses to the other two. "I trust your meeting with Fredrick went well, Joseph?"

"Went as expected. His next trade caravan leaves two days from now.

Once in Bulgar, they'll push off for the southern shore on one of Grendal's ships."

"Great! It'll be a comfortable distance from these wretched folks and close enough to my old home that my little ones can learn of their roots. And how are the little darlings? Behaving themselves, I should hope."

Joseph chuckled. "Fredrick didn't raise any concern with your untended crop. Would seem they take after their old man."

"Oh dear, no hope, then. Not to worry, mind you. My wife will be with us shortly enough, as will your family. And then there'll be enough of us to keep the little ones in line." He shook his head, a fat smile spreading across his cheeks and disbelief etched into his brow. "What were the chances my wife and your family would be picked up the very next day just north of here? One in a million, I'd say. And to think we had no idea until Fredrick told us."

"One in a million's probably not far off."

Dogner's face hardened. "I owe you, Joseph. And you, Evia. Let me finish, please. If it weren't for the two of you and your wits—well, I shan't like to think what would've happened to my family. Would've suffered the same end as the ones we couldn't reach, I reckon."

"You don't give yourself enough credit, Dogner," Evia spoke softly. "You're as much a part of this as we are. None of us would have gotten this far alone."

"That means a lot, Evia. Thank you. And you'll still have me right up until this lot are safe an' sound on that boat headed south."

"I'm glad."

"You know, Dogner," Joseph began, "we really could still use your help. Neither of us would put up a fuss if you decided to hang around a bit longer."

Dogner stared calculatingly at the man for a moment and then looked to Evia, who had only that morning relieved him of any duty he felt he owed her from the old days.

"Tell you what," Dogner said. "I'll have a think about it, but I'd be lying if I said I felt comfortable leaving the little ones all alone with my other half…she can be quite the handful also, you know. And you, Evia, sure you don't want to take a breather from the next couple of excursions? The brute caught you days ago, and you still look like a sore fruit."

"I'm old. I haven't got the reflexes I used to, or the abilities, and my folly lay in my complacency, but I assure you, that cretin's actions quite literally knocked it out of me. I'll be fine. Anyway, there'll be plenty of time to rest when this is over."

"Alright. Well, you won't be much use if you don't finish your meal."

"You couldn't have spared a little green?" she asked.

"What you want vegetables for? Don't get me wrong, I do like a nice roasted potato and grilled onion with a slab of meat, but if you're trying to build your strength, well, you can't go wrong with what I've given ya."

She chuckled. "Duly noted. Oh, and, Dogner, would you do the honours of accompanying me to Wispy Tavern tonight? Joseph will be preoccupied with final preparations, and I could do with a friendly face about."

"I assume this is in relation to the election, not your desire to down a couple of wet ones?"

"Right you are."

"Shame."

CHAPTER 15

Decembrix 28, 484; the Hunter's Passage, Zylencia—"Xander, wake up. Xander."

Beckoned to the waking world by the annoying voice piercing her dreamy cloud, Xander forced open a tired eye. Lying on her side amidst an army of pillows, she had an unimpeded view of the starry night through the window.

"It's not even morning…" she began frustratedly as she turned over, only to see the others fast asleep under the weak light of the firepit's glowing embers.

She frowned, convinced she had heard a voice, but not altogether certain it wasn't just her imagination. She shrugged it off and curled into the foetal position, ready to resume her slumber. To her irritation, though, after quite some time of trying, sleep remained elusive, deterred by the prior disruption. She let out a frustrated sigh and peered to Ricard and the others as they slept. She stifled a chuckle as the big man nearly choked on a snore, and then her gaze fell on the sketch of the triangles she had drawn for the twins.

She hadn't forgotten the images of the temple and the skeletal remains of its congregation. Neither had she forgotten the horrid dream from the other night, nor the book and its mysterious allure. An allure that was certainly at odds with the strange niggle that had urged her to leave when she was down there. "But what more was there to the situation?" she thought and had thought many a time since emerging from the eerie cave. A non-religious sect executed by a religious one. Simple. But if it was that simple, why had the niggle warned her from touching the book a second time? What harm could come from touching a book? And what if the dream was also a warning?

Another snore drew her gaze, but this time she spotted Aika staring at her. Careful not to make any noise, Aika got up and walked over to Xander.

"You're thinking about it again, aren't you?" Aika whispered.

"What?"

"You know what. You're thinking about that book."

Xander sat up with a raised eyebrow. "I am not that easy to read."

Aika chuckled. "You are. You really are. And I know you're thinking about it. How long before you go back down there and touch it?"

"Are you mad? I'm not going back down there."

"But you want to, don't you?"

Xander put her hand to Aika's forehead. It was cold. "Nope, no fever, but maybe the chill's made you delusional. Seriously, it sounds like you're trying to get me to go back down there."

"Me? Of course not. But I know you want to and eventually will. It's just a matter of time. All I can say is resist it. Resist that little voice in your head that's telling you to give in to your curiosity. This isn't like the enchantress of the forest beckoning you. It's something else down there. Maybe something sinister." She rubbed her chin thoughtfully. "Saying that, you were down there for nearly two days, and you got out fine."

"Not to mention, I was asleep for much of that time. I think if there were something sinister, it would've got me while I was passed out."

Aika shrugged. "Doesn't sound too bad when we put it like that. So, why haven't you gone back down already, given that you can't stop thinking about it?"

"Because I'm kind of scared to."

"Then maybe that should be a warning."

"Alone, that is. But if you were to—"

Aika put her finger to Xander's lips. "I shouldn't have come over here.

I saw you awake, same as the past two nights, and your every other waking moment, and knew you were dwelling on it."

"Wouldn't you?"

"Not my point. I came over here to tell you to leave it be."

"And what if I were to go down there and have a glimpse? No doubt you'd feel obliged to follow," Xander said with a cheeky grin.

"And what of the wolves?"

"Travelled north in search of game, according to the twins. Plus, the cave isn't too far from here. We could make it there and back before the others wake."

"I can't believe we're having this conversation."

"Come on, Aika. I can tell you're curious to check it out."

There was hesitation in the girl, but the seed had been sown.

"In and out," Aika said.

"In and out!"

The pair quietly donned their kits and tiptoed out, leaving the others none the wiser. The air was frigid, but despite the hour, the ground was visible under the moonlight. The trek was as quick as Xander remembered, and she was riddled with both fear and excitement as they came upon the burrow.

"Well?" Aika said.

"Well, what?"

"This is your idea. You can lead the way."

"Of course!" Xander retorted calmly, though she felt anything but. She got onto her knees and stopped short of crawling in. The burrow was dark, very dark, and creepily quiet. "Maybe this isn't a good idea."

"Really?"

"Really."

"In that case—" Aika got onto her knees and gently pushed Xander to the side.

"Really?"

"Yes, really. You'll be back tomorrow if we don't, so let's just get it out of the way."

Aika slid her bow into the hole and entered.

"Okay then," Xander whispered and got onto her belly.

The dirt was cold, borderline icy, and it stung the skin. She looked ahead and glimpsed Aika's feet as they disappeared into the black shadow. A tingle traversed her spine, urging her not to enter, but she was committed. She took a breath and poked her head into the strangely quiet tunnel. The air was stale, putrid almost, and quite unlike the earthy scent she remembered.

"Aika," she spoke, a growing sense of unease holding her back. "Aika."

But only silence responded. Not even the ruffle of Aika's movements. Xander squirmed, but she knew for certain she couldn't let her friend go it alone. With her teeth gritted, she reached a hand forward and inched into the burrow, sliding in over the loose dirt, and with the weight of the mountain soon to be above her. One metre and then two. She stopped. There was no noise. Nothing. No echo. No wind. Not even the sound of her own breathing. Painful goosebumps suddenly erupted up and down her legs, and a desperate urge to get out of the tunnel clasped around her stomach.

She couldn't do it. She had to get out. She shifted onto her elbows, ready to push back, when a flicker of movement in the dark ahead caught her eye. She stopped still as her breath jammed in her throat.

"Aika?" she whispered.

Nothing but the eerie quiet of the black abyss responded.

"Aika—"

Xander froze as another movement traversed the dark. With her eyebrows creased, she very, very slowly craned her head forward. Waiting and watching. Her heart thumping. Suddenly, something started scrambling towards her at pace, causing her to knock her head in a panic. Dazed, she screamed as something unseen grabbed her leg, pulling her roughly across the dirt and out of the burrow into the mountain air. Hysterical, she thrashed her legs and caught the culprit with her heel, causing it to let out a pained cry and release her.

"Xander! What the heck!"

She rolled onto her back, her chest heaving and eyes wide, and stared at Ricard as he stood over her, holding his bloody nose.

"What in Anemoi are you doing out here?" he said angrily.

Xander looked from Ricard to Aes on his right, and then to Malum and Gemin on his left, and then to Aika on their left. Her mouth dropped open as a terrifying dread abruptly took her. She clumsily scrambled from near the mouth of the burrow but away from the group, her eyes never wavering from Aika.

"Xander, what's—" Aika began worriedly.

"Who—what was that?" Xander spluttered, pointing at the opening.

"Um…"

They all looked a bit puzzled.

"What do you mean, kiddo?" Ricard asked with more confusion than anger.

"Aika! That's what I mean," she spat. "I was following Aika into that tunnel. It was you! I know it was you!"

"Xander—" Aika spoke.

"No, no—" She shuddered. "Something, something pretending to be you just tried to get me to follow it back into that cave."

The others exchanged worried glances and then peered to the black opening. At once, they all felt it. They were being watched by something lurking in the shadow.

"I think it's time we leave here," Gemin said sternly. "Malum, take the lead. I'll take the back."

Malum, his expression stark, didn't say anything. He simply nodded and hastily took to the front. Moments later he led them onto a path that hadn't been there before and waited until Gemin joined. With everybody accounted for, he visibly relaxed, though again did not speak as he led them back to the hut. With everyone in the hut, Gemin locked the door behind him. It was the first time Xander had seen him do this, and it left an uncomfortable feeling inside of her.

"What was that?" she said exhaustedly. "It was in this hut. It looked just like Aika. It spoke to me as if it were Aika. It knew of the enchantress and the wolves. It played to my curiosity." She shook her head with disbelief. "What don't I know, Gemin, Malum? Who scratched out that book? Who killed those people?"

"We can't tell you for certain who or what killed those people without taking a look," Gemin responded.

"Or who scratched out that book," Malum spoke.

"And that thing?" she said with growing agitation.

"That thing wasn't human. I think that much is evident now."

"What do you mean, 'not human'?" Ricard said, leaning forward. "As in, like a forest critter?"

"It wasn't human or critter," Malum said.

"Then what was it?" Aika asked.

Gemin rubbed the back of his head as he considered his answer. "In layman's terms, most would call it a bogeyman."

"A bogeyman?" Ricard scoffed. "You mean the kind that hides under your bed until you're asleep, then gobbles up your children in the dead of night? That kind of bogeyman?"

"Yes," Malum said. "And it wanted Xander."

"To do what?"

They looked at each other and then back to Xander.

"You disturbed that cave," Malum said. "Presumably it wanted to take you back."

"She was in that cave for two days without incident," Aika said. "Why now?"

They shrugged. "Time to dwell."

"I think it meant me harm," Xander responded quietly.

"We think that's a safe assessment," Gemin spoke.

"But why? Just for disturbing the cave? It doesn't make sense."

"We don't think there's really any more to it."

Xander couldn't tell if they were withholding something.

"Is she safe?" Ricard asked. "Are we safe?"

"In here, yes," Gemin said confidently. "It'll not get in again."

"Or anywhere near the camp," Malum added. "And whilst you're here, stick to our paths. It'll not breach them."

"And once we leave?" Aika asked.

"Once you're on the road with some distance between you and this area, you should be okay."

"Perhaps a word of caution, however," Gemin spoke. "In the future it may be best to avoid places that have been marked by death of that kind. Places that may have been cursed through bloodshed or other means."

"No telling what might linger in such abodes," Malum added.

"How?" Xander said nervously. "How can I possibly know if a place has been cursed or not? And what place hasn't been marked by death?"

"Trust the niggle."

She slumped onto the nearest pillow and had to force her hand from shaking. "Trust the niggle," she repeated sarcastically. "I need a drink."

Gemin nodded and got to brewing a tea.

"And you're sure that thing wasn't related to the visitor who appeared to me as a projection all those nights ago?" she asked as the others got comfortable, though it was apparent all of them were still uneasy.

"What does your gut tell you?" Malum asked.

She thought for a moment. "No. They're not related. One meant to warn me. The other meant to harm me."

"Then that's your answer."

CHAPTER 16

Decembrix 30, 484; the Hunter's Passage, Zylencia—The wind pulled at Xander's untied hair, and the sun browned her skin as Aes sprinted up the slope with her on top. They moved and flowed as one, and if not for the fact that Aes had antlers, from a distance one may have thought them one of the centaurs of legend.

Wearing a vest and without the inhibition of baggage or thought, she withdrew her blade and shield and feigned a sword dance taught to her by the late Haro—the tiny man who had accompanied her through the Great Forest with his equally tiny wife, Leila. Facing three invisible attackers head-on, Aes stepped to the side as Xander parried the first imagined blade and the next before unleashing a flurry of offensive and defensive swipes in synchronized, agile movements that resulted in imaginary victory.

Barely winded, they continued the rushed climb to the summit of their goal, and there they breathed the crisp air.

The rock on which they stood jutted out from the summit of the mountain and overlooked a deep and dark water, a sliver of an inland sea unknown to her and contained by grey stone and shallow grass on either side as it meandered through the inlet. It was a sight to behold in its own right but was made truly magnificent, and perhaps a tad strange, by the cluster of stars above that refused to slumber even during the waking hours.

"Hard to believe we're in Anemoi anymore…perhaps another illusion conjured by the twins."

She unmounted and trod to the edge. Euphoria took her as a sudden rush of adrenalin coursed through her, dampening the cloud of worry that had befallen her in the prior days. Calmly, she sat on the edge, legs over the ledge, and looked at Aes.

"Didn't take you to be scared of heights."

She turned back to the expanse and closed her eyes. Drawing a deep breath, she slowed her thoughts and the beat of her pulse, and then, just how the twins had taught her, she projected her mind, feeling for anything that desired to be touched, though it was something in particular that she searched for. Her previous attempts in the preceding days had been fruitless, the distance seemingly too great and the noise too much, but from this vantage point, one of height and serenity, again a suggestion of the twins, she could feel the distinct blue wisps of the aura she searched for. Though weak and fatigued in its brightness, the owner returned Xander's joy and surprise.

"Xander? They told me to expect you," the voice in her mind said, though it wasn't a voice in the conventional sense but a vibration of her mind and the mind's subconscious translation of the vibration.

She beamed. "Evia!"

"How good it is to hear you, my dear."

"And you."

"And you talk unassisted. I never suspected. Your mind was always so quiet."

Xander giggled. "Thank you, I think."

She felt her aunt's joyful laughter.

"I mean to say," Evia began, "I could always feel your wanted and unwanted emotions, but I never felt your mind flare as it does now, so strong and so vibrant. It goes without saying that you do possess the spark."

"But how did you know my touching Aes would allow us to speak all those weeks ago?"

"I didn't! However, after you saved Aes's life and we walked the forest together that night, I could feel the wisps of a connection between the two of you. I knew that if your connection held true with Aes, then my ability to communicate with him might allow you and I to talk."

Xander sensed her aunt's elation.

"Of course, now that we know you are a sky-whisperer," Evia continued, "you'll have to unravel what it is you're actually capable of and hone those abilities. And who knows, maybe your abilities will extend beyond just those of a sky-whisperer."

"You mean energy manipulation?"

"Yes, though I think I mentioned before, it is rare to possess both abilities. Controlling the energy around us, for example, isn't the same as speaking via the mind or listening in on another's thoughts—what's wrong?"

Xander hesitated, then chuckled nervously. "Speaking of thoughts—do you remember when you said you couldn't hear mine?"

"I do."

"Well, I'm fairly certain the twins *are* able to glimpse my thoughts. They have a habit of repeating things I haven't told them. I figured it's because my mind started to flare, opening it up or something."

Evia chortled. "And now you think everyone and anyone can simply hear your unfiltered, unprojected thoughts? Despite the twins enlightening you to the difference between intentionally speaking through the vibrations of your mind and the unrelated act of spying on someone's private thoughts?"

Xander shrugged. "I guess."

"Those two rascals really do struggle with boundaries sometimes. Yes, they did glimpse your thoughts, but not only did it take two of them—both very strong sky-whisperers—but what they saw was distorted at best. Don't worry. Your thoughts are still quite private—at least to us. And I did ask them to stop, though I'm doubtful they'll refrain."

Xander blew through pursed lips, relieved she still had some semblance of privacy from her aunt.

"That does remind me, though," Evia continued, "it'll be necessary for you to practice quietening and concealing your mind from hostile actors."

"Hostile sky-whisperers?"

"There are some out there so powerful that they can quite easily erase or plant thoughts and memories or control a person's actions and desires. Even if my inability to hear your thoughts is largely universal, you'll still want to work on limiting the ability of others to do damage where you can't see. There are many ways to permanently damage a person's mind."

Xander shuddered at the thought of someone erasing her memories, then the curiosity of a still-unanswered question struck. "You know, it was a different sensation the first time we spoke. I could see you, bloodied and hurt," she said sadly. "Now I can only hear the vibrations of your voice. Why is that?"

"I don't know. I had no intention of projecting an image of myself to you on that day of all days, and I certainly couldn't see you. I can only think the combination of you and Aes allowed it to be so. Nonetheless, how interesting!"

"Evia?"

"Yes?"

"I thought you were on your deathbed when I saw you that day. And the others—don't worry. After you spoke to the twins, they let me know that Joseph and Dogner are also okay. And their wives and children."

Evia sighed. "I'm sorry you had to see me like that. And the destruction wrought on Nhata. I can't imagine it would've been easy these past weeks after our connection ended so abruptly and without closure."

"It wasn't, no. Will you tell me what happened?"

"It's quite the story, and there's so much to tell. Where to possibly start?"

"I want to know everything. From the day I left Nhata right up to the day I saw you."

Evia chuckled. "I wouldn't expect any less from that curious mind of yours…"

And so, Evia took Xander through everything that had happened whilst apart. Starting on the day Xander left Nhata, right up to the meeting with Borlencia's fractured government.

"I would've been surprised if they hadn't agreed to the election," Xander said.

"Likewise. It took a little convincing and some assurances, but they agreed."

"You did so much in so little time. Your escape. Setting up the network for the refugees. Then getting not just the Borlencians but the Zylencians and the Eurencians to agree to an election. You make it seem, well, easy. And all I did was get a single shard."

"Easy? Ha! I don't know if that's the word to use. And definitely don't downplay the importance of gathering all the shards. It's becoming apparent that the election is only the first of many challenges Anemoi faces."

"The army in the north?" Xander asked.

"And the issues the eastern provinces struggle with, but more on that later. Let's not lose focus."

"Still feels like you'll change the world in the time it'll take me to complete the Rose."

"Persevere, Xander. Don't lose sight of the task. And it's certainly not been easy for us. We've had to tread very lightly for fear of provoking a violent response. That in itself has been completely exhausting. And don't get me started on the apparent indifference of the average Borlencian."

"Indifference to the election?" Xander queried curiously.

"The election. The Zylencians." She chortled tiredly. "The fools."

"You think they'll turn out to vote?"

"They will," Evia said with an exasperated undertone. "We'll just need to keep pushing."

"And they really show indifference to the Zylencians? Bit odd, isn't it?"

"Not so odd if we consider the dynamics on the ground and, just as importantly, the history."

"How so?"

"Let's think of the Borlencians as two separate groups. Those in the east along the lakeshore. They are the ones that didn't show indifference, and they paid the price," Evia began. "Unaccustomed to Zylencian influence, and unready to accept occupation, they showed their teeth and were quickly put down as a result. Their voice has been, for the most part, silenced."

Xander gritted her teeth at the thought.

"Then there are those in central and western Borlencia," Evia continued. "A lot of them aren't exactly crying over the occupation, but there are two reasons for this. Firstly, a significant portion of the population is still in the dark on the massacres and shady practices."

"Maybe it'd change their minds if they found out."

"I think you're right, but better to avoid violence at this point. Secondly, they're not being personally affected. The truth of the matter is, it's not that the Borlencians in the central and western counties don't dislike the Zylencians—it's that they've not been given a lot to shout about. The disruption to their lives has been minimal."

"How could the occupation not be disrupting their lives?"

"What's happened over the past decade, since Borealis fell?" Evia asked. "Long before this occupation."

There was quiet as Xander pondered the question. "Zyphyr was already taking over?"

"Yes, though not in the conventional sense. After Borealis fell, Zyphyr—the capital city of Zylencia and the seat of the Zylencian parliament—increased its trade ties with many of the larger towns in Borlencia. Zylencian merchants and accents became a commonplace feature in many of those town centres. Zyphyr's tried to fill the void of power. Granted, the results clearly weren't enough to satisfy Zylencian greed; otherwise, they probably wouldn't be an occupying force right now. Nonetheless, to many in the west and central Borlencia, those that have been exposed to that increased Zylencian trade, not much has changed. Except the presence of the soldiers."

"They've been conditioned," Xander commented.

"Inadvertently. Zyphyr's sphere of influence had already expanded into Borlencian territory. Though, like I just said, it wasn't enough, and Erzse now pursues administration under more assertive means. Fortunately, whilst the vast majority of Borlencia's people are just trying to get on with life, there's a growing number within the political, military, and mercantile ranks that have been rubbed the wrong way. They know what Erzse has done in the east and what she's capable of. A number of them are running or supporting the election, and then you've got the ones that have helped us build the network being used to free and hide the rescues. And the rest, well, they're biding their time until the election's completed and the Zylencian forces removed. Then the real fun will start."

"I can't wait to see that woman get what's deserved. Oh! And what of the Eurencians?" Xander could feel Evia's glee at the mention.

"Wiston and his counterpart, Robyn, arrived several weeks back. It was a bit later than we had originally expected, and the delay had us somewhat nervous. But they made it with some weeks to spare, given the election is mid-Januarix. After a brief meeting with myself, Dogner, and Joseph, in which they showed their shock at what they had witnessed on their journey to Crowton, they then met with Ronal and several of the other Borlencian mayors in close proximity. From there, they publicly endorsed the election."

"And what of Erzse?"

"Wiston sent a messenger to the commander of the occupying force with news of their endorsement. The message was then relayed to Zyphyr."

"And?"

"Wiston didn't have to wait long for a Zylencian messenger to find him, though the message wasn't quite what we expected…"

Decembrix 2, 484; Crowton, Zylencia; four weeks earlier—Born and raised in Eurus, the capital of Eurencia, Wiston was a man of two metres with rigid muscle, long blond hair, and the fair skin of the Eurencians. In his forties, he appeared every bit the solider and carried a confident demeanour that was quite unlike that of his counterpart—it was a rugged look accentuated by his strong chin and high cheekbones.

Robyn, the other man in question, was also a native of Eurus. He was a portly fellow with fair skin, and he wore a trim cut of thin, mousy brown hair. To some, his bashful eye when it came to members of the opposite sex was amusing. To others, it was a viable suitor to his sharp mind and often pensive features.

The pair took their seats at a round table where Evia, Joseph, and Dogner were already seated. In the living room of a townhouse being rented by the Eurencian delegation, they were eager to discuss business whilst nursing a spread of local delicacies.

"Well, lad, tell us—what does the witch say?" Dogner asked excitedly, grabbing himself a plate of smelly cheeses.

"It's not from Erzse," Wiston said.

"But it's from the Zylencian parliament, right?" Joseph said, confused.

"From a Zylencian senior minister, just not on behalf of his parliament. Do you know a man that goes by the name M. K.?

"I've heard of him," Evia said. "It's short for Mountain King, I believe."

"He's a good man," Joseph said. "I've done business with him in the past. He's honest and can't stand corruption."

"So not going to be a fan of Erzse, then?" Dogner queried.

"Certainly not," Wiston responded. "There's a bit of rambling in the letter, but to sum it up, he's pissed off at the woman. Mentions giving her the finger. And a bit more concerning, whilst she was somewhat annoyed by our endorsement of the election, she didn't seem overly fazed. In fact, M. K. says she plans to send news of her own very soon."

"What?" Evia asked worriedly.

"She's called a meeting of the Upper House," Robyn spoke. "To meet in Zyphyr as soon as the Borlencian Lower House is elected. He put the approximate date around early to mid-Marx."

Surprise took her and the others. "Why?"

"He doesn't know. But he's pretty clear with his concern. Says to be careful and expect the unexpected. He was particularly put off by her calmness in the face of it all."

"This isn't good," Evia fretted. "Are we able to find out more?"

Wiston nodded. "We've sent a messenger to liaise with one of our spies in Zyphyr. See what he can learn. But I'm guessing we'll hear soon enough from the Zylencians themselves, as it'll take the representatives from the different provinces some time to make the journey. She'll need to summon them now."

"What you thinking?" Joseph asked Evia as she sat back, her brow creased.

She looked at him. "Have we missed something?"

"You've led her to believe she's got the Borlencian ministers in her pocket. This is just her exercising that belief."

Evia drummed her fingers against the table as she puffed her cheeks. "Wiston, Robyn, will this meeting take precedence over any attempt by the Borlencians to call a meeting in support of removing Zylencian troops?"

"They can be done simultaneously," Robyn answered. "The Borlencians should lodge the issue immediately following their election."

"They could then hijack the same meeting," Wiston added.

"Probably nothing to worry about," Dogner said reassuringly to Evia. "The Borlencians aren't going to throw their lot in with the Zylencians, not if it's detrimental to themselves."

She bit her lip. "Let's hope that's the case. I don't like coincidences of this nature."

Wiston cleared his throat, discomfort etched into his brow. "There's more. Would appear that your suspicions regarding the young women weren't off the mark."

Concern took Evia. "What's she doing with them?"

"He can't say for sure. Whilst the older women, children, and what's left of the men are being transported to labour camps or abroad, the young girls are being kept under the city. M. K.'s trying in earnest to find out why, but in a court where no one can be trusted, it's a struggle. All he's had to go on is the odd disfigured corpse turning up in the sewers and alleys. All have the same scratched-out tattoo on their wrist. Though illegible, he says it's clear what was written. They're Borlencian prisoners."

"So she's murdering them!" Dogner spat. "I know you want to tread lightly, Evia, but once the election is completed, it'll not be a bad time to let Santos expand the network. Make sure to keep as many of the girls out of Erzse's reach as possible. Maybe even now we could increase our attempts a tad."

Evia was quiet as she contemplated. The balance between building the opposition without pushing Erzse to the brink of retaliation was a fine one, even with a soon-to-be elected parliament. But the partial confirmation of girls Xander's age being imprisoned and subjected to Erzse's cruel vices was absolutely terrifying and finally all too much. She looked at Dogner with pained reluctance. "Expand the network, but be careful not to give too much away in our movements."

"Santos already has it mapped out. Was just waiting for the all-clear."

"I should've expected as much. But like I said, keep it measured."

CHAPTER 17

Decembrix 31, 484; Crowton, Zylencia—Evia shifted the cushion under her bottom and then stifled an abrupt yawn. "Excuse me," she apologised, taking in Fredrick's and Santos's amused looks.

It was just the three of them in Fredrick's shed, a cosily warm refuge from the evening cool and the raucous celebrations outside. Sitting around the table with a detailed map of Borlencia unfurled across its top, they each nursed a small glass of warm ale.

"No need to apologise," Fredrick said. "The hour's later. Though I might say, I'm a bit surprised we found you at all. Thought you'd be out celebrating the new year at one of the taverns, not sitting in the den at your inn."

"I've lost count of the number of times I've cycled around the sun," she said. "It's all the same to me at this point. Now, Joseph and Dogner on the other hand, they could do with the respite."

"They were certainly on their way when we saw them," Santos remarked with a grin. "Of course, it was you we needed."

"Yes, yes. So, the three routes to the north—which one was compromised?"

Santos leant over the map. "This one."

"How so?"

"Foot patrol stopped one of our convoys. Didn't come to anything but was a close one. Our man said the sergeant made a note of all their names, residences, and occupations. Said he'd verify with the records office in Crowton to make sure all checked back. At which point he sent them on their way."

Evia gave them a perplexed look. "Then change the route and swap the papers next time around. Same as we've always done." She sat back, staring at them. "Why have you really called me here?" A rap came from the door, causing her to flinch. "What is this?" she said, alarmed.

A warm smile on his face, Santos lifted his hands into the air in a plea for calm. "Nothing to worry over."

She could tell he told the truth, but not in the mood for any more surprises, she reached her mind out to whoever stood the other side of the door. "Grendal!"

The door opened to reveal a sun-kissed man whose teeth shone brightly through a black but neatly trimmed beard. His nose carried a gradual hook, and his black hair was styled short and tidy. "Evia—how long's it been?" he asked as she got up and embraced him.

She pulled away from him. "Too long. Far too long. Please, sit."

Grendal closed the door behind him and pulled a seat up to the table.

Evia peered to Santos and Fredrick as she sat down. "And you couldn't tell me this, why?"

"Couldn't ruin the surprise of a good man," Fredrick responded.

"It was my idea," Grendal spoke. "Thought you could do with a little cheer after all you've been through."

She chuckled. "Bit presumptuous, don't you think?"

"Ha! Not after you hear what I've got to say."

Intrigue took her. "Do tell?"

"First, how's Xander?"

"She's in Zylencia. Don't worry. She's in good company. I expect we'll be seeing her soon enough."

"Very good!"

"And Hemish?" she asked him.

"I'm keeping him out of trouble. Plenty for him to learn in the merchant fleet. He's a fast learner but not one for orders. You're surprised?"

She laughed. "Always thought it was Xander getting them up to no good."

"Bad as each other, I'm sure. So, to business?"

"Yes, to business."

"Then let me start with the good," Grendal said. "Tell me, have you any idea who the commander of Zylencia's occupying force is?"

"Inexperienced general from Zyphyr. Goes by the name of…" She clicked her fingers as she searched her memory.

"Barton," Santos answered.

"Barton's the face of it," Grendal said. "There's someone else pulling the strings. Someone besides Erzse."

Evia shrugged. "I'm not entirely up to date on the line of succession in Zylencia. Please, enlighten us."

"Aiden."

"Aiden!" Her mind jumped to the man whose name she hadn't heard in years—a staunch Borlencian loyalist with a sharp mind, he had been Borealis's spymaster before its fall.

"Aiden?" Fredrick asked.

"He's thrown his lot in with the Zylencians?" Evia said in disbelief.

"That's as much as I know," Grendal said and then looked at Santos. "You're already familiar with his messenger, whether you realise it or not."

"Is he also Barton's?" Santos asked, unable to recall another Zylencian messenger he had encountered as much as Barton's in the preceding months.

"Yes. He's one and the same."

"This is news," Evia said, leaning back. "Good news, I'm not sure. Santos, can you arrange a meeting between me and Aiden?"

"For when?" Santos asked.

"As soon as feasible."

"It's done."

"Anything else I should know, Grendal?" Evia asked.

"That wasn't enough?" the sun-kissed man jibed, though his expression hardened. "I do have more news, but I wouldn't necessarily call it the kind that gets the blood warm. I'd dare say that the proliferation of Buto narcotics has pushed the entire province of Notencia to the brink of destabilisation. Greed and religious zealotry are rife. The whole of Notos has lost its wits."

"So you've told us."

"Unfortunately, I suspect a number of the ministers not succumbing to the ways of this new religious sect have in fact been bought out by Erzse. What they'll do for a pretty penny, given Notencia's coffers are depleted. Suffice to say, the Notencian parliament is compromised and beyond the point of redemption."

"Which doesn't bode well for the vote," Evia replied worriedly.

"No, but there is potential for hope. I've requested a meeting with several of Notencia's commanders and ministers, those not compromised. We're going to call a vote of no confidence against the compromised ministers in an attempt to remove their legitimacy before the meeting."

"Cutting it a bit close, don't you think?" Fredrick blurted. "I mean, the meeting's just around the corner. You're all the way out here in Borlencia, and your ministers are half a world away in Notencia."

Unfazed, Grendal continued, "The vote of no confidence will take place in Bulgar when the Notencian delegation arrives there by ship. They'll be en route to Zyphyr for the meeting and wholly unprepared. We'll have half the merchant navy there and a good portion of Anemoi's southern fleet. It'll be a public affair. One which they'll not be able to slip their way out of."

"Will it succeed?" Evia asked.

"I'm hopeful. I'm also hoping to meet the Eurencians whilst I'm here. I'd like to commandeer some of their marines to assist the southern fleet in blockading the Buto. See if we can blunt their stream of smugglers. But I can keep you updated on that front."

"I'd appreciate that. Thanks, Grendal."

"Anyway, that's the news from the east." He peered to Santos and Fredrick. "The three of us need to sit down before I leave and have a catch-up."

"Just say when," Santos said.

"Excellent." He turned back to Evia. "Fancy a drink? We can use the opportunity to reminisce and trade embarrassing stories of the little ones."

"Ha! Enough to get us through the night and then some. It'd be my pleasure."

CHAPTER 18

Januarix 6, 485; small village 270 kilometres north of the River Went, one hundred kilometres south of Zyphyr, the Black Mountains, Zylencia—Xander held out a crumb of warm, doughy bread, and the frazzled chick grabbed it and skilfully fled into the bush, its awkwardly long legs and its chirps of joy both somewhat amusing.

"You're a cute little thing, aren't you?"

The chick's coat was dirty and unkept, and the pure yellow of adolescence already gave way to the creep of the dirty blond and brown of adulthood. The chick poked its head from the bush and walked cautiously towards her, stubbornly wary despite the familiarity.

"Still feeding that thing?" Ricard had said to her the day prior. "Oscine would be jealous if he knew." She chuckled aloud at the thought.

"Maybe one day your mother will return," she said sadly as the chick took another crumb from her hand.

She had learned the hard way that, with a piece too big, the chick would struggle, and with a piece too small, the chick would nip her finger. Of course, she could just throw it to the ground, but then that would simply invite the larger chickens to come in and bully her new friend. No, she would take the time to break manageable pieces and ensure a full tummy. It was a wholesome task still wholly inadequate to fill the long hours of tedium entailed with keeping watch for a person only she knew how to identify.

She sighed a sigh of boredom and then peered across the dusty cobblestone road. She squirmed as a hen and her chicks sprinted across, darting between pedestrians and carts and horses, the little legs of the offspring nothing like their mother's. The evident vulnerability of the little family against the world exposed Xander's own sense of vulnerability, and she was quick to grit her teeth angrily as one of the villagers of the quaint mountain village kicked out at the labelled vermin.

"Poor things. Do people have no heart?" she muttered angrily.

A familiar voice spoke from beside her. "Some people forget what it is to have heart, and in this world, I don't blame them."

"Joseph!" she cried and jumped up and hugged the travel-weary man.

"How good it is to see you, and in one piece," he said joyously. "And you've grown in no time at all. Soon enough that jacket won't fit you. On that note, ever thought of getting it washed?"

"All these months and you want to talk to me about laundry?"

"Ha, you know how it is. So where are the others? I expected you and your new friends to be eagerly awaiting my arrival."

"Maybe the first couple days, but Evia was a bit off with your intended arrival. I expect you've got a good reason?" she teased.

"I've got many a good reason."

"Do tell?"

"How about we find your friends, and I'll tell you all one time? It'll save my breath."

"As you wish."

"And your little friend?" he asked, nodding to the chick.

"Isn't going anywhere. He's a resilient little bugger. Plus, I've caught a kind soul a little way down the street visiting many a time in my stead."

She looked at a shy girl of seven or eight years hidden behind a doorway and who hadn't stopped watching since her arrival that morning.

Joseph smiled softly. "You haven't changed."

▲ ▲ ▲

Ricard tossed a sweet in his mouth and then took a swig of his warm water. "And the news on the road?"

Joseph looked at him and Aika and then back across the stained, smelly table of the grotty tavern to Xander.

"After you spoke to your aunt several days ago and just before I hit the road to come down here, Erzse's reason for calling the meeting of the Upper House came to light. It'll be the first to be called since the attack on Borealis, and the first with all the representatives present since a couple years prior to that. You probably don't remember, Xander, but your father represented Borealis on that occasion, at least according to your aunt."

"I remember."

"You do?" Ricard asked, surprised. "You were probably only yay high," he said, motioning with his hand.

She nodded. "It was in Borealis, in the palace. My father had been… not himself in the lead up to it. He wouldn't tell us why, but we soon saw why for ourselves."

"We?" Aika asked.

"My mother and I. We were there, in the assembly. We saw it all…"

▲ ▲ ▲

Octobrix 5, 474; Borealis, Borlencia—"Hush now, Xander. They begin," Alya whispered.

Sitting amidst the audience of the plain yet magnificent parliament hall, Xander and Alya wore matching cream robes, and in many respects, Xander looked like a miniature copy of her mother.

"All rise," bellowed the man standing on the stage at the end of the room. He looked odd in his long grey robe and bizarre wig.

Moments later, the procession of elected politicians entered from the other end and proceeded through the pews of civilian onlookers to the stage where the wigged mediator sat.

At the head of the assembly were two men and a woman all wearing the blue robes of Borlencia, but they were absent the ridiculous wigs, and their names and districts eluded her. Immediately behind was Carolus in his blue robe, and with his hair sleeked back, he walked with an elegance and formality that usually escaped his gait when wearing his armour. Xander smiled warmly.

Beside him was a lady she did not recognise. The lady wore a green robe and held an air of familiarity, and though she was not the most beautiful of women, her dark, angular features were striking and not too unlike Carolus's—a distant relation, perhaps. She walked with a brazen arrogance that stood out to Xander, and she chatted to Carolus with obvious comfort despite his seeming disinterest. Behind them was a group of unfamiliar faces. Some Xander could identify by way of their garments and features, which were not of Borlencia, and others she couldn't.

"I thought there were only twelve ministers," Xander whispered innocently. "I count sixteen, and I don't recognise most of them."

"In Borlencia there are twelve, yes, but this is not a standard assembly. The group you see walking consists of only the four senior ministers from each of the four provinces."

"And the non-senior ministers?"

"You mean the eight common ministers. They sit amongst the audience in the front row."

"But why?"

Alya smiled. "Hush now. You'll soon find out."

With the procession seated, the mediator stood to address.

"The proposition that shall be discussed and decided upon in this session of parliament concerns the abolition of term limits for elected ministers—"

Surprise and confusion erupted from the audience, and even Alya, who had not been made privy by way of personal connection to Carolus, gasped at the prospect.

"Silence!" the mediator continued. "The abolition of term limits and the election of a prime minister outside of wartime. The proposition, as brought forward by the ministers of Zylencia, shall be debated henceforth. The proposer will now stand and present their argument."

The lady of similar appearance to Carolus stood and proposed her argument with the same arrogance that characterized her demeanour, but she held the audience's attention with her concise and well-presented argument, though an unspoken hostility emanated from the crowd.

"In summary, the abolition of term limits and the election of a prime minister will allow for greater efficiency in the decision-making process of the four capital cities and their provinces, greater unison in vision and governance, and less disruption from the obligatory election and handover process every five years."

"And what do you propose—that we make you prime minister?" roared a spectator.

Jeers and cries of disagreement spread through the crowd but quickly died down when the mediator raised his hand to open the floor for the next senior minister to debate, and one by one, the senior ministers gave their two shillings. Whilst none was steadfast in their spoken argument, the senior ministers from Zylencia appeared quietly decided.

Throughout, Carolus sat poised without a hint of expression. He listened intently and was the last to speak, and when he finally stood, the ministers and audience alike fell silent without prompting, their respect for him during this period of office infallible.

"I…I can't in all good conscience support this farce—"

"Silence!" the mediator bellowed as the entire forum descended into chaos.

"This farce that on the face appears sensible in its move to promote long-term strategy and better cooperation but, at the grain of it, is a blatant attempt to garner unmatched influence and power suited to one person's ideal. No, the abolition of term limits will erode the checks and balances that prevent corruption and give the people an opportunity to be heard. The election of a prime minister without fear of reprimand, supported and elevated by the same senior ministers that will be free from scrutiny, will pave the way for a dictatorship, a kingdom, an empire, if you will. No! I cannot support this blatant power grab that flies in the face of all we stand for and all that we have worked so hard to build."

This time the mediator did not silence the crowd as the city's inhabitants cheered their champion's input. For of all the ministers, it was Carolus who stood to gain the most from such a move due to his popularity, and still he had denied the proposition. Content with the reaction he wished for, Carolus took a seat, his gaze unwavering under the scowl of indignation that had stolen the woman's previously silent expression.

"They'll now deliberate and then vote," Alya said over the noise as the senior ministers and the common ministers seated in the audience vacated the forum. "This is a dangerous move by Erzse. She threatens our current government, and her move would create a system not much unlike what proceeded the Revolutionary Wars. I can't see the ministers or the people allowing this to happen. I daresay there would be riots if the vote returns unfavourable, though I suspect Carolus holds enough clout to sway the others with his sensibility."

"Riots?"

"Like I said, Xander, this is a dangerous situation, and it flies in the face of all the progress we've made since the near destruction of Anemoi all those years ago."

Calls for quiet made the rounds as the ministers re-entered and took their seats. The majority of them, the mediator included, appeared visibly relieved at the undeclared verdict, but Erzse made no attempt to hide the scowl directed at Carolus, and still he exuded an air of indifference in response.

Xander felt Alya relax as if the decision had already been announced.

"The motion has failed and is excluded from further proposition for no fewer than two terms of parliament…"

▲ ▲ ▲

Present day—"So, a dictator," Ricard hissed angrily.

"In all but name," Joseph responded.

"Why now, though?" Aika asked. "She's already skirted the law to remain in power as long as she has, and now she occupies half of Anemoi without retaliation from the other provinces. Why call a vote and risk undoing what's already been done, especially as the Borlencians not under her control can now vote against her? What's changed since the last vote that assures her of a win?"

"Everything's changed." Xander spoke up before Joseph could. The answer was painfully clear to her, and still her voice did not betray the hurt that bubbled beneath. "My father was her biggest opponent. He had the support of the other ministers and the people, at least up until the months before the attack. I don't know who it was, but someone or some group started to drag his name through the muck, trying to tarnish his reputation and his policies. And then, after Borealis fell, well, so did Erzse's opposition. All that's prevented another vote was the required time period of ten years, and now even that's gone."

"But lack of political support hasn't stopped her from pushing ahead with her armies. Why bother?"

"Appearance of legitimacy. At least to the other provinces," Joseph chimed in. "She's labelled her occupation 'the quell of an insurrection that risks the whole of Anemoi.' Although we've convinced two of the Eurencian senior ministers of the blatant lie, to the other provinces, it still seems as if western Anemoi is amidst the fires of civil strife. A reality that won't change until they can see the Borlencians managing their own affairs without issue.

Combine this with the army on Eurencia's eastern doorstep—"

"This is new!" Ricard blurted. "Who?"

"I don't know all the specifics, just that they're nomads from the distant east."

"Two armies on our doorstep, both within a decade," he uttered in disbelief.

Xander chuckled nervously. "Evia kept that one quiet when we spoke. I can see why."

Joseph's cheeks reddened from the slip, but he continued, "With the army in the east, the army in the north, and the perceived instability in Borlencia, we think Erzse will insist that additional resources and unity of leadership are a much-needed relief to these existential threats. Even if we can convince the other provinces that Borlencia isn't compromised and can manage its own affairs, those provinces have serious issues of their own. It recently came to light that the Eurencians have signed a hefty debt agreement with Zylencia to ensure they have the funding necessary to combat this army in the east."

"Which will call into question their loyalty," Ricard remarked.

"Exactly. And the Notencians are supposedly so disorganised and plagued by disease and rampant narcotics that it's been near impossible for anybody to get a meeting with their leaders. There is exploitable distraction and weakness in fractured states, and that's exactly what Anemoi is right now."

"She's played her hand well," Xander said.

"Is that admiration I sense?" Ricard taunted.

Xander shrugged. "She created and then sold a solid reason for forcefully roping the remnants of Borlencia into Zyphyr's administrative sphere and is now exploiting the other provinces' weaknesses to get what she wants. Not only will she hold the position of prime minister over all of Anemoi through election—"

"Assuming she wins the vote," Joseph interjected.

"She will also indirectly control the wealth and power of more than half of Anemoi by virtue of Zyphyr's reach."

"And by population alone, she could sway all voted legislation in her favour, assuming she keeps the right people happy."

"So, the plan?" Ricard asked sternly, clearly irritated by the topic at hand.

"Twofold," Joseph spoke. "Evia is adamant that Xander finds the other shards. Even if we subdue Erzse, the movement in the north and the army the Eurencians face mean there's too much at stake to give up that search."

"The next shard's in Zyphyr," Xander added.

"Great! Means you'll be seeing your aunt in no time," he said to Xander's delight. "Our second action, besides ensuring the Borlencian election is completed without issue and Zylencia's armies are removed from our borders, is needing to build the opposition to Erzse's proposal. If we can do this, we may be able to sway the vote in our favour."

"I imagine you'll have the full support of the Borlencians," Ricard said. "Can't see the ministers warming up to Erzse's trickery given what they know, even if the people on the street don't give two damns."

"We think they're a given. It's the Notencians and the rest of the Eurencians that'll be tricky. It doesn't help that Erzse can use these crises as arguments for her proposal."

"It'll be a difficult sell," Ricard pointed out.

"It will be. Especially as she's offering them a solution."

"When will they hold the meeting of the Upper House?"

"Two months from now," Joseph answered.

"A lot to accomplish in such a short time."

"Indeed!"

Ricard and Aika squirmed.

"What?" Joseph asked, intrigued by their expressions.

"*Indeed* seems to be the word of choice for two painful memories," Ricard said. "The twins that tended to the girl's every whim several weeks back led me and the princess on a bit of a trek through heck knows what. A memory best left forgotten."

Aika chortled. "Agree with the old man on this one. Those two were more nuisance than good."

Xander giggled. "Ah, you exaggerate. They gave you everything you needed to survive. Think of it as a forced lesson in bonding."

The two shot each other looks.

"It was certainly a lesson in toleration," Aika jibed.

"Agreed," Ricard said. "Still, we got out alive, and that's what matters."

"I'm surprised you let the two tricksters off so lightly. Didn't think restraint was in your blood."

Joseph, amused by the antics, cleared his throat. "Good to see you're all getting along. I was worried there may be tension on the road."

"Tension's healthy. It keeps you alert," Ricard said. "So then, next stop is Zyphyr?"

"Not quite."

"M. K.?" Xander asked, recalling Evia's brief mention of the man.

"M. K.," Joseph responded.

CHAPTER 19

Januarix 8, 485; the town of Flint, sixty-eight kilometres south of Zyphyr, the Black Mountains, Zylencia—Xander rubbed at her irritated eyes and nose with all emphasis on inhibiting the sneeze building in her itchy throat.

"It's the ash," Ricard said.

"Huh?"

"The ash, kiddo. Doesn't agree with you. There used to be a poor fellow in the town I grew up in that suffered the same affliction. Was very unfortunate."

"How so?"

"Well, we lived next to a volcano." He laughed. "There was no escaping it. Truth be told, I was always surprised he didn't just end it."

"Or leave."

"Not this one. Not an adventurous bone in his body. Would've been unthinkable to the boy."

"Then maybe death would've been too!" She sneezed.

"I'll pray for rain for you," he said. "Might help. Look, they return."

Aika and Joseph rode side by side on two mountain ponies. Xander jumped on Aes and Ricard his pony, though the poor thing seemed near collapse from his bulk.

"On the right track?" Ricard asked.

"Couple miles along. It's been a while. I had to jog my memory," Joseph said.

They started down the dusty road that wound across the desolate, rocky landscape of the smoky volcano, their destination the large mining town of Flint that was nestled into the slope, and Joseph pulled in beside Ricard.

"I think you'll like this lot." Joseph smiled. "But I'll tell you now, some of their customs are a bit dated. Wouldn't let it get to you, being an adopted man of Borealis and all."

"Ah yeah?"

"Yeah. I'm well acquainted with the town, having conducted business here in the past, and I still squirm at some of their odder traditions."

Ricard laughed. "And yet you think I'll fit right in."

"You'll see. Just try not to speak your mind."

"You know me well in such a short time. I'll behave…assuming they don't have a craving for good beer. Then I can't make any promises."

"That's what I was afraid of. Of course, difficult to argue if you can't help yourself to one. The air here is drier than any desert I know."

"And bitterly cold, despite the fact that we're climbing a volcano," Aika called from behind.

"The princess hasn't quite warmed up to the open air," Ricard said with a grin.

"I heard that."

"Don't worry, Your Highness. You'll get it sooner or later."

Aika turned to Xander. "The man's an ass. But he grows on you, albeit slowly and somewhat painfully."

▲ ▲ ▲

Town of Flint, Zylencia—Joseph and Dogner took in the large wooden hall brimming with rowdy men, still dirtied from the day's labour, strewn along the benches and on foot. The two of them were standing to one side of the room under a worn portrait of an unfamiliar man donning a thick beard, and they were casually gazing across the long wooden tables covered in food and beer that dotted the space. Aika and Xander were sitting around the central table, chatting away with a cluster of curious men, and at the doors waited lines of the local women, ready to cater to the feast.

Ricard took a swig of his beer, and unable to hide his revulsion for the bitter liquid, his lips curled. "You've got nothing to worry about. The beer, if you can call it that, tastes like baby's vomit."

"Could you say that any louder?" Joseph hushed.

"I'm sure I could, but I'm on my best behaviour, remember?"

"They're a rough bunch, and look how fascinated they are with the girls," Joseph observed.

"You've seen their women, and still you show surprise."

Joseph chuckled. "Valid point. I was shocked they let the girls attend the hall, if I must be honest. It's the first I've seen it so, not that I've ever encouraged female acquaintances to frequent this town or any other in this district."

"I assume that was the dated custom you referred to?"

Joseph nodded.

"A toast to our guests!" a large burly man in the centre of the room suddenly bellowed to raucous cheers. His thick black beard and clothes were sodden with beer, and his fair skin wore the soot of the mines. "And to my old friend, Joseph, an honest trader if there ever was one." He laughed boisterously and held his flask up to the two of them.

When the hall had quietened and the local women had cleared the floors and tables of spilt beer and drunkards, Xander and the others sat down with the man and his retinue at the centre table. Despite the copious amounts drunk that afternoon, the miners seemed unfazed by the ill effects of the beer.

"She insists on paying us the same in denomination, even though she dilutes her coin left, right, and centre," M. K., the large burly man, said with a sophistication that betrayed his gruff exterior. "She taxes everything that should rightfully fill our pockets, and she's gone ahead and nationalized all the ore refineries in the province to squeeze our every penny. You could say she's beaten us into a pathetic submission like disobedient little whelps, and now she strangles us between a rock and a hard place. I reckon it's just a matter of time before she attempts to nationalize the mines—"

Anger and frustration erupted from his retinue.

"And I reckon a reckoning is on the horizon," he bellowed to cheers of agreement. "Enough is enough. Like I said to the Eurencians, Erzse is no friend of ours," he said to Joseph. "And I know the same can be said for the majority of the other towns in the district. We may be under Zyphyr's administration, but that witch can stick it where the sun doesn't shine. She's shown her true colours, and now it's time to show ours!"

He signalled to one of his men to unroll a large, crudely drawn map across the table.

"Unfortunately, it's not enough to just refuse to sell, if we're going to significantly sap her coffers and erode her support base," he continued. "Erzse does have the ear of one town in particular, Ingleton, the largest town in the north of the district. Without them, we'll struggle to meaningfully affect supply, and for the right price, I don't doubt that they'd also jump at the opportunity to mine these deposits, whether Erzse legally acquires or not."

"Not to mention that every mine that halts supply will drive the price of ore up that much more. There's a hefty profit in store for those that resist," Joseph added.

"Is diplomacy with Ingleton an option?" Ricard asked.

"They're a stubborn bunch with a taste for the finer things," M. K. said. "Being so close to Zyphyr has rubbed them the wrong way. For them, money is diplomacy, and we have little to spare."

"Then we can't rule out the use of force."

"It's in nobody's interest to wage war against our neighbours."

"It'll play into Erzse's hands if you do," Xander commented with a confident demeanour, though inside she was a mess of nerves and excitement at the prospect of presenting her ideas to so many unfamiliar faces. "She'll just use it as another excuse for her cause. Same as she's doing with the Borlencians."

M. K. looked at her and, not at all bothered by her input, nodded in agreement. "Xander's right. If anybody's going to use force, best we let Erzse draw blood first. There's no justification in her attacking the southern districts because we've halted the supply of *our* own resources. It's a move that'll work against her. And in the event Erzse is the one that decides to go the violent route and send troops down here, we'll need the men fresh and ready."

"So we can't rely on Ingleton to affect supply," Ricard said, "nor rely on their support, by the sounds of it, if Erzse uses force, unless we can offer something in return?"

M. K. nodded.

"Curious. I take it Ingleton is not subject to the same tax policies the rest of the district is?" Joseph inquired.

"To a lesser degree," M. K. replied. "Hence the ear of Erzse."

"I bet that's not won them many friends." Ricard laughed.

"Would Ingleton raise a finger against you if unprovoked?" Xander asked, again a tangle of internal jitters.

"Unlikely, but it does depend on your definition of 'unprovoked,'" M. K. said.

She stood up and, controlling the nervous shake that had begun to transcend her arm, pointed to the map immediately above Ingleton.

"The Black Mouth?" M. K. observed.

"Yes," Xander said with forced firmness. She was barely able to control the excitement coursing through her, eager as she was to explain the learned military strategy that could be applied to the situation. "We don't need every town on our side to affect supply, Ingleton included. We simply need to control the trade route, and the gateway to the Black Mountains where all roads meet is the most defensible point in the range and the only way in besides an incursion from the deep south. And if there's a chance that Erzse will send in her armies if we cut off one of the city's lifelines, attempting the defence of individual mines is, well, silly."

"Starting to think like a strategist, kiddo," Ricard said proudly. "But your proposition's risky. We'll have Ingleton right on our backs, and interfering with their business might constitute the definition of 'provoked.' Not to mention, holding several of the larger mines and forcing Erzse to split her forces in difficult terrain makes it easier for the miners to hold their own rather than face a trained army head-on."

"Hush your mouth, little one," M. K. said to Ricard light-heartedly. "Where do you think Zylencia pulls the bulk of her hardest soldiers? Certainly not the valley or Zyphyr itself. Look at my men. Their forearms are the size of logs, and their endurance in these clouds is second to none. We've all seen service, and boy, can we fight."

"They also know the terrain," Aika added.

"And I'm certain our own currently in service will refuse commands to lay a hand on any of the mining towns," M. K. added.

"But if such disobedience is expected, I can't see why Erzse would use those troops," Joseph said.

"It'll deprive her of the backbone of her army," M. K. said. "I'll tell you that much. Holding our own, if it comes to it, is not the problem. It's making a meaningful difference through economic and political pressure that matters, and Ingleton still prevents this. Remember, they also have the second-largest population in the district and two of the twelve elected ministers, so we'll need their support."

"Well, what can we offer Ingleton besides your ore?" Ricard asked.

The miners all looked at one another and began mumbling something under their breaths.

"Didn't quite catch that," Ricard said amusedly when they finally stopped their indecipherable muttering.

M. K. put his elbows on the table and stared at the man. "Longmel."

"Honey as rare as diamonds," one of the miners with a great big beard grunted. "It's the only thing other than our mines that'll push the bastards to turn the cheek."

Another chorus of mumbling did the rounds before the room fell quiet.

Joseph held out his hands, expecting elaboration. "And where can we—"

"You're wasting your breath and your time," M. K. interjected. "Unless you're fool enough to cross the mouth of hell and dance with mountain bees the size of horses, you're out of luck. We'll need to figure something else out."

"Time's not on our side."

"As we're aware." Sternness took M. K. as he eyed Joseph. "I know Wiston and Robyn are opposed to Erzse's occupation of Borlencia, and they've given me their written reassurances that they don't support her reasoning for having called the Upper House. But tell me, as a friend, will their resolve hold?"

"It'll hold. They've already sent word and evidence to the other Eurencian senior ministers of what they've seen and what to expect. Once the election in Borlencia is concluded, they'll travel to Zyphyr with their expanded delegation and vote against Erzse when the time comes."

M. K. nodded and then glanced at Xander, his expression pensive. He turned back to Joseph. "Does she know?"

"Know what?" Joseph said cautiously.

"About her father?"

"His opposition to Erzse?" Xander asked before Joseph could. "I do."

"And do you know what's happened since?"

"Um…" She looked at Joseph, confused.

Joseph shifted uncomfortably. "I'm not sure what you mean, M. K."

Xander could sense Joseph told the truth and that his discomfort stemmed from the prospect of what was to come.

M. K. looked at Xander. "Erzse is in the process of rewriting the reasoning behind your father's stance."

"Wait—his stance on her proposition for the prime minister chair?" Xander stammered.

"And the term limits."

"That's ridiculous," Ricard blurted. "What fool would believe Erzse over a man like Carolus?"

"But I was there," Xander said angrily. "I know what he said. I know why he opposed her."

"Doesn't matter," M. K. said. "She's got her worms spreading word that in the months before Borealis's fall, Zylencian intelligence came across a plot by your father to overturn Anemoi's governing institutions and seize power for himself—by what means, we have yet to hear, but the accusation's doing the rounds at a blistering pace. To make matters worse, there's also a rumour that there's evidence to suggest he was being supported behind the scenes by a foreign power."

"His birth country?" Ricard asked bitterly.

"I believe so. I can only guess that she'll say he intended to use the existing political setup that is devoid of the centralisation of power, and thus susceptible to slow reaction times, to succeed in whatever this supposed plan of his was. After all, that was her argument for the seat in the first place. And my guess is, she'll likely go on to say that the only reason his plan didn't come to fruition was because of the attack on Borealis."

Xander balled her fists, and a dangerous expression wormed its way into her. In that moment, she could feel panic take Joseph and a nervous dread befall Ricard.

M. K. continued, "Because he's not here to defend his stance, and anybody that was close to him is dead, or thought to be dead, there's nobody to question otherwise."

"I know where you're going with this, M. K." Joseph spoke up swiftly and with forced calmness. "It'll not do Xander or us any good to paint her as a target."

"She—"

"What about Ricard?"

This time Xander could practically feel Ricard's stomach tighten.

"It's not the same." M. K. turned to Xander. "You're the only one that can stand up for your father's position and not be scoffed at. You were in that assembly. You knew the man right up until his final moments. I doubt any of these soon-to-be-elected Borlencian ministers were there. And the Eurencians and Notencians weren't as close to the man as his wretched sister to know his true intentions. It has to be you, his daughter."

Joseph was about to protest but stopped as Xander peered to Ricard, anger in her gaze. "You remember that army of slippery tongues in Borealis ruining my father's name?"

Ricard's expression betrayed no emotion. "I do, kiddo. You suppose it was her?"

"Stories questioning my father's origins. His loyalty to the people of Borealis. His political intentions. It reeks of that vile woman! I know it was her dragging his name like that!" She looked at Joseph and then back at M. K. "I'll do what needs doing."

"Hold on," Joseph spoke up. "This is still reliant on the other ministers believing Xander over Zylencian intelligence. Couldn't they just implicate Xander also? Or accuse her of trying to salvage her father's tarnished reputation under false pretences?"

M. K. sat back. "Difficult to implicate a girl who would've been a child at the time."

"It's also difficult to trust a child's word."

"A child not yet robbed of her innocence."

"But who would do anything to salvage her family name?" Joseph retorted. "Come on, M. K. Tell me. What's to stop Erzse's centre of intelligence—because let's be honest, they answer to Erzse—from implicating Xander also?"

"I can't say there's no risk—"

"Exactly! There's risk. Risk we can't afford. Xander's role in this is more important than being the mouthpiece for a decision made over a decade ago."

"Joseph—" Xander tried to protest.

"I'm sorry. I already know what your aunt would say, and as far as I'm concerned, she's got more experience in these kinds of matters than all the heads in this room combined. The risk of Erzse coming for you is just not one worth taking." He looked at Ricard. "You were Carolus's best friend and his right-hand man but also a champion of Borealis that was uncorrupted by politics. There's been no attempt on your reputation, and the Borlencians wouldn't have forgotten your evacuation of the city. It should be you to spearhead the opposition. And until we get Evia's say on this, Xander stays in the shadows."

The finality in his tone was enough for the others to simply nod their heads and accept the position, for now.

Xander struggled to hold her sneeze as she cupped her hands under a narrow stream of cold, cloudy water pouring from a pipe in the wall into a stone basin below. She was in a corridor directly outside the hall that was noisy with chatter and drunkards. Desperately, she splashed the cupped water onto her eyes and up her nose in the hope of relief from the irritants in the air. The effect was temporary and wholly insufficient.

"Here." A voice came from behind.

She turned around, conscious of her red nose and watery eyes. "M. K."

His arm was outstretched, and he held a glass of grey liquid in his hand.

"What is it?" she asked.

"It's a local plant. Helps with the runny nose and eyes. Will take a couple of minutes to kick in, but once it does, you'll feel as fresh as a newborn."

She clumsily grabbed the drink from him and downed it. The taste was foul, not too dissimilar to dirt, but she cared not. M. K. pointed to four chairs a couple of metres to the side of the fountain, and they sat down. There was a stout upright log in the middle of the chairs and an obscure animal head nailed to the wall behind.

M. K. looked at Xander, softness in his gaze. "Do you know why they call me the Mountain King?"

"I don't."

"They call me the Mountain King because in my youth I convinced the mining towns in the south to join in the enforcement of a law designed to protect the miners. They saw me as a champion and thus cursed me with a new name. It's a name that's meant to bestow praise, but I find it quite unfortunate. It gives the wrong impression. You see, I was elected to my position as senior minister like all those before me. I'm no king. And it's a tough job convincing this lot to give a man back his original name when cultural tradition dictates otherwise."

"What was your original name?"

"Brutus."

"I like it," she said softly, causing him to smile. "So you convinced them to call you M. K. for short?"

"Took a while, but yes. Xander, I wasn't in your father's inner circle, but I knew him to be a man of the people. All his policies were designed to protect the people. I'm not going to go over Joseph's or your aunt's heads, but you should know: If you do decide to stand up in favour of Carolus's policies, you won't be without support."

They turned to the sound of someone clearing their throat. It was Ricard. His eyes were slightly glazed from the alcohol, but he stood without swaying. He walked over with a nervousness quite unlike him and sat down. "M. K., kiddo," he greeted them without slurring.

"Ricard," M. K. responded. "Everything okay?"

Ricard sighed. "There's something you should know. Both of you." He paused. "There was this idea. Not born from your father, Xander, but one that we learned of on our travels. An idea that both Carolus and I viewed with sceptical eyes in our earlier days, but one that took hold with him after some years in positions of power." Again, he paused, his hands fidgety, his gaze elusive. "Carolus was a man of the people. Yes, his policies were designed to protect the people. But to him that also meant protecting the people from themselves."

Xander lifted an inquisitive eyebrow.

"In his later years, behind closed doors," Ricard began, "he discussed the possibility of a more technical government, one that could demonstrate some semblance of a democracy on the outside but with the majority of the important policies designed and implemented by the most qualified behind the scenes. Of course, even now, no city or town functions without its civil servants actioning the orders of the ministers and councilmen. Government and society would grind to a halt if that were the case. But those civil servants don't determine policy, and they certainly don't act independently. Their function is dictated by those elected and not by the collective interest of the people."

"He didn't think the elected politicians represented the collective interest?" Xander asked.

"Humans are easily corruptible. Doesn't take much for a person in power to sour and solely represent their own interests."

"Not saying much for the voter," M. K. spoke.

Ricard shrugged. "Your typical voter is short-sighted and inclined to vote on a whim or according to their own immediate needs. Carolus figured by making certain offices independent of those elected and giving them greater influence and efficiency in policy-making according to the long-term collective interest, he could limit the ability of any one person or group from overreaching and governing simply according to their own selfish needs."

"Who defines the long-term collective interest if both the voters and the elected are assumed to be untrustworthy?" Xander said suspiciously.

"There are some functions that should be left independent of those in power, kiddo. Control of a state's coin is an obvious example, as I'm sure you know, but one could also argue that tax policy, court nominations, and even ambitious construction projects should be left to independent review by the most qualified persons, not the politicians. Carolus's arguments had merit."

"But that doesn't answer my question. Who determines what the long-term interest is if the voters are not to be trusted?"

"I know what you're getting at, but hear me out. Voters are a guiding voice by way of the elections, but your average person doesn't have the know-how or experience to determine what's in their long-term interest, not in all matters, anyhow. Their vote might suggest a collective desire to proceed down a path, if they even know the path exists, but the hard work of identifying, measuring, building, and tracking the path is left to those behind the scenes. Those that are most qualified, which isn't necessarily the person elected."

Xander thought back to Aika's people and their method of government, whereby the decision-making fell on Aika and a small group of elders. It wasn't without its flaws, and the thought that something similar could've been dreamt up by her father to be implemented in Anemoi, of all places, made her uncomfortable. "What you describe is a world where the people don't have a say over how they are governed. Those groups working behind the scenes haven't been elected. They're left to interpret the direction of the elections and then design and implement policy without the input of the public."

"I think you fail to see the logic, especially when it concerns technical functions," Ricard said without meaning to be dismissive.

"I don't fail to see the logic," she said with growing agitation. "I just think it betrays the idea of a democracy, whereby the person on the street has no say over how they are governed, instead leaving it to interpretation." As young as Xander was, she was well versed on the various political theories and their pitfalls, thanks to Evia's teachings but also her own interest in her father's role in Borlencian politics. Consequentially, for someone her age, she was strongly opinionated in her views, and the thought of someone unelected and behind the scenes controlling her future to further their own interests was somewhat suffocating—the irony that her political ideology had been born from her father's earlier teachings also hadn't been lost on her.

"Democracies have their faults," Ricard said. "Your father knew this. All he wanted was to find a balance between sound management and popular interests, and to do this he wanted to weaken the power of elected ministers and the councilmen and transfer it to groups that are not self-interested. He also knew his push to remove the barb of populism would make him a lot of enemies, and still he proceeded with his initial plans, using Borealis as his test case. That's your father's unspoken legacy."

"Carolus was willing to use his popularity to limit his ability to use that popularity," M. K. said. "That'd make him a madman to those that stood to lose their power."

"Unfortunately," Ricard said.

Head down, Xander sat there quietly digesting a side to her father that conflicted with what she knew. She peered up at Ricard. "Why are you telling me this?"

"There's a reason people like Erzse disliked Carolus," he said sternly. "It wasn't just because he denied her, his own sister, the prime minister chair. It was because he threatened the power of the ministers altogether. And now, I suspect it's those same views she'll be using as ammunition against your father." His forehead creased with indignation. "His origins and this fabricated foreign allegiance will throw into question his loyalty and his character. And the political views of his twilight years, which would have weakened the power of our governing officials, can be used to muddy his intentions for power and thus his argument against the utilisation of the prime minister chair—assuming that's what Erzse intends to hijack."

Hunched over, M. K. swore as he shook his head. "She'll paint him as a corrupt, power-hungry foreign agent—a man so sly and conniving that he wanted to convince the whole of Anemoi to give up the power of the elected officials and hand him the opportunity to pull the strings from behind the scenes—a puppet master scheming out of the public's eye and away from scrutiny. Combine that with the multiple crises Anemoi faces and the efficiency and effectiveness of response the prime minister chair will provide, and she'll have her case for consolidating power under a more 'democratic' institution."

Xander squirmed, her head lost in the revelations.

M. K. peered at her, aware his words were likely akin to salt being pressed into an open wound. He spoke reassuringly. "We'll find a way to dilute the woman's spittle. And trust me when I say this, Carolus was a good man, regardless of how his views evolved. Even if against the grain, his reasoning was solid, and his intentions *were* true."

"The people were always top of mind," Ricard agreed. He cleared his throat. "I'm telling you this, Xander, because you need to know what it is you'd be supporting by throwing your lot behind your father's legacy. Those of us in his inner circle knew of his views and his intentions. But his teachings weren't confined to just us, and unfortunately, the wrong people found out." He stared at her, his uncharacteristically stern expression unnerving. "It's pretty clear your own views don't align with his, but I also don't think that matters. Even if you could look past it and we could somehow build an opposition on his political opinions—make sure those listening understand where he was coming from—once the truth comes out, there's no guarantee we'll get the support we need. And everyone standing behind those views could find themselves the uncomfortable target of public opinion."

She returned his gaze, unsure what to think or say. Softly, after several moments of silence, a single word escaped her breath. "Okay." Then, overwhelmed with confusion, guilt, and betrayal, she stood up and walked away.

Drawn to the bedroom made for her and Aika, she slumped onto the soft bed in the corner and lay her head against the stiff pillowcase. As she stared up at the wooden rafters, her mind raced through the revelations of that evening, and soon enough, her confusion and guilt gave way to anger. Anger at her father for his betrayal of the customs designed to create fairness amongst Anemoi's people. Customs that had become the envy of Anemoi's neighbours. And then there was her anger towards Erzse. An intense anger further inflamed by Erzse's readiness to twist Carolus's good intentions to further her cause.

How Xander despised that woman. How she wanted to inflict on Erzse the same cruelty the vile woman had inflicted against Nhata and the Borlencians. Against the critters of the Great Forest. Against the Zylencians. Against her own family.

"I'll do what I have to do to make you pay," Xander seethed through pursed lips. "I will make you pay."

It is in those moments, when a racing mind meshes with shallow sleep, that our dreams take on the veil of our most recent reality. But throw into the mix the consumption of the mountainous weedle plant—a herb characterised by its grey leaves, and one that's frequently used in the alleviation of nasal irritation and watery eyes brought on by volcanic and tree dust—and the line between dreamworld and reality can blur to the point of being one and the same in a very select handful of users. For an exceedingly, exceedingly rare side effect of the plant, unbeknownst to most, is its ability to temporarily warp the minds of young, untested sky-whisperers.

The breeze was light within the confines of the white-marble courtyard, which was somewhat unexpected given the walls and their windows and doors were very tall and what one would have thought an effective break against the winds.

A very young Xander skipped curiously into the deserted yard and onto the rectangular lawn that filled the centre, her little legs and inquisitive spirit joyous at the liberty she had mischievously afforded herself.

The soft padding of the grass was interrupted by four small squares brimming with soil and a colourful array of flowers, some of which she did not recognise—in her limited experience—as native to Borealis.

"Hello, Mr Bee!" She giggled at the insect so content to forage the innards of a particularly large sunflower.

Though another child may have been tempted in their adolescence to flick the honeybee from the flower in spite of its endeavour to feed, or to draw back from the fearsome hum of the wings, Xander felt neither impulse and instead instinctively and delicately offered forward her hand.

The bee, without wariness or hesitation, accepted the invitation and climbed onto her forefinger. And there it waited and observed for several heartbeats before clumsily launching into the air and up and over the garden and out of the courtyard as she stared after it, amazed and subdued by the interaction.

The voice from the wilds of the steppe spoke. "Their tranquil nature is so easily imprinted. Of course, few open themselves up to the opportunity to connect, as if the thought itself could sting."

She turned to see the clouded silhouette of the man from the steppe. Taking in the figure's height versus her line of sight, she peered down at her hands and her feet and saw that she was back to her normal size and age. She looked back up.

"You left me in a coma the last time."

"Not me. The process of communicating like this can be—"

"Draining for the unaccustomed. I know."

"You've had practice since the last time we spoke," the silhouetted man said.

"You've been spying?"

"Just an observation."

"You come to warn me again?"

"Ha! I should like to, but I see little point, seeing as you ignored my first warning." The silhouette spoke lightly and then walked towards her whilst taking in the vivid surroundings of her dream.

"You said I can't do it alone, but I'm not alone."

The obscured man chuckled, amused by her logic, and then reached towards the sunflower, but the sunflower flinched from his touch and left Xander with an uneasy chill. He retrieved his hand with a sense of melancholy and regret.

"The thing with bees is they're not unfamiliar to extortion with little regard for their feelings," he said. "Sometimes it's just a matter of asking—politely, that is. You'd be surprised at how ridiculously kind they can be if given the chance."

She stared at the figure that stood over her and exuded internal struggle. "You're suggesting I ask the horse-sized mountain bees for honey?"

"Of course not. It's simply an observation on the nature of bees."

"And will you tell me your name?"

"My name? I don't have a name, at least not anymore. There's no need for it where I am."

"Was it Hemish?"

"Ah! A long-disappeared friend, perhaps?"

"Something like that, yes," she said sadly.

"Sorry, I'm not Hemish. It's clear that you long for him."

"He was taken from me a long time ago. Not through death but by his overbearing mother."

"And you dream about him?" the silhouette asked.

"Sometimes, mostly old memories, though it's not always him that comes out. He's not always his usual kind and good-natured self."

"Sometimes our fears and anxieties manifest themselves in our dreams, often in the most peculiar of ways."

"And guilt?"

"It's not impossible—" The figure's head abruptly looked behind, though Xander could not see at what. "I must leave."

"But—"

"Remember, just ask politely." And the shroud vanished.

Xander turned back to the garden, beckoned by the sudden vibrant hum of a black hummingbird and its long and slender red beak as it drank the nectar of a stout bluebell nestled beneath the sunflower. Hypnotic in the melody that betrayed its size, the song of the wings seduced her near like a fly to light, and only when she stood close enough to cradle the little creature in her hand did she notice the intricate web of ivy that rose from the dirt in the corner of the courtyard. Clinging to the marble wall, it climbed up and through the open top of the quadrangle and onto the roof.

"I don't recall seeing that before..."

And as one does when uninhibited by the realm of reality, she reached out to the soft but sturdy plant and pulled herself up towards the skylight, the courtyard below forever growing smaller until it appeared no more than a neat little square that could fit within her palm.

The breeze of the open air was cooler, and it prickled the skin and ruffled the hair. From her vantage point atop the tiled roof of the building that so resembled the palace of Borealis, she beheld the bluish-purple sky of twilight and the swarm of stars that decorated it, and in the distance and all around, the horizon was marked as if the rays of the dormant sun lit the way. Her gaze fell to the figure lying comfortably on the ledge of the roof, content to let the world continue its spin without interference.

Xander's heart jumped upon closer inspection.

"Aika!"

The girl turned and smiled. "I was wondering when you were going to come up here."

"And I'm glad I did. What a view!" With a joyous grin, Xander took a seat beside her friend and let her now-adult-sized legs dangle over the ledge. "Though I don't think we're in Borealis anymore..."

Aika laughed. "You must be dreaming. We're in the Black Mountains, land where the men are loud and obnoxious and the women subdued and subservient. Still, what a view!"

Together they silently enjoyed the rising horizon of Anemoi to the east and the unfamiliar lands of the west. To the north where the bulbous moon donned a creamy glow that revealed the way ahead, they saw the long and winding road to Zyphyr and the mountain that towered over it, its lofty silhouette amidst the lunar glow so obstructive as to blanket the city in shadow.

"We're close," Aika said eventually.

"To Zyphyr?"

"To your aunt…the evil one, that is."

Xander breathed a sigh of uneasiness.

"You worry too much," Aika jibed playfully.

"So Aes tells me."

"Can I say I'm not surprised?"

Xander chortled embarrassedly. "He tells me: 'It's not a healthy response for someone searching out so many unknowns.'"

"Smart deer, but more to the point, why worry when you've got me looking over you?" Aika winked and then unslung her bow and aimed it playfully at the moon. "So, you figured it out yet?"

"Figured out what?"

"How you're going to do it?"

"Do what?"

"Reach the light."

Xander raised an inquisitive eyebrow, and Aika responded with a simple movement of her bow to the left. Xander followed Aika's line of sight to the little sparkle of white light atop a peak not far from where they sat.

"The light that unlocks the next step on your journey," Aika said.

About to speak, Xander peered at her, perplexed.

Aika stood. "You'll figure it out, and when you do, I'll be waiting. Anyway, Xander, I need to stretch my legs and loosen my shoulders, and what better way than to roam this cold and heartless rocky landscape in search of mischief, with maybe the odd episode of tormenting the slumbering bulk of Ricard thrown in for a laugh." She nodded her goodbye and then jumped from the ledge to the distant ground below.

Not resigned to waste an opportunity to explore, and equally keen to understand Aika's comment, Xander, too, leapt from the ledge to the grassy field at the base of the building, a prolonged but gentle descent that caused only a light flutter of the heart.

A soft smile took her as Aes emerged from the shadows. "Aes! My friend. And your coat—it glows like the night we first met. How long ago that was."

She stroked his neck as he nuzzled hers, and with a swift movement, she climbed on top of him. And what began as a gentle trot along the paved road that was the "backbone" of the Black Mountains quickly manifested into a mad gallop off-road through the forests and meadows of Borlencia towards the sparkling white that hugged the peak. It was a gallop unconstrained by fatigue or friction, and at a pace that invoked exhilaration of the mind and that blurred the thick grasses underfoot and the trees and stars overhead.

And when they had entered the meadow where Xander had first met Aes's herd, a once-magical space now unexpectedly tainted by pain and loss, he slowed to a wander and then stopped at the lifeless body of water in the centre. There she dismounted.

He turned to her. His eyes were heavy with sadness and yet burned with purpose. He spoke sadly into her mind, and her face dropped.

"You must find your kind before they're all lost," she uttered aloud, repeating his revelation. "Will you make it in time?" Her chest clenched at Aes's grim response: Half of his herd had already been slaughtered for sport and meat by a lone Zylencian regiment, and now the rest hid in what was left of central Borlencia's deep woods—desperate to journey south if not for the burden of the suckling fawns and the too few stags left to defend.

Anger swelled in her, as did concern for her friend, and then somewhat shamefully, longing for his continued companionship simmered to the surface.

"How long must you go for?" she said after several moments. "We still have so far to go and so much to accomplish, and yet I could never think to deny you this."

Aes spoke again into her mind. It was a stream of measured vibrations, carefully chosen to warm the girl's heart and instil confidence not only for his well-being but for her own arduous journey ahead.

"I will see you soon, my friend," she responded meekly, barely able to constrain her tears. "Good luck."

She wept as a sad loneliness enveloped her at the sight of his bronze glow disappearing into the night. Hesitantly, she peered into the pool stained by blood and darkness, and renewed anger and frustration and an unbreakable resolve stole her. Through gritted teeth, she sprinted into the tree line towards the white beacon of hope that still beckoned, her weapons and gear securely fastened, the moon and mountain that overshadowed Zyphyr watching intently from the north.

But no matter how much ground she covered or how quickly she moved her legs, the peak remained out of grasp, and eventually she pulled to a halt, the white light always taunting.

"There has to be a way," she muttered, frustrated.

"There is, but you're holding back. You've got to let your mind go," remarked a voice from the shadows.

She turned abruptly, though not from fright but recognition. "Hemish!"

"Who were you expecting?"

"It's been so long. And where are you now? What do you do?" she blurted excitedly to the partially concealed boy whose face had retained its childlike features.

"Keeping busy. So, you ready?"

"Wait. I've so many questions."

"Don't we all, but there isn't time. Now listen carefully. Look at the light… Do it, Xander! Okay, you need to bypass the limits of your mind and remove the passage of time. Focus on your destination, and imagine yourself in the new location."

"You what?"

"Just try it. It's the only way you'll reach it."

"And if it doesn't work?"

"Doesn't sound like the Xander I know."

She turned to the voice, only to be greeted by shadow.

"Hemish?"

There was no response. She turned back to the white light atop the peak.

"How can I imagine the destination if I've never been there…and remove *the passage of time…Does he mean the time to pass through the woods to reach there? How in Anemoi do I know that?"*

A bizarre, mischievous heckle emanated from nearby, and the thought of whatever lurked in the tomb near the twins' hut immediately popped to mind. She shuddered at the thought of that creature coming for her alone in the wilds and dragging her back to that cave.

"Maybe if I imagine the woods…"

The heckle grew closer, sending a shiver through her, and compelled by Hemish's urgency and her desperate desire to get out of there, she closed her eyes and envisioned her destination as well as the forests in between.

"And now…to remove the passage of time—"

Lifted off the ground and through the air at a speed she thought impossible, she felt as if an invisible lasso dragged her through the starry twilight sky towards the light. It was a gut-wrenching feeling exasperated by an inability to control the speed or direction.

"Too high! Too high!" she screamed when it seemed likely she would overshoot the sparkling white peak, and instinctively her mind pulled back, leaving her to drop the couple of hundred metres onto the peak below without any forward momentum.

But rather than meet with a hard bump, she landed comfortably in a luscious meadow of giant white daisies. They were the source of the sparkly white light and a nostalgic reminder of the Great Forest, where even the smallest of plants dwarfed miniaturized humans.

She scrambled to her feet and breathed relief. Wary of sudden gusts and awkwardly angled rocks, she wandered from the peculiar plants towards the edge of the peak and then did a circuit of the summit. The drop was vertical on all accounts, but it was on one particular side where the rock jutted out into an irregular cliff hang overlooking Anemoi to the east that her skin tingled and her hair rose from the assortment of vibrations in the air.

And then she spotted the first—a lone worker bee, quite literally the size of a horse, confounded by her presence on a peak thought unreachable by even the most determined of persons, but the reaction didn't manifest beyond a growing curiosity as another and then another joined the first until a swarm of workers and soldiers encircled her, the drone of their many wings both therapeutic and deafening.

Her face brightened as the bee from the courtyard approached and perched on her hand.

"I'm supposed to ask you for something," she called over the noise, and silence swiftly abounded. "I'm supposed to ask you for something, but I don't know what," she said in a softer voice and with slight embarrassment at her words. "Something to help me on my journey…to stand up against an evil that threatens my people. At least, that's what I think I mean."

The bee didn't respond but, along with the rest of the colony, swarmed over the cliff to the hives underneath and reappeared moments later with a hefty sachet filled with white honey.

"Longmel!" She gasped, wide-eyed. "Well, thank you, Mr Bee!"

Unsure of protocol, she bowed her head out of respect and motioned that she must be on her way, and at that, the bees returned to their business. Sachet tied to her back and feet on the cliff edge, Xander peered to the base of the peak. It was a drop that cried vertigo, but still, she took a deep breath and jumped.

CHAPTER 20

A sharp pain shot through Xander's arm as Aika yanked her wrist and swung her into the cliff face, causing her head to collide with the uneven surface.

"Grip the wall!" Aika screamed through gritted teeth, the strength in her aching hands rapidly evaporating. "Grip the damn wall!"

Xander roused herself from the dreary recess of her semi-conscious mind and reached clumsily for the rocky wall, but her limbs were slow to respond, and it was only after much effort that she was able to latch onto the rock and pull herself in close.

"What in Anemoi are you doing up here?" Aika cried angrily. "Trying to get yourself killed?"

"The white light…" Xander spluttered through short breaths.

"White light? What white light? Never mind, we need to get off this cliff before the next gust puts us in our graves—"

A stream of hot, scalding vapour scorched past them and added to the already-unbearable toxicity of the dry, dusty, sulphuric air prevalent even at that height.

"Damn it!" Aika coughed. "I'm not ready for this. I need a moment to rest."

Xander nodded, and they struggled the short distance back to the relative breathability of the summit.

"The white light," Xander whispered as they took in the meadow.

"Beautiful as they are, why cross through the underworld to reach them?" Aika muttered sternly in reference to the surrounding sea of jagged terrain that exuded death and uninhabitability. For there was not a speck of green amidst the desolate slopes of black-and-brown rock feeding into the peak, only rivers and pits of lava and the long-ago-destroyed remnants of an ancient town.

Instinctively, Xander reached to her back and felt both relief and surprise that the sachet was intact and, more importantly, real.

"Can you hear that?" Aika asked after several moments.

"It's the bees. They won't hurt us."

Aika reached into her pouch and withdrew two candies from the Great Forest. "I was saving these for a rainy day, but this'll have to do. We'll not get back down if we stay up here much longer, and it's a heck of a climb." She passed one to Xander. "It'll make you feel like you've had a full night's sleep and a good breakfast and should hopefully give us the strength we need to get off this rock."

"Fruity."

The indignation etched into Aika's brow released a tad, and her dirtied lips widened into a grin. "Savour it. I've only got a couple left."

The descent and subsequent trek to the cairn where the backbone of the Black Mountains joined the winding road to Flint was a brutal affair and left their bodies torn and drained.

It was the same cairn where yesterday the group had laughed at a wealthy tourist clad in furs as she barked her every whim to an army of cold serfs from under the protection of her carriage. In normal circumstances, the sight wouldn't have been wholly unusual given the backbone was a popular tourist route with the more adventurous city dwellers, but they were entering winter, when the biting cold deterred all but the borderline insane or those who could afford portable comfort.

Sitting in exhausted silence under the frigid morning sun, the girls tended the cuts on their hands and feet and the aches and pains in their limbs, and though the majestic views rarely lost their royalty except for during periods of heavy fog, this morning's view was lost on them.

"I saw him again last night," Xander said, disturbing the quiet.

"Ah, she speaks! Who did you see again last night?" Aika asked, still agitated.

"The man who warned me of the route we take."

"He warned you?" Aika said, surprised. "This is news to me. Who is he?"

"Before we met the twins, the night I fell into a deep sleep, the man that visited me in my dream—or at least I think it was a dream—he warned me that we face only loss on the path we take."

"That's slightly concerning, Xander. And was it he who told you to go climb a peak and throw yourself to the bottom?"

"No, you did and Hemish."

"Well, I certainly didn't tell you to climb a peak and jump off, and I highly doubt your childhood friend did either. Whoever this person is, he must've tricked you, and if it weren't for the fact that you nearly died, well, I'd say it's all just a dream."

"And you—how did you know to find me up there?"

Aika's cheeks reddened. "Um, well, funny story…a dream told me."

"A dream? And you're giving me a hard time?"

"I think there's a slight difference here. Anyway, Aes woke me and brought me near the base, where I spotted you part of the way up climbing. Just so you know, Aes ran off north, away from Flint." Aika caught the twitch of recollection in Xander's expression. "Everything okay?"

"He…he told me in the dream that he must return home."

"He told you this in the dream?" Aika shook her head, dumbfounded. "Okay. And did he say why?"

Sadness took Xander, but not wanting to burden her friend with Aes's personal tragedy, she held her composure. "He's gone to find his family and make sure they're okay. He said he'll join us once he's met with them."

"I guess it has been some time since he's seen them." Aika peered at Xander, a confused blend of apprehension and awe in her eyes. "Whatever this was—the conversations, the climb, the remarkably accurate recollections—all while you were not really awake, well, I'm not really sure what to make of it."

"That makes two of us."

"You know, I'm still fully expecting you to tell me that it's Longmel in that sachet you nearly died retrieving…"

CHAPTER 21

Back in Flint—"As simple as that?" M. K. queried, perplexed.

Sprawled across his chair, he basked in the warm sunlight that pierced the ash-clad sky of the mountain and cleansed the dank musk of the hall. Unlike the prior night, it was only him, Xander, Joseph, Ricard, and Aika in the room. Each had in front of them a heavy breakfast of eggs and bread, though only Ricard and M. K. washed it down with warm local ale.

"As simple as that," Xander said nonchalantly. "Was just a matter of asking politely."

"I've never heard anything like it," Joseph repeated in disbelief.

"Probably thought they were giving you a helping hand. Doubt they often encounter a stranger up there, a distraught lost soul unlikely to make it back," Ricard chided and took a sip of his beer.

"Be that as it may, this could be the payment we need to bring the mayor of Ingleton on board," M. K. said. "Assuming you're happy to relinquish some of it?"

Xander nodded.

"And you're sure about this?" Ricard asked M. K.

"We're soon to find out, but given the mayor's my cousin and I have a pretty good inclination of his tastes, I'm fairly certain this will work."

"Your cousin?" Ricard nearly spilt his drink. "And diplomacy wasn't an option?"

"He's a second cousin several times removed and not always the most reasonable."

"When will you present it?" Xander asked.

"Well, I would've thought it preferable you do it, considering you're the one who retrieved it."

"Me?"

M. K. glanced at Joseph. "In my experience, it's easier for your average person to latch on to a vision when there's actually something to visualize, especially if you're looking to persuade the other provinces to follow you. Those who have skin in the game need a reason to risk it all, and a leader is much easier to sympathize with than a group of so-called elected bureaucrats." Joseph was about to speak, but M. K. continued. "And, given what came to light last night, it might not hurt for us to build an opposition on Xander's ideologies rather than her father's. Seeing as she is a staunch supporter of his earlier policies."

"No," Xander declined politely before Joseph could speak. "I understand where you're coming from, M. K. But for the same reason I don't agree with my father's teachings in his later years, I can't take on such a role. I've done nothing to earn it. I have no official title. I've not been voted in. I'd be no better than him or Erzse if I chose such a path."

"You got that honey yourself. Nobody else did it for you."

She was quiet for a moment. "I have my role in all this, and it's not to debate politics. If you need me to vouch for or against my father or Erzse or whoever, I will, but that's not my purpose. My purpose lies shattered across Anemoi. Once I have what I need, maybe then I can be a face in this leadership. But until then, it has to be you, M. K., and Evia and Ricard and Aika. All of you have or had official positions from which to leverage. People like me and Joseph—we're here to help but in other ways."

Joseph could barely contain his proud smile, and even M. K. and Ricard found themselves in awe at her integrity.

"We're lucky to have you, Xander," Aika said softly.

"What says you?" M. K asked Ricard.

Ricard sat back with a curious grin. "Can't force the girl, can we? Nonetheless, I've been thinking about our little conversation last night, and you know, I don't think it'll hurt us to run with Carolus's later ideologies."

"How so?" Joseph asked. He and Aika had been brought up to speed that morning.

"We can't deny those teachings, because at the end of the day, they happened. But that doesn't mean we give Erzse the right to bend and twist his words to suit her needs. No—we need to sell it that his teachings were the mark of a selfless individual. That to truly give the people what they need and want, he felt we needed to remove the barb of populism. It's the complete opposite to Erzse's desire to create a permanent prime minister chair, which gives whoever's elected unreasonable power over the people."

"She'll argue that his goal *was* to deprive the people of a choice," Aika remarked. "More so than the prime minister chair ever could have."

"Doesn't matter," Ricard said nonchalantly. "We're not asking them to vote on his ideologies. We're simply portraying his viewpoint and intentions. Nothing more. Nothing less. Hopefully it'll reaffirm his original reasoning behind his vote against Erzse. Reasoning I, and maybe Xander if she so chooses, can attest to, given we were witnesses."

"And the foreign influence?" M. K. asked.

Ricard rubbed his eyes and spoke angrily through gritted teeth. "The man died protecting Borealis against a foreign army."

"A foreign army working against his own interests," M. K. said.

"I…we'll need to think about how to counter that one."

Aika stood and stretched the arm she had used to stop Xander from falling to a certain death.

"You okay?" Ricard asked.

"Just sore," she responded. "And all this talk of having to defend an honourable man that can no longer defend himself is exhausting." She looked at Xander. "I'm sorry you're having to go through this. But if you'll excuse me, I really need to stretch my legs and go to the…you know what."

Xander nodded and watched as Aika left the room. Without turning to the others, she spoke softly. "What do you think Erzse will do if she finds out I'm alive?"

There was silence. She looked to them, anger and frustration written in her brow.

"Nothing good if given the opportunity," Joseph spoke finally.

"She'd probably find a way to use you to further her cause," Ricard said. "She would see the danger you pose as Carolus's daughter and find a way to twist it to her own end. That's my thought anyway."

"Why?" Joseph asked Xander.

"Well, she's going to find out sooner or later if I end up speaking on behalf of my father. Maybe it wouldn't hurt to make it known who I am before she gets a chance to grab me in the dark. I imagine she's not too dissimilar to those bogeymen the twins spoke of."

M. K. chuckled. "Would be a fitting look for a woman so cruel. Don't think any of us know for sure if she has any idea you live. But assuming she doesn't, it'll be quite the show when you stand up and denounce the accusations. We'd need to get you into the assembly as a witness, of course. Perhaps with the protection of the Eurencian ministers to avoid any funny business. But I'd save your face and name until the very last moment, Xander. It'll have a greater shock value and reduce the chance of her making any attempt before you can give testimony, whatever that may be."

Joseph squirmed in his seat, clearly irritated by M. K.'s persistence. "We'll wait until we've regrouped with Evia before making any decisions of this kind."

"Naturally. 'Twas just a thought."

CHAPTER 22

Januarix 11, 485; Crowton, Borlencia—The crowd that was packed into the market square was raucous, and the steam of their three thousand hot bodies rose steadily into the frigid morning air. Evia was standing on one of a dozen elevated platforms along the edge of the square along with Dogner, Robyn, and a group of locals she didn't know. In the centre, there was a much larger platform where forty Borlencian candidates stood in eager anticipation, including Ronal and the woman from Bulgar, along with Wiston and a handful of election officials.

"I can feel the peoples' nerves," Robyn commented.

"Nerves?" Dogner said, surprised. "That's excitement, lad. And lots of it. This has been a long time coming."

"Wasn't that long ago that we were struggling to build the hype and undo the damage caused by Erzse's accusations."

"I don't think the damage is quite undone," Evia said sternly. "It'll take some time for those insurrectionist rumours to die and for the Borlencians to turn their full, undivided allegiance to their own ministers. Unfortunately, ridding the province of Zylencian troops and getting official recognition of the illegality of this occupation are both a must if we're to see any meaningful restoration."

"I don't doubt your words, Evia," Robyn remarked.

"And I don't doubt your commitment to the cause," she responded.

"Also," Dogner began, "I only see Crowton's residents packing the space, and Crowton's only got the one candidate. They'll be excited for Ronal, no doubt. And it'd take an impossible disaster for him not to take the seat."

Evia peered around the square as the other two continued to chat. She could see Zylencian soldiers posted on all the corners, but there were no captains or figures of authority, except for one man watching a little way off from the central podium. Santos had pointed him out as the main point of contact for Aiden—the Zylencian commander overseeing the occupation—the same messenger Grendal had informed them of. The man had a narrow chin and a weathered forehead but could be no older than thirty, Evia guessed.

A trumpet blared, silencing the throng, and a Eurencian official walked to the front of the central platform. He raised a copper acoustic megaphone to his mouth and unfurled a long parchment.

"The votes have been tallied—"

The crowd descended into chaotic gossip, and it took several moments of the orator gesturing with his hands for silence for the onlookers to fall quiet again.

The man, clearly irritated at the interruption, dutifully continued. "Borlencia's twelve ministers have been chosen, in addition to all the unfilled council positions. Congratulations."

Cheers abounded, and many in the audience stomped their feet against the hard winter ground. This time the orator seemed less annoyed and waited patiently for the noise to subside.

"The first senior minister position has been filled by"—he read the parchment in front of him—"Ronal of Crowton."

The throng went mad with excitement and cheers. A scene repeated, albeit not as enthusiastically, intermittently over the next half hour as the orator went through the full list of names. The woman from Bulgar had failed to take a senior minister position but was confirmed as a common minister. Only one other senior minister position was taken by one of the individuals brought in to appease Erzse as a phony crony, though all the schemers got one official position or another.

"That went well," Wiston said over the noise as he climbed onto Evia's platform. "Borlencia's got its parliament back. Should be interesting to see how everything unfolds from here."

"And all thanks to the two of you," Evia said to him and Robyn. "We're eternally grateful."

"It was a necessity for Anemoi. Can't repel invaders in the east and the north if we're fractured." He glanced around the square, then locked on to two Zylencian soldiers a short way off. "We're leaving for Zyphyr in the morning. Perhaps we can sow some goodwill with the Zylencian ministers in the lead-up to the meeting."

"That's new. So soon?" Evia asked, surprised. "The Borlencians have barely tasted their new reality."

"We decided it's best to work several fronts simultaneously. We're leaving a number of our officials in Crowton to oversee the transition and to help taper the rumours still circulating about insurrection. More are on the way with the two other Eurencian senior ministers." Indignation seemed to take him at this.

"What?"

"It's not the best time to be pulling our most senior officials from Eurencia."

"Your garrisons will manage with your commanders at the helm, I'm sure."

He nodded, though his expression was grim. "You're still committed to staying in the short-term?"

She peered around for snooping ears. The noise of the throng was deafening, and besides those she knew, the platform on which they stood had been abandoned. "The meeting of the Upper House is not for some weeks, and I need to ensure Ronal and the others get off to a good start, free of…encumbrances. And until the Zylencian army is removed, Fredrick and Santos will still need their continued support in ensuring the safety of the freed prisoners."

"Don't forget…" Dogner began, glancing at the Zylencian messenger with his thin chin and haggard forehead.

"Right! And there's another matter I must attend to," Evia said. "It so happens that the commander of Zylencia's occupying armies carries a name I've not heard in quite some time. If he is who I think he is, then he may be worth a trip."

"Very well," Wiston said. "Your hands are full. We'll keep you updated. And Joseph? Will we be seeing him before we see you again?"

"Very likely, given he and my niece will be arriving in Zyphyr this afternoon."

"You seem ill at ease," Robyn said.

"Well, my dear," Evia retorted with a shake of her head, "that's because I only found out a short while ago from two acquaintances of mine, and unfortunately, I'm not there to keep an eye."

"She's been running free the past couple months without harm."

"This time it's different."

"Then I assume it's her new proximity to Erzse?"

"You could say that, lad," Dogner spoke, displaying the same apprehension as Evia.

"We'll be sure to make haste, then," Wiston said reassuringly.

"Just don't make it too obvious who she is when you find her," Dogner cautioned.

Wiston grinned and patted the big man on the arm. "So little faith."

CHAPTER 23

Januarix 11, 485; city of Zyphyr, northern tip of the Black Mountains, Zylen-cia—Zyphyr was a city born from the black rock of Mount Camana in the sense that pretty much every building of old and new was constructed using the mountain's beautiful black stone. The city was an unnatural silhouette perched atop one of the most wonderous of Anemoi's skylines and was known not only as the city of the west but also the amber of Anemoi due to its famed trade in ore and refined metals.

"Zyphyr has a…distinct smell," Aika remarked as she, Xander, and Joseph turned onto another street carpeted in black cobblestone.

Narrower than the last, this street was relatively unbusy and certainly cleaner, with high-walled residences on either side.

"It's a blend of burnt soot, mountain air, and the linger of human excrement," Joseph said, referencing the volcano overshadowing the city.

"Leaves a mark on the nostrils and tongue, doesn't it?" Xander added to their amusement.

"I'm sure we'll get used to it in time. Sounds like we'll be here a little while. This must be us," he said, stopping in front of a tall, solidly built gate.

Behind the perimeter wall, they could make out the exterior of a large black villa spanning the width of forty to fifty metres.

"This is Evia's villa?" Aika said, stunned. "Can't say I'm familiar with how things work in your cities, but this must've cost quite a bit."

"I'd say so," Joseph responded.

"How could she afford it?" Xander asked curiously.

"You'll have to ask her," Joseph said as he fiddled in his bag. "Got it!" he said and withdrew a key. "She's been around quite a while. Who knows how much she's saved and invested over the years."

He inserted the key and unlocked the gate. "Ready?"

They nodded their heads excitedly. He opened the gate and ushered them in. Their shock and awe were immediate. Behind the wall was a pristine garden filled with neatly trimmed bushes and, behind it, an immaculately kept building covered in vines and wallflowers.

They trod up to the thick wooden front door, and Joseph rapped on it. Nothing. He shrugged and inserted the key and opened it.

"Hello!" he called to no response.

"Who you expecting?" Aika asked.

"Evia has a caretaker that looks after the property. Helps her rent it out. She sent word ahead of time that we'd be coming. Still, I'd rather us not sneak up on him and give him a fright."

They entered through the door and down a short, tiled hallway into a central, open-air courtyard brimming with luscious plants and miniature fountains dotted around its centre and bordered by a dozen spacious rooms with marble flooring. It was a design influenced by the wealthy villas and warmer climate of Borealis and one Xander recognised right off.

"She certainly is no ordinary aunt," Aika managed as they entered the villa's dining room.

Xander chuckled. "I couldn't think of anybody less ordinary at this point."

Aika brushed her hand over a giant mahogany table. "I'm excited to meet her."

They exited the dining room, and each trotted in different directions as they took in the marvellous construction.

"Ah! A bedroom," Joseph said, poking his head through an open door. "The first of many, no doubt."

Xander and Aika rushed over and peered into the room. Their mouths dropped. A king-sized bed draped in ornate cushions sat against one wall, and antique furniture lined the other walls. Aika walked over to a low-lying couch and sat on it.

She winced. "Looks prettier than it is comfy."

"Who wants this—" Joseph began when the two girls quickly said each other's names simultaneously.

They laughed.

"I'll take it," Aika said, "unless it's the nicest of the lot; then I'm happy to relinquish it to the almighty bearer."

"Hey! None of that, Your Highness," Xander retorted.

Joseph smiled warmly and then peered across the courtyard. "I suppose we should head out and get some food to bring back."

"Or surely we will wither and starve!"

"I third that," Aika spoke, rubbing her tummy.

"Right then, it's settled," Joseph agreed. "Find a room and leave your belongings. I'll leave a little note for the caretaker. Then we can head out."

The two girls nodded excitedly and swiftly did as they were told, while Joseph left a note near to the door. Entering back onto the street, they began in the direction from which they had come, having spotted several markets on their way in. But it wasn't long before Xander and Aika insisted they stop at a restaurant, their need for nourishment too much. No sooner had they voiced their concerns than they came across a quaint little hole in the wall.

An array of locals sat across the pavement on shoddy wooden stools, and all seemed to be eating the same dish from ceramic bowls. A brown goop with chunks of unrecognisable meat, forked into the mouth with doughy bread.

"What is it?" Aika asked Joseph under her breath.

"Stew."

"I know that much. What kind of stew?"

"Smells like goat," Xander said.

"The girl's got a noggin," said an old man with white whiskers, though he didn't make eye contact with them. He simply stared into the run-down store on the opposite side of the road as he tended his meal from one of the stools. "You ain't gonna go wrong givin' it a try, I'd say. The stuff fills your belly and's made of sturdy mountain goat."

Xander could tell Joseph was a tad wary of taking the only three vacant seats, which happened to be right next to the man, but before he could sway them to search out another spot, Aika spoke excitedly.

"It's a local dish, then?"

"As local as they come," the man grunted, again without looking at them.

"Sounds good to me!" she said, peering to Joseph and Xander.

Joseph blew through his cheeks, his discomfort blatant, but he reluctantly nodded his head. "Very well, then. Take a seat, and I'll get us three dishes."

The girls obliged and sat down on the rickety stools just as a squad of Zylencian soldiers entered the street. Neither flinched nor tensed, for they were unknowns in Zyphyr, but they still watched with interest as the local men and women parted way for the armed procession.

"Rodents," the old man said before taking a greedy bite of his bread. Though his gaze didn't deviate from the storefront, it was clear he was referring to the soldiers. "Tools of the wealthy as they sit in their palaces, eating and drinking their fine fare, whilst the rest of us makes a livin' off whateva scraps we can find. Worst of it, ya say a thing, and they'll take your life." He turned his head from the store and looked at them with deep-blue eyes. Beautiful eyes, but not unscathed. The girls hid their shock at the tiny scratches etched into the centre of his pupils. "They're a wretched lot, the royals of Zyphyr."

"Royals?" Aika queried. "I didn't think Anemoi had any royals left."

"The wealthy families of old never left. Where you think they went?

Just vanished? Gone extinct? No! They're still here. Ministers. Generals. Stingy business owners. Same in all them provinces. If a position can 'av' power, they've got it. And if I still 'ad my eyes, I'd stand up and give 'em a hiding. But then, that's what got me them taken away in the first place." He let out a sigh and went back to staring at the storefront.

"Everything okay?" Joseph asked, sitting down with three bowls of stew. He held them out, and the girls took theirs without the enthusiasm he was expecting. He glanced at the man, who had gone back to eating his goop, and then back to them. "Everything okay?"

They nodded and descended into a silent eating frenzy. The old man didn't speak again, and after a few minutes, he got up and shuffled away, leaving behind his empty bowl.

"What did he say to you?" Joseph asked once the man was out of earshot.

"He shared his dislike for the wealthy families of Zyphyr," Aika responded.

"No doubt Erzse—" Xander began when Joseph motioned with his hand for her to lower her voice. "No doubt she's one of them," she said quietly.

"If it's anything like M. K. said," Joseph began, "then a lot of your ordinary citizens aren't in the best place. But it's too dangerous to openly revolt or complain."

"Pretty much what that old man said," Aika said glumly. "Poor man. I wonder what he must've done to have been blinded so?"

"Blinded?" Joseph said, shocked, his mouth full.

"His eyes had been scratched."

A look of disgust and sadness took him. "Some can be so, so cruel." He blew through pursed lips. "Just because it should go without saying doesn't mean I won't say it again. We need to be careful. Stick to the villa until Evia—"

"What about the shard?" Xander interrupted.

"Until Evia arrives, unless it's to find the shard." He ripped off a piece of bread and dipped it into his stew. About to put it into his mouth, he stopped and looked at Xander. "Where do you think it is?"

She shrugged. "I think it's under the streets, but I won't know until I have a proper look at the map."

"Well, you've got us to help," he said and chucked the flavoured bread in his mouth.

"You're going to help?"

"I've got a few things to sort out for your aunt, but when I'm not busy with that, I'll join you and Aika."

"Three's a bit of a crowd, don't you think?" Aika said.

"I know the city. Won't hurt to have me with you." He wiped the residue of the stew from the bowl with the last of his bread and bit into it.

The girls had already finished theirs and were keen for something sweet to dampen the enduring saltiness.

"Cake?" Xander asked.

He chuckled. "Do you know me?"

"I knew I could count on you. And Aika."

"I know a place nearby. Only a couple of blocks."

The three of them stood and walked at a slower pace down the road, hobbled by the heavy meal in their bellies. Turning onto a narrow side street, they stopped as they took in the windowless walls completely covered in graffiti right up until the next crossroad. There were hundreds of caricatures drawn in a whole assortment of illuminous colours, bright against the backdrop of the black wall. Most of the faces were obscure and unknown to the trio, though every now and then one or another would have Joseph scratching his chin in recognition.

"Why haven't they cleaned it?" Aika asked when they were about half-way down the empty street.

He shrugged. "Who's there to clean it?"

"The people that live here."

"Don't think they care. And if they do, it's likely any attempt to clean the place has been temporary. You okay, Xander?"

She had stopped and was now standing a few metres behind the other two, her gaze locked on a shoddily drawn woman wearing the robes of a Zylencian senior minister. The woman's face was twisted into a scowl, and she held a small dagger in her right hand and a slain lamb in her other.

"I recognise her," Xander said as the others backtracked to where she stood. "From Borealis, also graffiti."

"Who is it?" Aika asked.

Xander looked at Joseph, sensing the palpitation of his mind. "You know who she is, don't you?"

He blew through pursed lips. "And I think you do too."

"Erzse?"

He nodded. "The one and only."

Anger rose through Xander.

"What was she doing in the drawing you saw in Borealis?" Aika asked.

"She was drawn as the saviour to my father's theft of Borealis." Fists balled, she shook her head and then turned to them. "I think I want to go back to the villa."

"Of course," Joseph said sympathetically. "I'll drop you both home and can find some sweets afterwards."

She nodded silently and followed Joseph as he led them back towards the villa. Her excitement at being in a new city with her friends had all but gone, and all she could think about was the retribution she so desperately wanted to inflict on her evil aunt.

Back in the villa, and eager to start searching for her best response to Erzse's nastiness, Xander went to the room she had assigned to herself and pulled the map from her sack. Subconsciously brushing her thumb against the ring on her finger, she unrolled the map across her lap. A bird's-eye view of Zyphyr gradually etched onto the parchment. She could make out the city's perimeter wall, its numerous market squares and residential districts, and even the various government buildings. The shard itself appeared to be in the centre of the city, beneath the city palace's walls. She had a rough idea of where Evia's villa was and, when confident of its whereabouts, zoomed in on its location. The road outside, the garden, the rooms, and the courtyard, all visible to her. And also, to her surprise, a tunnel.

A curious expression took her, and she stood up and walked into the courtyard. She counted off the multiple fountains and then strolled up to one that was just off-centre. There was no discernible difference between it and the others, except this was the only one marked on the map.

"The tunnel starts here," she murmured, taking in the floral pattern painted on the porcelain reservoir.

"You talking to yourself again?"

Xander turned to Aika, who was leaning against the living room door. She snorted, her excitement at what the map had shown her enough to brush away her previous anger. "Again?"

"It's not the first time I've heard you talking to yourself. Hence, again." Aika's gaze fell on the map that was blank to her eyes. "You find something?"

"You could say that," Xander said and placed the map on the ground. "It's showing me a tunnel under the fountain."

"Well, the water's got to come from somewhere."

"It's a pretty big tunnel."

She and Aika knelt down for a closer look and began combing the fountain for any sign of a switch or lever to stop the water.

"What?" Aika asked as a smile took Xander.

Xander slipped the ring from her finger, dipped her hand into the crisp water, and placed it on a crease marked by a faded broadleaf otherwise lost amidst the pattern's numerous flowers.

Not a moment later, a clicking noise sounded from below and the water stopped. Then, with a shudder, the fountain dropped into the ground, revealing an opening into the world beneath Zyphyr's streets.

CHAPTER 24

Januarix 15, 485; town five kilometres from the Zylencian eastern border, Borlencia—Evia gritted her teeth from the cold as she took in the dilapidated pub devoid of noise. It was nestled onto the bank of the only river meandering through the shoddy settlement on the road to Zyphyr. She blew steamy air through pursed lips and shot Dogner a hesitant glance. Both were soddened with the dirt of their journey.

"Unsavoury comes to mind," he said. "You're sure this is the place?"

She reread the lopsided sign. "The Crown. This is it."

"Alright, then. I'll only be a moment," he said and began for the door.

"No. We go in together."

"Could be a den of cutthroats."

"And it wouldn't make any difference whether I was accosted in there or out here."

He nodded. Hand never venturing far from his hammer, he trudged up to the door and opened it. Surprisingly, the waft that greeted them wasn't that of stale beer or dust, as one might suspect from the building's grotty appearance, but of richly scented candles and tobacco smoke.

"Fancy that," Dogner murmured as he entered cautiously.

Despite the complete lack of noise when outside, the cosy pub was filled with men and women smoking and talking quietly. They both glanced to the corner where a slender man with a hooked nose and tanned features had raised his arm. His hair wispy and his crow's feet pronounced, the man looked as if he was carved from one of the many ancient Borlencian busts depicting the quintessential merchant of old. Against the wall, a short distance away, was the slender man's messenger, the man with the thin chin and haggard forehead. Alert, the messenger looked on, a dagger strapped to his belt.

"Then it's true," Evia said of the slender man still sitting.

"Aiden," Dogner muttered under his breath.

Evia started towards the bare table, and Dogner was quick to follow, still vigilant of their surroundings.

The man stood up as the pair approached. "Evia," he said warmly and embraced her as if they were the best of friends. He pulled away and directed her to sit on the chair nearest himself. He then reached out a hand to Dogner. Not wanting to soil the introduction, Dogner clasped Aiden's hand and shook it. "It's been a while, old boy," Aiden greeted him.

"It has," Dogner responded without the same enthusiasm. He took the seat opposite Evia after manoeuvring it for an unobstructed view of the pub and the messenger.

Unlike their meetings with other prospective acquaintances, Evia did not reach into Aiden's mind in search of trickery or doubt. She knew the man was adept at concealing information from individuals with her gifts and that he was also fairly skilled at picking up on intrusions. Somewhat frustratingly, she would have to approach the conversation without the advantage of knowing his intentions. That, or risk souring a relationship before fruition.

"So you're the commander of Zylencia's armies in Borlencia?" she asked.

"One of many titles," Aiden responded.

"And what's Erzse got Borealis's old spymaster doing commanding Zylencia's armies?" Dogner grunted suspiciously. "You're no general."

Aiden sat back, and a smirk breached his cheeks. "General, no. Senior minister of Zylencia and master of logistics and subterfuge, yes. And who says Erzse has me doing anything?"

"You're—"

"Not Erzse's stooge, if that's what you're insinuating, old boy. Can't stand the old bag. It was at my own insistence that I took the helm after the man Erzse had appointed butchered a dozen settlements on the lakeshore at her behest."

"So it wasn't you?" Evia said, both surprised and relieved.

"No, it was a man called Barton," Aiden said. "I came in after the fact."

"We're familiar with the name."

"Unsurprising. Now, tell me, what's compelled the two of you to come out of retirement and seek me out? A need to relive—"

"An occupying army in Borlencia that's outstayed its welcome," Evia said bluntly. "And Zylencia's self-appointed leader's push to—"

"To establish a permanent prime minister's chair? And here I was thinking your insistence on meeting me was for old times' sake," he said as he took the pair in through the fresh eyes and light wrinkles that belied his seven decades. He leant forward as if to whisper. "So, will they stand steadfast?"

"Sorry?"

"The newly elected ministers and their colleagues. The ones you coached to deceive Erzse. Will they stand steadfast, or will they buckle under the pressure that'll inevitably come their way?"

The pair skilfully hid their shock.

"I'm not sure what you're referring to," Evia lied.

Smugly, Aiden sat back and opened his palms to the pub. "Tell me, do you always conduct your business in such establishments?"

"You've lost us, lad," Dogner said.

"The Wispy Tavern—the one in Crowton, in the central quarter, to be precise." Evia and Dogner tensed. Aiden was very clearly referring to the tavern in Crowton where they and Santos had first reacquainted and subsequently conducted much of their follow-up business. The cunning man continued nonchalantly, "Because let's be honest, most landlords seem content to recycle the same four or five names without remorse for their lack of originality, and thus we end up with a dozen Wispy Taverns across a town the size of Crowton. In this instance, however, the lack of originality requires no repentance, for the landlord is a friend of mine, and the tavern acts somewhat as a safehouse for weary messengers and spies in my employ. Apt given the high-ranking guests that tend to unwittingly frequent it."

A pocket of quiet enveloped the corner as they sized each other up. Finally, unable to glimpse Aiden's sharp mind, Evia spoke. "What do you know?"

"Don't worry, my dear," Aiden replied. "This isn't the word on the streets that knows no restraint."

"Just the word of your spies, who may or may not hold only your ear," Dogner said sternly.

"It's nothing to worry about, old boy. My men can be trusted."

"We do worry. We worry exactly how much she may know, and the last thing we need is the wrong person taking down some of the finer details," Evia said.

"She knows whatever I want her to know when it comes to the finer details of this particular matter," Aiden bragged. "Most of her men are really my men, and the ones who aren't hear what I want them to hear—the ones I let live, anyhow."

Dogner suppressed his revulsion at the dishonesty and trickery of the man's dark arts, but Evia invited explanation.

Aiden leaned forward. "You and I want the same thing, Evia. To see the woman's stranglehold on Zyphyr and Anemoi weakened, and what better way to place the first knife than to recognise the legitimate government of Borlencia and declare her occupation illegal. Fantastic idea of yours, really, to coax her into handing you the knife by schooling the candidates to lead her on. Of course, their success ultimately depends on their ability to stand up to the pressures that will inevitably come their way once Erzse catches on."

"If she catches on," Dogner retorted.

"The Borlencians are in the process of lodging a formal complaint against Erzse, no?" Aiden responded nonchalantly.

"It's a formal request to have the removal of Zylencia's troops added to the meeting agenda," Evia corrected, annoyed but ultimately not surprised he knew.

"At which point, I presume they'll declare the occupation illegal and try to muddy the water? Don't worry, Evia. She doesn't know the latter, but she will surely realise the former as soon as that request is lodged."

"It's not unreasonable for the Borlencians to want the troops removed, even the Borlencians secretly 'allied' to Erzse. It's about showing face to the voter base. Something she should understand if she wants puppets with some semblance of legitimacy."

Aiden shrugged. "Sure, but the woman's volatile and unreasonably cruel. It's a dangerous game you have that lot playing, Evia. You want to know what her initial reaction was when she first heard of the Borlencian desire to hold elections? It was to castrate the ringleaders. Imagine that—a senior minister of Anemoi suggesting castration as a means of cutting off the democratic process. Of course, I quickly stayed her hand, reminding her that Zylencia is not the only province with peeping eyes and that interference, insurrection or not, could in all likelihood be seen unfavourably. My nudge and the pledge of allegiance from a number of the Borlencian candidates were ultimately enough to convince her it was best to endorse the process, not hinder it. Whether this would work a second time, I couldn't tell you, especially if she feels betrayed."

"The woman has no business as a senior minister if killing legitimately elected officials is her first thought."

"Couldn't agree more," Aiden said.

"Then your suggestion?"

"Continue to risk the puppets, so as to keep her lulled into this false pretence," Aiden answered. "I'll not entertain any line of thought with her that could reaffirm suspicions regarding the integrity of her 'corrupted' Borlencian officials. In fact, I'll do my upmost to convince her they're reliable. That way she'll be blindsided on the day of the vote. Oh, the heartache as it pierces her withered bosom!"

Evia eyed him, curious as to his intentions. "That's very kind of you, Aiden. Thank you."

"It's for the greater good. But that brings me to you, Evia. Your presence has somewhat complicated matters."

"Evia?" Dogner said worriedly.

"Erzse has shown interest in Evia's whereabouts for some time now and vehemently believes that your ultimate intention is to build support against her cause. You could even say your appearance out of the weeds was one of her reasons for returning to Zyphyr so promptly from the Great Forest."

Her heart clenched, as did Dogner's.

"Your reputation transcends time," Aiden continued. "For even after the many years that you've been inactive, she thinks to neutralize you as a threat. Again, rest assured, I have stayed her hand. You can only remove so many enemies before it becomes too obvious, especially one as revered as yourself."

Evia held his gaze. Though it wasn't lost on her that he may know more than he just let on, she breathed shallow relief knowing that Xander wasn't on the tip of his tongue.

With a cheerful wave of his hand, Aiden smiled and relaxed into a slouch. "But back to business. Besides keeping Erzse in line, what do you need from me? I presume you'd like me to remove Zylencia's armies?"

"It would be a start," Evia spoke. "It's just one of several actions that need to happen to reverse this path to disintegration."

"It'll have to be during the meeting. Any attempt to do it before then will simply rile up Erzse."

"And if she wins the vote—" Dogner began.

"Then it doesn't matter what I say now," Aiden interjected, his expression grave. "But it's an eventuality both you and I are working to avoid. I, too, will be returning to Zyphyr shortly to continue the necessary work. You're welcome to travel with me."

"We…you know, that sounds like a good idea," Evia said.

Aiden smiled. "Where will you stay in Zyphyr? I hear that old villa of yours still stands."

She relaxed. "I've heard the same. And yes, that is where we'll be staying."

"And the Eurencians?"

"Nothing escapes you, does it?"

"Not everything," Aiden said. "You know, it's a good thing they're staying with you. One of the many drawbacks to Erzse's inability to maintain economic order is the steep increase in property prices and rent in all quarters of the city. A group of politicians and their retinue taking up residence in a fancy hotel would bankrupt what's left of Eurencia's coffers before the month was over."

"Let me guess," Dogner said agitatedly, breaking the calm. "The bone-crushing debt they owe Zylencia was co-signed by you?"

"Some of us have little choice but to bide our time," Aiden retorted.

"And what about the Notencians? What've you done to rope them in or cripple 'em?"

"You mean the drug-ridden crazies from Notencia? Nothing. But that's not for a lack of trying on my part."

"They've shown the same reluctance to engage with us also," Evia admitted.

"I suspect Erzse has Notencia's ministers in her pocket," Aiden said. "Though I can no longer trust the news coming out of that wicked swamp where hallucinogenic plants and ghastly illnesses rot the mind and body, and the way of the witch doctor shows resurgence in the towns and cities, a disease of the spirit no longer confined to the backwaters."

"I thought that wretched religion was long ago extinct," she said apprehensively. "It would appear that without the example of Borealis, the rest of Anemoi falls to ruin. And yet, surely it cannot be that the entirety of Notencia's government is compromised?" she said more to herself than to her company.

Aiden laughed. "Define compromised. I'm sure some still have a moral compass, if that's what you mean, but I wouldn't put all my eggs in that basket. A mind succumbed to rot, be it through indoctrination or chemical, is a mind that cannot be trusted."

"And yet you ask that we trust you," Dogner said suspiciously, evidently unwilling to give the man an easy pass.

"I think you'll trust whatever lead doesn't reek, old boy. Remember, I'm not from Zyphyr, though my wife and darling children may be, and I've not been exposed to the decades of decay that have infiltrated this once-dear city. Take faith in my roots and my unwavering lust for balance."

"Asking faith in Borealis's old spymaster is asking much."

"And asking civility from the marine general of Anemoi's now-disbanded, not to mention disgraced, raiding fleet isn't?"

Dogner clenched his fist, but Evia gently placed her hand on his to defuse the tension.

"Let bygones be bygones," she urged calmly. "Anemoi's northern fleets lie at the bottom of the straits along with their legacies," she said softly and looked to Aiden with conviction. "Aiden, you have the political support and Erzse's ear. Use your influence to build support for pulling Zylencia's troops from Borlencia and support against Erzse's propositions, even if behind closed doors. Inclusion of Borlencia's ministers in the Senior Council and Upper House, along with you and your allies, will increase our odds of preventing passage of the motion to introduce a prime minister."

"And the declaration of the occupation as illegal and the pain that'll surely be invoked on the Zylencians?" Aiden said. "It's a necessary move on your part, but I also need guarantees the damage will be…within reason."

"There has to be a cost, but that's not to say we can't work together to lessen any repercussions."

He stared at them, as if taking in their every little detail. "You have my word; I'll not let her bring back a throne only she can sit on. Unburdened unity is the only path forward for Anemoi."

"And what's in it for you?" Dogner asked, this time with less aggression.

"I'm a man of balance, an engineer of equilibrium, if you will, and I've spent most of this life as a saboteur and obstructer to those that might seek to disrupt said balance. But alas, the woman is a breathing reminder of my failure to pierce the fog of deception and ambition that now threatens to topple the equilibrium that has governed Anemoi since the Revolutionary Wars. It would be unforgivable of me to not, at the least, attempt redemption. Take pleasure in knowing that her proximity to absolute power causes me much aggravation at night."

"I'm sad to say, there's too much at stake to not hope for your redemption."

CHAPTER 25

Januarix 17, 485; Zyphyr, Zylencia—"Gross!" Aika said, nearly gagging. She clasped her nose and mouth and turned to Xander who already pinched her own.

"Quick, this way!" Xander managed, and they ran down the nearest tunnel using their torches to light the way.

Both carried light sacks with only the essentials, and Xander had purposely left her shield at the villa. Still, it was rough going through the slime-covered passage that was no taller than a metre. Breaching into a chamber on the other side, one lit by a drain to the street above, they released their fingers from their noses.

"Slightly more bearable." Xander laughed, grateful to be away from the stench of the previous room.

Aika shot her a disapproving glance and then chuckled. "Not sure the fate of Anemoi is worth this." She pointed to Xander's bag. "Sure you don't want to check the map and see if there's another way to the shard?"

"The only other tunnel near here that can get us close was the one we took yesterday. And that was a dead end."

"And beside that one? There must be something."

"There were dozens," Xander replied. "But they all require us to circle around the city's centre a bit. It'd take us hours."

"And you don't want to check?"

"Don't trust me?"

"Not if you're making me go back through there."

"Okay then," Xander said and withdrew the map. Using the light from above, she looked at the scribbles visible only to her. She sighed and looked up with regret etched into her brow. "Sorry, Aika. It's the only way, unless you want to put it off until tomorrow?"

Aika blew through pursed lips. "How did I go from the purity of the forest to this sewer? When you said let's get the next shard, I thought it'd be as…"

"Magical and fun as the last?"

"Something like that," Aika said, pulling a rag seeped in oil from her sack.

"Really a good time to oil your knives?"

"I'd rather poison my lungs with the fumes of this cloth than with whatever it is that lies at the end of that tunnel."

Xander chuckled and pulled her own from her sack. "Good idea."

Faces wrapped against the odour that awaited them, they ducked back into the tunnel and made for the stink-ridden chamber. They entered the space that natural light could not permeate and cautiously stepped into the shallow recess of the ground that was carpeted in gunk. Waving the torches around, they scanned for the next opening.

Xander's gaze caught on the shadow of the next tunnel. She turned around and tapped Aika's shoulder, then turned back to the opening. She stepped towards it and abruptly slipped to the ground with a thump. She cursed through gritted teeth and got to righting herself. But as she stood up, she stopped all movement and stared at the partially decomposed body strewn in a heap next to her fallen torch.

Aika, also in shock, stretched her torch out in front, and they both gasped. The young girl's face had been mutilated. Matted locks of golden hair stuck to the ground in what appeared to be a pool of dried blood, and the girl's wrists and ankles bore the bruises that could be inflicted only by heavy shackles. Aika put her hand to her mouth and swiftly darted out of the chamber, back the way they had come, taking her torch with her.

But Xander stayed, unable to pull her eyes from the victim's tattoo that flickered under the light of her fallen torch. She reached down and picked the stick up, then brought the flame close to the ink permanently etched into the girl's shoulder.

She read the inscription. "Etlinga."

She craned closer, determined to make out the rest that was obscured by dirt and blood. It was too difficult. She clumsily retrieved her flask from her sack and poured a sliver of the cold liquid over the marking. "AG Fifteen. DS One." Her eyes wandered up to the neck, where a smudge-covered square of sorts had been carved into the skin.

As she craned closer for a better look, a noise sounded from the tunnel she was moments ago ready to enter, startling her dead still. She listened for another. There was a voice. How far off, she couldn't tell, but not wanting to stay and potentially meet the girl's abuser, or whoever else lingered in such an eerie place, she quietly and swiftly vacated the chamber, back the way she had come.

She joined with Aika and, finger to her mouth, ushered Aika back towards the villa an hour's walk away. Partly shocked into silence, and partly keen to not betray their location, the journey was a quiet one. It wasn't until they neared their marker signalling the last bend to Evia's villa that Aika stopped, forcing Xander to follow suit.

"That girl was murdered," Aika said. "Someone cut into her flesh and then saw good to dump her body in the sewer to rot."

Xander frowned, the same image painfully imprinted into her mind. "Who do you suppose did it?"

"I'd like to think no man or woman capable. That maybe it was a creature like the one that tried to lure you back into the grave by the twins." Xander shuddered at the thought. "But I think it's likely the murderer was human. Someone corrupt enough on the inside to torture and kill that girl."

"She was from the lakeshore."

"How do you know?" Aika said, her eyes widening in shock.

"She had a tattoo that said as much."

"A war prisoner?"

Xander nodded. "I think so."

"But why kill her?"

"I don't know."

Aika gritted her teeth. "I fear it's far more dangerous down here than we realise. I think something bad is going to happen if we keep coming down here."

Xander shifted uncomfortably. "What choice do I have? It's the only way to get to that shard."

"I think the map tricks you. You said it won't show you a direct route. That the shard's always a bit out of reach in the centre of the city, no matter which tunnel you follow with your mind."

"I don't get it either. That's why I need to follow every possible path until one rings true."

Aika was about to speak, but excited murmurs from the direction of the villa stayed her tongue. They looked at each other and then began in haste for the entrance to the villa. Closer approach revealed a myriad of voices, Joseph's and the Eurencians, who had arrived the day before, and another voice, much fainter and quite undecipherable from the tunnel.

Ready to climb up, Xander felt Aika's hand tug at her trousers.

"Next time we close the entrance before wandering off," Aika said. "Now that we know we're not the only ones down here."

"Agreed," Xander said, and she poked her head through the collapsed fountain into the courtyard.

Pulling herself through, she peered to the group of bodies crowded by the door, and a fat smile took her.

"Evia!"

The congregation went quiet and, as one, turned to the site of the filthy girl running excitedly across the garden. Evia trudged to the front and swallowed Xander in her arms as the two gracefully collided. Neither spoke as they gripped each other. It was a long, emotional reunion that left Xander feeling a sense of security she never knew she had been without. Finally, as she released her grip and pulled away from her aunt, she saw Dogner. Wiping a tear from her watery eye, she walked up to him and embraced him.

"Little one," he said softly as he wrapped her in a big, burly hug.

▲ ▲ ▲

"She was from Etlinga," Xander said to Evia.

The pair was sitting on Xander's bed. Facing them, Dogner, Aika, and Joseph lounged on small chairs dotted around the room.

"Did you recognise her?" Evia asked, her sadness evident.

"No. The rest of the tattoo read 'AG Fifteen. DS One.'"

"One of the prisoners, then," Dogner remarked. "Age fifteen. District one."

"District one?" Aika asked curiously.

"Zyphyr. Her ultimate destination." He sighed. "She likely would've come through our network, but with too few of us, we've not been able to rescue them all. A damn shame we missed her."

"Another one chosen for Erzse," Joseph said angrily.

"Chosen for Erzse," Aika repeated sadly. "Then it's been confirmed—they're not just political prisoners?"

Evia looked fondly at the girl that had become near inseparable from Xander and who had clearly been kept abreast of the situation. "If not chosen for Erzse, then someone affiliated with her. There's a plateau a short distance from the city where the groups are broken up and the prisoners given their assignment. We've had reports that most have been drafted to work the mines the regular miners refuse to work out of protest. A small few have been transported across the border—"

"Transported out of Anemoi—you mean to be sold as slaves?" Xander said, clenching her fists, her memory of the inhumane trade in the aftermath of Borealis's fall still vivid.

"We still don't know for what, but that's a reasonable assumption."

"And then the rest become Erzse's, or some other Zylencian minister's, playthings?" Aika spoke.

"They're being kept in Zyphyr in cells under the streets." Evia hesitated. "They're always the youngest of the lot. Never older than nineteen or twenty."

"But why?"

"We still don't know."

"I can already tell you there's nothing good in store for them," Xander said in disgust.

"Your sources know they're being kept here as more than political prisoners, and yet they do nothing?" Aika asked with growing frustration.

"What can they do without knowing exactly what she's doing to them?" Evia responded. "As far as Zyphyr's politicians have been told, the ones not in the know that is, the girls are simply—as you say—political prisoners."

"And the ones being transported out of Anemoi?" Xander said. "What about them? It's pretty obvious—"

A rap came from the door.

"Yes," Evia called.

Robyn popped his head through. "Dinner's ready."

▲ ▲ ▲

"Tell me more, Wiston," Evia said in stunned curiosity, peering across the polished marble floor and through the prancing rays of the skylight to her gathered assortment of guests.

Seated on old mahogany furniture, Evia, Xander, and Aika were positioned to one side of the spacious room, with Joseph, Wiston, Robyn, and Aiden on the other side. Despite the odd comment from the Eurencian ministers in the preceding weeks regarding the new adversary from the east, the full light of the Eurencian predicament hadn't been discussed at length with Evia and the others—a not-so-surprising reality given the time and energy commitment of rebuilding Borlencia's government. Coupled with the almost complete lack of gossip on the streets of the large Borlencian towns, Evia, Joseph, and Dogner were, like the others who had travelled from the south, hearing most of the shocking details for the first time.

"What's strange is that this army from the east—the Cent as we've come to know them—travels with mother and child, as if one day they decided to just pack their lives and migrate west," Wiston continued. "They never venture far from their caravans, and in every skirmish, they've thrown all they've got at us as if they have nothing to lose," he said with uncharacteristic apprehension. "And their skill on horseback makes some of our younger horsemen look like amateurs…I can already see them using their mobility to devastating effect against Anemoi's infantry if the other provinces ever manage to commit, and that is assuming we can catch them head-on."

Wiston's confident demeanour that was already a hit with the wealthy housewives of Zyphyr had all but disappeared in the matter concerned.

"Horse archers?" Dogner squirmed, aware of the devastation a contingent of the highly mobile archers could cause on those unaccustomed to the deadly volleys.

"We've seen some, but to date they've primarily used their lancers. Still, I've never seen such effectiveness in a charge, and there's so damn many of them." A steely expression befell him. "They've taken two of the outer districts on our eastern border and evicted all who worked the land. Though they're still a significant distance east of our capital—Eurus—we've spotted their scouts as far west as the Pass of Eurus."

"So close to the city!" Joseph said.

"Too close," Wiston said. "We tried to push their main force out of

Eurencia early on, utilising our eastern garrison and a tranche of mercenaries, but with their women and teens also taking up the sword, their numbers proved too great. Fortunately, with so many mouths to feed, they've had no choice but to strip the sustenance from what's left of our neighbour to the east—the Sterling—in addition to our own two lost outer districts, and that has given us some time to bring in forces from the west and to build our coffers. Without the other provinces committing troops, however, we've not been in a position to expel them, though we have been able to largely hold them in check, for now."

"For now?" Dogner repeated.

"Putting it bluntly, we're spread too thin to cover the line of attrition, and though we've bloodied them on several occasions now, our losses outweigh theirs," Wiston said sombrely. "And this doesn't even take into account any smaller forces they've still got ravaging the Sterling, those that have yet to join their main force. On the outside it might look like we've slowed or even stopped their advance, but it's only a matter of time before we lose the ability to hold them near the border. When that line fails, the only choke point between them and Eurus where we could maybe hold their numbers sufficiently, and maybe deliver a decisive blow, is the Pass of Eurus—"

"But we'd lose half of Eurencia if you were pushed back to that line," Joseph blurted, aghast.

Wiston nodded. "It's the kind of dilemma wholly unfit for sleep. We retreat to a more defensible point but lose half of the province in doing so, or we continue to put up a front in the hope that reinforcements arrive in time whilst slowly bleeding out at the saddle as we do."

"How many would have to be evacuated?" Dogner asked.

"Some have migrated west already, but it's still half a million at the low end."

Dogner cursed, and the group fell silent. Wiston's unease was contagious, and it proliferated through the room like wildfire as the ramifications of such a loss dawned on them all. It took Evia clearing her throat to jerk them from their brooding.

"Interesting that they chose eviction over slaughter with your two outer districts," she remarked, eager to better understand their newfound enemy.

"Depends on the adversary and whether they've crossed what happens to be a very fine line," Wiston said. "The Sterling resisted, and they paid the price. And I worry we're about to cross it, if we haven't already. The day that horde is fully regrouped and facing starvation, they'll throw their all at our weakened lines and breach through, and at that point our people may no longer be afforded the luxury of walking away."

"Still, with their entire uprooted civilisation reliant on continued success in battle on foreign territory, it sounds like they have everything to lose, and that's why they fight the way they do. And yet they look to not inflict more damage than necessary," Evia responded curiously.

"That's perhaps an optimistic assessment. Eviction is not far behind death when you have nowhere else to go."

"But it shines a light onto their motive. So my question is this: What drove them to pick up their belongings and seek a new home?"

"You assume they're in search of a new home," Robyn said.

"And you don't?" Evia asked him.

"To assume they're in search of a new home is to assume they're content to work the same piece of land through the generations, but maybe these people are more similar to the nomadic locust. A creature that consumes all the resources in a given area to the point where it becomes a 'move on or die' scenario."

Aiden spoke up from the corner of the room. "The evidence would suggest this to be a realistic assumption." Until then, he had been happy to silently admire the art on the wall of Evia's living room.

"Ah, the spymaster speaks," Dogner said. "Please, enlighten us as to how you came to know the ways of this unknown and mysterious foe now threatening Anemoi's borders."

"With pleasure, old boy. Like yourselves, I was blindsided by the arrival of this horde on Anemoi's doorstep, but I was never one to shirk my responsibility to understand a threat, nor one to sign a contract to commit funds and troops without first understanding the implications. I took it upon myself to study these people and their origins. And the evidence shows that they live and move like other nomadic peoples, all their belongings in tow, always following the ripeness of the picking ground. Testimonies from other affected peoples left in their wake have shown this to be the case."

"But that begs another question: Why have we not heard of these nomads before?" Evia said. "Most nomadic tribes tread the same migratory route, and as this is our first encounter with their caravans, I think it safe to say we're not situated on their regular migratory route. So why now? Why deviate, unless something or someone has disrupted their usual path?"

"Aye, sounds like the displacer could've been displaced," Dogner chimed in.

"Well, whatever their reason for turning this way," Robyn began sternly, "I think we can all agree that time is scarce, and you need only ask what's left of the Sterling to fully grasp the magnitude of the situation Anemoi faces. The Sterling are a people content to trade and deal with themselves, and our relationship with them has been guided by a mutual recognition of one another's presence rather than any shared history, trade, or fear. Truth be told, I'm sure you could count the centuries of cohabitation on the same plain without a raised quip or strike or whisper between us and them, and yet, in the final days of their collapse, they sent an emissary to our palace begging for military assistance and the opening of our borders to their refugees. It was the first time we'd heard of this tribe from the east. And it was a desperate and fearful plea that, though impactful on our sentiment, was too late to buy them the time needed to stem the slaughter."

Dogner scoffed. "The horde offered eviction to your two outer districts all while the blood of an entire civilisation to the east of you was still wet on the ground. There's no middle ground with this lot. You oblige or you die. It's enough to turn the stomach when you think on it."

"We don't know how much of the Sterling civilisation survived," Robyn admitted. "We've not been able to survey the far reaches of their land, and the ones that came over as refugees had been cut off from their brethren for some time, but there were several instances where they were given the option of eviction. The Sterling cities directly across our border continued to present a wall of fierce resistance, however, and that unfortunately invited their eventual destruction."

"Which doesn't bode well for us in the long run, given we have little desire to remove ourselves from our own land," Wiston said coldly.

"The Sterling referred to them as the Centaurus, or Cent for short," Robyn continued. "Testament to their skill on horseback. And we were lucky in those early days. The Sterling's warning, plus the time it took the Cent to regather their main force, bought us the time we needed to bolster our eastern garrison sufficiently enough to hold them after the fall of those two districts. The message was clear, though, that the consumption of acquired resources was the aim of the game, not settlement. And eviction is an option, albeit one we're unlikely to pursue or be afforded at this rate."

"And we have no idea how many are yet to join their main force?" Dogner asked.

"Worryingly, no."

"So we are to assume, then, that once they've sucked Eurencia dry, they'll turn their attention to Notencia or Borlencia?" Evia queried worriedly.

"More likely Borlencia, given the unhindered route via the plains. I can't see their horsemen faring well in the jungles and swamps of Notencia. That and they'd need to cross the Buto Jungle, which is a demon of its own."

"Then why the steep terms from Zyphyr to support Eurencia in what I would deem a threat to the whole of Anemoi?" Evia asked Aiden. "Why not call the Special Council and vote to assemble Anemoi's armies in defiance of a common enemy?"

Wiston and Robyn looked on in fascination at Evia's ability to disregard subtleties.

Aiden shrugged matter-of-factly. "With a significant portion of Zylencia's armies already occupied fighting the 'insurrection' in Borlencia, Erzse thought it reasonable to insist on terms of her own before she commit. The debt agreement being the first in a list of demands."

"Did the situation not give Erzse the opportunity she desired from the outset?" Xander spoke up. Though in the company of senior politicians, her nerves were less fraught than when she had spoken to M. K. and his retinue, thanks in part to the allure of Evia's calming presence. "The opportunity to call together the Special Council, invoke the position of prime minister against a wartime threat, and then retain the seat once the matter resolved."

"Alas, Evia's handmaiden knows more than her title would suggest," Aiden said, referencing the title Evia had introduced Xander under. He turned to Aika. "And, Princess, you've been so quiet. Not even a greeting. Do you still speak?"

"You know I do," Aika retorted.

"Hadn't realised you'd met each other," Evia said, surprised. "I thought this may be the first time."

"He knew my father," Aika said with what seemed like borderline disgust.

"My condolences." Aiden bowed his head. "I heard only recently of his passing."

Aika nodded, and an awkward silence abounded before Aiden looked to Xander.

"To your point, Xander, that's not an unreasonable observation. It would've given her the seat but only temporarily, for it's not a legitimate means from which to permanently secure the position. Much better to demand the amendment of the constitution to eliminate the term limits and make the seat a permanent one prior to committing a full-fledged campaign to strengthen the border."

"And still, why dream up a contract designed to cripple? Why not just demand the position outright and prevent the continued bloodshed?"

Evia said.

"Must I really remind you of Erzse's desire to control? The more Eurencia struggles, the easier it is for her to make additional demands. There was no guarantee they'd support her proposition outright, so she chose to weaken their resolve instead."

"You co-signed the debt agreement," Dogner muttered. "You speak as if you're not complicit."

"Such a large quantity of coin required the signature of two ministers from Zyphyr. It was a necessary action to be seen as her legitimate ally."

"And an effective means to give her power to sway future votes," Evia added.

"Evia, my dear," Aiden began. "We could argue about this all day long, but the agreement is signed and has been for quite some time now. At this point, it's important to pre-empt the next move, not dwell on history."

"It makes me uncomfortable, how much power it has given her over some of the ministers. What were they thinking?"

Wiston interjected. "With their homes at stake and Zyphyr the only city with sufficient coin or a battle-ready garrison besides our own, it's little wonder they were quick to agree. I myself was keen to get the funds and troops needed at any cost. Of course, much has come to light since, and principle now dictates my hand."

A knock came from the door, and all turned to an official from the Eurencian delegation.

"Yes?" Wiston asked the man.

"I saw M. K.'s messenger to the gate. He'll be in Ingleton by morning. He seemed pleased to be on his way, something about having no desire to be stuck in the city for the procession this weekend."

"Yes, the streets tend to get a bit clogged when Erzse holds her charitable events," Aiden said. "Certainly not an event for the claustrophobic." As the messenger left, Aiden turned to the others. "And how is M. K.'s push to rally Zylencia's south against Zyphyr coming along?"

Despite inviting Aiden to join them for dinner and the group's willingness to work with him in most matters Erzse related, there was still a veil of distrust towards him. Their reluctance to indulge his question swiftly morphed into an uncomfortable silence.

Aiden laughed, breaking the quiet, and he peered to Dogner. "You, too, old boy?"

"I'm sorry, Aiden," Evia spoke softly. "I'm not versed on M. K.'s plans, but it's his journey, not ours. I don't think he'd appreciate us giving away details to another senior minister of Zylencia, however trivial."

"Say no more, Evia. It's an understandable predicament, though I would say keeping me in the loop can only work to his, and your, advantage."

"That may be so, lad," Dogner said. "But one step at a time. You're barely back from the dead and under Zylencia's colours, no less. Will take a bit of getting used to."

"Never one to withhold, old boy," Aiden said, standing up.

"You're leaving?" Evia asked, her worry of having overstepped clear to Xander.

"That I am, but not on account of the conversation. I've been back in Zyphyr several hours now and haven't checked in with the wife or my own. Some would call that suspiciously overdue." He bowed his head and walked to the door. "I'll see you soon." And at that, he left the villa.

"Aiden?" Joseph said to Evia in disbelief.

"Aiden."

"How did this happen?"

"Quite the coincidence, isn't it?" she said, still a tad bewildered herself.

"And you trust him?"

"As much as is sensible. He's already well versed in our plans, and not on account of our loose tongues. So not much we can hide from the man."

Joseph cracked his knuckles and then shook his head. "I think we're playing a dangerous game involving him. The man's a senior minister of Zylencia. His loyalty will be to his own, not us."

"He sees the danger in Erzse taking power. That much is obvious."

"I don't trust him," Xander said.

Evia looked at the girl inquisitively. "Your gut tells you this?"

"My gut. My logic."

"Do tell?"

"I agree with you. I don't think he can stand Erzse. But something tells me he's looking out for himself. His motivation is to further himself. Not Erzse. Not us."

"I don't think it hurts to have a senior Zylencian other than M. K. on our side," Wiston mused.

"The trick will be to feed him what we want without divulging more than is necessary," Robyn added.

"Cautious openness," Dogner said. "What's not to like?"

"Cautious openness," Evia repeated, ponderingly. "And how do you suggest we lead him astray without betraying his trust in us?"

There was quiet, everybody in the room diving for an answer.

"Let him in on M. K.'s plans," Xander said after several moments.

"His plan being?" Evia asked, having not been brought up to speed on the most recent developments.

"He and his cousin have levelled half the forest east of Ingleton," Wiston said.

"War then?" Dogner asked.

"A blockade. Bring Erzse to the table."

"Risky."

"But smart. And he's in good hands with Commander Ricard by his side," Robyn added.

"Ricard!" Dogner chuffed loudly. "Been a long time since I've heard that name. That's a pair of very good hands right there."

"He's our hidden weapon," Joseph said. "Supporting M. K.'s military effort and vouching for Carolus's stand against Erzse's ideology on the day of the vote."

"The lad truly is as hardy and cunning as an ox, even as an oldling."

Aika chuckled. "He's definitely as stubborn."

Xander looked at Evia. "Let Aiden in, but not enough to give away anything important. Feed him the sentiment on the streets. That if he or Erzse want to win the votes in the south, they'll need to come to the table. Give the stolen mines back and lower the taxes on their minerals."

Dogner nodded his head as he contemplated. "Demands Erzse would hardly go for, if not for the blockade exasperating the pain at home."

"She may still not go for it," Wiston observed.

"She might if we let Aiden try and talk some sense into her," Xander said. "The same way you had some of the Borlencian candidates convince her it was the best and only way to secure additional votes."

Joseph grunted as he massaged his chin with his thumb. "Xander could be on to something."

"And what if M. K. and his followers end up throwing their votes behind her?" Robyn asked.

"They won't," Joseph said. "They can't stand the woman. But we can talk to M. K., tell him what we've discussed here, get him to play along."

"Then that's what we'll do," Evia said, sitting back. "We'll use Aiden the same way he's likely using us."

"The lad's got a lifetime of subterfuge behind him," Dogner commented. "Are you sure you want to try and play him at his own game?"

"If it's a game worth playing, it's worth a try."

▲ ▲ ▲

That evening—Xander turned over in her bed so that she was facing the window. Even through the dimly lit night, she could make out the network of a flowery vine crisscrossing the bricks of the perimeter wall. Light chatter came from the street, and the mellow drone of an unfamiliar brass instrument emanated from the end of the block. The ambience was wholesome, and still, her thoughts raced.

The distorted image of the maimed girl they had found earlier was seared into her mind, plucking away at her guilty conscience. Left to wither away, alone and unknown, a world away from home. She felt guilt for not at least attempting to identify the dead girl or pull her body out of the sewer and onto the street where maybe, just maybe, the girl could be afforded the justice she surely deserved.

Xander clenched her fists and ground her teeth in frustration, then flipped onto her back so that the plain, unjudgmental ceiling was all that stared back. Her guilt was compounded by the inaction of those that had the means to help the prisoners on the plateau. They knew, they all knew what was going on, and still they did nothing. But what if she could, even if it saved the life of just one innocent? Her mind jumped to the shard in the centre of the city. She sighed. That was her priority. Not the Borlencian prisoners. Her duty was to get the shard and complete the Rose. Not even the vote could be her priority.

Tears welled up in her eyes.

The guilt for not wanting to support her father's legacy was the worst of all, searing through her like molten rock. The shame of not wanting to support a man, her own father, that only wanted the best for Anemoi was unbearable. After all he had done for both her and their people, still she couldn't do him this one favour. Was she a fool to bind herself to a principle that mattered not if it could oust Erzse, or was she right to stand by her beliefs? How she wished her father, her mother, and her brother could be there right now to guide her. To hold her hand and tell her she was no fool for standing behind her values. But they were long dead. Their bodies cold and bare in the ground, the same as would happen to the dead girl they had discovered in the undercity.

Their memories were too painful, too cold. She needed warmth. No, she craved warmth. Warmth that could someday be more than memory. Her longing to see Hemish came to the fore. It had been years since she had seen him. He was probably not the same person she had known as a child. But his goofy presence was as comforting as it was amusing. A ray of light desired when the weight of her responsibility darkened her mood so. And he still lived, as far as she knew, anyhow. Maybe one day she would run into him again. Maybe during this journey to find the shard. Maybe many years later when they were all old and fat and content.

She sighed and twisted back onto her side. One could dream, but until then, she knew what needed to be done. Rescuing the prisoners or vouching for her father may not be on the table, but finding the shard sure was. And she would do all in her power to make it happen.

CHAPTER 26

Januarix 18, 485; Zyphyr, Zylencia—Xander gripped the map and frowned. The city's sewers, crypts, dungeons, cellars, long-forgotten temples, and tunnels of seemingly no purpose or origin all connected into one vast network of confusion and darkness underneath the comparatively simple grid system of Zyphyr's streets. Some throughways were sturdy in their design and others nothing more than hollowed dirt. Some were vented by outlets to the city above, and others tainted by excrement, humidity, and ancient decay. She found herself again longing for the liberty brought by daylight, a world apart from the frustrations of her search that even the map seemed unable to comprehend.

"How much of this was built since the last bearer entered?" she muttered to herself in exasperation and for the umpteenth time as she scraped a drop of dried slime from her cheek. She nearly heaved at the stench it released. "Disgusting! Let's take a—"

She frowned. Aika had been only too happy to take up Evia's request to run an errand that involved both stealth and the opportunity to part ways with the search. But despite both Evia's and Aika's insistence that Xander wait for Aika and not go into the tunnels alone, Xander's restless determination had compelled her to ignore the warning.

She peered down at the map and traced her finger along the route she had taken. She was near the inner districts of the city, less than a mile from the shard dotted in the centre of the metropolis seemingly under the municipal buildings. And yet, like the incursions before, the throughway marked on the map was non-existent. Instead of a continuation of the tunnel, she was faced with a brick wall to the front and a small hole, partially concealed by weeds, burrowed into the ground at the wall's bottom right corner.

"You're looking in the wrong place," a voice echoed from behind, causing her to jerk around and withdraw her blade.

"It's you," she said to the tall silhouette leaning against the filthy wall.

"It's me. I see you're in the city. Should've known you wouldn't listen."

She could tell he grinned even through the obscurity. "Why are you here?"

"Like I said, you're looking in the wrong place."

"And what exactly do you think I'm looking for?"

"If you want the shard—" Her posture hardened, but before she could speak, he continued. "I mean you no harm, Xander. I'm only trying to help."

"But how do you know about the shard?"

"It's quite the tale. Listen, if your map is older than a decade, which I'm guessing it is, it'll be wrong. Much has changed down here in that time."

"Then how—"

"If you want the shard, follow the Borlencian prisoners…What's wrong?" he asked as she abruptly clipped her nose.

"I just got a whiff of…of…rotting meat." She nearly gagged. About to quip, she stood still as the man shifted from the wall and peered down the dark tunnel the way Xander had come, his posture rigid.

"What?" she asked nervously.

"Something's down here."

"One of Erzse's minions—"

"No, something else." He looked at her and pointed to the burrow. "Get in there."

"What?"

"Just do it!"

The silhouette abruptly faded away, leaving her alone in the dark. Goosebumps prickled up and down her legs, and not wanting to see what lurked, she quickly stuffed the map into her sack and flung herself into the narrow opening of the burrow.

Made of the mountain's earth, sharp rocks protruded from the tunnel's uneven sides, and ancient, long-unused roots wove through the formation like a spider's web not quite content to catch its prey. Coupled with the throughway's downward gradient, there was little wonder Xander emerged on the other side with a myriad of cuts and bruises on her knees and hands. Still, not wanting to wait and find out what exactly had spooked her new friend, it was an inconsequential price.

As she stood, she withdrew her blade and peered around the circular chamber she had crawled into. It was no larger than one of the rooms in Evia's villa and was carved from the mountain itself. Light protruded from a small slit in the ground overhead, enough to illuminate a space of that size, and at the opposite end there was a wooden altar pushed up against the wall. Other than the opening she had come through, there was no other visible exit.

Fretting, she withdrew the map. Hope took her. Though the chamber wasn't on there, she could still make out another tunnel leading from the chamber. She looked up at the altar and trudged over to it.

"What in Anemoi?" she said of the five two-inch-high figurines positioned across its top.

With no discernible gender, each was complete with a pair of horns, a tail, and a pot belly, and each carried a silly expression and pose. She pulled in close, eager to make out their every detail, when a noise came from behind. She abruptly turned, blade at the ready.

"You're back," she said to the silhouette standing on the opposite side. "What was it?"

"Whatever it was, it's gone, but you should leave before it comes back and you lose your chance to get out." The silhouette turned around suddenly to face one of the nondescript walls and then disappeared.

"Bye to you too!"

She turned back to the altar. Curiosity begged for her to move it and see what lay in the tunnel on the other side, but the thought of something eerie creeping up on her unawares from behind was enough to tear away any interest.

Instead, she grabbed the figurines and stuffed them into her sack, then made for the tunnel from which she had come. It took only minutes for her to clamber back up and find the nearest manhole to the surface, and still, it felt like much longer, with every gust and echo putting her on edge.

She breached the horizontal entrance of the manhole into an empty, narrow street and shut the drain behind her. Confused by what had just transpired, she stood up and sucked in a gulp of comparatively untainted mountain air. As her eyes adjusted, she took in the black stone street on which she stood, where small houses and stores lined the edges. Though it was marked on the map, she felt no familiarity. Her gaze fell on the noisy procession coursing through the adjacent street, and she approached the fuss, her prior bewilderment slipping from thought.

The street was much, much wider than the previous one, and thankfully, too, for the excited crowds that lined the pavement on either side of the march were at least ten people deep and stretched to the horizon of the grim industrial settlement.

"What is this?" Xander asked a soft-featured girl standing beside her whose skin and hair were a stark blond and eyes a piercing grey.

To the girl's side stood a boy similar in appearance and stature. Neither looked to be more than eighteen years old. The girl took in Xander's dirty appearance, but instead of showing disgust at the grime of the tunnels that had latched to her skin and clothes, she exuded nervousness and sudden suspicion at the inquiry.

"Not from around 'ere?" she asked guardedly after a moment's contemplation.

"No, I'm from out of town. I'm visiting my aunt."

"She keeping ya well?"

"Huh? Ah, the clothes, yes. Just a part-time job to earn some extra coin," Xander lied.

"What made her think to bring ya here at such a—" She stopped midsentence when the boy nudged her.

Xander ignored the interrupted question. "So what is this?" she repeated.

"The men and women on the carts are ministers and 'ired servants," the boy said. "The soldiers ya see are Lady Erzse's personal guard."

Xander's stomach tightened.

"Everything okay?" he asked.

"Yes, just a bit nauseous from the job," Xander fibbed again, staring into the procession.

The girl leaned over. "Needn't worry yourself over Erzse's guards, if you are. The worst of the lot ain't in town from what I 'ear."

"The worst of the lot?"

"The man that wears the silver mask. Erzse's right-hand man. A real brute he is. We've both seen it. When he's around, ya know Erzse is up to no good."

"And where's Erzse?"

"Coming, of course."

The knot in Xander's stomach twisted painfully. She was suddenly nervous to see the woman who had caused so much strife and who she still had yet to glimpse after nearly a decade. But she also felt an uncomfortable blend of fear and hatred and disgust for the woman, the product of rumoured wickedness and treachery and the recently witnessed atrocities in the city underneath the streets.

The crowd pressed around them and grew more frantic, the perspiration and warmth of the squish of bodies therapeutic against her rapidly cooling skin, but it had taken several moments more before the smell of warm bread revealed the reason for the excitement.

To the left, men straddling large carts pulled by teams of horses tossed loaves of the soft stuff into the onlookers, and the results were instantaneous and savage in their effect. Men and women trampled one another as they lunged at the gifts, in addition to the few unlucky children caught in the melee, and it took a fair degree of strength from Xander and the duo to hold their own against the rush.

The boy scowled. "She buys votes like there's no tomorrow. A scourge if eva there was one!"

"Soon enough, brother," the girl whispered and gripped his hand.

"I see her! I see her!" a child on his father's shoulders screamed excitedly, arousing Xander from her silent inquiry into what had just played out.

Excited curiosity quickly overwhelmed the dread, and Xander lurched forward through the throng in search of a better vantage point. Nearer the front, the press was such that significant movement was laughable, but her height amongst the most impoverished of the city's inhabitants was advantageous.

The weight of the behemoth bread carts shook the stone underneath as they wheeled past, and they were immediately followed by ranks of bodyguards, their uniform that of the Anemoi regulars but their insignia tailored to Zyphyr's colours. At the tail end, standing atop a chariot akin to a throne and purposely oblivious to the bought worship lining the streets, Erzse stared ahead with a hardened scowl etched into the thin, leathery skin of what, one would have assumed, should have been the defined features of a middle-aged woman rather than the weathered face of a sickly bat. Even her body seemed a decrepit betrayal of her years, and Xander found little resemblance to what she had seen all those years past when the woman walked alongside Carolus to make her argument for a prime minister. Even the caricature from the alley did little to capture the reality. Pity wormed its head into her array of emotions.

Like a pebble skipped across a pond, the approach of Erzse's chariot beckoned waves of onlookers to reach their hands forward in some futile attempt to brush fingertips with her perceived sanctity, and what little pity had arisen in Xander's gut swiftly fell to revulsion and then panic as the woman who had remained unflinching in her stature up until then locked eyes with her.

Xander's muscles tightened, and her mind screamed for immediate flight, but the faint voice of caution called for calm. Could she be sure it was her the woman looked at? How would Erzse even know what she looked like? And still, proximity only seemed to enhance the look of curiosity that had overtaken Erzse's unrelenting scowl.

At five metres, Erzse's curious gaze still bore into the increasingly nervous girl, but as Xander prepared to flee down the nearest side street at the slightest provocation, the woman's eyes darted past her into the mass of people, and urgency and fright suddenly took her.

"In the crowd! The two brats!" Erzse howled frantically, pointing with her claw.

Xander sighted the brother and sister as they pushed their way through the confusion, the faint whiff of lit gunpowder a betrayal of their motive. Fully aware of what was to come, she swiftly darted onto the road away from the siblings and through the procession towards the other side of the street. She had just thrown several distracted soldiers from her path when she caught sight of a man bounding towards Erzse's other flank with the same hostile intent.

"Damn it!" she cursed and made desperately towards the bread carts ahead.

The first explosion emanated from the unfamiliar man and ravaged an area of ten square metres, maiming and killing soldiers and civilians alike, the force of the blast indiscriminate in its approach. Xander reeled on the ground, dazed and bruised and bloodied from the impact. Her immediate instinct was to climb from the mess of limbs and torn bodies that now littered the road and pavements, but the memory of three attackers swiftly stayed her impulse, and she pulled the limp body of a fallen soldier over herself.

The second explosion detonated from where the siblings had approached, the felling of the bodies like the felling of a forest under the force of an avalanche, the weight of the fallen suffocating to anyone stuck underneath. And still, despite the longing to gasp for air, Xander braced for a third impact, but this time it didn't come from where she expected but farther down the line, and followed by a fourth, then a fifth, and too many to count. Screams and cries and shouts of anger and fear and loss and confusion abounded through the city.

If Erzse had been intent on Xander, she now found herself readily occupied by the massacre of so many innocents in the city under her charge, the beginnings of an insurrection in her home base. Xander took this opportunity as an afterthought to climb through the clutter and make towards home, her bloodied appearance not unordinary given the situation.

▲ ▲ ▲

"This may complicate matters," Wiston said with a mouth full of smoke from his pipe, taking in Robyn, Evia, Joseph, and Xander as they lounged in Evia's living room.

"I imagine she'll come snivelling to us, using the attack as support for her cause," Robyn said with disdain, his and Wiston's vicious dislike and suspicion of the witch always apparent. "Perhaps another reason why she must keep troops in Borlencia or why we must elect a prime minister that can bridge the growing gap between the provinces. Same old story we've heard a dozen times, just a different pretence. How boring!"

"Ouch!" Xander flinched from her aunt's touch, the gash on her head swollen and raw.

Evia pouted. "It'll get infected if you don't let me clean it."

"And yet it doesn't hurt to be gentle."

"And yet! Isn't it a good thing you bathed as soon as you did. I can't see the filth of the sewers being kind to even the slightest graze."

"I had motivation," Xander said numbly, the stench and stain of blood unforgivingly stubborn.

About to rebuke the girl for going into the sewers alone, Evia held her tongue.

Joseph stood from his chair and crossed the marble floor to the large mahogany table covered in city maps and crudely written communications and poured himself a sharp drink. He peered thoughtfully into the villa's courtyard.

"First drink I've seen you take, Joseph. What might be the matter?" Evia queried.

"You say she looked directly at you?" he asked Xander.

"Yes, but I can't be sure if it was because she knew who I was or because of her cruel tastes…"

"Either one could be my worry right now."

He turned to the two men slumped on the couch and then back to Evia.

"What if she knows that we lobby the more reasonable ministers in Notencia and Zylencia with the goal of rejecting her proposition? Or that Ricard will be recounting Carolus's ideologies to shore up support? Or, and this is what twists my gut the most, that Xander lives and could potentially vouch for her father? This is Erzse's base. She has spies. It can't be ruled out."

"Erzse already knows we lobby the other ministers with the promise of rejecting her proposition," Evia responded. "Ricard is in Ingleton, away from prying eyes. And I don't see how she could connect Xander to this."

"Plus, none of our spies have picked up on gossip that would suggest otherwise," Robyn added.

"Agreed. She's done nothing to suggest she knows Ricard or Xander are the cards we'll play or that Xander even lives," Evia said. "And her outspoken annoyance at my presence in Zyphyr doesn't mean she suspects a distant relative of mine lives…As far as anybody's concerned, Xander is my handmaiden."

Unconvinced, Joseph rubbed his chin as he peered into the wall. "Maybe M. K.'s suggestion wasn't such a bad one." He looked at them. "Perhaps we *should* bring Xander from behind the scenes in support of her father. And sooner rather than later."

"I thought you were against me standing up before Erzse in support of my father?" Xander remarked, surprised.

"On account of not wanting to paint you as a target. But if Erzse already knows you live—"

"There's still no proof that she does," Robyn interjected gently.

"Okay, but let's assume for a moment that she does know, and we've just not picked up on it," Joseph said. "It would mean Xander has already been painted as a target. My counter is this—if the people and the other ministers know who Xander is and that she intends on vouching for some of her father's policies, it'll make it difficult for Erzse to silence her without drawing suspicion on herself. And playing to the underlying theme of M. K.'s idea, it can't hurt to rope in would-be allies that have yet to reveal themselves to us."

Evia frowned, her unwillingness to draw Xander into the open so soon undiminished.

"I don't think you've grasped the ramifications of what happened on the streets today," Robyn responded. "The attacks have done us no favours. Erzse will want blood, and anybody tied to those she suspects responsible will be in for a rough time. And whilst it's possible she'll accuse Borlencian rebels or M. K. and his militia regardless, the burden of proof still lies with her, and that will stay her hand temporarily. But I think to reveal Xander now—and it would be a revelation, because all evidence points to her not knowing—may push the woman to rashly, and openly, insinuate a connection with the attackers and undo our progress."

"Not too different from your worries about Zylencian intelligence coming after me, Joseph," Xander added.

Joseph peered into the wall again, his expression pensive.

"I'm thinking the same," Wiston said. "We should stick with the plan to present the girl on the day of the vote." He looked at Xander. "If she even wishes to. It's no secret to those in this room that she doesn't see eye to eye with her father's later ideologies." Xander nodded her head appreciatively. "The decision to allow Borlencia autonomy was won by a hair's breadth, and other developments have demonstrated to us that there's only a small minority of ministers in either camp that can be trusted to act reasonably. Ultimately, I'd rather not tempt Erzse's hand. Better the girl remains hidden."

Joseph slumped back in his chair. It was obvious that his adoration for Xander was stoking his uncharacteristic agitation. After a long, drawn-out moment of reflection, his face relaxed as a sigh escaped his lips. "There's a reason they say to remove emotion from critical decisions. Don't get me wrong, I do think there's logic behind what I suggested, but you're right. It's a rash decision based on what we know, or don't know. And it's also one seemingly at odds with what Xander even wants." He turned to her. "Sorry. It's not my intention to force you down this route. I just want—"

"The best for me," Xander answered warmly. "I know."

"It never hurts to talk these things out," Evia said.

He forced a smile. "No, I guess it doesn't."

▲ ▲ ▲

"I thought I told you not to go into the tunnels alone," Evia scolded.

She and Xander were sitting alone in one of the villa's many rooms.

"I didn't want to lose a day," Xander protested.

"But maybe now you'll listen. Now it's not just Erzse you need to worry about apparently. Whatever this person tried to warn you of in the tunnels clearly isn't friendly."

"He didn't know what it was or that it was after me."

"He knew enough to tell you to get out. And I don't like that we still don't know who this man that keeps appearing to you is. Was there any hint as to who he may be?"

Xander shook her head. "Do you think he saw the same creature from that chamber near the twins?" she asked worriedly after several moments.

There was silence as Evia stared at her. "Do you know where the bogeymen come from, my dear?"

Xander shrugged.

"They're most often summoned," Evia spoke.

"Summoned? As in, conjured from the dead?" She shuddered at the thought.

"Some are conjured from the underworld, though they're not necessarily the dead. Others from planes we do not know of."

"Do you think it was Erzse?" Xander asked.

"Erzse wouldn't have known of your presence near the twins. No, something else conjured that creature. Someone else knew who you were and sent that vile thing to lure you back into that tomb."

"Who?"

"I don't know."

"But you do think it could be related to that creature, don't you?"

"I don't know. It's a possibility." Evia glanced at the blade strapped to Xander's back. "Your blade is very special. Perhaps maybe even akin to the Rhineblades of old—fierce weapons capable of slaying the creatures we speak of now. Whether it has the same power, we won't know until you test it. But that is an eventuality I'd rather put off for as long as possible."

"I can't not go into the tunnels, or I'll never find the next shard."

"I know—" Evia began.

"And it doesn't help that you know nothing about how and where this one was hidden," Xander said with sudden agitation. "How could you be so in the dark regarding its location? Maybe I wouldn't have to scour the undercity if you could just recall something."

"I told you—my direct involvement with this one was limited at best.

And all I ask is that you take company when you go down there."

"And what the man from the shroud told me of the prisoners?"

"Can you be sure he doesn't lead you on?"

"I don't think he does."

Evia bit her lip. "I'm not sure how he knows of the shard, and though you feel no distrust towards him, maybe it's best you continue as you have."

"So ignore his words?"

"If the map takes you to the prisoners, so be it, but there may be another route that doesn't require you to breathe down the neck of Erzse and her ghastly henchmen."

"He warned me of something in that tunnel today," Xander said. "He didn't have to do that."

"And how do you know he didn't do it to gain your trust?"

Xander pondered for a moment. There was a familiarity about the man she couldn't pinpoint and a voice inside her own mind that whispered with all sincerity that she could trust him. Of all the tricks and fallacies of life, she knew this one to be neither. "I just know."

CHAPTER 27

Januarix 20, 485; Zyphyr, Zylencia—Xander flinched as another explosion rocked the city streets outside Evia's villa, causing the ground underneath to tremble and dust to descend from the ceiling above. She turned to the others sitting in the cold living room: Evia, Aika, Joseph, Dogner, and Robyn. All looked uneasy under the dim flicker of candlelight dancing across the walls, with each shout or explosion or clash of weapons in the rioting city putting them on edge.

"It's been two days," Dogner grunted. "You'd think—" He gritted his teeth as a scream pierced the twilight of evening.

"It'll continue for as long as Erzse and her supporters round up their enemies," Robyn said, "and for as long as those not succumbed to her purse have the energy."

"The entire city will be razed before then."

"The city's seen worse," Evia commented solemnly. The others peered to her. "Even before Erzse's time, the city's been a hotbed of strife. Whether it's the breed of leaders or the religious tensions always bubbling under the surface, the city's prone to violence of this sort."

Dogner cleared his throat. "In your time?"

She lifted an amused brow. "In my time?"

"You know what I mean, lass! Don't make me say it."

She chuckled. "Yes, in my time. I think it was maybe a hundred years ago—"

They turned to the door as Wiston entered. Behind him, in the courtyard, they could see a dozen Eurencian soldiers sitting around in their armour, prepared for any possible breach. "Don't stop on account of me," he said, taking a seat.

"A hundred years ago, maybe a bit less," Evia continued. "It was a time when one of the city's ministers, a man by the name of Bralyn, had full authority over the city's parliament."

"He had compromised the other ministers," Wiston remarked, familiar with the history.

"Yes."

"How?" Joseph asked.

Evia shrugged. "How else? Money. Wealth like you've never seen from one man in a place like Anemoi. I remember him still. He was a portly thing with thin wisps of golden hair, a crooked smile, and ridiculously oily skin. He owned a number of the mines in the south and controlled the tolls in and out of Zylencia to the kingdoms in the west and to Anemoi in the east."

"And let me guess, he had a love for the finer things?" Dogner asked.

"No. His love was for control. And therein lay the problem. He was very religious and absolutely despised what Anemoi had become."

"A non-religious state?" Aika said.

Evia nodded. "A non-religious state."

"But that happened before his time."

"It did, but that doesn't mean he didn't see it within his remit to fix the situation. Of course, by that time, what you see now as Anemoi had already become ingrained in the collective consciousness. That's not to say there weren't some that craved his dreams to become a reality, but the majority were opposed to his drives to impose his religious beliefs. His rule ended after he burned hundreds of non-believers, inciting a month of riots whereby the city nearly burned to the ground. The unrest culminated only when his own guards arrested him and his followers at the behest of the other provinces, all via secret communications, of course."

"What happened to him?" Aika queried.

"He was hung. As were the other ministers complicit."

"A bit old fashioned, wouldn't you say?" Robyn said.

"It was an old-fashioned time," Evia responded. "Not to say I agree with it, however."

"And were you involved in his arrest?"

"I was one of many involved in his eventual arrest."

Dogner scratched his chin. "A woman of history. Always gets me."

Evia shrugged. "And me, on occasion."

"What was the religion?" Xander asked Evia curiously.

"I must admit I can't recall exactly. There are many, some the same, others quite different."

"A product of Anemoi's sometimes-loose borders," Wiston said.

"Yes." Evia nodded. "And Bralyn's wasn't anything special. It was one of a number all derived from the same religion. The sister sects were natural supporters to his, of course, but they found allies in other religious sects that wanted to overturn Anemoi's ban on religion in politics, hoping to pave the way for their own ascension." She looked at Xander. "In the run-up to his rise and in the aftermath, his supporters and several of the other religious sects eager for control took to the tunnels under the city. Expanding them. Erecting places of worship. Building underground settlements from which to wait out assaults. Places from which to plot. The same that's been done by a hundred others for a multitude of reasons across the centuries."

"Ha! Explains the nonsensical maze down there," Aika said.

"So the altar I found may have been one of Bralyn's?" Xander asked.

"Hard to tell for sure without some sort of—where are you going?" Evia said as Xander shot up.

"There was something! And I completely forgot about it."

Xander ran from the room and reappeared moments later with the five figurines in her hand. She carefully placed them on a table in the centre, and the others gravitated closer for a peek.

"Well, that's an oddity!" Dogner grunted amusedly. "Never seen anything quite like it."

"Very odd," Evia said, scooping one into her palm. "Just the five?"

"I think so," Xander responded. "Do you know what they mean?"

"I don't recognise them, but I think five statuettes or figurines were associated with one of the old pagan religions. Really can't recall there being anything nefarious about it, if it's the one I'm thinking of. Also, I can't recall if it was Bralyn's. Either way, seems you simply stumbled upon one of the old rooms of worship."

"The map showed a corridor on the other side of the altar, even though it didn't show the room specifically. It means one of the old bearers must have come close to entering from the other side."

"And why not enter?" Aika asked.

"Who knows?" Xander said. "Maybe they didn't need to. I'll tell you this much, though, I'm dying to see what's on the other side. Maybe it's the entrance I've been looking for."

"Did you check the map?"

"It was hard to tell where the tunnel leads. It's like someone took a pencil and viciously scratched into the paper. There are so many down there, crisscrossing, overlapping, collapsed, filled in, or stopping at vertical drops into old mines."

Dogner chuckled. "Comforting to know!"

"You're still going to go down there, even with that thing running around?" Joseph queried.

"I don't know what was running around down there," Xander responded as she sat back down. "I don't even know if it was looking for me. Anyway, I still need to get the shard, so I don't have much choice."

Evia cleared her throat and peered to Xander with a look of disapproval.

"Whilst that is correct, I thought we had agreed—"

"Yes, yes. Not alone." Xander subconsciously scratched at the cut on her forehead. As she continued to speak, Evia got up and walked over to examine the wound. "Hopefully we won't have to wait too long—what?"

"It's still a bit raw," Evia said worriedly. She took a step back. "And you've been applying—"

"You know I have."

"Give it a chance," Dogner said. "It'll take a little while for something like that to heal."

Evia sat back down. "Of course. Sorry, Xander, please continue."

"Hopefully we won't have to wait too long before we can get back down there."

"And wait you should," Robyn said. "Last we heard, a number of the rioters—"

A loud bang emanated from the end of the road.

"Rifles," Wiston observed curiously. "It's becoming quite the crackdown."

"It is," Robyn agreed. "To the point, Xander. Last we heard, a number of the rioters and individuals being persecuted are hiding down in the tunnels. Best avoid them and the streets until this all calms down."

"Have you tried to reach out to Erzse?" Joseph asked Robyn.

"Erzse and the other Zylencian ministers in the city. We offered our condolences for those killed and our assistance in finding the perpetrators."

"And?"

"We were told that the perpetrators had already been identified and that at this point it was a Zylencian matter," Robyn responded.

"Dismissive."

"A bit, yes."

"So no indication as to who she was accusing?"

"None."

Joseph grunted. "Will be interesting to see how this plays out. To mirror your words several days back, I'm sure Erzse will find a way to use this to

her benefit on the day of the vote."
    "No doubt."

CHAPTER 28

Januarix 23, 485; Ingleton, Zylencia—"Unlikely to hold against advanced siege weapons but should delay enough if she attempts a surprise attack before the vote," Ricard said of the wooden palisade that spanned the paved road.

Built from thick, blackened tree trunks with spikes carved of the tips and hemmed in by two vertical rockfaces that even the most adventurous would hesitate to venture, the palisade gave the appearance of sharpened teeth grinning across the Black Mouth.

"She won't." Joseph squinted through the wind and the glare of the peaks as he took in the road ahead.

"You seem sure of yourself," M. K. said as he and Ricard followed Joseph's gaze. The trio had spent the past thirty minutes inspecting the newly built defences constructed to block the flow of ore into Zyphyr and beyond.

"Wouldn't be sensible of her to disrupt the vote in such a manner. Civil conflict, if induced by her without legitimate cause, will distract from her agenda. Besides, the other ministers would have a field day. Of course, if she wins the vote, then it might be a different story."

"Might be a different story if she sees things going sideways after we cut off the city's life source."

"Diplomacy is key. You'll need—"

"Heard you the first time," M. K. interjected. "Lead the snake and the wench on with words, not violence."

"The blockade is the perfect tool to get them to the table. Make them think you'll vote—"

"Like I said, heard you the first time. And if they resort to violence?"

"A bridge we'll cross when it happens," Joseph remarked.

Ricard spoke, "Here comes your cousin."

M. K. waved Acro and his retinue to where they stood. Except for the red beard, Acro was nearly identical to M. K. in all aspects, and Ricard and Joseph found it difficult to believe they were not siblings.

"The tallies are in. Barring several that are content to support from the sideline, the majority of the towns will commit men, just in case," Acro informed them.

"This is good. We've got our blockade and the strength to hold it. When can we expect full strength?" M. K. asked.

One of Acro's retinue spoke up eagerly. "End of the week. And we've dispatched two riders to two of our commanders currently serving. If a fight breaks out, they'll be ready to counter with our own."

"Yes, I passed them on the way up. They were fast, faster than I'd expect from those that tend to outweigh the mounts," Joseph said.

M. K. laughed. "Careful, you. Anyway, doubt they're true mining folk, right, cousin? You often find some of the soft out-of-towners taking up residence in Ingleton looking to twist the way of the locals."

"It's as you say. Can't keep them out, though I trust these two to deliver the message…even if I don't agree with the move."

"If you trust them to deliver the message, don't fret over whatever intent you think might be discovered," M. K. responded with frustration. "Like we discussed, we're covering our options."

"Right. Anyway, I'm in need of a cold one before the day loses us," Acro said dismissively and bounded back towards the town with his men.

"On the bright side, at least we have his support," Ricard said once the group was out of earshot.

"However laboured," M. K. retorted. "Who would've thought paying him a pretty penny would nearly not be enough to persuade him to our cause."

"*Hypocritical* was the word he spat, if I recall."

"He's not wrong. We're technically buying his support…Of course, Erzse would've done the same, but we're meant to be the 'righteous opposition with a moral compass.' To think we had my cousin lecturing us on principles when I don't doubt that our payment is the only reason he agreed to stand up for what's right."

"In my experience, bought support can't be trusted. No matter what high ground he pretends to take, you should keep an eye on him," Joseph observed.

"I've got him covered, but I doubt he'd take up arms against us, even for another pretty penny. Renege on the agreement, perhaps. Withhold his men from a fight? Again, maybe, but intentionally bring harm to his brethren? I don't think so."

"It's the unintentional we should worry about," Joseph said, unconvinced. "And he'll travel with us for the vote?"

"Yes, he'll travel with us."

Ricard sighed.

"Thought I just heard a woman's whimper." M. K. grinned with his hand cupped over his ear.

Ricard shrugged. "Didn't think I'd miss the girls so. Shame I can't come in until the day."

"With me and my cousin on the road, we'll need you keeping an eye on this lot."

"Yep, I know, and I've got it covered. I trust the girls are looking after themselves, Joseph?"

"As much as can be expected."

"And up to no good?"

Joseph chortled. "Of course. Can't keep them from continuing their search, no matter what dingy hole that takes them down."

Ricard sighed again.

M. K. grinned. "Cheer up, brother. I'll be back to hold your hand before you know it."

"And who knows, maybe we can get them down for a visit," Joseph said.

Ricard's eyes lit up. "Better to not toy with me."

"I don't," Joseph said and slapped the stocky man's back.

M. K. grunted. "Got the cheese festival in a few weeks. Could get them down for that if they're not busy."

"There you go, big guy, something to look forward to," Joseph said, smiling.

Ricard squeezed Joseph's shoulder. "Make it happen, little man, and I'll owe you one!"

"I'll make it happen. Come on, we should join the cousin for a wet one."

"Now you're talking!" M. K. roared and slumped his heavy arms over their shoulders as he led them in the direction of the town.

CHAPTER 29

Januarix 29, 485; Zyphyr, Zylencia—"Are you okay?" Aika's suppressed voice carried down the vertical shaft.

Xander stopped her descent down the metal ladder shoddily hammered into the brick wall and took a breath. Her forehead itched like nothing she had known before, and a dull ache pierced her skull. She peered up to where Aika's torch lit the top of the shaft. "I'm good," she called in as quiet a breath as she could manage.

She restarted her descent and moments later touched her foot to the slippery ground at the base of the shaft.

"Ready!" Aika whispered down.

Xander stepped to the side and caught Aika's torch just before it hit the floor. Moments later, Aika reached the bottom.

"Well?" Aika asked as Xander began scouring the map.

Xander looked up and pointed down the farthest of the three tunnels adjoined to the shaft. "That'll take us to where I found the altar."

"Excellent! Come on then—"

A chorus of voices rang through the chamber, emanating from one of the three tunnels. Aika quickly put out her torch, and they both darted into the shadows and crouched to make themselves small. The voices continued to grow until a dozen men in nondescript garments appeared from the middle corridor. There was no torch between them, and all carried weapons and walked like soldiers used to physical exertion. But despite their proximity, neither girl felt threatened by the group, hidden as they were. Using what little light there was, the group climbed up the shaft whilst chatting amongst themselves. As the last of the men disappeared over the vertical wall, the pair emerged from the shadows.

"Will be a pain relighting this," Aika said glumly, torch in hand.

"Then don't. They managed without."

"And how do you expect to read that map of yours?"

Xander tapped her head with her finger. "Memory. I can get us to the altar without it. We're close enough."

"If ever there was a string of final words."

"No faith!" Xander said as she began down the middle tunnel with Aika in tow.

For several minutes they combed through a connected series of tunnels and chambers, most illuminated by the grey sun piercing through the drains overhead, until they emerged into the tunnel where Xander's friendly silhouette had warned her of the other presence.

"Seems eerie enough," Aika said of the dank space.

"Look. There's the wall and the burrow," Xander said, pointing to the concealed opening.

"Hold on a second," Aika said, her face horrified as she peered back the way they had come.

Xander grabbed her blade as her nerves tightened. "What is it?" she whispered.

Aika was quiet, her shoulders rigid, her hand slowly moving towards her bow. Abruptly, she turned around with a mischievous smile. "Just making sure. Come on, let's get in there before someone finds us."

"Cretin! What if something was really there?"

"Then I would've skewered it with an arrow. Satisfied?"

"Hardly! And you're still a cretin," Xander mumbled light-heartedly as she led them to the small opening.

She crouched into the burrow and began down the tight space, but without the threat of something sinister lurking behind, the distance seemed less palpable. Breaching into the chamber with the altar, she stood up and stretched.

A second later, Aika popped her head out and stood up. "Quaint. And that's it?" she said, walking over to the wooden structure.

"That's it," Xander replied, withdrawing the map.

"Well?"

"It's long."

"How long?"

Xander pulled the map closer. "Hard to tell."

"And what's on the other side?"

"I see a chamber. It's large. And…" Xander looked up excitedly. "There's a tunnel leading from it to right under the palace. It gets us near the shard."

"Then maybe this is what we've been looking for."

"I think so! Come on, help me move the altar," Xander said, putting the map away.

Together they stood to one end of the wood structure and heaved it to the side. Barely had they revealed the opening when an acidic odour hit them.

Irritation took Aika. "Gross! I sometimes wonder if the fate of Anemoi and the Great Forest is worth all the bad smells that seem to greet us at every door."

"You'll get used to it."

"And for that, I'll let you do the honours."

Xander nodded and entered the newly revealed opening. She could feel Aika enter behind her. Unlike the last tunnel, there was an absence of tangled roots and protruding rocks, and instead the walls were made of damp dirt. The smell of standing water hung heavy in the air, and visibility was wholly absent.

For ten minutes they crawled through the space, unable to determine how long until they would reach the chamber, a desired escape from the suffocating squeeze of the burrow. Knee over knee, hand over hand, they persisted forward until—*thud*. Xander held her forehead where she had collided with an unseen object to her front. Hardly a moment had passed, and she could feel Aika's increasing nervousness behind her.

Carefully, Xander put her hand forward and brushed her fingers over whatever it was that blocked their route. The texture was similar to the walls of the structure. Coarse, damp sand. A collapsed tunnel perhaps, she pondered. Worry enveloped her at the thought of having to backtrack backwards or even the tunnel collapsing in on them. She was unsure what to do—when an idea struck. She put a lone finger to the top of the blockage and drilled it forward. A second later she pierced the two-inch-thick wall, and a thin sliver of light invaded the darkness, along with a whiff of the acidic odour.

She peeked through the hole, and elation took her. It was the chamber. She brushed her finger down the surface of the blockage. It was uneven and quite a bit thicker at the bottom.

"The entrance collapsed."

Very careful not to bring the burrow down on top of them, she widened the hole with her fingers until she could fit a hand through and then, clump by clump, cautiously dismantled the blockage. Relief washed over her as she climbed into the chamber with Aika right behind. They brushed off the sand as they stood up and took in the circular space.

It was large. Much larger than Xander had anticipated. And more akin to a cavern with the ceiling some fifty metres overhead. Natural light shone in through various holes in the roof and refracted throughout the space via mirrors nailed to the walls. A wide pool of still water fully dominated one half of the cavern and thick, bristly blue grass the other half. A dirty white cottage with a partially submerged water mill stood on the pool's far edge, and on the two opposing ends of the chamber were stone arches that had seemingly buckled under the weight of the rock, blocking whatever lay the other side.

Xander withdrew the map. "Ah no!"

"What?"

She pointed to the collapsed arch at the far end. "That's our tunnel."

"Like all the others. Collapsed or blocked. Definitely a pattern."

Xander sighed frustratedly. "It's starting to look like someone's gone and blocked every throughway into the centre of the city."

"Why do you think?"

"I don't know. Maybe let's just head back—"

"What's that?"

Xander followed Aika's outstretched finger to the cottage. "What?"

"There's a mark beside the door."

Curious, they began across the bristly grass towards the cottage.

"Thought you needed running water for a water mill," Aika murmured of the placid pool.

"Look." Xander motioned to two low-lying collapsed arches where the rocky wall of the cavern met the water on either end of the pool. "No current if there's no throughway."

"Really odd."

"Whoever did it was keen to seal this place. I wonder—"

Aika gripped Xander's wrist and pulled her to a stop. "The marking beside the door."

"Is it…?"

Even at thirty metres' distance, the smeared crimson handprint was obvious.

Quietly, and suddenly much warier of their surroundings, they crept forward until the building overshadowed them. There was a single window to the top, and the structure was quite like the one Xander and Hemish had stumbled upon outside of Etlinga all those years ago. A twinge of nostalgia momentarily wormed its way into Xander's mind before scattering.

"It looks like blood," Aika said. She turned to Xander. Their collective desire to be out of there was as obvious as their need to see what was inside.

As one, they withdrew their weapons. Cautiously, Xander walked up to the door and grabbed the cool knob. Slowly she turned it and then with one swoop threw the door open and barged in with her blade raised. She lowered it.

"It's nearly identical," she said softly as Aika came up to her side.

"To what?"

"To the one outside Etlinga. Even the trapdoor."

Vivid images of her and Hemish toying with the room from what seemed like another life tugged at her emotions. Happiness for a simpler time, sadness for what had been lost. And guilt. Guilt reared by the almost complete absence of the boy from recent memory. She brushed it aside and walked up to the massive wooden gears to the side of the room.

"They're in place," she observed, recalling how one out of sync could render the whole system useless.

"For what?"

"For the mill to work. Which means…" Xander walked over to the dust-covered trapdoor.

As she was about to open it, Aika spoke, "Wait, what's that?" She walked up to something drawn on the wall. Something obscured by the accumulated grit of time. She took her hand and brushed away the filth to reveal a symbol. A square with a horizontal line drawn through its centre. "Another sect?" she asked as Xander came up beside her.

"Must be," Xander responded, recalling its familiarity to the square etched into the girl they had discovered under the streets all those days ago.

"One to ask Evia, I guess," Aika said and wandered over to the trapdoor.

"Five figurines."

"Huh?"

"That old pagan religion Evia told us about was signified by five figurines," Xander continued. "Well, what about five lines? Would explain why this place was joined to the other room with the altar."

"Could be," Aika said as she knelt down. "Must be dozens if not hundreds of those symbols." She slipped her fingers into a small rectangular opening to one end of the trapdoor and began to open it. "Maybe the library—"

Xander jumped and turned around as Aika slammed the trapdoor shut. "What?"

Aika looked up, her skin drained of colour, her mouth agape with horror.

"What?" Xander repeated with growing agitation as the acidic odour from outside filled the room.

Silently, Aika slowly reached her hand down to the trapdoor and, after a long, drawn-out breath, opened it.

Xander nervously glanced at Aika and then to the trapdoor. Wary of what awaited her, she edged over ever so slowly until the first body came into sight. "How…how many?"

Aika shook her head, her eyes on the brink of tears.

A sharp twinge tore into Xander's stomach, but she had to know. She took a breath of courage and stepped the rest of the distance for an unimpeded view. Dozens. Dozens of bodies piled in a heap in the cellar. Young. Old. Some rotten, some less. Some disfigured beyond recognition. Others carrying only the slightest of wounds. And all female.

Xander retched onto the ground beside the opening.

"I need to get out of here," Aika said quietly, standing up. "We need to get out of here."

As Aika stumbled for the door, Xander knelt down, grabbed the trapdoor, and slammed it shut. But rather than follow Aika out, Xander stayed kneeling as bewilderment took her.

"What?" Aika asked nervously from the doorway. "What's wrong?"

Xander looked up, eyes wide.

"What? Xander?"

"I…I saw something move."

"Impossible."

"I know what I saw."

Aika cursed under her breath and rushed back over as Xander grabbed the trapdoor and opened it.

"Which one?" Aika asked.

"I thought it was that one," she responded, pointing at a lady near the top, whose lower body was submerged under the pile of flesh.

Unlike the others, the woman was older. She had matted red hair, and her pale face was relatively unscathed compared to the unhealed wounds across her torso. They watched intently for even the slightest murmur of the chest or flicker of the eyelids. Ten seconds passed. Then a minute.

"There's nothing," Aika said finally. "Your eyes were—"

"Look—her finger, it moved!"

"I saw it!" Aika fumbled through her bag and withdrew a rope. "I'll lower you down."

Xander glanced into the dim cellar that reeked of death and cursed under her breath. "Argh! What choice do I have?"

With no obvious way down, they dropped their sacks to one side and began the process of measuring out the rescue. Decided, they looped the rope around the sturdiest of the gears and then tied a foothold at the bottom of the line.

Xander sat on the edge of the trapdoor and slipped her foot into the foothold. She then lowered herself into the opening until the rope was taut. From there, Aika slowly released the line until Xander's foot was nearly level with the woman. One hand gripped to the line, Xander crouched awkwardly and reached the other hand down, stretching and manoeuvring until her finger brushed against the woman's hand.

"Give me an inch," she hissed through gritted teeth. Aika released an inch, enough for Xander to grip the woman's cold wrist. She looked up. "I've got—"

Something grabbed her arm and pulled her downwards with a tug.

Caught unaware, she lost her grip on the rope and tumbled down the pile of bodies, smacking her head against the brick wall of the cellar. Blood gushed from the reopened wound on her forehead, matting her hair and smearing into her eyes and face.

Dazed and struggling for sight, she stood up and withdrew her blade. The numb repetition of her name rang from Aika above and, to her horror, somewhere in between. Her hair rose on end, and her back tightened with fear. But all that stared back were the lifeless faces of the innocent dead, their eyes forever closed, their skin forever cold.

"Aika," she spluttered.

"Xander?" her friend responded, as did the voice within the chamber.

"Quiet!"

"But…" Aika did as she was told, though the other voice heeded not.

"Xander. Xander. Xander," it cooed.

Xander glanced around the room, across the mound of restful dead. The peace of their stillness was at odds with the chaos of their marked bodies. All at peace. All with their eyes sealed closed. Except for one.

Xander's grip on her blade tightened, and her breath caught in her throat as the woman with red hair began descending the pile of corpses like a spider untethered by gravity. The woman's naked body was soiled in blood and muck and scars, and her dead eyes were unquestionably intent on Xander's position.

"What…what is this?" Xander managed as the woman reached the bottom and stood up to face her.

The woman's mouth creased into a snarl. "Necessity."

She suddenly charged and swiped at Xander's neck with an outreached hand. Instinctively, Xander flinched backwards out of reach and thrust her blade into the woman's chest. An audible gasp escaped the woman's lips, but rather than fall down limp, she pulled the blade deeper and grabbed Xander's throat. Using her other hand, she pressed Xander into the wall and brought her face right up to Xander's. Her grip was impossibly strong.

Tongue out, the woman licked Xander's bloodied forehead and then put her lips to Xander's. The woman's eyes rolled into the back of her head with unbound euphoria as she pulled away. Try as she might, Xander couldn't hold it in, and she instantly vomited on the woman, the rotten stench too much. But this only seemed to add to the woman's ecstasy. Then, to Xander's utter panic, the woman smiled a smile of sharp fangs.

The woman's jaw suddenly unhinged and her mouth gaped wide open, revealing a set of yellow animal-like teeth. Absolutely terrified of the prospect of being eaten alive, Xander placed one foot on the wall behind her and threw herself forward. Both crashed into the pile of bodies. But despite the dizziness, Xander scrambled up first and managed to pull her blade from the woman's chest before the woman could right herself. She then stabbed it back into the woman's chest, again and again until the woman went limp, the creepy smile morphing into a crease of irritation.

"Xander!"

She peered up to see Aika standing at the top of the mound, her bow ready, the rope hanging beside her.

"Get up here, now!" Aika called.

Xander nodded through laboured breaths and clumsily climbed over the nearest of the bodies. And then the next and the next. So absorbed in the task at hand, she barely noticed the arrows flying past her head into the woman clambering up behind her.

When she reached the top of the mound, she felt Aika grip her collar and pull her to a stand. She turned around to see the woman snarling from the bottom, her teeth gnashing like a wild beast.

"Die!" the creature kept uttering as arrow after arrow thudded into its chest.

"Climb up!" Aika ordered.

"What about—"

"Just do it. It'll take you longer."

Xander nodded and grabbed on to the rope. Though it was only several metres, the smack to her head had sapped her strength, and it took nearly thirty seconds to make the climb. All the while the thud of Aika's dwindling arrows and the howls of the creature filled the space below.

"I'm out!" Xander called down once free of the line.

Not a second later, Aika leapt as high she could and grabbed the rope and within a couple of seconds was clear of the trapdoor. She swiftly pulled the rope out, and they both peered down to see the woman at the top of the mound, scratching at the air.

"Die! Die—"

Aika slammed the trapdoor shut. "We need to go. Right now!"

Xander peered around the room for something to put on the trapdoor but could see nothing. "The hell with it. Let's get out!"

Desperate to be out of there, they grabbed their kits and sprinted across the bristly grass back to the tunnel from which they had come. Xander first, Aika second. The uphill battle and the frightening dread of what gave chase made ten minutes feel more like an hour. As Xander emerged back into the chamber with the altar, she shuffled to the side of the wooden structure.

"Help me!" she called as soon as Aika passed through.

Together the girls pushed the altar back over the opening, and not a second later, a loud thud rang from the other side. This was immediately followed by a series of violent bangs and ghoulish cries interwoven with the shaking of the altar and the same repeated word: *die.*

Petrified of the prospect of getting caught down there, the pair immediately made for the burrow and clambered up it into the tunnel above and then onto the street, near where Xander had witnessed the attack on Erzse several days prior. Winded and shaken, they pushed the manhole cover over the last opening between them and the creature below. Slumped on the ground, they glanced at each other in disbelief.

"Did that just happen?" Aika said quietly.

Xander nodded numbly.

"What the heck was it?" Aika asked as she stood up. She gripped

Xander's arm and helped her up.

"The same creature that tried to lure me into that cave by the twins."

"You're serious?"

"Yes. We need to talk to Evia."

Aika nodded and looked up. "It's late afternoon. It'll be curfew soon, and there's half a city between us and the villa. We don't exactly look, well, like we've been up to only good. But unless you want to go back down there, we'll need to risk the city's soldiers."

"Right now, I'd much rather a squad of soldiers than that thing."

▲ ▲ ▲

"It's after Xander. That much is obvious," Evia said worriedly, pacing the living room.

Only Evia, Aika, Xander, and Joseph were in the villa, with everybody else out on errands. Night had fallen, and the trio was sitting on the chairs whilst Evia paced the floor. Both girls had damp hair and wore fresh clothes, having cleaned themselves of the grit and blood of the excursion, and Xander held a cloth covered in one of Evia's ointments to her forehead.

"But how did it get here?" Joseph asked, confused.

"It was summoned," Evia responded. "That place was marked by death, and I think, given the nature of the mutilated bodies, they had been tortured and killed in a manner that left them or the place itself cursed."

"Meaning?"

Evia stopped pacing and looked at them. "Erzse or somebody else killed those women in such a way that the bogeymen of our nightmares could crawl from the tainted fabric if willed. Intentional or not, it's not safe for you under the city anymore, Xander. Not without me."

Xander had little desire to protest. "So only when you're available?"

"Yes. And only after much examination of a route for all throughways and exits. That labyrinth of tunnels is a miscalculated disaster waiting to happen."

Xander could suddenly feel the angst spilling from Evia's every pore, consuming her aunt's every sense and thought. It was a fear she hadn't felt from the usually sturdy woman before. And something niggled at her that Evia would find every opportunity to delay her going back into the tunnels, at least until there was more clarity as to what was down there.

"So it's possible those women were murdered for someone to gain access to some other world?" Aika asked.

"Or even for something to gain access here," Evia said. "But more likely it was some sort of offering or ritual, with one of the consequences being the access point."

"Why?"

Weariness took her. "Strength. Youth. Assistance. I'd need to see the bodies firsthand to know for sure, and even then, we may never know."

"Does the symbol mean anything?" Xander asked, referring to the square with a horizontal line through its centre, a detail they had already told Evia about when recanting the incident.

"You were right in that it's another sect's representation. But that doesn't signify any link between the religion, the creature, or the deaths."

"Could be random?" Joseph said, surprised.

"Could be," Evia responded. "Only way to know is to do some research that doesn't involve trawling the undercity."

CHAPTER 30

Januarix 31, 485; Zyphyr, Zylencia—The early afternoon was chilly, with each breath of icy wind enough to cause ache in the bones and the sensation of sharp needles on the skin. Xander and Aika, heeding Evia's advice to stay out of the tunnels, but not content to wither away in boredom on such an uneventful day, had taken to the streets in their thickest winter jackets.

Despite the blanket of strife that had befallen the city, the flow of merchants was hearty throughout. Moving unassumingly with the traffic, the pair had crossed half the city unbothered by the miserable soldiers standing exposed to the elements. But now, with the East Gate in sight, Aika thought to repeat the same question she had asked when Xander first put forth the idea to travel to the field outside Zyphyr's perimeter wall.

"You're sure your aunt won't skin us for leaving the villa?"

"We're not in the tunnels."

"Maybe not, but this place is still a hotbed of unrest. Even if we're back before curfew, it's dangerous."

"I've—" Xander recovered her balance after knocking into a trader coming from the other direction. "I've got to try. There's too much noise in the city."

"Noise? The villa seems pretty quiet to me."

Xander tapped her forehead beside the gash. "Not in here, it's not."

She noticed Aika's gaze had caught on the wound, which had worsened. "Thought you were going to stop staring?"

"Bit hard when it looks like it's throbbing. Probably another reason we should've just stayed put, don't you think? You know, the hot flushes, the headaches, the swollen flesh."

"Ha! I'm fine."

Unconvinced, Aika lifted an eyebrow. Xander chuckled and peered ahead. A hundred metres from the gate, the traffic was slowing.

"Checkpoint?" Aika asked, craning for a view.

"Probably. Good thing you didn't bring that bow of yours."

"And you that clunky shield."

Twenty metres from the gate, the crowd had swelled, and though there were numerous soldiers dotted throughout the square directly behind the gate, the people around carried on uncaring. As the pair approached the opening, two soldiers looked them up and down and then waved them through.

"Do you think they'll give us grief when we're passing back through?" Aika pondered as they continued along the lone road dug into the vast grassy field to the east of the city.

A foot tall, the grass bent with the wind and was a calming view for both of the girls, who had grown a bit bored of the city's characteristic black stone.

"I doubt it. Probably thousands coming and going every day," Xander responded.

"How far out do you want to go?"

"Maybe where the forest meets the field? Think that's a kilometre."

"You're asking me? This is your little excursion."

Xander glanced back towards the wall and then back east. "Too close to the city and the guards on the wall might think it a bit strange."

"To the forest edge, then. We've got plenty of time."

They continued with the traffic along the road leading east to Borlencia, chatting and gossiping until they arrived at the forest's edge. At that point, they veered off into the woods. Despite the sparseness of the trees and the litter plastered along the road's edge, Xander could feel immediate relief emanating from Aika. She in turn smiled at the comfort it brought. After another ten minutes, where the road was no longer visible and the noise of the caravans absent, they pulled to a stop.

"This'll do," Xander said. She took off her sack and handed it to Aika. "I brought some bread and cheese, if you fancy?"

"So thoughtful!" Aika said delightedly, and she scrummaged through the sack and withdrew two sandwiches. "You want yours now or in a bit?"

"I'll wait—actually, maybe just a bite."

Mouth full, Xander sat on the hard ground and closed her eyes. She could feel Aika watching, but it didn't bother her. The two were incredibly comfortable in each other's company, having been on the road together for so long. Her breathing calm and thoughts clear, Xander reached out with her mind in the general direction of Nhata and the surrounding woodland, scouring and scouring until a sad frown took her. She could feel some of the familiar presences of her childhood, from the librarian to one of her old teachers. But the loss and pain were blindingly clear, and the absence of so many she had known was absolutely devastating.

A light gasp released from her lips, and she dove back into the search. First to Etlinga and then farther north to where she had met Aes's herd. For two hours Xander scanned the area with her mind, searching and calling for her friend. But there was no response. Aes wasn't there, or if he was, he couldn't hear her. Her head sore from a mixture of the exertion and the cold, Xander blew through pursed lips and stood up with some effort.

She peered to her friend, who had fallen asleep against a nearby tree. "Aika."

The girl opened a single groggy eye. "Nothing?"

"Nothing."

Aika opened her other eye. "It's probably nothing to worry about. Evia said herself that he's fine. Just busy."

"I know. Just thought he would've kept in contact, that's all." She rubbed her temples with her hands as a sharp pain pierced through.

"It hurts?" Aika asked worriedly.

"Guess the pain's not quite gone."

"Maybe time to head back. We can always try again tomorrow."

"Probably for the best," Xander said, scooping up her sack.

The trek back to the villa was sombre compared to the excitement of their outbound journey, and though the sun had some hours yet until it would set, the city was a tad quieter than earlier. Besides a light interrogation at the gate as to their purpose in the metropolis, they made it home without incident and without discovery, for Evia and the others had their own errands to run that day.

Despite this, however, the lack of response from Aes, coupled with the gnawing ache in her head, left Xander in an irritable mood come evening. So much so that all she could think of after dinner was the insatiable need to climb into bed and sleep off the draining annoyance—an endeavour she greedily welcomed.

CHAPTER 31

Februarix 7, 485; Zyphyr, Zylencia—"*Irate* is the word I would use, old boy," Aiden said exhaustedly to Dogner.

The pair was sitting with Evia in a small, unassuming tavern on the edge of the city. Owned by Aiden and purposely geared towards meetings of this kind, the establishment was absent the stench of stale beer and its wait staff were few. Despite being the only patrons, their voices did not carry through the quiet.

"But there's nothing she can do, not without starting a conflict," Evia said as she toyed with the small bowl of nuts on the table.

Aiden glanced at her fidgeting fingers and then looked into her eyes. "Who knows what goes on behind that woman's scowl." He sat back and stretched his tight neck. "The attack. The blockade. It's all a bit much. For her. For the city. Heck, even my wife and brats." He leant forward as if to whisper. "Did I tell you she up and left?"

"Who?" Dogner asked. "The wife?"

"Yes, old boy. Left the city with the kids. In the maddening aftermath of the attack on Erzse, I was sucked into the mayhem. Who did it? Why? How to respond? *Chaos* was the mystery word. 'Twas a full two days before I managed back to the house, only to find it empty. My wife's messenger turns up not an hour later telling me my wife couldn't bear to be in the city with all the violence."

"Where did they go?"

"This is the funny part. Her mother's. She can't stand the woman, and yet she still went to her mother's house in the east. What a joke! Saying that, hard to argue. Even I felt a bit of a quiver in my chest when news of the attack reached me. Of course, then I realised the perpetrator very nearly solved our problem for us. Still, her mother." He sat back, his features tired.

"It'll get worse before it gets better," Evia said.

"That blockade of M. K.'s certainly won't help. Been barely a blink of an eye and it's already having a devastating impact."

"But will she come to the table?" she asked him. "M. K. said himself that if she would just work with him, he could give her what she wants."

A youthful mischievousness flashed in Aiden's eyes, and though Evia could sense his mind was racing a dozen a second, she couldn't see or hear his thoughts. "The woman is as stubborn as a whippet is fast. Her dislike for M. K. is staunch."

"But you'll keep trying?"

"Of course, of course. If only to save the poor and impoverished that suffer the most from M. K.'s action."

"He has his reason, lad," Dogner said, crossing his arms. "They all do. And they're within their right."

"Absolutely. My poor and impoverished. His poor and impoverished. Everybody has their champion, however adept. That reminds me," he said, looking at Evia. "I heard your handmaiden has come down with something a tad nasty."

"Is even my villa not off limits to you, Aiden?"

"The villa, yes. Your caretaker rushing to the nearest pharmacy and the gossip of the Eurencians out on the town, not so much. Ganarellia, or so they think. Nasty illness, though it's usually only the homeless and sewer workers that come down with it. Still, should I send my physician?"

"No, it's quite alright, though I thank you for the offer. She just needs to work it out of her system, that's all."

"As you wish," he said with a curious squint.

▲ ▲ ▲

The heavy odour born from a dozen tangy herbs meshed into a thick paste designed to fight infection, coupled with the airy incense of eucalyptus oil, worked only to amplify the insufferable stuffiness of Xander's bedroom. Even with the window open to the cool afternoon air outside, she felt like she was suffocating.

Sitting at the desk with the map and charts of the city unfurled in front of her, she had ignored her aunt's advice to rest and instead pored over the routes she had taken and the routes yet to take under the city. It was her only distraction from the burning sensation that gripped the gash on her forehead and the delirium and aches of the fever that ravaged her body. It was also her only escape from the eerie hallucinations that relished in plaguing her slumber. From painful memories of her parents, Lawrence, and Hemish, to the unnerving imaginings of a creature stalking her every movement. She'd had enough of the rest prescribed by her aunt.

And still, even in her element cross-referencing her search to date, she was restless. Eager for fresh air and open sky. She sat back and rubbed her temples in a pointless attempt to soothe the faint headache that had taken hold in the days since she fell ill and then glanced at the ghastly concoction that had numbed the pain from the likes of a thorn bush growing within her skull to the numb afterthought of what she felt now. Through pursed lips she blew and then, holding her nose to counter the horrid taste, grabbed the glass and drank the brew. She reached over, slabbed some more paste on the infected wound, and then struggled up.

She pulled off her sweaty undergarments and splashed cool water over her cheeks and under her pits. She staggered over to the wardrobe and, about to don her clothes, caught her gaunt face staring back from the mirror. The wound was red and swollen and her cheeks pale and bony. She lifted her hand to her head and attempted to fluff the oily hair matted to her scalp. It was as good as it was going to get, all things considered, and she trudged back to the wardrobe and began to retrieve her clothes.

Not a moment later, however, a light knock came from the door followed by Aika's face appearing from behind it. The girl lifted an eyebrow as she took in Xander and then walked in.

"Going somewhere?" she said, her soft smile not enough to hide her worry.

"Anywhere," Xander muttered tiredly.

"Maybe not your brightest response."

"I need to get out. I've been stuck in here for five days—"

Aika cleared her throat. "It's been over a week now."

"A week! How?"

Aika shrugged. "You fell ill pretty quickly. Your aunt told you to keep that cut clean. You didn't listen even though we were climbing through the sewers—"

"It was that thing's spittle. I'm sure of it. And what about the shard? It can't wait."

"I know. But unfortunately, we've paid the price."

"We?"

Aika chuckled. "Who do you think's been caring for your every whim? Your aunt's busy building a resistance with her friends. And I'm certainly not going into those tunnels alone. Not without you and that map."

"Sorry."

"Ha! It's been a pleasure. Any excuse for a break from the stench of Zyphyr's toilet. Anyway, to the point, where do you think you're going?"

"For a walk. Coming?"

Aika grinned as she took in the haggard girl standing before her. "Sure."

The streets were quiet, though not empty. City folk still walked this way and that as they completed their business, but a cautious air hung heavy. Soldiers dotted every street corner, eyeing the pedestrians for any sign of what, the girls didn't know. Still, the pair was able to pass block after block unbothered at a pace no faster than a hobble.

"Are you okay?" Aika asked as Xander stopped to catch her breath.

"Just about," she managed. She followed Aika's gaze as the girl peered down the nearby side street.

Quieter than the last, but not without its hustle, they walked over to two boys graffitiing something onto the wall.

"Who is it?" Xander asked of the demonic-like individual coming to fruition on the black stone, though she already figured who it was.

One of the boys, in his early teens, peered both ways down the street and then looked at them. "Erzse the rat."

Aika held her chuckle. "Erzse the rat?"

"That's her name," the other boy, of the same age, said with a naughty smirk. "Erzse the rat."

"The witch can stick it where the sun don't—" the first had begun when a shout came from the other end of the street.

"Damn it!" the boy swore as two soldiers pounded towards them. "See ya!" he yelled, and the pair quickly darted in the opposite direction onto the road Xander and Aika had just come from.

As the soldiers approached, skirting the unbothered city folk, Xander and Aika stepped to the side out of their way. They were clearly not the target, as the first, much fitter soldier ran by without even a glance at them and disappeared around the corner. And still, even with the clear pass to continue on unhindered, Xander couldn't stop the impulsive delirium of the fever as it urged her to stick out her foot and trip the second. The man fell with a loud crash onto the cobblestones below, smashing his hands and face in the process.

Aika looked at Xander, open-mouthed. "Have you lost your—" She stepped forward and kicked the man unconscious as he turned around to look at his tripper. "You've bloody—" She rushed forward and punched the other soldier out cold as he reappeared from around the corner to find the cause of the commotion. "Damn it, girl! Come on, let's—"

Shouts emanated from the adjacent street as the alarm was raised by a distant soldier who had just witnessed the second soldier stumble back and collapse. Aika grabbed Xander's hand and pulled her halfway down the street before leading her onto a perpendicular one no wider than a metre. But they had only made it a few metres when Xander stopped still.

"I—I—" she spluttered, unable to catch her breath.

Aika cursed as more shouts rang out from the road. Then her eyes widened. "In here," she said and, propping Xander up, casually led them into the nearest store.

It was large, much larger than one would have assumed from the lone door to the outside world. Incense and polish carried in the air, and wares of a vast variety of types and origins carpeted the floor and shelves. There were dozens of patrons combing the interesting selection as the girls wandered in, trying to look as normal as possible despite the exhausting exertion not a minute before.

"Look at that carpet," Aika said, in awe of a twenty-metre-long rug stained red and purple and covered in a myriad of gold and blue ink in intricate designs.

"It's from the desert," Xander said weakly.

"The Ignis?"

"I think."

Aika brushed her hand over it and marvelled at the flecks of sand flicking up in the wake of her fingers' path. "It still carries the sand of the desert. Maybe the first and last time I'll have to touch it."

Xander chuckled. "Don't speak too soon. Who knows where the shards will take us."

Aika's face hardened into a mocking scowl. "Not very far if you're thinking to trip every soldier that crosses our path."

"Sorry. Really couldn't help myself. It was just so—"

"Tempting?"

"Yes!"

"That's the fever speaking," Aika remarked.

"And can you blame me?"

"I'll get back to you on that one. Come on, let's see if we can find another way out before those soldiers—what?"

Aika followed Xander's gaze to a shelf a short way off. On the shelf there were three vases, a rusty sword, and a mask.

"It's like the ones the attackers wore when they took Borealis," Xander murmured of the mask. As she drew closer, her anger at the soldiers who had killed her parents frothed to the surface. She reached out her hand and picked it up, and an immediate sense of homesickness and guilt took her, causing her to jerk her hand away.

"That there is Cresedi." A voice came from behind them. They turned to see a stout man with grey hair and glasses watching them. He carried an armful of books under one arm and leant on a cane held by the other. "Couldn't tell you with absolute certainty if it was one of the ones worn in the attack, but it was found in the vicinity. So, my guess is, if it wasn't worn by one of the assailants, it was certainly carried by their army given there's no other recorded instance of the Cresedi coming this far south."

"I thought they hadn't confirmed it was the Cresedi that attacked?" Xander asked, surprised.

"Who's *they*?" he said, placing the books on a nearby table. "I think at this point it's fairly obvious it was the Cresedi. Anybody with an ounce of intelligence could've picked up a history book and figured it out for themselves. There's only a handful of armies in history that've worn masks like this in combat, and none of them are around today but the Cresedi. Then there's an army of that size just left to occupy with seemingly no purpose. To a place the size of Anemoi, that'd be disastrously expensive. Both in manpower and financial resources, given our soldiers are volunteers and paid a living wage. But to the Cresedi, with its class system, vassal states, and conscription, it's inconsequential. Oh! And what about where they came from? The north! And yet, there's been a complete absence of any chatter about the army's origins from any of our northern neighbours. I'd say it's fair to assume that army's certainly not from around here."

"Or the neighbours to the north wore the masks to throw off Anemoi's attempts to identify them," Aika pondered.

He chortled. "An interesting thought, but no, I don't think so."

"Okay, a bit far-fetched. But why wouldn't your leaders—"

"Our," Xander corrected Aika playfully.

"*Our*," Aika said mockingly. "Why not just come out and say it was the Cresedi?"

The man shrugged. "One for the politicians."

"And why come all this way south to attack Borealis and leave an army to sit behind those walls?" Xander asked.

"Who knows. An empire of that size—one so big that it needs three concurrent emperors simply to govern—can play the long game, even with its grievances."

"Grievances?"

"You can't become that big without becoming a target," he said. "And their royal customs are a bit odd. They tend to create periods of instability before much longer periods of stability. Throw the two into the mix and on occasion you'll have yourself trouble. Not something that's going to fell the mighty empire—really I should say the three sub-empires—in one night, but enough to whittle them down over time if not tended to."

"But isn't that a contradiction?"

"What? To leave an army of that size here with grievances at home?"

"Yes."

"Like I said, the Cresedi operate on a much grander scale than we do," he answered. "Seventy-five thousand men for them was likely a drop in the well. And every move the emperors make is strategic. They wouldn't have attacked and occupied Borealis without reason. Unfortunately for us, we'll have to wait for the nature of their game to reveal itself. Could be tomorrow. Could be twenty years from now."

Xander coughed violently into the nook of her arm and then rubbed her eyes. "I'm tired."

The man glanced at the wound on her head. "Infection?"

She nodded. "Ganarellia."

"And it's being treated?"

"With herbs from the pharmacy."

"I'm glad." He eyed her for a moment. "You seem to have a keen interest in the Cresedi."

She shrugged. "I'm interested in whomever killed my parents. If they're Cresedi, then so be it."

"Ah. I'm sorry to hear that. Well, if you're ever in the mood for learning a bit more on them, or anything else for that matter, you should visit the city's public library. It's a couple of blocks east of here and an absolute treasure cove of information. Gives Borealis's ruined collection a run for its money."

The memories of the quaint library in Nhata suddenly rose to the fore, filling Xander with a sense of joy. "I'll check it out."

"If you don't mind me asking," Aika said, "have you another exit besides the one over there?" She pointed at the door they had come through. "We should be headed home, and there were a couple of creeps—"

"Say no more. It's been a delightful conversation, and I give little care to who I might be inconveniencing by sending you in the other direction," he said, nodding his head in the direction of a second door in the far corner.

"Thank you," the girls said in unison.

"You're quite welcome. And help yourselves to a jug of water on the way out. A lack of it will kill you with that affliction."

The girls stumbled towards the door with Aika supporting Xander. Just as they opened the door, Xander glanced back to see the man wave them farewell and return to his business.

CHAPTER 32

Februarix 9, 485; Zyphyr, Zylencia—"You'll not receive another warning," the officer snarled as he took in the wooden palisade. "Dismantle the damn blockade, and let the carts through, and we'll forget ya dared—"

"Dared what?" M. K. said threateningly, to the man's surprise. "Refuse to sell our ore?"

"Your ore!" he spat, his wiry build and rat face shaking with indignation, but he quickly regained himself, much to the relief of his small entourage of soldiers dwarfed by the men in their way.

"Right, our ore—you know, the valuable stuff that lies under our towns and that's mined by our men. The same stuff your boss seems eager to get for free."

"And now ya dare throw false accusations at—"

"My accusations are not false. If Erzse had it her way, we'd be mining the ore for nothing. Now, do yourself and your men a favour and return to Zyphyr or whatever rathole you crawled out of and leave us be. If Erzse wants to discuss, she already knows she's welcome to come herself. If not, we'll see her soon enough."

The officer took in the burly man and his two fearsome companions. The taller of the two was similar in appearance and size and sported a thick red beard; the shorter wore a silver mane, rested a wicked axe across his shoulders, and looked especially eager for confrontation.

"And me right of way?" the officer asked.

"Huh?" M. K. goaded.

"Ya 'av' no right to block the Black Mouth. It's not yours to block." He stood up bolder, suddenly sure of his point. "You can refuse to sell, but you can't refuse us access."

"I can do whatever I damn well please. You think those men camped behind the wall are just from Flint or Ingleton? No, we have support from the entire district, and until our terms are met, we're closed for business to all crooks and their muscle. Understood?"

The officer glared at M. K., and then a cruel smile took his expression. "I'll be seein' ya soon. All of ya."

The officer mounted his horse with emphasized arrogance and sped back towards Zyphyr with his retinue.

"We openly state we're going to vote against her, and we refuse to sell. Is it necessary to threaten her men also?" Acro said as they watched the soldiers kick dirt into the distance.

"Last thing we need is some of the smaller mines buckling under the sight of a couple scrawny grunts and weakening our position," M. K. said. "We're too close to the vote to leave anything to chance."

"And you've thought beyond that? We win the vote and prevent her election of a prime minister, and then what? You piss her off, and she'll not forget the slight. Trust me—I know her ways."

"She occupies half the towns in Borlencia, cousin. And it's been weeks now since the Borlencian ministers lodged their formal request to have the matter added to the meeting's agenda. You would've thought she'd have taken the initiative and removed Zylencia's soldiers by now, wouldn't you?"

"She likely waits for the meeting."

"Why? Why wait? Do you really think it likely she has any intention of removing them? And what about us? I've asked her to come to the table and decide Zylencia's fate. I've told her we're willing to compromise. Has she responded? No."

Acro shook his head, unconvinced. "It'll take time."

"No doubt. But let me put it this way. If she won't compromise, then at the least by winning the vote we can go some way towards stopping her grab for power over the whole of Anemoi. Beyond that, well, I reckon she'll be turning her attention towards us anyway. Every day we halt shipments is another day of lost revenue for her, and soon enough she'll struggle to bring an army to the table or buy support at home. She'll have two options: negotiate or fight."

"It'll make her desperate," Ricard observed.

"And reckless and more likely to make mistakes. All key ingredients for pushing her out."

"A vote of no confidence?" Acro asked.

M. K. smiled cunningly. "You ever wondered how she still holds her seat despite the term limits?"

"Because she knows how to woo."

"Because she knows how to lie creatively. We win the vote, it'll be easier for us to convince the other ministers that there is no threat and that it's time for her to step down, as per the law. We cut her off to the point of declaring war on her own or losing support of the army or being able to buy votes, and we'll finish her."

"Might get messy before then," Ricard said.

"I'm counting on it."

CHAPTER 33

Februarix 18, 485; Zyphyr, Zylencia—Dressed to protect from the cold, Xander sniffed the frigid air as another whiff of fresh bread carried on the wintery wind.

It was early afternoon, and the square plaza in which she stood was relatively busy with merchants and tourists alike. A light layer of frost carpeted the black stone underfoot, and stalls selling hot wine, pastries, and small gifts lined one of the edges. Municipal buildings stood on two of the other edges. She peered to the fourth side where a large red-brick building stood. One of the few in the city not constructed from the black stone of the mountain, it was two stories high, and a decent number of clear glass windows adorned both floors. The sign above the door read "Public Library."

She began for the building that had become a regular visit in the weeks prior. With Evia too busy building influence to accompany the girls into the undercity, and Aika eager to join and familiarise herself with Anemoi's political undertakings, Xander had been left to her own devices. Health permitting, of course, for she was still a tad weak. As she was about to ascend the stairs at the library's entrance, commotion from a small crowd not far off drew her attention.

Curious, she wandered closer until the source of the excitement was revealed. It was a man or a woman—she couldn't tell—draped in a shiny silver sheet and holding the colourful mask of a canine. The individual commanded the attention of the onlookers with a peculiar crouching dance of abrupt, awkward movements hypnotic in their execution. So strange and mesmerising was the routine that it took several moments for Xander to realise that the performer no longer performed but instead stared at her through the mask. It was an unsettling stare broken by the sudden rambling of a man sitting on the library steps, drawing her attention.

Donned in rags and a long grey beard, the old man was mumbling about some religion, so far as she could tell. She peered back to where the person draped in silver danced and was relieved to see that he or she was headed in the opposite direction and the crowd dispersing. Unbothered by the encounter, she pounced excitedly up the steps past the old man and entered the library.

The man from the store hadn't lied about its impressiveness, and each time she entered the vast building, she was filled with awe. Hundreds of shelves crammed with books, old and new, dominated the landscape. Tables and chairs were nestled against each wall under the windows and everywhere in between. And unlike libraries she had visited in the past, the warm air was fresh and absent the odour of old furniture and decayed paper.

She waved to the man sitting behind the front desk, and he nodded indifferently. Eager to jump back into her investigations, Xander climbed the stairs to the upper level and cantered over to the history section. Brushing her fingers across the spines of multiple tomes, she stopped on the one that had garnered her attention only yesterday: *A History of the Cresedi*. It was a heavy tome whose faded red was at odds with the sharp, unblemished green of a book on ancient coins incorrectly placed beside it. Though dated, the red tome was still filled with a vast reservoir of interesting knowledge and observations and was written in a conversational tone quite unlike the mundane history books she had read in the past.

Book in hand, she traversed the floor to her preferred spot. It was a table by one of the many windows overlooking the plaza but the only one with an unimpeded view of the steps. As she sat down, she noticed the old man still perched on the steps. Even from up there she could hear the drone of his voice reverberate through the glass, though not enough to disturb.

She opened the book to the page she had sneakily folded in the top right corner the day prior and scanned to the paragraph midway down:

"The unwritten custom of the Cresedi royal family is that no two sons should survive to inherit the throne. Implicitly, what this means is this: In the event an emperor bears more than one male son, the sons must attempt to remove one another through whatever means they find at their disposal. Given that this should, at preference, play out before the emperor dies, they would not have at their disposal the official standing armies of the Cresedi Empire.

Instead, the sons would attempt to raise their own armies or employ other, less obvious means to dispose of their competitors. Despite the barbarity of the practice, however, there are, interestingly, several unwritten rules. One, young children without the means to partake are off limits. Poisoned food is frowned upon. And, in times of existential threats to the empire, the sons put aside their deadly contest for the greater good.

A primary criticism of the custom, besides the obvious damage to the line of succession if all the sons were to die without heirs, is the instability it can create. To the emperors of old, however, it became a necessary means through which to avoid contestations against sitting emperors and the far grander, much more devastating battles that followed under such circumstances. In this author's opinion…"

Xander peered outside to the library steps where the ragged man was swearing loudly at two soldiers walking past. However, rather than confront the man they clearly recognised, the soldiers continued on, uncaring. She chuckled and looked back down to the page.

"In this author's opinion, having observed the customs of a number of governments, royal and not, the custom holds weight. The empire's wealth is vast, and its greed permeates all levels of society. So much so that the checks

and balances effective in other societies have little to no effect in containing the wanton desire of multiple sons born to the throne. Better to lose all but one before ascension than risk the empire splitting.

And all this said, the custom does not prevent the sons from making a name for themselves during their sometimes-short lives, for to lead, or to even outlive the custom, they must still build a reputation and skill set that will serve them as emperor."

Xander sat back in her chair, struck into thought by the custom that seemed so far from anything she knew. As she sat there, staring ponderously into the sky's clear blue, a shallow draft blew through the massive room and lifted the pages of the book. She put her hand down to stop the flow and withdrew it to reveal the page. Her eyes widened at the symbol staring back.

A square with a horizontal line through its centre, the two ends of the line curled upwards. Though different to the square with a flat horizontal line through its centre, the similarity between the two was undeniable. She craned closer and read the passage beneath:

"Of the numerous Cresedi religions, the Zorforiat religion is, contradictorily, the most widely known and the least used. Supposedly born from the planes of the afterlife (underworld, heaven, or spirit world, in other vernaculars), the ancient religion is characterised by practices often described as both mystical and brutal. Maiming, sacrifices, and dead worshipping are not uncommon within the religion.

Despite the religion's prevalence across the empire, and even within the ruling class, the religion was eventually outlawed after the group grew too powerful and made an attempt on an emperor of the second dynasty. Whilst not uncommon for vassal states or political groups within the empire to revolt, it was the fact that the religion's leadership was able to convert and will the emperor's daughter to make the attempt herself that invoked such a harsh response. The group's leadership was culled and the practise made punishable by death.

In the centuries since the ban, however, a handful of pockets of the original group have remained intact, and multiple sister sects have arisen under various aliases across the empire and beyond its borders. To this day, the ruling class remains incredibly wary of the proliferation of the religion and its derivatives. So much so that, on occasion, an emperor or his governing officials will enact bans on any derivative deemed too big to leave intact, usually entailing harsh punishment."

"Sister sects," Xander murmured under her breath. She turned the page to find the chapter's end.

Curious for more on the Zorforiat, she peered into the vast landscape of books and shelves. Recollection jogged her memory, and she got up and made for the far end of that floor where the section on religions sat. "But what to look for?" she wondered as she combed her finger across the three unrelated books arranged in the "Z" section. Like tossing a pebble into the ocean, she began to scan each and every book across the nearest shelves until her eye caught on one in particular.

She read the title aloud. "*Religions of Anemoi: Past and Present.*" This would do.

She grabbed the hefty tome and eagerly trekked back to the desk, but as she sat down, she noticed the man on the step staring up in her direction. She glanced left and then right, but she was the only one in the vicinity. She looked back down, and he held her gaze for a couple of moments more before stepping into the square and wandering off. Not thinking anything of it, for the man was clearly in his own world, she opened the book.

The first chapter portrayed several dozen family trees, with each religious sect's associated symbol, name, and page reference. Looking in particular for the square with the horizontal line through it, her eye caught on another equally interesting symbol. It was the three triangles standing atop one another. The symbol was near the bottom of its family tree.

She read the name aloud. "Aesthyo. Page one hundred and three."

Curious as to why it would be in a book on religions, given the twins had called it a non-religious sect, she eagerly skipped through the pages until a larger drawing of the triangles stared back at her.

"Aesthyo is derived from the Aesth religion and is local to Anemoi. Like its parent and sister sects, it is a subtle ideology rooted in spirituality rather than the worship of a deity or deities. Similar to its sister groups of the same generation, the sect played a critical role in the Revolutionary Wars and in the removal of religion from politics in Anemoi during the Upheaval. It has since played some role in maintaining the status quo. As such, it is considered a non-religious sect.

Unlike other sects derived from the Aesth religion, Aesthyo was considered pacifist prior to the Revolutionary Wars. Only during and since has the sect resorted to violence to protect its interests."

Xander thought back to the grotto by the twins. There had been no evidence of a struggle, only the remnants of an unchallenged slaughter. But the twins' testament that the sect fought the religious sects behind the scenes supported the text.

She flipped back to the front of the book, where the family tree diagrams were, and began to work her way through the pages. So many religions and sects, she wondered how many still existed and how many the book may not have picked up. Finally, drifting through tree after tree of colourful symbols, she spotted what she was looking for and then some.

Not only had she found the square with the line through its centre but also the symbol's ultimate parent. At the top of the page was the symbol of the Zorforiat. They were related. She traced her finger back down to the symbol she had seen in the water mill under the city.

"Zora," she said aloud.

"Zora is derived from the ancient Cresedi religion, Zorforiat, and arrived in Anemoi during the Revolutionary Wars. It is the only sect within this family to have arrived and existed in Anemoi. Like its parent and sister sects, the teachings of Zora centre around sacrifices, the underworld, communicating with the dead, and the channelling of the dead's energy into the user. (There is only one other religious tree, that of the witch doctor [page 345], that preaches the same, though that is where the similarities end.)

The Zora religion is often characterised by five statuettes representing death, life, the underworld, our world, and the medium. The Zora religion played a prominent opposing role in the Revolutionary Wars and in the removal of religion from politics in Anemoi during the Upheaval. Upon its loss, it was widely disbanded, though remnants of the religion can be found all over Anemoi."

The seed was sown. Keen for more, she began to flip through the book, taking in anything even remotely interesting. From the sister sects of the Zora to the scrimpy paragraphs on the frightening practices of the witch doctor and their supposed ability to summon from the underworld, she scoured through it all. Hours passed, and when she was finally able to tear her eyes away, the sun had already dropped below quarter mast and dusk had taken hold.

She peered around the library, and several shuttered lamps had been lit in sections where readers still lingered, including in her own section. She couldn't recall the transition but was thankful for the librarian's vigilance that had allowed her to feed her curiosity. Still, the hour was late, and though the curfew was nothing more than a recommended guideline these days, she could imagine Evia giving her a mouthful at so late an hour.

Eager to head home, she gathered her belongings and put the books away. As she departed the library into the icy cold, she took in the light puffs of snow that drifted through the air and the torchlit square that was empty but for a few stragglers hastily treading through the space. Walking in the direction of the villa, Xander was about to step out of the square when motion near the closest corner caught her eye. It was a cart on the next street along. Moving in the direction of the city's centre, a handful of guards trailed it. Her mind immediately jumped to Borlencian prisoners and what the silhouette had told her.

About to follow, she hesitated as the imagined scolding she was going to receive resurfaced. Stuck in inaction, she watched as the cart rounded the corner out of view. A silent curse carried on her steamy breath, and she began towards the corner she had glimpsed the vehicle traversing. Walking with speed, but not with enough impetus to draw attention, she followed the cart from a sizable distance, right up until it passed through one of four gates on the palace's fortified wall.

Casually, and as nonthreateningly as she could manage, she strolled right up to the gate. This was the first time she had seen the building and its stone perimeter up close, and she was stunned by the sheer height of the fortification. Two guards stood atop the gate, but neither seemed to notice her presence below.

She glanced around and noted that the surrounding houses and businesses sprawled right up to the wall. There was no gap. Her gaze locked on a three-story building a short distance to the right whose upper floor poked above the rooftops lining the road she was on. Curious, she began down the closest road leading to the right until she was standing outside the tall building. Its gate was open, and she could see into a courtyard that opened on to the wall itself. Light chatter and the clatter of cutlery and plates came from a small café another ten metres down the road on the opposite side of the building.

Confident no one was looking, she entered through the gate into the space and was immediately struck by its familiarity. The windows and doors were lofty, and the building's three walls stretched nearly to the same level as the fortified wall's peak. In the yard's centre was a perfectly rectangular lawn, though the grass was frosty white. All that was missing from her dream the night she found the mountain bees was the marble white of the structure and the four squares brimming with soil and flowers.

Both delightfully surprised and somewhat confounded, she wandered up to the fortified wall at the opposite end of the courtyard. A thick vine of sorts snaked up the stones right to the wall's peak, as far as she could tell. She put a hand to the plant and tugged. It was strong, very strong.

"Oi! What ya doing?" a gruff voice penetrated the quiet.

She turned around to see a round old man staring at her from the open gate. "Sorry, I got lost."

"Ha! It happens. Best you be on your way, nevertheless."

She scurried back through the courtyard and dipped her head as she passed him. "Thank you."

"Nothing to worry ya'self over," he said as she exited onto the street. "Just be careful of the ruffians as ya head home."

About to walk away, she turned to the man. "What is this place?"

"Can't ya tell by the doors? It's a stable."

"Ah! I guess that makes sense when you think about it. Thank you."

"'Tis my pleasure."

Thankfully, the trek home was uneventful, with the few soldiers she crossed more concerned with keeping warm than a young woman wandering around alone. The villa itself was dark and empty but for a single lit torch by the entrance. A pang of worry took her, her immediate assumption that Evia and the others were currently searching for her. But the hour wasn't that late. She grabbed the torch and entered the kitchen, her stomach guiding her to the pantry. About to enter, she spotted a note on the table.

"Xander, your aunt's running a little late, and the rest of us have a meeting to attend. She said it might happen and to not worry. Be sure to try the pie Robyn made when you're back. Wiston."

She smiled at the warm gesture and made straight for the pantry, moments later emerging with a slice of minced pie. As she sat down, it occurred to her that she hadn't eaten since lunch and thus proceeded to lambast herself for the oversight, her recovery predicated on healthy meals and strength training. As she munched away in the dim room, her mind drifted to what she had read on the Cresedi succession customs and the Zora.

"Perhaps there is a tie between the creature, the prisoners, Erzse, and the Zora," she pondered quietly. Still, she would need more than a chance occurrence to establish a connection.

CHAPTER 34

Februarix 21, 485; Zyphyr, Zylencia—Evia looked up from the documents on the kitchen table to the source of the knock on the door. It was early afternoon, and though the villa was full with all its residents, it was largely quiet.

"Wiston," she said, taking in the man who carried a pensive expression. "You needn't knock to enter the kitchen. It's as much yours as mine whilst you're a guest here."

"Just trying to be polite," he said, taking a seat opposite her.

"And what's bothering you?"

"That obvious?"

"Should I go with your less cheery demeanour or that look of concern?"

He leant forward and lowered his voice. "One of my men found another room full of—you know."

"How many?"

"Nine. Borlencian. All young women. The chamber was sealed like most of the others. That makes eight, including the room the girls found."

"And the square symbol?"

"Etched into one of the girls' arms."

Evia glanced into the courtyard and back. "Have you told her?"

"Wanted to speak to you first. I know you've been apprehensive about her going into the tunnels so soon, even with you by her side. So I wanted to make certain—"

"To be frank, I don't want her anywhere near an opening into the undercity, even with me present. Not until we figure out what it is that attacked her."

"That's why you've been avoiding the topic with her?"

"What topic?"

"Anything to do with the religions she's become fascinated with, the prisoners, the search for the shard," he said. "Every chance you get, you find a new mission that takes your time from her."

"That obvious?"

"To a rock. She knows you avoid her because you fear for her."

"You don't?" she asked.

"I do, but you've said yourself numerous times that the shard is critical to our success. At some point we're just going to have to accept there's a risk down there that we can't manage. At least with you by her side, and a couple of my men, if not me, she'll have good company." Evia was about to speak, but Wiston continued. "Plus, what about mapping out the exits and finding ways to increase the certainty of the tunnels she'd explore? You said it was acceptable to go down if we reduce the risk."

She bit her cheek and sat back. "I've not quite kept my word, have I? I—"

"You're scared for her. But you knew this journey would take her across all sorts of paths."

There was a moment of quiet before she spoke again. "Will you join me?"

"Where?"

"I think it's time I paid a visit into the undercity," she said. "Without the girls. You, me, Dogner, and a group of your men. I'll send the girls on an errand so they're far from us and our antics."

"And if we don't find anything?"

"We have to; otherwise I'll be forced to let Xander venture back down there without being any wiser as to the threat."

He nodded. "When?"

"Tomorrow, before somebody else stumbles on the bodies."

The man seemed relieved as he stood. "I'll start making arrangements."

"Thank you, Wiston. And I'll have a think about where to send the girls."

"I'll take them to Ingleton." A voice came from the doorway.

"Joseph," Evia said, surprised.

"It's their annual cheese festival. Could be quite the distraction for the girls. I actually meant to mention it before, but it slipped my mind. Anyway, I'm sure they'd love to see Ricard. Don't worry, Evia. I could only hear because I was sitting in the courtyard by the flowers."

"Would explain why I missed you," Wiston remarked.

Evia lifted an amused eyebrow. "And you didn't think to let on sooner, Joseph?"

He smiled mischievously. "So, Ingleton tomorrow?"

She chortled. "Thank you. That sounds like a good idea."

CHAPTER 35

Februarix 22, 485; Ingleton, Zylencia—Xander peered down the steep, grassy hill lined with throngs of rowdy people along the sides, at the bottom, and at the top where she and the others stood. She looked back at Ricard and M. K., disbelief on her face. "They're crazy."

"That's an understatement," Aika echoed, her expression also one of shock.

"You know, they've got similar traditions in Borlencia," Joseph commented. "Not around Nhata, mind you. And certainly not in winter when the ground's as hard as a rock."

M. K. grinned. "No surprises there. The Zylencians in the mountains come from hardier stock than your average Borlencian."

"And if by hardier you mean less prone to common sense, then yes, I think that's something we can all agree on," Ricard jibed. He turned to the girls. "So, you going to partake?"

Aika chuckled. "In a cheese-rolling competition? Doesn't make much sense to me, but sure, why not."

Xander hesitated. She wanted to but knew Evia would scold her for risking her recovery over something so trivial.

"She doesn't need to know," Aika said, guessing Xander's thought process.

"And if I get hurt?" Xander responded.

"Coming from the girl that climbed a mountain just to get some honey?" M. K. scoffed.

"Well, you said so yourself—it wasn't just any honey," Xander retorted.

"True, I did say that. So?"

Xander peered back down the grassy hill littered with knolls and rocky crags. "Hope I don't regret this—"

"You'll only regret not trying," M. K. interrupted.

"Okay, okay. Let's do it."

"Yes, atta girl!" He turned to a nearby mediator. "We've got two more victims for the grind."

The girls winced at that and wandered over to the starting line with M. K. and Ricard. Joseph, content to just watch, remained with the spectators. Unlike the traditional customs that ordinarily permeated the Zylencian miners and farmers, both men and women stood ready to race.

Raucous cheers swept up and down the throng as M. K. took to the centre, left of Acro. The two men gripped hands and seemed happy to be taking part together. Xander and Aika were immediately behind the pair, and Ricard had opted to stand on the wing of the line.

"It's really just a matter of grabbing the cheese first?" Aika asked over the deafening noise.

Acro turned around. "Some would say it's just a matter of making it down the slope without breaking a leg."

"Is that really sensible given you might be"—she leant forward as if to whisper—"fighting soon?"

M. K. looked back. "They'll have fought through worse. Plus, always good to keep the soldiers happy."

A horn blared from nearby, silencing the crowd.

"Are ya ready for the eight hundred and eleventh cheese-rolling contest?" a man hidden from the girls called out. Screams abounded for a good two minutes before dying down. "A competition won last year by yours truly, the Mountain King!"

The girls peered at M. K. as the crowd's screams turned euphoric, and they saw Acro whisper something in the man's ear. M. K., in response, laughed boisterously and patted his cousin on the back.

"Didn't realise we were in the presence of the champion," Aika whispered to Xander, to the latter's amusement.

Again, it took several minutes for the noise to die down, but this time, without prompt, the contestants simply readied themselves for the descent. A tense air hung heavy as they all awaited the signal to begin.

Suddenly the girls saw the nine-pound wheel of cheese ten metres from the hill's crest, hurtling down at speed, and not a second later heard the horn's piercing blare. Instantly the line lurched forward and the weight of the bodies behind pushed those in front over the crest.

Xander immediately took to trailing M. K. and Aika to trailing Acro. Pounding down the long slope at speed, Xander could feel every thump on the frozen ground reverberating through her legs and core. In the peripheral she could see men and women falling over one another, some rolling from momentum, others coming to a hard stop as they crashed to the ground.

Seventy metres down, Xander saw Acro fall and Aika leap over him. M. K., despite his size, was leading the line, running and jumping like a dancer. Keen to overtake, however, Xander manoeuvred a tad to the left, clipping an unseen man as she did. The man fell to the ground, and she also found herself falling headfirst. Instinctively, though, she put her hands down and rolled forward smoothly over the ground, coming back to an upright position, albeit with even more momentum. It was enough to edge M. K., and she could hear the man's competitive grunts follow her as she crossed in front of him.

Still, she was nowhere near the cheese wheel, which was already two-thirds of the distance, a full hundred metres in front of her position. Dodging divots and drops and outcrops like her life depended on it, she felt Aika pull up beside her. She managed a glance and could see Aika smiling from the exhilaration.

When they were three-quarters of the way down, the wheel of cheese had already completed its journey and was waiting stationarily at the bottom for a victor to put their hand to its rough surface. The blur of faces at the bottom cheered and cried in frenzy, and much of the racing line had diminished until only a dozen or so still stumbled down.

Fifty metres from the finish line, the gradient was gentler and the ground smoother, forcing the contestants to transition from an awkward stumble into a running gait. Thirty metres from the line, Xander again glanced to the right and could see Aika edging her ever so slightly. It wouldn't do, and she abruptly put her all into her stride despite the burn that had enveloped her muscles and chest.

With twenty metres left, Xander couldn't help the grin forming on her flustered face, the excitement all too much. Suddenly she crashed to the ground, as did Aika, both taken out by M. K.'s bulk stumbling to the grass in a chaotic flounder.

Once the dust settled, Xander peered up to see Ricard swooping in at an angle and diving onto the cheese before the next contestant could. Cheers rang through the throng up and down the hill, both onlookers and contestants absolutely thrilled by the spectacle. And though Xander could sense that M. K. was a bit disappointed at losing the crown, the man still laughed and cried with the rest of them as Ricard stood up victoriously with the cheese lifted overhead.

▲ ▲ ▲

Xander, Aika, Joseph, and Ricard took their seats at a long wooden table, one of many nestled under a huge pavilion. And the pavilion itself was one of a dozen perched at the edge of a sea of military tents erected on the moor between the town's northern reach and the palisade wall. The pavilions brimmed with stalls and festival-goers, and the noise of a thousand chattering mouths and the heavy odour of cheese and meat filled the air. And despite the frigid temperature of the winter day, with numerous firepits dotted around the tent and the squash of so many bodies in close proximity, they and the crowds were comfortably warm.

"My eyes still play tricks," Ricard said warmly.

Aika laughed. "It's barely been a month."

"And how it's felt much, much longer. And as you can see, we've been busy," he said, pointing to the palisade in the background. "The army now numbers in the tens of thousands. Enough, I'd say, to give the woman a run for her money."

Joseph glanced around nervously.

"Don't worry," Ricard said to him. "Nobody's listening, and even if they wanted to, they'll not hear over this racket."

"Can never be too careful," Joseph cautioned.

"So, now that we've got a moment to chat, what's the news in the city? Your search coming along well, kiddo? And what about you, Princess—finally figured out the sky's not going to fall onto your head?"

"Glad to see you've matured during our time apart," Aika retorted.

They looked up as M. K. approached the bench with a large tray in hand. He skilfully placed it onto the table, and the others quickly marvelled at the offering. A big pot of melted cheese with bread, beer, and sliced boar to the side.

"Dig in," he grunted, taking a seat next to Ricard.

"Is it…?" Ricard asked, motioning to the pot.

M. K. looked at him, his earlier disappointment gone. "It is. Finest wheel of cheese to be served today. Congratulations, Zylencia's new winner of the cheese-rolling contest."

Ricard proudly ripped a handful of bread and dunked it into the pot. As he withdrew it, strands of gooey cheese dripped back into the container, and not a second later, he tore into the cheesy bread with his teeth.

"Amazing," he managed in between chews. He turned to the girls and again spoke with his mouth full. "Well then, don't keep me waiting. What's the gossip?"

"The blockade's working better than expected," Joseph said. "Lot of angry people since the trade of ore dried up. The resistance and the riots are keeping Erzse and the other corrupt ministers on their toes."

"Music to my ears," M. K. said, and he took a long swig of his beer.

"Have you made any progress in your talks with Erzse?" Joseph asked him.

"What talks?" M. K. scoffed. "Every time she's come to the table, it's been nothing more than a staring contest. It's like talking to a petulant toddler. There's been nothing productive said, not since my first proposal to work with her if she leaves our mines be and lowers those unnecessary taxes. Not sure what she's convinced herself of, but it certainly doesn't revolve around working with us."

"What about Aiden? Has he—"

"The man's trying, I'll give him that, but it's starting to look like he's got no influence with the woman." M. K.'s expression transitioned to one of annoyance. "I know we're just trying to lead them on with these talks, get them to believe we're wanting to negotiate and work with them, but it's becoming blatantly obvious that she'd cut off her own foot to win the race. She's irrationally stubborn." He sat back, his expression sombre. "War's looking more and more likely with her at the helm."

Again, Joseph peered around, but nobody was listening. "Only if we lose the vote."

"And how are we coming along on that front? I've not heard much from you or Evia since I was in the city last."

"We think we've got a way to hamstring the Notencians and get their vote," Joseph said. "Along with the Borlencian vote, and a majority of the Eurencians. Time will tell how many Zylencians we can get on our side, but it's starting to look positive."

"Good to know my talks with Erzse are irrelevant," M. K. stated.

"Doesn't hurt to cover our bases, make Aiden and any other sensible

Zylencian think we're trying to align with them."

"All good until she strings me up in one of our meetings, never mind the implied armistice. Just waiting for the day."

Joseph shook his head in disbelief. "She wouldn't."

"She just might," M. K. retorted and proceeded to down the rest of his beer whilst motioning to a handmaiden nearby to fetch him another.

"A lot of moving pieces," Ricard chimed in. "All with a purpose. And you, kiddo, how's your search coming along?"

"It's not," Xander replied.

"Oh!"

"We've run into a slight problem. You know that creature near the twins?"

Ricard's eyes widened in horror. "You're kidding?"

"She's not," Aika said. "It followed us to the city and attacked Xander whilst we were in the tunnels searching for the shard. It nearly got her when we stumbled on a mass grave like the one Xander found before. We were lucky to get out alive."

"And you're okay?" Ricard asked Xander worriedly.

"I'm fine, but Evia's not let us into the tunnels since. She says it's too dangerous without her, but she's preoccupied with the vote, so she's not been able to join."

"And I'd say the woman's bloody right! I wouldn't let you anywhere near that thing if it were up to me. Not a chance. Unfortunate that it means there's been no progress on that front, mind you."

"Not much, no," Xander said disappointedly. "I've been able to trace a couple of tunnels using the map that I think could lead us to the centre. It's all a blur, though. As if the map's playing tricks. Until we get down there, I won't know for sure." She was about to mention the silhouette's suggestion but thought better of it. A strange man no one could see but her, giving her directions to follow Borlencian prisoners into what so happened to be Erzse's stronghold. They would think she was mad. Even with everything she had told Evia, her aunt had still had a hard time believing it could be anything more than a distraction, and at worst a malicious attempt to get her into trouble.

Ricard rapped his knuckles on the table. "In that case, thank the gods and their minions we're making progress with the ministers. Otherwise, we'd have a lost cause." He looked at Xander, hesitation etched into his shoulders. "Have you given any more thought about the day of the vote?"

She hadn't. At least nothing more than a courtesy nod. Her mind was already set, and it had been since that night in Flint when she discovered her father's less-known legacy. "I'll not be vouching for my father."

The man looked pained, as if he had failed his dead friend. "I understand. It's the last you'll hear of it from me."

"And me," M. K. said, "given I was about to bring it up too."

She could sense that Joseph was still somewhat conflicted by the whole idea. That part of him agreed the right move was to take the stand with Ricard and speak up for her father's legacy. The legacy she remembered, anyway. And in doing so, make it more difficult for Erzse to act maliciously. But she could also tell he knew better than to rehash the conversation and thus was content to drop it once and for all.

A horn blared from the field, interrupting the emotional quiet.

"Ah!" M. K. said, rubbing his hands gleefully. "Time for the armed combat."

"Armed?" Aika said, puzzled.

"Wooden swords, don't you worry. Still, no ladies allowed to partake in this one, sadly. An old tradition reluctant to die. Anyway, finish your grub and let's head over. I've got prime seating for us."

Excited, the group greedily scoffed down their food and drink and headed over to the growing swarm that was deliriously eager for the next round of entertainment.

CHAPTER 36

Februarix 22, 485; Zyphyr, Zylencia—Evia felt her knee pop as she stood up from her crouch. Upright, she let out a sombre sigh and then peered around the torchlit room. The pungent stench of blood and sewage permeated the space, and except for a lone table and chair in one corner, all that filled the area was the maimed remnants of nine Borlencian women strewn at her feet near the adjacent corner. She turned to the doorway where Dogner and Wiston looked on.

"Well?" Dogner asked, barely able to contain his anger.

"They've got the same markings," she managed. "From Borlencia. Destined for Zyphyr. Two of them have the symbol of the Zora etched into their skin."

"And it's a sacrifice?"

She turned back to the bodies and took in the gaunt, lifeless expressions. "It appears so."

"But why? Why kill so many?" Wiston said agitatedly.

She turned to the door and walked over, keen to be out of the room. Together, the three of them exited into a massive chamber outside where a dozen houses lined a narrow cobblestone street built under the city. The massive room itself was illuminated by a series of drains in the shallow ceiling connecting to the world above. She glanced to the end of the road where the only exit was. Two plain-clothes Eurencian soldiers guarded it, and she could see another five stood sporadically along the street. She turned back to the pair.

"I took the liberty of doing a bit of reading on the Zora religion after Xander's revelation," she said. "And from what I've gathered, the practitioners make the sacrifices in return for energy or strength from a provider in the underworld."

"What bastard could bring themselves to do that?" Dogner roared, putting the soldiers on edge. "Send innocents to that blasted place for eternity in return for something so selfish."

"I don't know who or what, but the sealed burials suggest to me that it's an ongoing trade. Even now I can feel something emanating from the channel connecting this chamber to the underworld. The energy is transferring to someone or something in this city."

"Our culprit?"

"Must be."

"Can you stop it?"

"I don't know. I've only encountered something like this once before, and that was with the witch doctor many, many years ago."

"Before they were banished from Anemoi?" Wiston asked.

"After," she responded. "As old as I am, I wasn't around during the time of the initial culls."

"And you're certain it's not that wretched lot back from the dead?" Dogner said.

"The two religions are unrelated, and I see no markings to suggest it was the witch doctor."

Wiston's expression hardened from one of shock and sympathy. "Could it be Erzse?"

"We'll know only if we catch her in the act," she said.

"Then what? What are our options?" Dogner asked with growing frustration.

"We can station soldiers around the undercity," Wiston suggested. "We might get lucky."

Evia shook her head. "It's a labyrinth down here, and I've seen no pattern from where the burials have been placed. You haven't got enough men to cover every tunnel."

"We'll have more with the arrival of the Eurencian delegation."

"That's still a week from now, and even with a thousand down here, which you won't have, it'd be a long shot."

"Then what?"

Evia bit her cheek as she pondered. Slowly, she peered around the chamber to the grimy houses that hadn't seen the full light of day and the six Eurencian soldiers waiting for them. "Maybe the creature knows."

"The creature after Xander?"

"Yes," she said, not taking her eyes from the guards. "It can enter and exit through the channel when summoned. It may know who we search for. Plus, isn't it the reason we're here?"

Dogner cleared his throat. "No disrespect meant, but what makes you think that bloody thing will listen to you if you try to summon it?"

"Because I don't need to conjure it."

"Then how will you—"

"Wiston, remind me—how many soldiers did we enter with?" She interrupted Dogner's question, her gaze not averting from the guards.

"Eight," he responded, confused.

"And some are on patrol? Maybe in the houses?"

"The search was completed. Their orders are to stand watch on the street. Why?"

"Call your men over," she said calmly.

Puzzled, he looked to his men and called out, "Gather on me!"

Six soldiers jogged towards the trio, stopping a metre from their position. None spoke, and all waited for their next order.

The realisation was immediate. "Where're Gareth and Harry?" Wiston asked.

The soldiers looked at each other and then back at him, their confusion apparent.

"In pairs, spread out," he said quietly, and at once the men split off, the patter of their footsteps all that filled the echoey space as they began to scour the closest of the houses.

"You two should help them," Evia said.

"You must be mad," Dogner scolded. "Not a chance I'll leave you alone."

"I'm fine, and you need me to keep watch on the street—"

"We've found Gareth!" one of the soldiers called from the second house on the right. "He's…he's…just come see for yourselves!"

"Go on," Evia urged.

Dogner peered at her, confounded by her insistence. But her oddly relaxed demeanour spoke volumes. "Let's go, Wiston," he said, and the pair began towards the house.

Evia watched them as they disappeared into the abode, leaving her alone on the street.

"That was a mistake," cooed a raspy voice behind her.

"Was it?" she said without turning around.

The voice cackled in her ear like a strangled dog. "A grave mistake."

"For whom?"

"You."

A hand gripped Evia by the neck, but rather than squirm or scratch for release, she swiftly grabbed the hand with her own and whispered something. The perpetrator instantly squealed in pain. Shouts came from down the street as the others reacted to the commotion. Evia peeled the perpetrator's hand off her and turned around. Harry, the Eurencian guard, stared back at her, his once brown eyes now cloudy blue, his skin pale and bloodied. His face was creased into one of agony, revealing mangled animal teeth unlike that of any man or woman Evia knew.

"What are you?" the creature hissed as the others reached the pair.

"What's gotten into you, man?" Wiston yelled, levelling his sword against the creature's throat.

The creature tried to writhe free of Evia's grip, but each pull or jerk simply worked to compound its distress. Instinctively, it howled and hissed and barked as the perplexed soldiers formed a circle around it.

Overwhelmed with pain, it collapsed to its knees, its head craned to the floor, its shoulders slumped. A sob escaped its lips, and again it repeated its question: "What are you?"

"Conjurer and vanquisher," Evia replied coldly. "Why do you seek my niece?"

It hooted, its gaze still to the ground. "And who is your niece?"

She tightened her grip, and the creature arched its back and looked up, its yellow teeth clamped together, its face creased to the point that Harry's features no longer reflected true.

"Tell me, creature, and I'll spare you a prolonged death."

She released her grip a tad, and it snapped its teeth at her. "What niece? What niece? What do I know about any niece? Nothing! Die, you—" Spittle escaped its lips as Evia grabbed it by the throat.

"Talk to me, creature of Zora. Who are you? What do you want with my niece?"

Its nostrils flared, and its eyes narrowed as it bared its fangs again.

"Let me put the thing out of its misery," Dogner spoke, readying his cudgel.

"No. I need an answer," she said sternly and lessened her grip on its throat.

"Zora! Zora! Ha! Ha!" It cackled and then spat on her.

Without hesitation, Dogner smashed his knuckles into the creature's temple, causing it to shake awkwardly.

"Talk to me, or I'll make sure you never step foot in the underworld again," Evia said angrily. "You will spend an eternity writhing in pain. Tell me, who are you? What do you want with my niece?"

Suddenly it began to squirm, its head thrashing from side to side.

"What's it doing?" Wiston said cautiously.

"The girl will die!" it hissed. "She'll die, and you'll not stop it!" The creature abruptly began to murmur in a language unlike any in Anemoi—a punishingly screechy language that had the men covering their ears to block out the piercing sound.

Evia gasped, and she let go of the creature and jumped backwards. The others swiftly followed suit as the creature began to melt, its skin and flesh oozing into a pile of bubbling blood and guts. The group stood around the puddle in silent shock as the last residues of Harry's face dissolved completely.

"What the heck just happened?" Wiston uttered, breaking the quiet.

"It…it killed itself," Evia said, baffled.

"As in, went back to the underworld?"

"No, it's dead. There's no coming back for it."

"This was the same thing that attacked Xander?"

She nodded. "It was strongly guarded, but I could read some semblance of its thoughts. It's the same one that attacked her."

"And the person that summoned it?" Dogner asked.

"I don't know," Evia admitted.

"Can they summon another like it?"

She looked up at him and then the others. "I'm not sure. Maybe."

"What was it?" one of the guards asked, his cheeks white and his brow crinkled. "That language—I've never heard anything like it."

Evia's fear was clear to them all as she glanced around the group. "It was a demon from the underworld, permitted to enter through the channel."

"Then conjured by the same that made the channel?" Wiston asked.

"I don't think so. The channel was built by a practitioner of the Zora religion, but the creature seemed to mock us when I mentioned the Zora. I think something else conjured it."

"Then it must be the witch doctor. What other religion plays with the underworld as such?"

Evia cursed under her breath. "That's the last thing we need. For all our sakes."

CHAPTER 37

Februarix 24, 485; Ingleton, Zylencia—Xander stifled the chuckle trying to escape through her pursed lips and peered from the playing card in her hand to Ricard. Sitting on the opposite side of the long wooden table, he carried an air of annoyance under his forced grin as he scanned the five cards in his hand.

To Xander's right, M. K. looked on excitedly, in his hands a pint of lager and a turkey thigh. To her left was Aika, her hands empty, her gaze intent. And to Ricard's left, Joseph, his hands empty and distractingly fidgety. Sitting under one of the many tents, all of them were bundled in thick woollen jumpers to protect from the frigid evening air, despite the close proximity of one of the dozen bonfires raging across the moor under the dimming light.

Still, all were joyfully content and brimming with rich food and a bit too much drink. Amidst the light chatter of the thinning crowds, and eager for a change of pace on their final night in town, they had resigned themselves to the slightly less demanding activity of a Borlencian card game called The Duck & The Goat.

A game as old as Borealis, supposedly, each player was required to rid themselves of their cards using the dizzying array of rules at their disposal. But only the second to last to do so could be declared the winner—The

Duck. Leaving the last one to do so the declared loser—The Goat. And whilst there was no prize for coming first, there was certainly a penalty for coming last. The declared loser, per the rules, was always required to perform some embarrassing feat dreamt up by the other players on the spot.

And to Ricard's growing frustration, this round was looking more and more likely to be the third notch in his belt. Given he had only very reluctantly agreed to join to quell the girls' incessant whining, he was now violently kicking himself for having agreed.

"You needn't worry this time," M. K. said, breaking Ricard's nervous tension. "We'll not have you crawling around like a baby again. Think we all saw enough of—"

Ricard shot him a dangerous glare.

M. K. smirked. "If a glare could kill, I'd have been a dead man long ago."

"It's never too late," Ricard retorted.

"Be that as it may," Joseph began, "are you going to take all day? It's getting a bit—"

"Oh, heck with it!" Ricard roared, placing one of his cards on the table.

Xander's mouth creased as she gave her all to force down the smile itching to appear. She turned to Aika, who also struggled to hold a laugh craving for life.

"Let me guess," Ricard said grumpily. "It's done? I've lost again?"

The girls looked at him and back to each other and then burst into laughter along with the others.

After a good minute of giggling, Aika wiped her tears, leant across the table, and took the last four cards from his hands. As she peered at the hand, her mouth straightened, and she looked at him wide-eyed. "You had a winning hand, old man."

Xander took the cards, and she, too, looked at him with surprise. "You could've beaten M. K. with these. Maybe even Joseph."

Ricard's flat expression didn't brighten or even twitch. His features remained straight and emotionless as he leant forward, his gaze locked on the pair. "You bloodthirsty harpies. I may not be able to read minds, but I know you're both winding me up. I can see right through the two of you." He turned to Joseph. "Can you believe this? Scoundrels if I've ever met one."

Joseph laughed. "It's just a game, big man."

"I know. But look at these two conniving vultures." He started to grin, mirroring the beams etching onto their faces. "It'll get you far in life, I don't doubt. Just need a bit more—"

"M. K." They turned to a soldier appearing from the direction of the palisade. It was one of the miners from Flint. "A rider approaches."

"Do you know who?" M. K. asked, standing up. The others followed suit, keen to witness the development for themselves.

Concern was etched into his brow. "It's him. Erzse's man."

M. K.'s expression hardened. "I was wondering when he would make an appearance." He climbed from the table and began in the direction of the palisade through the sea of military tents and the soldiers asleep in them. The others were quick to follow. "You're sure he's alone?"

"As sure as can be."

"Alright. Well, just in case, grab our kit and the rest of my unit. And make sure they're armed."

"Sir," the soldier responded before running off towards a cluster of marginally larger military tents situated in the centre of the camp.

"Probably not the smartest move to ban weapons from the pavilions," Joseph remarked as the rest of them continued along the rough grass towards the wall.

"Had to after an incident when I was just a youngling," M. K. said. "Nearly half the miners were cut down over some argument nobody could quite recall the next day. Can't let it happen on my watch now, can I?"

The ground directly behind the palisade was largely bare and torn up. Likely, Xander figured, due to the numerous drills M. K. and Ricard had had the soldiers performing along the defensive front in the prior weeks. Torches marked the length of the wall at ten-metre intervals, dual sentries every fifty metres, and one-hundred-man units manned each of the three gates.

At the main entrance in the middle of the wall, the group climbed the wooden staircase onto the ramparts where five guards also stood, providing them an unobstructed view of the dusk-covered landscape. As one, their eyes fell to a man on his horse some twenty metres from the gate. The man was lean, though muscular, and he wore a menacing silver mask. He made no attempt to approach or signal to the group that had appeared. He only stared through the mask's slits at M. K. standing in the centre.

"Erzse's bodyguard?" Xander asked quietly, recalling what the blond girl had told her moments before she blew herself up all those weeks ago.

"Henchman, right-hand man, doer of evil," M. K. muttered as he took in the lone figure. "All befit the bastard." He cupped his hands to his mouth. "And what can we do for you?" No response. "Well, I'm sure you didn't come all the way out here to catch a cold. What can we do for you? Fancy a beer? Maybe a woman? Come on, man. Speak up."

Ricard leant into M. K. "Nobody else about. Wouldn't be too hard to make him disappear."

M. K. gritted his teeth, clearly uneasy under the man's stare. "It's tempting." He cupped his hand again. "You've had your fun. If you're not here on business, and I'm certainly not letting you through these gates, you've got just the one option. Go back the way you came. What say you?"

A gust tore through the field, causing the torches to flicker and their clothes to tug. As the man's cloak whipped with the wind, he craned his head ever so slightly in Xander's direction. It was seemingly a reaction to the elements, but as the seconds passed, Xander felt an uncomfortable knot clamp onto her innards. She stepped to the side away from the apparent onslaught, and the man turned back to M. K. Moments later, he turned around altogether and, at a gallop, rode off in the direction of Zyphyr.

"One for theatrics, clearly," Joseph remarked.

"In this instance, no," M. K. said. "He was sizing us up." He looked at

Xander but didn't say anything, then made for the stairs. "I need to convene my captains. That man's presence is never a good omen."

Xander watched as M. K. and the others began down the stairs, leaving her alone on the breezy ramparts. She peered to the horizon, wondering if she could catch a glimpse of the man's shadow. He was no longer in sight, and yet she couldn't help but feel he watched her from afar. Suddenly uneasy at how exposed she was, she hurriedly descended the stairs onto the moor.

CHAPTER 38

Februarix 25, 485; Zyphyr, Zylencia—Evia turned to her bedroom door as laughter emanated from the villa's courtyard. She stood up and wandered over to the door to see Xander embracing Dogner and Joseph and Aika clasping hands with Wiston and Robyn. Despite the worry that had enveloped her in the preceding days, the sight of the girls was enough to brighten her mood.

"Evia!" Xander called, spotting her aunt standing in the doorframe. She raced over and hugged the woman. "Miss me?"

"You know I did!" she said as they released their embrace. "Was starting to wonder if you'd ever come back."

"What can I say, that cheese festival was something else. Oh! And I've got something for you." She rummaged through her sack and pulled out a small wheel of cheese. "M. K. says it's a special one."

A warm smile took Evia, and she embraced Xander again, this time not letting go.

"What happened?" Xander said, sensing her aunt's turmoil.

Evia pulled away and looked at her. "Let's talk in my room." She peered over to Joseph who was about to walk over. "I'll only be a moment!"

"And there I was, hoping for a hug," the man jibed.

"I'm sure a couple of minutes won't kill you," Evia retorted and ushered

Xander into her room. Closing the door behind her, she took a seat at the edge of the bed.

"What's wrong?" Xander asked with growing apprehension, sitting down on one of the chairs.

"Seems we've run into a bit of a problem. That creature that was after you, well, we found it under the city—"

"You went without me?" Xander blurted, shocked.

"We did."

"Then the cheese festival—what was that, a means to get me away?"

"Sorry, Xander. But I couldn't risk taking you down there without knowing what it was you were facing," Evia said crossly.

Though a tad annoyed her aunt hadn't trusted her enough to at least tell her, she let it go. "Okay. And what happened?"

"It killed itself."

"Killed itself?"

"Yes, as I said."

"But how? Or why? How odd."

Evia shrugged. "It didn't want to give answers. And I presume it figured out I was going to get them sooner or later."

"What were you able to find out?"

"Firstly, the sacrifices were made by a practitioner of the Zora to open a channel to the underworld in return for some sort of energy."

"Vile!"

"Indeed," Evia agreed. "Secondly, and just as concerning, the creature wasn't summoned by any practitioner of the Zora. Which means whoever's been sacrificing those girls wasn't the one to summon it. Problem is, I don't know who summoned it."

"All we know is that it can't be Erzse that summoned the creature?"

"Correct—besides the fact that I'm not even sure she knows who you are, she wouldn't have known your location by the twins. I think at this point we can conclude that something else has you in their sights."

"That's good to know," Xander muttered sarcastically, gaze to the floor. She peered up to Evia. "What can we do?"

"I can't risk you going back into those tunnels—"

"But you said yourself, the creature killed itself."

"Doesn't mean another can't be conjured. I'm too far in the dark to know for certain."

"Then come with me into the tunnels."

Evia shook her head. "The vote's in two weeks. There's too much that needs doing. And even if I had the time, where would we start?"

"Then what? I just wait here until when? You're building a political alliance against Erzse. Ricard and M. K. have an army. Dogner is your guardian. Aika represents the Great Forest in supporting your cause. And Joseph is using his network and skills to do all the above. Then there's me. Outside of this villa, nobody knows my name. I can't help you build your alliance or M. K.'s army. I don't have a network of spies and traders or a nation of people behind me that I can use to fight. Heck, I can't even—I *won't* support my father's legacy on the day of the vote. So let me ask you this—what use am I if I can't search for the shard?"

"I'm sorry, Xander. We'll have to figure something out, but for now, I can't have you in those tunnels."

Xander stared at her aunt. The joy of the festival was gone from the stern expression that had formed. Without a word, she got up and marched to the bedroom door and opened it. About to leave, she turned to Evia. "I *will* find another way."

At that, she left the room, leaving Evia alone and worried as to the ramifications of the girl's words.

CHAPTER 39

Februarix 27, 485; Zyphyr, Zylencia—Xander looked up from the candlelit maps on her desk, drawn to the sound of light chatter coming from the kitchen. Curious about who could be up at such an hour, she got up and poked her head through her bedroom door. A mist of light drizzle enveloped the courtyard, and a lone torch on the wall illuminated the space.

Unable to make out the speakers or the topic, she slipped out of her room and began for the kitchen along the slightly damp tiles. Pulling up to the door, she stopped short of walking in as Joseph's voice pierced the late-night quiet.

"My man can't get any closer," he said frustratedly. "As soon as the carts enter through the eastern gate, they veer north along a stretch of road with the palace to one side and the fortified wall to the other. Problem is, there are no windows, no doors, and the only means of getting onto the stretch is by passing through a checkpoint to the immediate right of the gate. Anybody trailing the carts will stick out like a sore toe."

"What about trying to access from the other end?" Robyn's voice carried.

"The area is cordoned off from the other direction. Only way is through the palace, but that section of the palace is also blocked off. Deserted and in disrepair from what I've heard."

"But if you could get a man in there, they'd be able to glide through without being apprehended."

"*If.* It's guarded. And there's no plausible excuse if discovered."

"Which is also suspect," Wiston spoke. "Obvious question coming your way, but you've tried getting a man into one of the carts?"

Joseph chuckled. "Obvious and insulting, perhaps?"

"Had to ask."

"Right. The carts leaving the plateau for the city centre carry only Erzse's closest soldiers. Haven't been able to infiltrate. Can't say the same for those caravans going to the mines or abroad."

"She's covering herself where she risks the most," Robyn commented.

"It's a dangerous game," Wiston said. "If her own were to find out she's butchering innocents for something so sinister, there'd be an uproar."

"Begs the worn question, why not just expose—"

A clang from the courtyard's garden shocked them into silence and Xander into a nervous crouch. A fountain ornament had slipped from its perch onto a stone, the result of the wet surface. Xander heard the muffled screech of a chair from the kitchen, and she swiftly turned and sprinted to her room, leaving the door slightly ajar as she rushed to her table and sat down.

Moments later a light rap came from the door, and she turned around. It was Joseph.

"You're up late," he said curiously.

"Could say the same of you," she responded innocently.

"Ah! Just catching up with the Eurencians." He peered to the table. "Still trying to figure out a route?"

"Trying. It's a bit of a lost cause at this point, though, wouldn't you say?" She picked up on the guilty feeling permeating him at what he had said, and she quickly sought to change the topic. "I happened across something today." She reached into her sack and pulled out the green book on coins that had been wedged beside the tome on Cresedi history. "It's a book on ancient coins."

"Oh?"

"You remember that coin you gave me for my seventeenth birthday?"

"How could I forget?"

"It was minted in an old Cresedi vassal state, from an era before the empires split." She looked at him with a suspicious grin. "Something you were trying to tell me?"

He laughed. "Nothing more than coincidence. Given what we've learned of late, seems the borders of that empire have shifted as much as they've expanded over the millennia. I'm sure there's not a nation or state in that region that's not had some interaction with the Cresedi."

"Well, seems a little more than coincidence to me, but okay."

"People can find causality in anything they put their mind to," he remarked as she offered the book to him. "Surely you'll need to return it?"

"Soon enough but thought you might want to read it. The librarian told me it's a rare one. Lots of coins in there you'll not find descriptions on for quite some distance."

A warm smile took him. "Thank you. I'll be sure to scan through it. Learn as much as I can before we're on the road again."

"You're welcome. And who knows—maybe you'll find a few more coincidences in there."

"Becoming quite the sarcastic monster, aren't you?" he jibed.

"I have good examples," she said with a wink.

"Careful, you. Anyway, best I get back to business. Won't do keeping them up waiting for me. See you in the morning?"

"We shall see."

He chuckled and left the room, leaving Xander to digest what she had overheard.

"Maybe there really is another way," she said ponderously, her mind drifting to what the man behind the silhouette had told her: "Follow the prisoners." The man who spoke in riddles. The man who, to her growing angst, hadn't appeared to her since the tunnels.

CHAPTER 40

Marx 2, 485; Zyphyr, Zylencia—Even from within the conference room, where the heat of the fire and the aroma of the teapot warmed the ambience, the grim weather outside was depressing to Evia. She, Dogner, and Aika had travelled to the eastern fringe of the city to join the first meeting of the recently arrived Eurencian senior ministers, Varela and Glandenhier. Born and raised in Eurus, Varela was a clean-shaven, wiry old man with a permanent scowl and fierce temper. Glandenhier, on the other hand, was an old man with a pointy beard from the plains of eastern Eurencia, and he was, for the most part, softer in features and personality than his counterpart.

"Listen to me, boy," Varela said to Wiston. "If giving her the position of prime minister will get her to commit her army, then it's a necessary action."

"You've read our reports, Varela," Robyn chimed in. "You saw the devastation yourself when you crossed through Borlencia. It'd be a grave mistake to vote her in. She's rash and not sound of mind. The old adage of 'beware inviting the wolf into the coop' couldn't ring truer when it comes to Erzse."

Varela peered to Glandenhier. "And what say you?"

Glandenhier contemplated for a moment and then directed a question to Wiston. "It comes back to this—can we beat the Cent without the support of the Zylencians?"

"We've already slowed their advance considerably with our horsemen. And Eurus and the pass stand between the horde and the west. We can prevent any further advance. To repel them altogether, though, will be tough. But it's also not impossible."

Varela scoffed. "Not impossible? Hardly words of encouragement."

"Nobody's saying you have to forgo help if you don't vote for Erzse," Aika spoke, irritated by the bickering.

"The woman's the definition of scorned," Varela retorted. "If we don't vote for her, she'd gladly see the destruction of Eurencia."

"And by extension, the whole of west Anemoi, because from what we've heard, the Cent will trample right through into Borlencia and eventually Zylencia."

"And your troops, Princess, will you commit them if Erzse turns her back on us?"

"Whoever we can spare, yes."

"Who you can spare? Promising."

"They have their own battle to win, Minister," Evia said. "Courtesy, again, of Erzse's war."

Varela bowed his head to Evia, his respect for the woman going back many decades. "She co-signed our debt agreement," he said. "She's loaned us a lifeline. If it takes a vote for her to get us her army, then I think it's a step we might have to consider."

"It'll be the end of Anemoi," Wiston said bluntly. "She'll consolidate her power. You know it's true."

"Then we use her to repel the Cent, and when the time is right, force her to dissolve the position. We could then make a move to prosecute her for her crimes."

"So let me get this straight, lad," Dogner said, leaning forward. "You'd accept her help and then go back on your word once the deed was done?"

Varela took in the man who held no official title. "I'm not sure which rock you've been hiding under, boy, but honesty isn't always synonymous with politics. Not when the survival of your people is at stake. Anyway, how's it any different from what the Borlencians are doing?"

Wiston stood up, his expression stern. "Please, Varela, I beg of you, do not give that woman the position of prime minister. It'll do more harm than good. If we block her vote, we can oust her and still get the Zylencians on our side."

"How?"

"M. K., Acro, and Aiden. All three senior ministers will support our cause. We don't need Erzse."

Varela shook his head. "But she has the support of the majority of Zylencia's common ministers and a large chunk of the councilmen."

"Many are loyal to Aiden, and he's loyal to us. She will be ousted, man. Don't fall on the wrong side of history."

"And if she wins and we've voted against her? We can say goodbye to any favourable terms. That much is certain."

"The alternative—"

A rap came from the door and a Eurencian guard poked his head through. "Aiden of the Zylencians and Ronal of the Borlencians are here."

Evia perked up, not having realised the two were acquainted beyond middlemen or that Ronal was even in town.

"Aiden?" Varela spoke. "Better late than never. Let him in."

"Will be useful picking the mind of a Borlencian senior minister," Glandenhier commented as Wiston sat back down and the guard left. "And should we also expect the rest of the Borlencian entourage?"

"None of them were due until the night before the vote," Evia said. "He's early."

The door opened and in stepped Aiden and Ronal. Aiden seemed less tired than he had the last time Evia saw him, and Ronal was obviously excited to have been invited to such a meeting.

"Gentlemen, ladies," Aiden greeted them as he took a seat. "Quite the pleasure."

Ronal strolled up to Evia and Dogner and shook their hands. "It's good to see you both."

"And you," Evia said. "We weren't expecting to see you for several days yet."

"Aiden invited me." He turned to the others, and they all introduced themselves one at a time.

With the greetings out of the way, everybody took their seats.

"What's the news in Borlencia?" Dogner asked Ronal.

Ronal, still new to such a senior role, spoke with an insecure undertone. "Erzse's troops are still stationed around the province—"

"Not for lack of trying on my part," Aiden interjected. "I think we initially agreed to wait until the day of the vote, didn't we, Evia? But sensing it might help to build some good faith, I tried to arrange a meeting of the Zylencian Lower House to discuss and vote on the topic. Was told it wouldn't happen before the meeting of the Upper House."

"Blocked by Erzse?" Evia asked.

"Presumably."

"A sign of Erzse's ingrained influence, perhaps," Varela commented nonchalantly, an obvious attempt to poke holes in Wiston's argument.

"It's politics, old boy," Aiden retorted. "She wants the Borlencian vote, and this is her leverage. And a number of the other ministers want the same assurances that I can't provide. Whatever way you look at it, the troops are there until the meeting of the Upper House."

"Have you met with her since you arrived?" Evia asked Ronal.

"This morning."

"The first since the Borlencians lodged the formal request to remove the troops?"

"It was. And got to say, it was a bit strange, but she seemed not to care. I was expecting a less civil reaction."

"I'd say a combination of time to digest and arrogance," Aiden said. "To her, winning the vote's a given."

"And your Borlencians?" Varela asked Ronal. "Any change in their leaning with respect to the vote?"

"She's got no friends amongst us. We tell her what she wants to hear but have no intention of giving her what she wants."

"That's good to hear," Glandenhier said. "I'd hate to think she had installed a puppet government after all that's transpired in Borlencia. As it is, it sounds like you and your colleagues can be relied upon. Which brings us to the vote, Varela. If the Borlencians can be relied upon to vote against her, it'd not be unreasonable for us to do the same."

The old man scratched the dead skin from his lips as he thought on it. "This only works if Erzse is ousted. We still need the Zylencians to fight. If we deny her the position, she will still have control of Zylencia's government and army."

"And suppose I gave you my assurance that she can and will be ousted?" Aiden asked.

"How?"

"Those loyal to me, including M. K. and Acro and their followers, will vote to have her removed from office."

"Have you got enough support?" Varela asked.

"I wouldn't be suggesting it, old boy, if I didn't think it possible."

Varela ground his teeth as he stared at Aiden, his unwillingness to trust clear to Evia. "Names. Give me the names of those who will support you, and I will consider it."

"Some may not be too happy to know their position has been given up so freely."

"Which begs the question, how invested are they in ousting the woman?"

Aiden deliberated quietly, and suddenly, for the first time, Evia could sense vulnerability in a man usually unreadable. It wasn't the words of his thoughts, or a glimpse of an image, but simply the raw emotion of vulnerability that told all. And then it was gone. His expression calculated and stern, Aiden spoke. "With their families at stake, I'll need their permission before I can divulge such information."

"If you give me names," Varela said, "I'll make sure every like-minded Eurencian votes in line with us. You risk your back, and I'll risk mine."

"So be it. I'll use my reservoir of goodwill to get you what you want. When ready, I'll arrange a meeting with you and your lot. In return, I'll need the same. Fair?"

Varela didn't have the same qualm. The risk of retaliation targeted at individual Eurencian ministers by Erzse was highly unlikely. "Fair."

"Thanks, Aiden, this is appreciated," said Glandenhier. "It will certainly help us to strategize when building the case."

The conversation was more subdued after this, with them touching on the finer details of the vote, the war casualties in Borlencia and Eurencia, the limited contact with the Notencians, and the bubbling unrest on the streets of Zyphyr. Due to Aiden's presence, Evia and the team remained tight-lipped about Grendal's plan to oust the Notencian parliament and Ricard's plan to vouch for Carolus on the day of the vote.

As the assembly began to pack up, Evia motioned to Aiden for a private word. He nodded, and they stepped outside onto the street, where prying ears were few and far between and the steam of their breath reached high.

"Is everything okay?" Evia asked him.

Neither his expression nor his mind revealed the angst of before. "Is this about Zylencia's army in Borlencia? I know—"

"Though I *am* a tad shocked you jumped ahead on that one, given your dismissal when we spoke on it initially, it's not what I'm referring to."

"Then what?" he asked with a hint of weariness.

"It's dangerous business dealing with Erzse. I just want to make sure you're okay. That she's—"

"Not compromised me?"

"That's…not what I was going to say." There was silence as she took the man in. "Did she?"

His tiredness evaporated, replaced by his usual keen sharpness. He raised an eyebrow. "Do you really think that possible, Evia? Please give more credit where it's due."

"You're the one that said it, Aiden, not me."

He looked at her, his expression straight. "Are you asking that I'm all dandy? That I'm not exhausted dealing with a woman I'm fairly certain has already descended into that cursed pit of madness? The woman's oblivious to the growing resistance in her ranks. She'll have nothing to stand on when the dust clears. What needs doing will be done. Enough for you?"

She nodded. "Yes. Thank you."

"Anyway, I must be going. I've got quite the to-do list to get through today. If you don't mind?" He lowered his head courteously and began back for the room to get Ronal.

"Oh, Aiden! I meant to ask, how's your family?"

She felt it again, the vulnerability.

He turned around and smiled. "They're great. Still hard to believe the wife would choose her mother over a little civil unrest. Madness permeates where madness is tolerated. I'll be seeing you soon, Evia."

At that, he entered back into the room, leaving Evia watching on uneasily.

▲ ▲ ▲

"What do you suggest?" Joseph asked Evia.

Evia and Dogner had found Joseph at his temporary office by the city's largest forum. It was here that he coordinated with traders doubling as messengers, traffickers, and spies. The space was unassuming, with a simple desk and a handful of chairs. Not what someone would expect to be the centre of a growing network tasked with rescuing Borlencia's refugees and undermining Erzse's authority. And altogether easy enough to discard on short notice.

"Can you have someone follow him?" Evia responded. "See what you can find out about his family? I need to know that they're okay."

"If he's been compromised, it could unravel everything we've built," Joseph said.

"I know, and that's why I need to find out as soon as possible."

Joseph picked up a book full of scribbled jargon and scanned through the most recent page. "I've got someone that can look into his family, but I'm short on hands if you need him followed." He peered up at her and Dogner. "I'm happy to do the legwork, but I'll need a cover here. Up to the task, Dogner?"

"You really can't spare a man?" Evia asked, unconvinced.

"For this, no. So, Dogner, what say you?"

"Where in Anemoi do I get started, lad?" he asked apprehensively. "And what about Evia—"

"Don't worry about me," she interjected. "I'll keep in Aika's company or the Eurencians'. I'll be okay."

Dogner shifted nervously on his feet. "Doesn't change the fact I've no idea where to get started with running whatever sort of outfit this is!"

"I'll run you through it," Joseph offered. "Anyway, you'll have a quiet couple of days from here, so I don't think you'll be too overwhelmed."

Dogner puffed his cheeks as he took in the scribbled jargon. "Can't say I'm too excited about this. You sure you'd leave it to me, lad?"

Joseph patted the man on the back. "I've got the utmost faith in you, my friend."

"Aye? Well, at least someone does."

▲ ▲ ▲

That evening—Xander glanced subtly behind her to the market square with the library and then back down the street leading towards the palace. Though the natural darkness of night had yet to fully descend, low-lying clouds from that afternoon's drizzle had blanketed the city in obscurity. It was a most perfect veil from which to sneak and pry.

Comfortable the coast was clear, she turned onto the street, away from the square. Casual in her movements, she traced her footsteps from the night she had followed the cart from the library, and almost every night since she had arrived back from the cheese festival, until the palace wall was in sight. She then veered off towards the stable that bordered the wall. Once outside, she entered the small, cosy café nearly opposite and ordered a glass of hot chocolate. With the frothy drink in hand, she took a seat by the window, where she had an unobstructed view of the stable entrance.

The clock on the café's mantle read fifteen minutes until seven, which meant she had another quarter-hour until the portly stable keeper would pack up and leave for the night. But not before coming into the same café for his takeaway dinner. From then, she would have another thirty to forty minutes to scale the wall and observe her intended target. Without fail, each and every evening, two prisoner carts would arrive from the plateau. The first would have already come and gone that night, but it was the second transport that she was after.

A tad nervous but altogether excited, she sipped her drink and opened her ears to the chatter of the café's patrons. Absent the slurred conniving of Zyphyr's stale taverns, the gossip was innocent and less depressing. Watching as she eavesdropped, and unable to avoid the inadvertent glance at the clock every minute on the minute, seven o'clock came and went. Ten past. Then twenty past. And still the stable keeper hadn't emerged from the courtyard for his dinner.

She bit her lip. Maybe she had timed it wrong. Or maybe today was his day off, and it was somebody else in his place. But who? She hadn't seen anybody else coming and going except for the odd patron. Frustration took her, but as she was about to get up and see if she could spot anything amiss, the man emerged in less of a rush than usual. Still, as predicted, he entered the café and trudged up to the counter.

She exited the café and started towards the gate but nearly stumbled as someone else emerged from the stable. Whoever it was, they had their back to her as they led two horses by the reins.

Trying to appear as inconspicuous as possible, Xander hopped to the building wall as she pulled her hood over her head and then slumped to the ground with her hands held out. The man, whose feet were the only part visible to Xander's averted gaze, slowly walked by, but not before dropping a shilling into her outreached hand.

Rather than speak and give up her Borlencian accent, Xander simply nodded her appreciation. But as the man continued on with his mounts, she noticed something strangely familiar about the character's gait and cloak.

"Joseph?" she mumbled under her breath.

Movement from inside the café caught her eye. Unsure if it was the stable hand or another customer, she got up and slipped into the stable. Desperate to make up for lost time, she sprinted across the courtyard after only a brief peep around and leapt onto the thick vine. Feet against the fortified wall, and half expecting the man to come back and raise the alarm at any moment, she pulled herself up.

She was two-thirds of the way up when the slam of the gate closing reached her. She paused and risked a look down. The courtyard was still and absent of noise. Cautiously, she restarted her ascent, each pull bringing her closer to the wall's summit. With ten metres to go, she was level with the adjoined building's roof. And to her surprise, she was relatively unbothered by the exertion, the aftereffects of the illness for the most part gone.

Two metres from the summit, the long strand of vine intertwined with a hardy, flowery bush burrowed into the wall's cracks. The viny bush sprawled in both directions like a wooden spider's web and gave no indication of strain under her weight. Carefully she pulled herself the rest of the way, stopping just short of poking her head over the armament.

Ears open, she ever so slowly edged her head over for a clear view. Chatter emanated from atop the gate to her left, where the wall continued south, and the flicker of torchlight revealed a small, fortified guard post on top of the gate. Whatever guards there were, all were situated inside. To the right, where the wall continued north, there was no movement for the length of the wall—it was quiet, dark, and concealed all the way to the next barely visible corner. And she was certain it was the same stretch of wall that overlooked the road of Joseph's conversation. Decided on what she wanted to do, but in need of a plan, she lowered her head and threaded her arms tightly through the bush.

Keen to see how far the mesh of vines flowed, she carefully leant back and peered right, along the vertical flat of the wall. It was difficult to determine, but from what she could tell, she had a good twenty to thirty metres of length. It would do. Constantly fumbling for a secure grip, she slowly shifted along the wall. Legs dangling, and grateful for the blanket of darkness, she navigated the width of the bush until the flowery web of vines ended.

Then, with a bit of a grunt, she lifted herself up and climbed over the wall. In the distance she could hear the continued chatter of the guards to the south, oblivious to her shadowy presence on the wall. Confident they wouldn't spot her but no less cautious, she continued along the fortification at a crouch. The farther she went, the darker it became, clearly supporting Joseph's assertation that the area was deserted. At the corner of the wall where it veered sharply to her left, or west as she figured, there was no sentry or fortification, only a clear line of sight onto the empty street below. The wall to the west was obscured by shadow, and not a sound emanated.

It was here that she would wait. Crouched on her knees and staring in the general direction of the gate, she inadvertently began to count the beats of her racing heart for every second that passed. As Dogner had taught her, it wouldn't do, and so she slowed her breath and cleared her thoughts until the thumps in her chest lessened in frequency and intensity.

A result instantly undone by the tremble of the gate opening. A cart entered the palace grounds. From her vantage point, she could see one of the sentries by the gate hand the driver a lantern and the cart start towards her. Anxiously waiting for it to near, a thought occurred to her. As it drew close, she again attempted to calm her breath, and this time, she reached out with her mind. Hopelessness greeted her. Utter hopelessness. Without a shred of doubt, it was the cart she was expecting.

At the corner, the vehicle veered west, and she slinked after it, always concealed by the obscurities on the wall. It was a game of chase that continued for ten minutes as the cart followed the zigzag of the palace boundary. There were no guards on the wall or in the street below, much to her surprise, and thus there was no artificial light. If not for the single lantern tied to the cart, the section would have been nearly pitch black.

The cart eventually came to a stop on the north side of the palace where the street had been blocked off. She figured it to still be some distance from the palace wall's north gate. Subtly, she peeked onto the road below and watched as a man in a silver mask emerged from the shadows.

"Him again," she murmured.

Unlike on the moor, she could feel his aura, and it was almost akin to a blank canvas, devoid of history, devoid of memory. She watched as he approached the cart whilst the driver hopped down, lantern in hand. Together they moved to the rear and unbolted the carriage door. Words were exchanged, and two guards emerged, slowly followed by five young women bound by the neck. Their faces were bruised and their postures exhausted. Xander had to quell the anger rising within.

More inaudible words were exchanged between the captors, and then the two soldiers and the driver led the women away from the cart towards the palace wall. The masked man trailed behind, vigilant. Thanks to the light, Xander could see the women disappearing through a trapdoor along with the soldiers until only the masked man stood outside. Again Xander noted that there was something odd about him, his movements somewhat unhuman. As he was in the process of entering the abyss, an odd curiosity suddenly beckoned Xander. Like a whisper in her ear, it asked her to reach out to the man in the mask with her mind.

As strange as it was, she was all too happy to give in to her innate inquisitiveness, and thus she projected her mind forward. But the man stopped still and turned around, causing her to stumble back before she could find his thoughts. Unsure if he had seen her, and too nervous to lift her head for a clear view, she kept to her crouch. And it wasn't until she heard the trapdoor close that she knew she had missed her chance. She crept back to the wall's edge. The masked man had gone and, with him, her chance to answer the beckoning.

Disappointed but no less pleased with the productiveness of her adventure, she climbed to her feet and jogged towards the east palace gate without the same caution as before. There she made quick work of the vine and didn't slow until within the confines of the villa. But rather than seek out Evia or the others and tell them what happened, she went directly to her bedroom, closed the door behind her, and slumped onto her bed.

She knew where the prisoners were being taken. She knew there were scant guards. Regardless of the risk, she knew what needed to be done. Whether through that trapdoor or the tunnels directly north of that position, she would enter the palace's underworld and discover with her own eyes what was down there.

CHAPTER 41

Marx 3, 485; Zyphyr, Zylencia—"How come you never told me about the twins?" Xander asked over the noise of the market, her arm interlocked with Evia's as she inspected a tray of fruits imported from the west.

In the weeks since the attack on Erzse and the subsequent unrest, daytime had regained much of its commercial and civilian bustle and differed only in the sinewy tension that still hung in the air. It was a tension that edged into the realm of eerie silence and anxious anticipation after sunset each day, for even though the arrests and riots had quelled to nothing more than a whisper, there was always that lingering memory of soldiers with malicious intent terrorising the city's inhabitants. Still, the day was young, and the pair felt comfort hugging a quarter not usually frequented by large numbers of soldiers.

"Theirs is a story for the ages and one not so easy to delve into if you're not wanting to reveal your truth."

Xander chuckled. "As in, you're a bit older than most would think possible?"

"Something like that! Difficult to fathom that they're nearly as old as me. They were just little sprouts when we first met. I was three, maybe four times their age back then. I can't recall exactly. What?"

"They insinuated you were, you know, maybe a bit older than that."

"Rascals! Well, whoever's in the right, most would likely argue that we're of the same generation."

"Ancient?" Xander jibed playfully.

"Hey, you! Anyway, they're a mischievous duo, those two."

"That they are!"

"I'll take a bag," Evia said to the trader and handed over a coin as Xander picked up the goods.

"So how did you meet?"

"Similar circumstances to you, if I can remember correctly. I was minding my own business on some errand that needed doing in the Great Forest when they took the opportunity to delve into trickery of the mind. Took me a good couple of days to realise that I'd taken the same stretch of road nearly a dozen times without any progress. It all looked the same, you see, with no landmarks to speak of. My only tell-tale sign was the length of time. Anyway, when I figured out somebody or someone had had me walking the same route over and over, I took it upon myself to teach them a lesson, and searching out the wisps of their minds, I located them and returned the favour. Really was quite fun."

"Truly are rascals!"

"Of course, when I found out they were orphans abandoned by their village to a life of squalor and barbarism, I took pity on the little cretins. I decided to take them under my wing and teach them the ways of civility, sky-whispering, and energy manipulation, not that they needed much help in the latter two."

"They're very gifted."

"Exactly." Evia pointed to a side street quainter than the last, and they rounded the corner. "It was not soon after that I met my dear friend Marcus, who you encountered under the lake. The four of us rode together for some time, getting into all sorts of trouble in the name of justice."

"Were there others?" Xander asked, eager for more.

"Yes. You can't live that long and partake in that many adventures without gravitating to others of a similar mindedness. A number of friends and allies came and went over the years. Some extraordinary and others ordinary but capable of the extraordinary. Oh! And here's a fun little fact. One of Aes's ancestors rode with us for a while. A prince uncaring of the antler crown that could be his. Really was a beautiful soul from what I recall."

"Have you heard from Aes? I've tried to reach out to him but with no luck." Xander felt the joy evaporate from Evia, though her aunt showed little reaction.

"As a matter of fact, I spoke to him only recently," she said nonchalantly. "He seemed fine. Something about—"

"No need to protect me. I know he's not fine."

Evia stopped and led Xander to the side of the street, out of the way of the traffic. "You're really getting very good at feeling out emotion and reading thoughts, aren't you?" she said with a mixture of pride and embarrassment.

"Emotions, yes, thoughts, not so much. But that's not the only reason I know you're not telling me the truth. He told me not all is fine the last time I saw him."

"Ah! Should've known."

"What's the update, then? Did he manage to find what was left of his herd?"

Evia frowned. "He found them. The ones that survived. And now he leads them to safety."

"Where?"

"Down to the Great Forest. At least there they'll have greater protection from Erzse's soldiers than could be afforded in Borlencia where the locals run scared."

"But there's a war in the Great Forest."

"South, where it's too wild for the humans. That's their destination."

"Then the bronzed deer is officially extinct in Borlencia," Xander said sadly, her shoulders slumping.

"Some of the herds will remain. And I've no doubt Aes will lead them home when it's safe to do so. As plentiful as the Great Forest is, it's not their habitat. It's a temporary refuge only."

"Will he return to join us?"

Evia pouted as she considered. "I…I don't know. That's for him to decide."

"I wish he'd have kept in touch."

"Aes feared it would be too much. With how your mind links to his, he worried that maybe his current emotional state would filter through to you and drive you to pick up and join him."

About to respond, Xander bit her lip. "I know what's required of me. I think I would've resisted. And if I were pushed to the point of insistence, Aika would've stopped me. She's good like that."

Evia chortled. "I'm sure she would have. Shall we continue?"

Xander nodded, and they merged back into the foot traffic.

Keen to brighten the mood, Evia jumped back into the conversation. "You know, one of our adventures brought me, the twins, and Marcus to Zyphyr. If I recall, it was in one of the buildings in this quarter that we conducted our business."

"And did they all have the pleasure of residing in your villa here? I assume it's been in the family for quite some time now?"

"Ha! I was wondering when you were going to ask me about it. I thought you might burst—you'd kept it bottled so long. Down here." She pointed to another side street.

"It's beautiful, and I can't imagine it, well, being an easy buy."

"No, but back then property was certainly cheaper. As you've discovered, Xander, I'm very old. I've had plenty of time to accumulate wealth, explore Anemoi and beyond, dabble in politics, and see the world evolve. I've seen loved ones move on, good people sour, and sour people sweeten. I've got more stories than there are stars in the sky and, once upon a time, networks as extensive as the most travelled traders. And it was only a short while before you arrived on my doorstep as a malnourished little girl that I had partially retired from such a life."

"How long's it been?"

"From today, twenty years or so."

"And Dogner played a part?"

"He was my strong arm for several years towards the end." Evia smiled warmly. "And, it would appear, still is."

"It must be lonely—to live so long, that is."

"Initially, but maintaining emotional distance made it easier. That and my work kept me busy. Not to mention the brief but frequent company of some very interesting people could make time fly."

They entered a busy market square filled with traders and tourists and soldiers.

"Evia!" called a woman from a stall on the corner.

"I'll only be a moment," Evia said excitedly to Xander and wandered over to the woman who looked of another land and carried an accent Xander didn't recognise.

Xander, in turn, wandered the square and eventually resolved to simply observe the business of the crowd, and though not as diverse or as big as the markets in Borealis, to her unaccustomed eyes, it was enough to invoke apprehensive excitement.

Slowly, her gaze drifted towards the far corner of the market square where the bustle was lighter. She tensed. Staring at her through the throng was the performer from outside the library. Draped in silver and wearing the colourful canine mask, the individual was sitting on a small crate with their back against the wall of a building.

The stare was as uncomfortable as the last time, but as she averted her gaze, a sudden curiousness not unlike the night before swelled inside of her. A desire to try to read the mind behind the mask. She turned back to the stare that hadn't wavered, calmed her breath, and cautiously began to reach out with her mind. Gently, like one would touch a newborn, she navigated the field of thoughts by lightly brushing past the people jostling between her and the performer. It was of little surprise to her that anger and frustration simmered beneath the surface of each and every person in that square. Like a sealed oven vent ready to explode.

And then she found it. A world a solar system apart, situated on the other side of the square. A world that, even in its unexplored state, exuded an incredibly powerful internal conflict unlike anything she had seen or felt. As if one hemisphere, completely devoid of feeling, emotion, or anything even resembling human thought raged over the other much-weaker human half. But what was most surprising to Xander was not the absence of life on the one side but the absolute familiarity of the human side, the man behind the veil of chaos. Intrigue took her, then dread.

The man got up and walked towards her. Unsure if he had felt her intrusion, she instinctively took a step back as the adrenalin coursed through her. But the worry was short-lived, for a sudden wobble in the field of emotions drew her attention. She peered to the side of the square where a ripple of commotion had emerged. Angry shouts and a wave of erratic movements betrayed the violence that was spilling into the space.

She jerked her head to the right as Evia grabbed her shoulder.

"We need to get out of here!" her aunt said sternly over the compounding noise.

Xander looked back to the other side of the square where the masked man had been and found no evidence of his presence. She turned back to her aunt and nodded, and the two swiftly left down an avenue on the side opposite to the forming unrest.

Every look back as they made the journey to the villa showed a scene of the discontent spreading across the city. Parents with children escaping the risk. Soldiers and ordinary citizens intent on a fight, either bounding towards the fray or tackling one another in the streets.

Safe in the villa, Xander and Evia immediately did a count on who was present and who had yet to return. Except for a few members of the

Eurencian delegation who returned a short while later, everybody else was already there.

Though not as violent as some of the previous riots, the destruction was still notable and continued well into the night. It later emerged that a number of political prisoners had been executed by the palace wall, sending an understandable wave of shock through the city.

However, despite the fires and screams and explosions emanating from outside the villa that evening, Xander's focus never wandered far from the man behind the mask. The man whose familiarity had come to unnerve her. A familiarity she just couldn't put her finger on.

CHAPTER 42

Marx 4, 485; small town ten kilometres east of the Zylencian border, Borlencia—"Pint o' laga," Joseph grunted in the deepest, most obscure voice he could muster, a determined attempt to not seem at odds with the carefully designed face he wore over his own.

"Mighty choice, that. And anythin' to eat whilst you're at it?"

Joseph waved his hand.

"Right! I won't be two moments. Oh! And if ya wouldn't mind removin' your 'ood, that'd be great. Tavern policy 'n' all."

Joseph reluctantly downed his hood, and the old tavern rat grinned with what was left of his yellow teeth before scurrying off to get the lager. Joseph rubbed his finger over an obscenity carved into the grotty wooden table and sneaked a glance behind, then abruptly brought his gaze forward.

"Bandi, pleasant of you to finally join." Aiden's voice rung clear. "Was starting to think the highwayman got the better of you."

"Ha! You a dee highwayman, brotha Aiden." A man with a dark-brown complexion and long angular features sneered as he took his seat opposite.

"Surely that depends on who you ask, old boy."

"Perhaps dis be true, but den, where be dis person dat says different? I don't no see him, not here, no way." The soft but strongly built man grinned broadly.

"Noted. So, Bandi, tell me what bothers you. Your letter suggested an uncomfortable urgency on your part."

"Yes, dis be true, brotha Aiden."

"Do tell?"

"Ya woman, she speaks to Grendal of Notos. She interferes with dis business."

"My woman?"

"De one dat goes by the name of Evia."

"And?"

"And does dis not botha you?"

"How could it? Grendal is but one man, a sheep amongst wolves, a mouse amongst rats, a—"

"Yas, yas, so you say, but he not very like the Buto, naw Bandi. What you say to dis?"

"I say—"

"Pint o' lager, as promised." The tavern rat interrupted Joseph's eavesdropping.

"Cheers," Joseph grunted, but the man didn't budge. "Yes?"

"That'll be a quarta shillin'."

"Reasonable," Joseph muttered.

"Try to keep the patrons 'appy," the wrinkled man said and walked off with coin in hand.

"Look, Bandi, let me put it this way," Aiden said. "How does a woman with no real power and who is far too late to the table have the resources or clout to win the vote and, more to your point, I'm sure, disrupt your valuable trade? She doesn't."

"Clout, what is dis?"

"Influence, clout means influence," he said with carefully hidden impatience.

The big man stared backed ponderously.

"Listen, Bandi. I can't stress this enough. Grendal is a non-entity that deserves no further qualm. He's already being dealt with." Joseph tensed at Aiden's words. "And neither woman you seem so intent—you'll have to excuse me, my messenger's arrived, and I have several urgent requests of him."

Joseph peered at Aiden's reflection across the tavern to the door and glimpsed the messenger with a thin chin and haggard forehead he and the others had first seen in Crowton. Aiden slipped the man a letter and began to whisper something in his ear.

Besides this encounter, Joseph had been unable to get any sort of close proximity to Aiden since the minister had left his home two days prior. The journey had seen Joseph tailing the man from afar to various suburbs and towns in the vicinity, presumably Aiden gathering permissions from his wealthy followers to divulge their names to the Eurencians. But Joseph had yet to land a snippet that could prove his assumptions right. Evidence contrary to Evia's misplaced faith. Aiden was being careful, as was to be expected. But the messenger, a man not bound by the restraints of image, could prove valuable.

"Excuse me, Bandi, old boy," Aiden spoke, bringing Joseph to. "It would seem something has come to light that requires my attention back in the city."

"What is da—"

"Yes, yes, I know. It was quite the trip for you," he said as he donned his coat. "Rest assured your worries are misplaced. I'll let my men know to make sure you're unbothered on your journey back to Buto, and if anything nefarious comes to light—"

The large man kissed his teeth, his annoyance at the dismissal blatant.

"You're in good hands, brother," Aiden said. "Our triad's survived a decade. It'll survive this. Trust me."

"We will see if dis is true soon enough, brotha."

"Farewell for now, Bandi."

There was no response as Aiden departed the tavern, leaving the big man alone at his table.

"Time to leave," Joseph whispered and downed his pint before following to the door.

He casually left the building and strode to the stable. From there he rode to the edge of town along the only road in and out of the settlement snuggled into the meander of a river. Concealed within the bush, he watched as Aiden galloped past with his entourage but didn't follow. No, he wanted the man not tethered by restraint. He wanted the messenger.

CHAPTER 43

Marx 6, 485; Zyphyr, Zylencia—It was early evening, and Xander was on her bed, tracing her finger between her map and a blueprint of the tunnels to the north of the city, when an eruption of voices from the villa courtyard drew her attention. She could hear Varela's interwoven with Wiston's and Evia's, along with a chorus of fiery mumblings in the background.

She got up, walked to the door, and stuck her head through. All the Eurencians were gathered in the dim courtyard along with Evia.

"What do you think's going on?" Aika asked. She was standing in her own doorway to the left of Xander's.

"Whatever it is, it doesn't sound good. Come on, let's see."

The pair slipped from their rooms and headed for the jittery congregation.

"If the Notencians have arrived," Varela began, red-faced, "it means that Grendal's failed."

A clearly alarmed Evia turned to Wiston. "And you're absolutely sure?"

"I'm certain, Evia. The entire Notencian delegation. All their senior and common ministers entered the city today. Even the ones supposedly loyal to Grendal."

"And Grendal himself?"

"Not with them."

Evia's expression hardened, and her eyes creased with worry. "We need to find out what happened."

"Naturally," Varela spoke. "But this does change things. Last I recall, we were relying on Grendal's success to not only get the votes to stop Erzse's play but to put the necessary pressure on her to withdraw her forces, and to ultimately support Aiden's plan to oust her. Without the Notencians, none of that is assured."

Xander could feel Evia's anger, even if she outwardly exuded calmness.

"What are you suggesting, Varela, that we simply hand Anemoi to Erzse?" Evia asked sternly.

Bickering flared through the group but quickly died down as Varela raised his hand for quiet. "It's not what I'm saying, but I do think it prudent to prepare for the possibility. The whole of Anemoi is at stake if we don't stop the Cent. We need to put our infighting to the side—"

"You've lost your mind, man," Wiston said coldly. "This isn't some little childish squabble. We're trading one threat for another. Do we again need to go through the risks to Anemoi if Erzse were to get that chair?"

Varela was about to retort when Robyn spoke up. "We don't know where the Notencians lie. We don't know with any certainty that they'll vote in favour of Erzse's motion. Our intelligence said only a couple had been confirmed as compromised by Erzse."

"Agreed. I think it's safe to say we don't know anything for sure about that peculiar group," Glandenhier said measuredly. "The Notencians might as well be another nation altogether, but that does suggest to me that there may be some hope. How likely are they to vote in favour of a motion that'll give a bureaucrat in the west even more power over their business? Not likely, I'd say."

"It's a gamble," Varela said bluntly.

"Then we play it by ear. We do our homework. And we hear out the arguments on the day. Let's make an educated guess as to which way they'll vote. If they're going to vote in favour of Erzse's motion, then perhaps it is such that we must also vote in favour. But if our judgment on the day suggests they may vote against her, then we can and should follow suit."

Evia shook her head, her frustration starting to show. "You already have the Borlencians. You have a chunk of the Zylencians. Even without the Notencians, you have a majority."

"It's not just the vote, Evia," Varela said. "It's the ramifications of Erzse losing the vote but still holding power in Zylencia. That's our fear right now."

"Aiden's furnished you the names of his supporters, has he not?"

"He has, but—"

"The only ones that can oust Erzse, short of direct political or military intervention from the other provinces, are the Zylencians. They already have the numbers to do it from within, but if Aiden's supporters see you, the Eurencians, turning cheek, that resolve may evaporate. We don't need the Notencians to do this, but we do need you and the Borlencians. It's the only way. We can make it work, *if* we stick together."

There was quiet as the Eurencians took in Evia's words.

Finally, Varela nodded. "We stick with the plan, but I'll need reassurance from Aiden. Seems we've recklessly placed too much on the shoulders of a single man who could turn coat at any moment."

"Do what you need to do, Varela," Evia said. "But I beg you, if you do find yourself backtracking from doubt, please consult us so that we can strategize together. We're in this together and should see this through together. I hope you can understand this."

Lips pursed, Varela put his hand to Evia's shoulder. "I trust you. I have every intention to do what's in the interest of my people, and if that requires me to follow you, then so be it."

Xander could sense the sincerity in the man's words, but she could also feel the growing worry stemming from his inability to control the situation. That in itself made Xander doubt the man's resolution. And she knew Evia felt it too.

CHAPTER 44

Marx 8, 485; Zyphyr, Zylencia—The library was quiet that afternoon, with only three of the regulars sitting in their usual spots around the building. Even the librarian seemed to not be quite there, drifting in and out of slumber, his snores disrupting the peace every little while.

In the preceding days, Xander's investigation had narrowed down to a single tunnel that could take her into the palace cellar under the northern wing. It wasn't marked on her special map, only on several other documents she had at her disposal. And there was also no guarantee it still stood, which left the trapdoor as her only known means of entry. A trapdoor with no telling how many guards stood behind it. Fatigued from the monotony of trying to figure it out, she had found herself increasingly hungry for the solace synonymous with researching the Cresedi. That morning, finally unable to resist the call anymore, she had simply upped and left the villa for the library.

Of course, like every other visit in those past months, her borderline obsession had translated into a marathon study session without the requisite meals and bathroom breaks. And now she sat there, desperate to finish a chapter on one of several Cresedi civil wars whilst her full bladder insisted on pressing painfully against her abdomen.

Fidgeting and shifting on the chair to distract from the discomfort, she was a paragraph from the end when it abruptly became a bit too much. Clambering up from the unfinished chapter, she yelped as she smashed her knee into the table leg and then rushed to the well-kept bathroom with a hobble. Inside, she closed the door behind her and dropped onto the toilet with a measured thud. The wave of relief to follow was immediate and lay somewhere between euphoria and ecstasy, as she internally described it.

Once again able to stand without impediment, she smiled as she pulled her pants up and then casually passed through the stall to the sink. Hands lathered and ready for the cold-water basin, she dipped them in as she peered into the mirror and then jerked them out.

"It's you!" she stammered in a hushed tone.

In the reflection, staring back, was the man hidden in obscurity. Her silhouette.

He dipped his head as she turned around. "Xander."

"I thought something had happened to you."

"Something did, but it's…let's just say it's resolved now."

"And you're okay?"

"Of sorts. Xander—"

"We've learned about the creature. The one you chased off."

"Oh?"

"It was summoned. We think from the underworld." Expecting some kind of reaction from the man, Xander grew suspicious when he didn't respond. "You know what it was, don't you?"

"Unfortunately. The creature was summoned by a witch doctor. A dangerous witch doctor at that."

Goosebumps erupted down Xander's legs. "A witch doctor? You're… you're sure?"

"I am."

"But how can you know this?"

"It's quite the—"

"No—no, quite the tale. How?"

"I've only a couple of minutes before I need to leave, and it would take me a literal evening to walk you through it."

"But—"

"An evening I will gladly give you, but not today."

Xander held her annoyance in check. "Then why are you here?"

"Tomorrow night will be your last chance to enter into the northern wing of the palace and get to the prisoners."

"Wait, how do you know—"

"Long—"

"Story. Right. What happens after tomorrow?"

"There's one tunnel still intact that leads to the rest of the undercity, but it's going to be collapsed the morning of the vote with what's left of the prisoners. Then the chambers directly under the palace will be flooded and sealed."

"Why?"

"Hide the evidence your friends need to tie her to the mass graves. Erzse is paranoid but no fool. She knows there's a chance she'll lose the vote and her position."

"Which means I need to try by tomorrow night," Xander mumbled. "There's no way I'll be able to do it then. It's the night before the vote."

"The tunnel is the same you've already identified under the northern wing. Take it—it won't be guarded. Anybody trying to enter through there needs to crawl through a good kilometre of sludge just to get to the entrance, so they see no point in manning it."

"Sludge?"

"Lots of it."

"Again, why are you telling me this?" she asked frustratedly. "Just tell me who you are."

"Like I said, you'll get that evening where I can walk you through everything. But until then, know this—this is the only way you can reach the shard. And you'll not get another chance like this. Not anytime soon."

"You're certain?"

"As certain as a weighted dice."

Suddenly the same unplaced familiarity she had felt in the man before rose to the surface, and then something clicked.

"You were the one in the square several afternoons ago?"

"I—"

"The one wearing the canine mask. The man trapped within his own mind." Heart racing, realisation struck again. This wasn't just any man from her past—this was someone important. Someone that had been close to her. She was absolutely sure of it. But his face, his face was still clouded in obscurity. Like a dream always out of reach, she couldn't reveal it. He wouldn't let her reveal it. "Stop blocking me!"

"You're not ready, Xander," he responded sternly.

"That's not your—"

He turned around and abruptly faded into nothingness, leaving her angry and severely irritated by the encounter. Grumbling to herself, she trekked back to her desk and slumped on the chair. Arms crossed, she stared out the window as she tried to grapple with the revelations and the truth that still eluded her. And even though there was no doubt as to the man's sincerity, she began to question her desire to keep the others in the dark. She breathed.

"There's too much at stake. I have to tell Evia."

Back at the villa—"What did you find out?" Evia asked Joseph as she poured a bowl of gruel for him.

"Aiden knows you schemed with Grendal," he responded wearily. He sat at the kitchen table, his clothes and hair matted with filth and his cheeks swollen from fatigue.

Evia's expression hardened, and she put the half-filled bowl down on the counter. "What else did he say?"

"Just that Grendal's being taken care of." He looked at the bowl. "I can—" he started, standing up.

"Sorry." Evia filled the bowl and then passed it to him before taking a seat opposite. The man practically scarfed it down as Evia continued. "The Notencians arrived several days prior. It seems Grendal failed in his mission, and now we know why."

"Any news of him?"

"None."

"Well, I think it's safe to say that Aiden played his part."

Anger wormed its way into Evia's already-stern expression. "What else did you find out?"

"His daughter and son are not with their mother. My guy couldn't find any trace of them. It's like they vanished."

"How odd. Why lie about that?"

"I don't know," he said.

"I need it to make sense. What else did you find out?"

"I followed him to one of his dingy ratholes in Borlencia and spied him talking with a dangerous man not of Anemoi. A smuggler and murderer that goes by the name of Bandi. He's of—"

"The Buto."

He scraped the last of the gruel from the bowl and swallowed it. "I'm guessing Grendal's updates had all the finer details?"

"They did. Bandi and his nation of thieves and outcasts and pirates are actively working to destabilise Notencia with their supply of narcotics. You know, my initial thought would've been that Aiden's conversation with the fiend is simply an extension of Erzse's attempt to sow more discord. Buy the ministers through their addiction and create a plight that begs intervention from the other provinces. But his admission regarding Grendal's well-being is concerningly drastic."

"Grendal must've already had some success in blockading the Buto ports, then, to invoke such a reaction."

"The Eurencians hadn't reached any agreement with him to supply marines. It was a work in progress."

"Then someone leaked the plan?" he said, sitting back, arms crossed. "You know, even a hint of it would've been enough for the Buto to take it as a declaration of war, especially as Bandi is revered in some parts."

Evia rubbed the bridge of her nose. "A blockade on its own was unlikely to push either party into total war. The consequences would be too great. And to take out Grendal, whilst not beyond Erzse, is certainly not in Aiden's character. To date, he's been the more measured of the two, keeping her in check. And to what end anyway? The region teeters on destabilisation, and a portion of the ministers are suspected as already being compromised by Erzse. We're on the eve of the vote. So why go through the trouble of removing Grendal because of a blockade that has yet to be enforced? Unless…oh my."

"Unless it's Grendal's plan to push out the Notencian ministers in Bulgar that's been revealed."

Sadness took her. "That would be…unfortunate. If Erzse has part of Notencia's leadership in her pocket, then it makes sense that Grendal was too dangerous to leave unobstructed. Poor Grendal. It would also mean someone he trusted threw him to the wolves before he could enact it."

"The Eurencians?" Joseph queried.

"Or even the Borlencians. Santos, Fredrick, heck, maybe even Ronal. All were acquainted with Grendal. Could've been anybody." She looked at him, his reaction to the mention of the mayor's name intriguing. "What else?"

"I followed Aiden's messenger over a three-day period. The man took me through various towns in the two provinces and then brought me back here. It was a route that took him to one of the garrison's commanders that's loyal to M. K., to three other riders perched at different intervals on the road between Zyphyr and the south and east, to Ronal—what's wrong?"

"Ronal's relationship with Aiden has me uncomfortable, given we no longer know where the latter stands. It leaves a frightening cloud over our so-called alliance."

"Then you can decide what to make of it from this next piece of news." He reached a hand into his pocket, and for the first time Evia spotted Joseph's bloodied knuckles.

"Your hand. What happened?"

"I intercepted him."

"Who? The messenger?" she asked with growing alarm.

"He has no idea it was me. It was dark, he was drunk, and I returned everything to where he would rightfully expect it to be. He had only two letters on him," he said, putting the traces of the letters he had made onto the table. "I caught him after a meeting with Acro."

"Acro—M. K.'s cousin?"

"Yes."

About to cuss, she held her tongue. "What do the letters say?"

"The one from Acro says that M. K. will be attending the preliminary meeting the morning of the vote."

"Which doesn't suggest foul play. They're all Zylencian ministers working to oust Erzse. Communication's to be expected."

"The other is from Ronal. 'The Borlencian vote is confirmed.'"

Evia bit her lip as she sat back. "Again, that doesn't mean anything malicious. If Aiden *is* still aligned with us, then all that means is nothing's changed."

"Is he, though? His ties with Bandi suggest he's linked to the Notencians in a nefarious manner. And Grendal's—"

"Bandi could simply be a pawn. And Grendal would've thrown into disarray any plan they had to use the existing Notencian leadership," Evia remarked. "Grendal's also a natural enemy of the Notencians in power. This could be Aiden's means of appeasing them."

"Then why not tell us?"

"We're friends with Grendal. It wouldn't make sense for him to do that."

"Possibly," he said, unconvinced. "But just the way he spoke about you, Evia—I don't think he's aligned with you. I really don't. And we already know he despises Erzse. I honestly think he's looking out for himself."

"You never did warm up to him, did you?"

"I'm being serious."

"Okay. Then to what purpose?"

"Maybe he wants the chair for himself."

She puffed her cheeks and then blew through pursed lips. "Everything you've told me suggests he still appeases Erzse whilst building the resistance to her. One's a continuation of her plan, and the other is support for our own."

"Okay, then what of his family? Why give us that whole ruse?"

"That's the part that we need to work out."

"Fine. What did he actually tell you?" he asked.

"That they'd moved to the countryside to avoid the violence of the riots."

"And?"

"I could feel his vulnerability and unadulterated fear at the mention of them," Evia admitted.

"Of course, he was vulnerable. He fears for their safety."

"But why lie about their whereabouts?"

"For the same reason we've lied to him. Because he doesn't trust us."

There was an uncomfortable quiet as they both contemplated, with the dull noise of the street all that filled the air. Finally, after a number of minutes, Joseph spoke.

"Why continue to pursue destabilisation in the east so close to the vote when you wish anything but?"

"The facade of allegiance to Erzse."

"Or perhaps Aiden's work to destabilise the east is not simply him biding his time and demonstrating a false allegiance. Either he's in cahoots with Erzse, or he's doing it to further his own agenda. His meeting with Bandi and the removal of Grendal both keep the door open to intervention in a failed state. It also ensures that the compromised Notencians continue to rely on the Zylencians. The same could be said of the Eurencians and co-signing their debt agreement. And what about the Borlencians? We have no idea what happened in those meetings between him and them. He purported to play the middleman, helping Ronal to convince Erzse of the brilliance of allowing the Borlencian election, but what if both he and Erzse secretly played us? Heck, even his alliance with M. K. and Acro could be suspect at this point."

Evia balled her fists. "What are you up to, Aiden?"

Joseph leant forward, his eyes intent. "We have to consider the possibility that we'll lose this vote. That Erzse will get her chair and full dominion of Anemoi. If that happens, the city, heck, western Anemoi will no longer be safe for Xander or yourself. I'm sure all that's stayed Erzse's hand against you is the need to appear unblemished. Perhaps…perhaps it's time to start thinking about getting out of the city when the time comes."

The front door clicked shut, and a moment later Xander entered into the kitchen. Her determined gaze brightened at the sight of Joseph's tired form but swiftly reverted to its former intensity.

"What's happened?" Evia asked before Xander could speak.

Xander glanced at Joseph, then back at Evia. "The man visited me again. The last of the prisoners will be executed—sacrificed—the day of the vote, and then the prison filled in. Erzse killed all those girls, and now she fully intends on hiding any connection that could lead to her."

Confusion took Joseph. "Who told you this?"

Xander hesitated, unsure how to tell him.

Evia cleared her throat. "A man's been visiting Xander in her…" Also uncertain how to put it, she simply tapped her head.

"In your dreams?" he asked.

"In her mind," Evia answered.

"And he told you the prisoners are going to be executed?" he asked Xander.

"He told me that once the chamber is filled, it'll prevent me from getting to the shard. That it's now or never."

"What chamber?" He stood up as his weariness rapidly morphed into obvious concern for the girl and her words. "How do you know where the prisoners are? I don't understand." His mouth dropped. "You heard every word I told the Eurencians, didn't you?"

"Most of it."

"And?"

"I climbed into the palace—"

"Xander!" Evia blurted angrily.

"I followed the cart to the north wall," Xander continued, "and saw the exact door they were being taken into. I then made note of the landmarks and have spent the past few days identifying all the possible entry points through the tunnels. I know where they are. I know how to get to them. And I know it's the only set of tunnels that have gotten me anywhere near to that shard on the map. And if what he says is true—"

"A man who, by the sounds of it, you've never physically met?" Joseph said in disbelief. "Do you even know who he is?"

"If what he says is true, the day after tomorrow I'll lose any chance of getting to the shard."

Evia bit her lip as her shoulders slumped with worry. "Bring me the maps you have. Ignoring the fact that I've had no direct involvement in the hiding of this particular shard, and that I can't read the special map you carry, I'll at least be able to give you a second pair of eyes with what you can show me."

"Evia?" Joseph said, alarmed.

"I'm sorry, Joseph," Evia said. "It seems our options are quickly dwindling. We'll need every chance we can get." Xander threw Evia a questioning look. "I'll explain later. Bring me what you have."

Xander disappeared and then reappeared with the bundle of maps and scribblings she had made in the prior days. She rolled them across the table, and they began to pore over them.

"This is the tunnel I found," Xander said, pointing to one of the maps. "It's the same one he told me to take."

"Is this before or after you found it yourself?" Joseph asked distrustfully.

"I found it before him. He reaffirmed it."

"And how do we know he wasn't watching you and has decided to lure you in there? Catch you off guard?"

"It's not true that I haven't seen him in person. I didn't know it at the time, but twice he's been near to me, and twice he didn't do anything. If he wanted to do something to me, I think he'd have done it already."

Joseph swore an old Borlencian curse word. "The lot of us will've gone mad if we were to let you go ahead with this."

"When will you go?" Evia asked to both Xander's and Joseph's surprise.

"Evia, please—" Joseph began.

"Tonight, maybe?" Xander interrupted.

Evia squirmed. "No planning—"

"I've planned it all."

"Okay, then too rushed. You'll need Aika and some of Wiston's men. None of whom have been briefed."

"Wiston's men? They'll—"

"What? Slow you down? What do you expect to do when you get to that prison and you're confronted by guards? Or run into another one of those creatures?" About to continue her scold, Evia seemed to pale. "Is it true?"

"I didn't say anything," Xander said, confused.

"You practically shouted it, dear. Something you'll need to work on. Tell me then, is it true?"

"It's what he told me."

Evia slumped into her chair. "Then what I feared is correct."

"You know what I fear?" Joseph began. "Or dislike, I suppose. It's suspense. Do you care to enlighten me?"

"The creature was summoned by a witch doctor."

"The same religion that was run out of town and is now looking for a foothold in Notencia?"

"Anemoi, it would seem."

"And why would this witch doctor summon the creature to go after Xander?" Joseph said worriedly.

"I have no idea. But it—"

"Doesn't change anything," Xander spoke. "It doesn't matter who summoned it. This is my window. I'll take Aika, but I won't take Wiston's soldiers."

"But—"

"I need to sneak in there. Not take the place. Aika's a natural. Clunky horsemen on foot aren't."

Evia held Xander's stare and then looked at Joseph. "Seems neither of us will fully get our way. Both of you, let's start preparing our belongings in the event we need to leave the city at pace. Xander, go tomorrow night when we meet with our allies. Erzse and her own will be doing the same. You're less likely to encounter the woman down there."

"Smart choice," Aika said from the doorway. "Also, it's not ideal in light of the soldiers on the streets, but we should enter through one of the manholes close to the tunnel. It'd take an age from here at night."

"How long have you been standing there?" Joseph asked.

"Long enough." She grinned. "Like Xander said, I'm a natural."

CHAPTER 45

Marx 9, 485; Zyphyr, Zylencia—Worry ate at Evia as she took in the guests assembled in the rented hall. The entire Borlencian and Eurencian delegations sat at a large circular table in the centre, eating and chatting away. Ronal, as the nominated head of the Borlencian delegation and a born political influencer, was all too happy to take his place next to Varela and Glandenhier on the opposite side. Wiston, Robyn, and Joseph sat apart from Evia, keen to make inroads with Borlencian unknowns, and Dogner stood in the corner, watching over the lot of them.

Evia was sitting between a severely inebriated Borlencian common minister to her left and a Eurencian councilman to her right who had little, if any, say or opinion on the upcoming event. It was a temporary wall of solitude she had purposely designed to allow herself an opportunity to pry. That is, if the incessant angst that was wholly distracting would just allow her.

Again, she tried to calm her nerves, to pay vigilance to her surroundings and the trove of information that could be delved into. And again, she found herself weighed not just by the gnawing doubt that had been sown by Joseph's words but by her shocking inability to part the veil of distortion that had clouded her mind and the air of the room. Something wasn't right. Her gut screamed as much. But what?

Struggling for focus, she jumped as a hand tapped her shoulder. "Santos. When did you…how good it is to see you!" she said, getting up and hugging the man.

He smiled. "And you, Evia." He peered around the room and then back at her. "Not like you to not mingle."

"I needed a break. When did you arrive?"

"With this lot. But I had a few things to take care of." His face hardened. "Have you got a minute?"

"Um…" She glanced around. Nobody watched. Nobody cared. "Okay."

The pair vacated the room into the corridor outside.

"What's wrong?" Evia asked.

"Grendal's been arrested."

"Where?"

"You don't seem surprised."

"I had already deduced something had happened."

"He was arrested on the road to Bulgar," Santos replied. "At least that's what I heard. Word is the Notencians believed he was riding there to stage a coup."

"Any hint as to who made the allegation?"

"No. So, is it true?"

"Coup is a stretch," Evia said. "He's a Notencian merchant doing what he thinks is in the best interest of the Notencians."

"Guess it depends on perspective. I don't know who his accuser is, but the soldiers who took him were Zylencian, if that helps."

"Not sure it matters at this point."

His sternness didn't waver. "There's more."

"I'm not sure I can take any more bad news."

"You need to hear it."

She nodded her head, inviting him to continue.

"It's Borealis," he began. "It's not just movement on the walls. My contact tells of fast riders to and from the city and the desert. These aren't your average traders. Something stirs, and it can't be good."

"Then I imagine they've begun the next phase of their conquest."

"Conquest? You think—"

"Why else?"

He shuddered. "Now that's a foe I'd rather not encounter again. The cunning black holes that bore the masks of those beasts and that screamed of a collective desire to win at all costs—it made for a frightening experience I'd like to forget."

"As would we all. Tell me, what's the new parliament's reaction?"

"They're too busy with the vote. Not sure I could say they've done much leading, if any, to date. Fredrick and I, on the other hand, we've not been idle."

"Oh?"

"You're probably not going to like what I'm about to tell you, but here it is. We've been expanding the number of groups and multiplying our routes. The network now spans most of the northern half of Borlencia, and we creep farther south every day."

"Sounds a bit more extensive than what we had agreed to, no?"

"*You* had agreed," he retorted. "But you've also not been in the picture for some weeks now. Much of the traffic in prisoners around Crowton dried up. The Zylencians were taking wider routes and drastically smaller groups. We had no choice but to expand the net or not catch any of them. But we've got the beginnings of a region-wide militia now. Still small but well trained in counterinsurgency. And word has spread of the danger to the north. With time, and without the threat of repercussion from Erzse, we could transform it into an army."

"This is good news, Santos. Finally, something to be hopeful of."

He looked puzzled. "You've got half of Anemoi's Upper House in that room ready to vote in line with you. I don't understand what more we could ask for."

"I don't know. Something's not right. And I can't put my finger on it. Something—someone, maybe—isn't what it appears to be, and I can't figure it out." She shook her head with frustration. "I'm worried I've missed something. That we all have. And that whatever it is, it won't be revealed to us until tomorrow."

"Then let's hope for the best."

"That's the worst part; I think that's all we can do now." She looked at him. "Shall we go back in?"

"Sure. Oh, where's Xander? I was hoping to see her tonight."

"She's doing what she must, as are we."

CHAPTER 46

The tunnel into the palace's underworld was, as had been aptly described, plastered in grime. Horrid smells clung to every corner and chamber, and the structure itself seemed to enjoy throwing its two intruders into disarray at every bend with unseen drops, pools of stagnant water, and vertical climbs up and down onto different levels. It was quite unlike any they had come across in the preceding weeks, and it left Xander doubtful of them encountering any sort of resistance.

"Pass the torch," she called up to the level above where, for the umpteenth time, the architect had seemingly decided to change the tunnel's depth without reason.

Aika leaned over and dropped the torch to Xander, and then she climbed down the slippery moss of the brick wall into the unnatural darkness of the chamber.

"Can't blame the last bearer for hiding the shard down here. Smells absolutely rotten at the best of times. Nobody in their right mind would dare linger. Of course, we're not in our right minds," she said and stretched her back, thankful for the opportunity to stand.

"The bearer didn't come down this tunnel," Xander said, peering into the blackness ahead.

"Nonetheless, it's all the same—"

The girl dropped through an opening in the grimy brick floor into a chamber below.

"Aika!" Xander shouted.

"I'm okay! Not far enough to break a leg…just enough for a sore bottom."

"What do you see?"

"Not much. Drop the torch…It's high enough to stand. There's a ladder knocked into the brick, but it's broken. We'll need to use the rope to get me out."

Xander withdrew the line and scanned the floor for a wedge.

"Hey, do you hear that?" Aika called.

"What is it?"

"I can't tell. It's distant. Sounds like it's coming from up there."

Xander tensed as she peered around. "I don't hear anything," she whispered down.

"Either way, might be a good time to pull me out."

Xander tied one end of the knotted rope around her waist, dropped the loose end into the chamber, and then leaned back so that the rope was taut against the opening. Even with the torch squeezed between her legs, Aika made quick work of the rope.

As Aika stood upright, they both turned and stared into the darkness.

"You heard it this time?" Aika asked quietly.

"I did."

"What was it?"

"I've no idea," Xander replied sternly.

"We must be close by now, right?"

"It's so hard to tell."

Aika looked at her. "If we're near, it wouldn't be sensible to take the torch."

"And if we're not?"

"Then let's just leave it here, propped up," Aika suggested. "Worst case, we come back and get it."

"If we can't see their light, they can't see ours. And what if it's one of those creatures?"

"Didn't think this part through, did we?"

Xander shrugged. "I didn't think it'd be pitch black. Pretty much every other tunnel we've been down has had some light."

"Crazy to think they've been dragging those bodies along here."

"Must have whole teams doing it. How about this? You hover a short distance behind me with the torch, and I'll scout ahead. I can give warning, and if anything happens I either run to the light or you run ahead to me. Whenever I hit a bend or drop, I'll wait until you catch up."

"It'll have to do."

"Glad you approve."

"After you, then," Aika said, inviting Xander to continue with her hand.

Wary of her footing, Xander crept ahead whilst Aika lingered behind. Once there was a full thirty-metre gap, Aika, too, began to creep ahead. It was a setup they held for only three minutes before Xander came to a stop in a narrow tunnel. Ahead in the distance was an orange glow so faint that one might mistake it for trickery of the eyes. She swiftly turned around and backtracked, startling Aika as she appeared out of the dark.

"What's wrong?" Aika asked.

"I think we're near the end. Leave the torch."

Without the torch, they continued cautiously towards the dim flicker of light and shadows.

"What the..." Aika unintentionally heaved at the rotten stench that lingered metres from the opening, and Xander swiftly clasped her hand over the other's mouth.

Both tensed in nervous anticipation as a passing silhouette abruptly froze in the opening, and only when they had verged on collapse under the weight of their gag reflexes did the figure continue on and provide them the opportunity to regress far enough to be free of the onslaught.

"That's not natural!" Aika spat. "It clings to my tongue and burns my nostrils."

Xander took a swig of the water bottle and then passed it to Aika, who greedily took it in her mouth and spat it back out to cleanse her palate.

"How do you suppose we get past that?" Aika said with disgust.

"Hold our breath again and hope there's nobody on the other side when we exit the tunnel?"

"And if it doesn't disappear?"

"Then we'll just have to get used to it."

"That's the smell of death, Xander. Have you ever heard the saying—"

A loud, agonising scream emanated from the opening, followed by wicked laughter and the rattle of metal.

"Must be one of the prisoners," Xander whispered. "We're so close. Still want to leave?"

"No," Aika replied solemnly and tied her oil-clad cloth over her mouth.

They tossed their sacks to the mucky ground and drew their weapons, and then they crept to the opening of the next tunnel, which was not more than a hundred metres in length.

"I think that's the exit." Aika pointed to the door at the end of the tunnel on the left. "And see the doors along the walls? Cells maybe?" she whispered when another scream rang out.

"It came from that end." Xander pointed to the open door at the end of the tunnel to the right. "Wait here and cover my rear. I'll check it out."

She edged along, wary of her shadow's tendency to dance enthusiastically under the gaze of the torches hung on the walls. Pressed against the wall, she had passed only three doors when curiosity overwhelmed her, and she took a risky glance in the nearest room.

"Empty." She breathed in relief.

"Why?" a girl's voice cried. "Why ya doin' this, ya monster?"

Xander's stomach clenched, and her spine tingled. With greater urgency, but no less caution, she crept to within a metre of the opening and dropped to her stomach. Carefully, she pulled herself to the edge and peered into the circular chamber. Horror took her.

In the pit below, the girl that had attacked Erzse at the procession squirmed from wall chains that gripped her wrists and suspended her off the floor. Her hands had been brutally mangled and her once-soft features cruelly mutilated. Dried and fresh blood matted her torn blond hair, and similar to some of the discarded bodies they had happened across in the dank, frightening undercity, a vicious design had been scratched into the girl's skin. And still the cloaked tormentor stood before her, hungry for more.

"Please!" The girl sobbed through her disfigured mouth, and again the demented tormentor, whose face Xander could not see, took to their work with no reservation or qualm over the agony caused.

Xander's hair stood on end, and a sudden rush of anger and hatred flared within, but as she was about to draw her blade, the tormentor's hand stopped, leaving the crude tool still stuck in the girl's flesh. Xander, too, stayed her hand and observed with barely contained fury as the object was slowly and agonisingly withdrawn.

The tormentor stood unmoving for a dozen heartbeats, as if admiring the crumbling brick wall, and then, with their face still undiscernible from the door, dropped the tool and casually reached for a rusted saw. Xander drew her blade and stepped towards the monster now taking aim at the girl's hand, but barely had she entered the foul-smelling room when she was gripped firmly from behind and put to sleep by a pungent metallic odour.

CHAPTER 47

Marx 10, 485; Zyphyr, Zylencia—Evia took a deep breath as she readied to leave the bathroom directly outside the palace hall. Worry gnawed ferociously at her stomach, and her heart felt as if it would give out at any moment. She shakily turned the doorknob and then exited the room with as straight a face as she could muster.

Only a couple of hours earlier, as she, Dogner, and Joseph were preparing to make the journey to the hall that would accommodate the vote, Aika had appeared bloodied and covered in grime. Welts plastered her face, and the blood of others matted her hair and clothes. In her hand was Xander's sack containing the map. Evia didn't need to wait for Aika to catch her breath or to even pry into the girl's mind. It was obvious what had happened.

Xander had been captured. And Aika, having failed to rescue her friend, had been forced into a long and dangerous chase through the undercity, pursued by the same henchmen—an exhausting ordeal that had left the poor girl a tired mess inflicted with guilt.

Evia, as desperate as she had been in those initial moments, had had little choice but to swallow her worst fear, subdue her own guilt, and make for the hall. For today was a day that they had all fought too hard to make happen. Leaving Dogner with Aika, Joseph and Evia had made the walk with haste, sombrely contemplating every conceivable outcome until the ominous black structure of their destination loomed overhead.

The diamond-shaped hall was gigantic, and tall stained glass windows lined all its walls. Throngs of standing Zylencian citizens crowded the rear, and in the centre of the room there were hundreds of seats filled with individuals like Evia—someone who held, or had held, a position of note. Someone who was perhaps acquainted with the process or the ministers.

The ministers themselves sat to the front on an elevated stage for all to see. Sixteen senior ministers and thirty-two common ministers. Each province adorned in its colours and insignia, all sitting amongst their own. The Eurencians were gathered to the far right, opposite the Borlencians to the far left. The Notencians were huddled off-centre to the left, and the Zylencians were dead centre, Evia presumed deliberately. To the side stood a decrepit old man resting on a podium: the mediator. A scar ran the length of his left cheek, from the edge of his lip right up to the tip of his ear.

Wearily, Evia navigated the rows of chairs and slumped beside Joseph. Not a moment later, and despite the noisy chatter, Joseph leaned over and whispered cautiously into her ear, "Notice anything amiss?"

"No games, Joseph. Tell it as it is."

"M. K.'s not up there."

She immediately peered up to the Zylencian gathering. "And yet there's—"

"Twelve ministers sitting up there."

Her gaze caught on Erzse. With the distance she couldn't quite tell if the woman was staring back or if her scowl was simply aimless. Nonetheless, Evia sensed nothing but a black hole of emotion and thought emanating from the woman. A dark veil of mystery that was a tad unnerving. Curious if the woman's counterparts would give up something, Evia scanned the rest of the delegation. Aiden was sitting next to Erzse, as was who she assumed to be Acro, given he was the only Zylencian minister with a thick red beard. They, too, seemed to exude no emotion or thought. A slightly odd coincidence, Evia concluded.

"Then he's been replaced?" she asked.

"That'd be my conclusion."

"But how? Who voted and when?"

"My guess is as good as yours," he replied.

"I don't like this."

"Me neither. Fancy doing a little digging?"

"Naturally."

Slowly, she worked her way through the other provinces, determined to suss out any further unexpected surprises. Wiston and Robyn sat quietly with Varela and Glandenhier to the front of the Eurencian congregation. Nothing seemed out of place in what little internal chatter arose from that sphere of stern men. She looked to the far left where the Borlencians sat. Ronal was in the second row speaking busily with a woman Evia recognised from the Borlencian election. There were others, some she recognised, others she couldn't quite make out. Gently she delved into the minds of the entourage she had helped get into power and again found nothing out of the ordinary. No nerves beyond what might be expected of fresh politicians eager to make a name, no thoughts of malice or betrayal. All was normal on the Borlencian front.

"Now the Notencians," Joseph said.

She looked at him, eyebrow raised.

He shrugged. "I may not be a mind reader, but your sequence is pretty obvious."

If not for the hurt that weighed so heavily on her, she may have smiled. Instead, she directed her hardened expression towards the Notencians. The group was of darker complexion than the rest, and besides the one man she vaguely recalled from some prior encounter she couldn't place, the others were unknowns. At least, as far as she could tell.

Still, she reached her mind forward, eager to explore and understand those who could sway Anemoi's future on that day. Gliding through the thoughts and emotions that reeked of inebriation and the rot of corruption. Touching and glimpsing their histories. But finding nothing. There wasn't even a whisper of where their decision swayed. How could it be that not a single one of them dwelt on the vote to come? Unconvinced, she dove back in with less caution.

"You okay?" Joseph asked as she flinched backwards.

"Someone caught me snooping," she said, alarmed.

"Which one?"

"I…I'm not sure."

None looked her way. None seemed to have stopped in their friendly banter. Evia was about to speak when the mediator stepped to the front of the stage with his hands raised for quiet. Slowly the chorus of voices died down until an anxious silence held the room.

"Today, at eleven o'clock on the tenth of Marx, we hold the long-awaited meeting of the Upper House to discuss and vote on the abolition of term limits and the election of a prime minister outside of wartime as a means to ensure Anemoi's future." To Evia's surprise, the room remained hushed at the blatant biasness just demonstrated by the man. "And the removal of the peacekeeping force from Borlencia. Each minister will have his or her opportunity to put forth their argument. Once all those who wish to speak have spoken, the ministers will then leave the room to vote. First to the podium, Common Minister Francis of the Zylencians."

The man stood up and ventured over to the podium. In his fifties, he was well built and had a trim white beard.

"I don't recognise him," Joseph whispered.

"On the grand stage, he's a nobody. In Zylencia, he's one of Erzse's mouthpieces."

Francis nodded his thanks to the mediator and then took in the room. "My fellow citizens." His voice carried without effort. "I'd like to begin with a history lesson. Ten years ago, in a room not too dissimilar to this one, there was a man—a respected man. For his time, anyway. He was a senior minister of Borlencia, and he stood before the four provinces eager to reject the motion of setting up and utilising a prime minister chair. His argument being that it would betray the principles of our great nation. That it would focus too much power into too few hands. A noble act at the heart of it. But not all was what it seemed. This man's name was Commander Carolus—"

A vicious tide of zealous boos ripped through the audience, startling Evia and Joseph.

"Did I miss something?" Joseph asked over the roar of the crowd. "Since when was Carolus a hated man?"

Evia looked around the room, the snarls and jeers almost demonic. "She's poisoned their minds."

"All of them?"

"The ones in this room." A grim realisation took her by the throat. "This is a setup, Joseph."

"So, what? She planted the audience. It's a cheap trick that'll not sway the ministers."

Unconvinced, Evia simply nodded and watched as the ruckus died out at the behest of the mediator.

"Commander Carolus was," Francis continued, "as many of you know, the estranged brother to our brilliant leader, Senior Minister Erzse—"

This time the congregation erupted with applause and cheers.

"They've lost their senses," Joseph muttered.

Evia didn't respond.

"Estranged brother and, to my personal dismay when I found out, abhorrent schemer," the man shouted elegantly over the noise. The racket subsided, with the spectators eager for more. "Much has come to light since that solemn day. As most of you are likely already aware, the man that championed democracy and the power of the people, at the heart of it, sought to weaken Anemoi's ability to function. He was a foreigner who refused to assimilate—"

The throng jeered nastily, stopping only when Francis raised his hand.

"And unlike his sister, your marvellous Senior Minister Erzse, he was wholly averse to honouring Anemoi's values. He did not answer to the people of Anemoi more than was required to obtain power. And power was what he sought. Authority was his overlord and foreign coin his enabler."

Another round of boos traversed the hall.

"It was a grim reality evidenced by his actions. Recall, he did not hesitate in denying the kind of integration that could make Anemoi a superstate. In fact, he was vehemently opposed to Anemoi becoming a vessel of envy amidst her peers—a nation that could respond swiftly and seamlessly to all threats, external and internal. He wanted absolute control over an Anemoi that could not depose him."

"Then why not just take the chair for himself?" someone called from the audience.

"What? And be held publicly accountable? No, that'd require honour and integrity. Traits the man was devoid of. No, his plan was much more sinister."

He was quiet for a moment as he took in the room, keen to build suspense.

"Our intelligence has since discovered that he wanted to dissolve the ministerial positions, thus taking the vote away from your average citizen, you the people—"

"That bastard!" a random person spat.

"Good thing the man's dead!" another cried.

Francis continued, "And he was going to install his own cronies into positions of power. Cronies that, on the face of it, served Anemoi, but behind the scenes secretly answered to him and him alone. There would've been no accountability in this world of Carolus's. No sharing of power."

He shook his head with exaggerated disappointment.

"How ironic that all that upset his plan was the attack on Borealis. Imagine that..." He paused as an audible sigh of feigned disbelief escaped his thin lips. "All that stopped this miscreant—this vile thief—from taking absolute power was an army of strangers from the north."

He held up his hand and squeezed his forefinger and thumb together for all to see.

"This close. This is how close we came to losing our beloved country as we know it. Let's face the facts. Are there risks to erecting a prime minister chair outside of wartime and by the abolition of term limits? Undoubtedly. But can those risks be mitigated? Of course. Look at our reality. We're hemmed in by armies in the north and east. Borlencia has been swallowed by the flames of internal strife. We have pirates eating away at our trade in the southeast. And cockroaches decimating the forests on our southern border. The threat to our way of life is clear. And the solution to this threat is also clear. We need a consolidation of power. Someone who can act quickly and seamlessly. Not just now, but always. My fine ladies and gentlemen, I propose we not only permanently erect the prime minister chair, but that we put the vote to this room of ministers—"

Commotion swallowed the crowd and the ministers as Evia peered to Erzse. The woman was unreadable and wholly unfazed by the proposition of a vote as to who would hold the chair.

"If he's putting it to a vote, it means she's confident she'll win," Joseph said.

Evia gritted her teeth. "There's no other explanation for her nonchalance."

Both Francis and the mediator raised their hands into the air, and again the room fell silent.

"I propose that on this day," Francis continued, "we elect our new prime minister. Someone who has the wits and know-how to take the mantle and immediately drive the remedies to our ills. That is all."

He bowed his head to the audience and then to the mediator, then took his seat behind the Zylencian senior ministers.

"That was quite the speech," Joseph remarked.

"She still needs to win the vote for the chair to be erected," Evia said sternly.

"Next up," the mediator bellowed, "Wiston of the Eurencians."

There was light conversation over the slight directed at the senior minister. As Wiston took his position at the podium, Evia could sense something was off.

"It was my hope today," Wiston began with conviction, "that I could bring before you the Battle Ox of Borealis…" Joseph and Evia exchanged concerned glances at the implication, just as murmurs spread through the crowd, Ricard's name still renowned amongst the masses. "Commander Ricard of Borlencia was not only a fantastic warrior that held the invaders of Borealis at bay until the city could be evacuated, but he was also an acute politician and a true people's champion. His name is known not just in Borlencia but throughout the four provinces. He was meant to be here today to attest to his friend's—"

"But he ain't!" someone jeered from behind Evia and Joseph. "He ain't here! And he's as much a snivelling shite as the other if he intended to support the bastard's plan to strip us of our vote."

"Quiet!" the mediator roared. "There'll be order in this hall."

Irritation stole Wiston's features at the interruption, and Evia could tell it took some effort for the man to rein in his overwhelming desire to bash the heckler's head in. Recomposed, he continued. "Ricard was a great man. As was Carolus. You've been fed lies about where their loyalties lay—"

"Nonsense!" Francis spat, standing up. "Are you telling us Carolus had no intention of installing a government that answered to him alone? That he had no intention of removing the power from the ministers and the people? Tell us, horseman, what was Carolus's truth?"

Wiston didn't look away from the sea of eyes as he spoke. "Carolus's truth was that he wanted to assemble a group of Anemoi's best and brightest to lead this nation forward. It was not born out of a desire to weaken Anemoi—"

"But it was designed to take the power from the people."

Again, Wiston did not look at the instigator as he spoke. "It was born out of a desire to strengthen Anemoi. You, the people, would've still had the opportunity to vote in your leaders, who would in turn have worked with this group of scientists, economists, and soldiers to run Anemoi. It would've—"

"Would've what, horseman? Dilution of power is dilution of power. And what about his ties abroad? Are you just going to ignore that he was—"

This time Wiston turned around, his glare enough to silence the minister. "Let me finish." Francis nodded meekly as he sat down, and Wiston returned to facing the crowd. "There's no substantiated evidence to suggest Carolus was aligned with a foreign adversary. Heck—he died defending Anemoi against one. And as for his idea. It would've created a checks and balances system. Technical experts to advise Anemoi's politicians. Technical experts to manage those areas not within a layman's expertise. Carolus's mission was honest. It was genuine. It's also the reason he couldn't get behind the creation of a permanent prime minister chair. Or the abolition of term limits. Either would've given those in power too much control. Look, we can debate all day about whether such a government would've worked, but that's beside the point. The technocracy of Carolus's government and the populism that'd undoubtedly come about from electing a prime minister pull us to opposite sides of the spectrum. As the arrangement stands, somewhere in the middle, the true power still lies with the people."

He turned around to face the ministers. His expression was fierce, and several of the ministers, including Francis, balked under his gaze.

"I won't support the proposition," Wiston said. "And neither should you if you value any semblance of a democracy. Put the people before yourselves. I urge you." At that he walked back to his chair and sat down.

"What do you suppose happened to Ricard?" Joseph whispered as the mediator took to the podium.

"I don't know," Evia said nervously.

"Next up, Senior Minister Ronal of the Borlencians," the mediator called.

"Now that's a surprise," Joseph muttered. "Did you sense any—"

"I've sensed nothing, Joseph," she gently snapped, her eyes intent on Ronal as he approached the front of the platform. "Either I've completely lost my touch or someone's blocking me. Unfortunately, I'm starting to suspect both."

"Thank you, sir," Ronal said to the mediator. He turned to the audience and seemed to glance at Evia before locking on a group closer to the front. "There's an assortment of faces here today. A true reflection of Anemoi's diversity. A melting pot. A disparity of cultures. Of religions. Of ways of thought. It's one of Anemoi's greatest strengths. And one of her greatest weaknesses. A pervasiveness that permeates all levels of our society, including our government." He turned to the Borlencians. "An army in the north." Then to the Eurencians. "An army in the east." Then back to the audience. "A government such as ours is a brilliant representation of each province's interests. And therein lies the problem.

"Each province has its own concerns. Its own challenges. But with a unified government, one headed by a single, elected individual at the helm, the inefficiencies of today could become the lessons of yesterday. I wholeheartedly believe that Anemoi can access the absolute power and wealth derived from an efficient, unified people if we vote to go this route. As such, not only do I and all my fellow Borlencians support the notion of erecting a prime minister chair, but we also propose the notion to have Senior Minister Aiden of the Eurencians take the helm for the first term—"

The entire hall erupted with cheers and mumblings and chatter.

"The bloody snakes," Joseph hissed. "When do you suppose Aiden got to him? Must've promised the removal of Zylencian troops or something equally as appealing."

Evia didn't respond, intrigued as she was by Erzse's lack of reaction.

"Evia?" he said.

"Doesn't matter."

"But—"

"What's done is done," she said sternly, dumfounded as to how she could have missed the deception. "All we can hope now is that enough of the others don't throw their weight behind the proponents."

It took several moments for the mediator to regain control, and all the while Ronal stood at the podium patiently waiting and pretty obviously avoiding Evia's stare. When the hall was his, he simply said, "Thank you," and returned to his seat.

The mediator, clearly chuffed by the flow of events, looked to the Eurencians. "Next up, Senior Minister Varela."

Evia tensed, and she could also feel Joseph's discomfort at what was potentially to come. Varela took his time as he strode up to the podium and, even when there, didn't speak for several moments. For once, Evia could read what was to come. As if a small window had opened in the invisible veil strung across the stage. The hesitation in Varela's aura was so blindingly clear, as was the brief glance in Aiden's direction. It was a combination that could mean only one thing.

"I," Varela began, "second the motion to erect the chair. I second the motion to"—again he looked at Aiden—"have Senior Minister Aiden stand for the first term. But…" He turned to the audience. "I do not second the motion for the abolition of term limits. True abuse of power lies in complacency. I will not allow it. Not under my watch."

Without another word he hobbled back to his chair, ignoring the confoundment etched into Wiston's and Robyn's brows and the grumblings of the hall.

"I think it's safe to say we've lost this vote," Evia said softly.

"Wait, what? That's four representatives. We've still got—"

"The rest won't matter." She looked at him, the graveness of the situation painfully written into her eyes. "The Eurencians and the Borlencians were key. We've lost half the former and all the latter. It doesn't matter which way the Notencians vote at this point. We—"

"Should at least wait for the vote to finalise."

"Absolutely. And we should also start making plans to leave as soon as possible."

"And Xander?"

Evia sighed. "There's not much we can do for her until we get our bearings on the situation. And we can't do that in this city."

He nodded, the colour draining from his cheeks. "Should I head—"

"No. Like you said. Let's wait for the verdict."

"Okay."

A number of other ministers stood up and gave their two shillings after Varela, though the Notencian congregation had yet to contribute anything. The consensus was clear. Unification was key, although there was friction across all ranks regarding the term limits. Several of the Borlencians even used their opportunity to hit on the occupying force in Borlencia, a matter that had, until then, seemingly been rendered unimportant. All in all, it was a daunting spectacle to watch for the pair as their nerves wound tighter and tighter. And just as they thought they might be afforded some reprieve from the annoyances by way of the vote itself, a woman sitting amidst the Notencians raised her hand.

"Senior Minister Nala," the mediator greeted. "Please approach."

The voluptuous woman was beautiful, her black hair radiant against her brown skin. And whilst every man in there was ogling over the sight, Evia was more intrigued by the shroud exuding from the woman and the irritation that had stolen Erzse's nonchalant demeanour.

"There must be history," Joseph remarked, having also spotted Erzse's glare.

"Must be," Evia said curiously.

Not a single eye deviated from Nala's confident presence as she took to the front of the stage. "I can speak for all Notencians when I tell you this: Our fleet and our funds have been severely depleted after the commitment to the Borlencians ten years ago and through the protection of the trade fleet from continuous attack by Buto pirates every day since. We are weakened. Our calls for help have found only deaf ears. If you want the bedrock of

Anemoi, the home of Anemoi's southern fleet and the trade fleet to see through the next decade, you will erect the chair. And you will vote in Senior Minister Aiden, the only man to have heeded our call."

"What in Anemoi?" Joseph muttered as the woman returned to her seat. "The bloody man orchestrated the whole ordeal. He's in bed with the pirates. Why the chuckle, Evia? Hardly seems the time."

"Nala's the only one that's apparently irked Erzse."

"Could you read her?"

"No. Other than the Eurencians, I've not been able to read any of them."

"Be that as it may, not really a time to be chuckling, don't you think?"

"We've been played, Joseph. Someone, or something, has completely and utterly blocked me. Shown me only what's been deemed necessary. If I can't laugh or smile, then what can I do? Cry? At this point I'm just wondering what else I've missed."

"Esteemed citizens! Ministers." It was Aiden. "What can I say? This… all this has been quite the surprise."

"Liar!" Joseph muttered under his breath.

"So let me begin with this. I see the logic in the prime minister chair. It is a logical solution to our existing inefficiencies. It can help us rebuild the Anemoi we want and need. But…" There was a pause, pulling each and every onlooker to the edge of their seats. "I can't accept it's our only solution."

"What?"

A sliver of hope wormed its way into Evia's gut.

"No. Too many have died for what we have currently," Aiden continued. "It's a system with flaws, but it works. It prevents the concentration of power in too few hands. A permanent prime minister chair has no place in Anemoi—"

"And that's why it must be you!" yelled a Eurencian common minister.

"Why, my good man?"

"Because you don't want it. You won't abuse it."

"And when my term is done? Who's to say the next won't hold on to the power?"

"Keep the term limits."

"And what if the next decides to use their power to abolish them?"

"We'll vote them out if they try," a Borlencian minister spoke.

Aiden blew through pursed lips, as if in contemplation, but Evia could see the farce. The man knew what he was doing.

"And now he'll accept it," she murmured.

Though Joseph suspected as much, he vehemently hoped it wouldn't be the case.

Aiden's mouth was strewn with conflict, the weight of Anemoi's future apparently resting on a decision he must make in that split second. Of course, to those in the know or who had caught on, it was a decision that had long been made. "Alright then. I support the proposition, on the condition that the term limits remain intact for at least two terms of parliament. During which we can collect and analyse the evidence that'll allow us to make an informed decision. Thank you."

Applause abounded as Aiden returned to his seat. Still the black hole of nothingness surrounded the Zylencian sphere, but there was one thing Evia could tell with certainty. Erzse was wholly unbothered by Aiden's ascension.

Aiden had been the last to speak before all the ministers got up and left the room. The noise of the babble was nearly deafening as the rest sat there waiting.

"What do you think will happen?" Joseph asked.

"I think Aiden will be our new prime minister."

"And then?"

She chewed her lip. "He played us, but he's the lesser of two evils. The safety of Anemoi is still in his best interest and, because of that, perhaps he can still be our ally."

"The man threw half the country into turmoil to get to this stage. How can you be so sure?"

"What's the point in having power over Anemoi if the nation breaks apart? This is still his home."

"I guess there is none," Joseph admitted.

"He's of clearer mind than the other. Like I said, the lesser of two evils. They return."

"That was fast!"

"Not if you're already decided."

The mediator didn't need to raise his hands for calm this time, with every observer eager to hear the verdict. Taking his place by the podium, the man unrolled a small parchment. "For the motion of erecting a permanent prime minister chair, ten ministers say nay—"

The hall rang with cries of joy, fading only when the mediator put his finger to his mouth.

"Four from Notencia, one from Zylencia—"

"What are you doing?" Wiston abruptly scolded the man as he and a swathe of the Eurencian ministers stood up threateningly. "The ballot's private."

"Should our citizens not know who voted for and who voted against said motion?" he queried accusingly. "Or would you hide the truth from the people you claim to serve?"

Wiston's cheeks glowed crimson red with anger. Slowly, and with obvious agitation, he and the other Eurencians sat down.

"As I was saying," the mediator continued. "One from Zylencia. And five from Eurencia. All others voted in favour. The list of names will be published in the forum for all to see after this meeting is adjourned. Now, on to the proposition of term limits." A chuffed grin took the man. "An overwhelming majority have, again, voted in favour of the abolition of term limits. The naysayers: four from Notencia, two from Zylencia, and twelve from Eurencia."

The mediator seemed less pleased with the absolution from the Eurencian ranks but was visibly happy nonetheless. He peered to Aiden as he read the next result.

"And the proposition to have Senior Minister Aiden take the seat. Wow! Can this be right?" He turned to the audience, hands in the air as if in shock. "Our naysayers: four from Notencia, one from Zylencia, and surprise, five from Eurencia. Ladies and gentlemen, I present to you, your new prime minister."

A standing ovation swiftly followed with screams of excitement, not just amongst the plebs to the rear but also across the rows of informed to the centre and front. Even Joseph and Evia stood up, not because of any desire to celebrate, but because of a need to witness Aiden's reaction as he took to the podium. It was a good three minutes before the noise finally settled, allowing Aiden to speak.

The man's first gesture was to signal to the mediator to put down the parchment. Next, he peered to the throng. "I…reluctantly accept." Another wave of applause and cheers did the rounds. "And, as my first action, I will withdraw the bulk of the peacekeeping force from Borlencia, keeping just—" More shouts of joy. "Keeping just two battalions to the north to provide a degree of protection against the army that occupies Borealis. One battalion to the south. And our growing fleet on the lake that'll be used to combat the surging piracy that has darkened our shores. And now, we adjourn."

"Let's get out of here," Joseph said as the politicians and citizens grew rowdy with joy and gossip.

"Not yet."

Uncaring of the mass of bodies that had gathered around the stage, Evia pushed her way through the crowd until she was at the foot of the platform with Joseph standing beside her.

"You're trying for an audience with him?" Joseph asked, following her gaze to Aiden.

"I need to know."

"Might be waiting a while."

"It takes as long as it takes."

"Evia," Wiston called as he descended the steps onto the floor with Robyn close behind.

"Wiston," she responded, somewhat buoyed by the big man's presence.

He spoke in a hushed tone. "Not the result we had hoped for."

"No, it's not."

"But perhaps not the worst outcome. Still, might be time for you to consider getting yourselves and the girls out of town, at least until we understand the consequences. We can regroup—"

"Xander…" She glanced around for prying ears but those closest were nobodies speaking loudly amongst themselves, eagerly awaiting an opportunity to touch or glimpse the new prime minister up close. "Xander was taken. Aika—"

"Taken? By whom?" Robyn asked worriedly.

"I assume the one we've all suspected, but we can't know for sure."

"And Aika?"

"Is safe at the villa with Dogner."

"That's a start," Wiston spoke. "Let's join them—"

"I need to talk to Aiden first," she said.

"Talk to the scoundrel? The man can't be trusted."

"And yet we, too, would be wise to give our congratulations," Robyn urged his counterpart. "He'll be expecting it, and we *will* need him sooner or later."

Wiston could barely conceal his disgust as he peered back up to the stage where the majority of the Zylencians had already left. Evia followed his gaze and locked on the mysterious woman from Notencia who was kissing Aiden on both cheeks. Again she found herself fascinated by the only person on that stage who had bothered Erzse. And again she found herself somewhat tempted to pry. But before she could, the woman and her entourage disappeared towards the exit, to be replaced by the thick of the crowd.

"We'll join the Eurencians," Wiston said as Aiden began for the

Borlencians. "I doubt they'll have to wait long for Aiden to find them and give his thanks, given how many voted his way."

"Did you suspect anything?" Joseph said as the four of them climbed the steps onto the platform.

"Varela's vote wasn't surprising," Robyn admitted. "The others were a bit shocking, yes."

As they pulled up to the Eurencians, Varela was swift to approach Evia.

"I am sorry," he said sincerely. "I think we could all see what direction this was headed, and better Aiden—"

Evia held her hand up to the man. "I understand, Varela. You did what was necessary by your people. No one can fault you for that, and time will tell if it was the correct decision or not."

Lips pursed, expression grateful, he nodded his thanks. "I assume you wish to speak with the man?"

"I do."

"Though I suspect not simply to congratulate him?"

"Congratulate who?" Aiden's cheerful voice interrupted.

Varela turned around and immediately held out his hand. Aiden was quick to clasp it and careful to avoid eye contact with Evia and the others.

"Congratulations, Prime Minister Aiden," Varela said sternly. "I trust you will be a fair leader who will do right by *all* his citizens."

"Absolutely, old boy, absolutely. And Aiden is fine." In swift succession, he shook the hand of every Eurencian, leaving Wiston and Robyn for last. "No ill feelings, I should hope?" he said to the pair, still avoiding Evia's fierce gaze.

Robyn shrugged and shook the man's hand. "You did what you needed to do, it would seem."

"As should we all. Wiston?"

The big man hesitated a moment and then held out his hand. "It's a sentiment I can get behind if you'll live up to the promises you undoubtedly made to my colleagues."

Aiden smiled and gripped the man's hand. "I'll do what's within my power, old boy." Pulling away, he reluctantly turned to Evia. "I know this wasn't what you expected."

"Understatement?" she retorted.

"I've always had the best intentions for Anemoi. I want you to know this. And this power that's been given to me, I never intended for it to be on my cards."

She knew the lie. And she could tell he knew that she knew he lied. Of course, he couldn't say as much. And neither could she, not in public, not without implicating herself in some form. But maybe it didn't matter, she suddenly pondered to herself. The man had seized power, but he wasn't a monster. He was just hungry. And if that hunger encouraged the cooperation necessary to ensure the survival of Anemoi, then maybe it could work.

Her expression softened, and she held out her hand. "Congratulations, Prime Minister Aiden."

A smile took the man, and he clasped Evia's hand in his own. And then, unexpectedly, all was revealed. The veil of obscurity that had plagued Evia that day, and unknowingly in the weeks preceding, had been lifted until all shone clear. Her mouth dropped in horror, and she stumbled back from the man as if assaulted.

"Evia!" Joseph said alarmedly, gripping her arm.

"Is it true?" Evia blurted.

Aiden's eyes widened as he realised something had been revealed to the woman with abilities beyond his own, but he quickly found his composure. "Not sure what you mean, old friend. Anyway, as it is—"

"Is it true?" she said with a raised voice, drawing in looks from those nearby.

Aiden faltered in his rebuke, and then, uncharacteristically uncaring of those that watched, pulled up close to her until his lips practically kissed her ears. "I'm sorry, Evia. There was no other way."

CHAPTER 48

Februarix 19, 485; three weeks before the vote; Zyphyr, Zylencia—"With the Eurencians, she still has the votes to stop me," Erzse said with quiet disdain from across the long oak table, her eyes unreadable as they took in Aiden.

The dark room reeked of incense and something metallic that Aiden couldn't quite put his finger on. Despite the wide windows, Erzse's lair, as he had come to call it, always seemed to be swamped by a perpetual blanket of bleakness.

"This is true," he began. "She does, and whilst the Eurencians have shown little willingness to align themselves with us, I have made some headway in impeding the conversations between them and Evia. As it is—"

"Hush, please." She stood up and ventured over to the window overlooking the street—a favourite vantage point from which to observe the scurry of the black city below. "Perhaps we should have cut them down whilst they were still on the road in Borlencia."

"The two Eurencians? Or Evia?"

"Both."

"And what would that have accomplished? Sometimes the art of controlling requires subtleties in letting the controlled think they actually have control."

Her wicked grin caught the reflection of the window and sent a shudder down Aiden's spine. She turned to face him.

"So you think by allowing them to live, we've shown them a semblance of control that'll make it easier for us to sway the Upper House?" she said mockingly.

"Evia's disappearance wouldn't go unnoticed. Nor the Eurencians'. And Evia's actions have greatly facilitated our plan. It was her idea to legitimise the Borlencians. If it weren't for that, we likely wouldn't have been presented the opportunity to get you an official vote with the potential backing of all the provinces—"

She raised her hand, signalling him to stop, and then returned to the table and took her seat opposite him.

"With the damned goats in the mountains and the fools from Eurencia aligning behind Evia, our majority is no longer guaranteed," she said. "Every day of that damned blockade worsens the sentiment on the street and in my army. And now the beggars are out in force wondering why their free coin has dried up. Please tell me, wretched worm, what is your plan?"

"First, might I point out, not all the ministers in Eurencia have irrevocably thrown their lot behind Evia and her cause when it comes to the vote. Don't forget that with their current predicament and their desperate need for additional funding and troops—well, to put it bluntly, they're as good as in your pocket, and I actively pursue this route. Secondly, I might also like to point out that we've still got a few weeks before the meeting. Even the staunchest of human minds can be re-educated in four weeks."

"And what of M. K. and that brute sleeping with him—what's his name?"

"Ricard."

"Ricard. Maybe it's time to cut their throats?"

"A rash decision that'll hurt us, I'd guess."

"Is that so?"

"You know it is." He watched her, wary of her temper, but also keen to move on to the real reason he was there. "I hear your man's returned from the desert."

"What of it?"

"What business does he have up there?"

She laughed a cruel laugh. "I bet it makes you seethe to not have your tentacles in something, doesn't it?"

"But the desert, Erzse. Nothing good comes from up there."

"No, nothing good does come from up there, and the news he brings is no different. But be that as it may, it's not for your ears or any other."

"As prime minister, you'll be expected to—" Her scowl hardened, and the unnerving pierce of her gaze compelled him to stop. "What's the matter?"

"Your games, Aiden."

"Sorry?"

"Your games. They tire me."

"I don't follow."

"On the day of the vote," she began, "all the ministers you've gathered, and continue to gather, will pass their votes to create the chair."

"Of course, as discussed—"

"And, as you've seen fit to arrange, they'll elect *you* to the newly created position—"

"Erzse—"

"Spare me," she said dangerously. "You'll proceed with your plan as if I never interfered, and you'll take the position you've worked so hard to secure for yourself."

"Erzse, let me explain."

"There's no need. I've known your scheme since it first appeared as a glimmer of an idea in that weaselly little mind of yours. There's little else you can explain to me. And once you've accepted your congratulations, attended your ceremonies, and further inflated that pompous head of yours, you and your cretins will vote me in as your second, with complete control of Anemoi's armies."

About to protest, he held his tongue and then, suddenly emboldened, stared her down defiantly.

"You've nothing of substance on me, and you'll have even less once I'm elected. And why, you withered serpent, do you think I'd dare make you my second only to be murdered in my sleep at a time of your choosing, leaving you uncaged to spew your wretched venom over all of Anemoi?" He stood to leave, but as he turned, he caught her cautionary glance to a box on the table corner. "What is this?"

"A gift."

The cruel snicker barely stifled by her reptilian lips sent an involuntary shudder down his spine. "I'll not be bought, Erzse."

"Everybody has their price. This is yours. Go on, open it, you wretch."

Hesitantly, he pulled the box towards him and carefully removed the lid.

He stumbled backwards, mouth agape. "You're…you're a monster. How…how can this—" He abruptly lunged towards her but was stayed by the show of her hand and the glimmer of the silver mask concealed in the shadowy corner of the room.

The fury in Aiden's eyes gradually dissipated into a murky cloud of desperation and sorrow, and he collapsed onto his knees and whimpered into the sodden box, the severed finger and familial ring adorning it like a knife in his heart.

"Your gift," Erzse cooed, "is the survival of your daughter. Once I have my army, you will have your daughter."

"Erzse—"

"Quiet! The girl nearly killed me. She should've been executed the day my men dragged her to me. But I kept her alive—"

"As a bargaining tool. She's just a girl. A child. Have you no morals?"

"Your success is now linked to mine, Aiden. Fail me and you'll know pain."

He shook his head in disbelief, as if it might wake him from the nightmare utterly consuming him in that moment. "What of Evia?"

"What about her?"

"Her abilities. She'll see this."

"You've held her at bay this far. What makes this any different?" she asked with a curious expression.

"Look at what you've done. It's raw emotion. I can't guarantee—"

She waved her hand. "Enough."

He looked puzzled.

"The woman's mind is as fuzzy as a mole's eyes," Erzse said dismissively. "She's too old and is too close to my centre…" Her distrust for him was blatant. "You're adept at hiding your thoughts from her kind, Aiden. And you've carefully led the ministers in such a way to avoid detection by her. But you're a fool if you think that's enough. I may not be able to dive into that decrepit little head of hers, but I've certainly been able to shield others from her attempts to spy. The truth will not be revealed until I see fit. Understood?"

"Yes."

CHAPTER 49

Marx 10, 485; two hours before the vote; Zyphyr, Zylencia—"Acro," M. K. greeted the man wedged between Erzse and Aiden on the elevated table that towered over him even as he stood. The collective expression of the ministers perched behind the table was dark and uncompromising and a fair representation of the grand but morbid room of the Parliament Palace's courthouse. Acro's lack of response added to the menace. "Better not let this set the tone for this evening's dinner."

M. K. looked to two ministers from the south. Miners and vocal supporters to the cause. One nodded to him. The other, Acro's counterpart in Ingleton, simply looked away.

Determined to invoke a reaction, M. K. spoke. "I notice two of the twelve seats are vacant, not including mine."

Erzse nodded to a decrepit old man sitting beside the table, the mediator. The man rose with feigned anguish.

"It is this assembly's understanding," he began, "an assembly consisting of the active senior ministers and common ministers of Zylencia, that on the seventeenth of Januarix, that you and several accomplices, most notably two ministers of Zylencia, entered into one of two known rebel strongholds in the south quarter and ordered the attempted—"

"Hold on!" M. K. said with growing alarm, but he was abruptly gripped by the escort of guards and swiftly disarmed.

"Ordered the attempted assassination of Senior Minister Erzse—"

"I wasn't even in the bloody city! You've flipping lost the plot—" He was violently punched in the chest by a tall muscular man wearing a silver mask and then grabbed by the neck and shoved to the floor.

"And subsequently fled the confines of the city to give the appearance of an alibi as the attack was carried out with significant loss to the city's inhabitants. It is with this charge that you and the others accused are to be suspended from your positions and held until a trial can so be arranged to prove, without a doubt, your guilt in the matter discussed."

"Who's my accuser?" He coughed, still winded from the blow.

The decrepit man looked to Erzse, and she nodded her approval.

"Senior Minister Acro is your accuser and your witness," the old man said to a howl of despair and anger.

M. K. was subsequently dragged from the room by five men and beaten outside as Erzse turned to the waiting ministers.

"Everybody out, except you three," she said, pointing to Aiden, Acro, and the mediator. The man in the silver mask also remained.

"Fill M. K.'s position and the two others with the ones I've selected," she said to the mediator.

"There's no legitimacy," Aiden retorted.

"Of course there is," the mediator said, pulling a long parchment from his bag. "The votes were tallied last night."

"Fraud then?"

Erzse chuckled. "After everything you've helped build, that's your concern?"

"It still leaves the one friendly that won't vote for the chair," Acro commented in reference to the minister from the south that had nodded to M. K.

"You've spoken to him about the merits of voting for you?" the mediator asked Aiden.

Aiden shifted uncomfortably. "My attempt was less than productive."

"And after what he just saw," Acro began, "I doubt he'll be cooperative anytime soon."

"Look, it'd be too obvious if you removed every minister sympathetic to M. K's cause," Aiden said sternly. "That's already three simply vanished and replaced, not including you and your counterpart, Acro. There'll be an expectation of some naysayers, given the reality on the ground. Let's not detract from the legitimacy."

"I agree with that sentiment," the mediator said.

Erzse pondered for a moment and then nodded. "So be it. And Ricard was dealt with?"

"This morning."

"Good. Acro, give the order for the garrison to mobilise."

"The garrison?" Aiden asked, confused.

"Their ministers are removed, and their general disappeared. Tonight we'll delimb what's left of the weathered goat."

CHAPTER 50

Earlier that morning, two kilometres north of Ingleton, Zylencia—Ricard peered east and raised his hand against the sunrays peeking over the crest of the mountain range. The morning frost gnawed bitterly into his bones, and the steam on his breath and that of his stocky horse carried into the air.

In the distance, at the end of the wide, muddy road on which he rode, he could just make out the black speck of Zyphyr, a sprawling dwarf amidst Mount Camana's shadow. Grassland and the odd haggard farmstead hugged the throughway and forests the peripheral to the west.

He was nervous for the event to come but equally keen to defend his friend's honour and keep ultimate power out of reach of the witch of the west. He was also a tad worried he had left too late, delayed by the rough onslaught of the prior night's overconsumption. He shook his groggy head and reached into his pouch, withdrawing a leather flask from within. Greedily, he licked his lips as he undid the cap and angled the container up. The first drop of chilled beer against his tongue was glorious, and if not for the snort of a horse carrying on the wind from somewhere ahead, it would have taken quite the impetus to pull the elixir from his mouth.

A dozen riders from the forest to the west grew quickly with each metre trodden. Careful to recap his flask, he slid it back into his pouch, tightened his left fist on his rein, and swung his axe from his shoulder. Precaution would not desert him, no matter the state of his pounding head.

"Who goes there?" he called as the riders approached hearing distance. No response. "Who goes there?" he called again, readying his weapon with obvious intent.

At twenty metres' distance, the group slowed and spread twelve across. The thought occurred to him to turn and run, but he was comfortable that his riding abilities were insufficient to keep any sort of lead. Neither did he want to present an undefended target on his back.

At ten metres, the core of the group ground to a halt, whilst those on the edges continued until they had him surrounded. All were soldiers, and all wore chain mail and helmets. Other than the restless movement of the horses, none edged closer, except for one. The man crept forward until he was five metres in front of Ricard. Slowly, to avoid alarm, the man raised his hands and withdrew his helmet.

"Aiden?" Ricard said, squinting. "Is that you? Bloody heck! Haven't seen you in how long? Nine, maybe ten years?"

"Something like that," Aiden responded.

"And to what do I owe this pleasure?"

Aiden didn't respond immediately, instead wanting to size up his opponent. It was obvious to Ricard that Aiden knew he would lose men in any confrontation.

"Turn back, Ricard," Aiden said, almost pleadingly.

"Sorry, what? Think I might've misheard you there. Did you just tell me to turn back?"

"I did. Turn back and leave today's event be."

"Well, who said anything about an event?"

Frustration instantly gripped Aiden's expression. "Erzse has your friend."

Ricard inwardly tensed but carefully betrayed no emotion. "Which friend? Reckon you've got me confused. You see, I'm running a tad short on friends."

"She's got your friend, and she will kill the girl if you make any attempt to reach the city on this day."

Ricard's face suddenly hardened, sending a quiver through the antagonists. "You threaten me?"

"I ask you politely. Let's not waste life today. There'll be enough of it in the weeks and months to come. I can sadly guarantee you that."

"You're certainly right about that." He shifted on his horse, causing several of the soldiers to step back.

"I don't want to kill you—"

"But it sounds like she does," Ricard said, referring to Erzse.

"Will you leave?" Aiden asked with growing impatience.

Ricard didn't respond as he took in his opposers and calculated his chances.

Aiden sighed and turned to the nearest soldier. "Keep him here until sunset. Do not let him leave. If he tries anything, kill him."

"But Erzse said—"

"Who's your commander?"

The soldier nodded. "He'll not move from this spot, and if he tries—"

"You'll do what, exactly?" Ricard taunted the man dangerously.

"Kill you," the soldier said coldly, the eyes behind the helmet not wavering.

Aiden swivelled his horse, about to leave, when Ricard called to him. "And the others?"

He turned to face Ricard. "I'll do everything in my power to ensure they get out of the city unharmed. Beyond that, they're on their own."

Ricard gritted his teeth. "Why the betrayal?"

"Erzse has your friend. And she has my daughter. Look after yourself, Ricard. And live to fight another day. This one is already lost for you and your kin."

At that, Aiden turned around and galloped towards Zyphyr, leaving Ricard alone but unrestrained amongst his captors.

CHAPTER 51

That afternoon, back in Zyphyr—"Ricard's alive as far as I can tell," Evia said to Joseph, Wiston, and Robyn.

The four of them were standing in the villa's front garden as a few Eurencian soldiers entered the residence, ready to pack anything that belonged to the delegation.

"Then we'll need to warn him what Erzse plans," Joseph said, alarmed.

"What's she got planned?" Aika asked from the front door. Cleaned up, the welts on her face were even more pronounced. Dogner was standing beside her, and the pair had been about to leave and grab some much-needed comfort food.

Evia hesitated, as did Joseph.

But Wiston did not withhold. "Erzse will sack Ingleton using the Zylencian garrison and those loyal to Acro."

"Then she won?" Dogner asked.

"That's putting it—" Joseph had begun when Aika interrupted.

"Wait, Acro?" she said, confused. "He's M. K.'s cousin. Why would his men—"

"M. K. and those ministers loyal to him have been arrested," Evia responded. "Aiden has been made prime minister but is simply a pawn in

413

Erzse's grand design. She is now de facto leader of Anemoi. And we're all in danger. We must leave as soon as possible."

"But when will she attack?" Aika asked.

"We think tonight."

"I need to warn Ricard," Aika said, turning towards the villa.

"You need to pack. We'll make sure word gets to him."

Aika turned to face them. Her expression was dangerous. "Which also means you intend to leave Zyphyr without Xander?"

"There's nothing we can do for her if we're captured."

"We'll keep spies in the city to find and track her whereabouts," Robyn said reassuringly.

"And you'll leave with us," Wiston added. "They'll not dare touch a Eurencian delegation, and we're armed enough to take on anything designed to be inconspicuous."

"And where will we go?" Aika asked uncertainly.

"Bulgar and then Eurencia," Evia said.

Disbelief took Aika. "So far. What can we do from there?"

"We'll figure it out. But it's—"

"What about the Borlencians?" Aika said. "We have friends there. At least—"

"The Borlencians sided with Aiden."

"But not Erzse. There must be somewhere else we can go that isn't the other side of Anemoi."

Evia chewed her lip. "We'll work it out on the road. In the meantime, it's imperative we leave the city before it gets locked down. Once that garrison is fully mobilised and marching—"

Aika turned around and disappeared into the villa.

Evia cursed. "She'll not leave Ricard and Xander."

"We can't force her anywhere," Joseph admitted.

"No, we can't."

"And you're sure we should go?" Dogner asked, also questioning the decision to leave Xander.

"You know it as well as we do." Evia sighed. "Pack what you can. We leave before nightfall."

CHAPTER 52

That evening, on Ingleton's northern moor—Ricard withdrew his gaze from the map on his desk and subtly reached for his axe beside the chair. He froze at the sound of bending wood.

"You're getting slow, old man," Aika said from the shadow of the tent.

"And you must be eating too much because I could hear the mountain creaking under your foot," he said, turning to her.

He got up as she walked up to him, and they embraced. As they released, she took in the map of Zyphyr and the pieces depicting military units that he had been poring over.

"Looks like you heard, then?" she said.

"Not enough to go on. Just that you or Xander were apprehended and the vote likely lost."

"The garrison marches."

"How long?" he asked sternly.

"Couple hours."

"And M. K.?"

"He's been arrested. Betrayed by Acro."

Ricard cursed in a tongue she didn't recognise.

"I found one of your sentries a kilometre north of here with his throat cut," she continued. "The marks were fresh—maybe a couple minutes old. Same with the sentries by the gate."

"Must be the garrison's forward party as those were Acro's…"

He paused as Aika hopped lightly to the wall of the tent and placed her ear on the leathery material.

"Expecting anyone?" she whispered as she stepped to the centre of the room and drew her bow.

"Not this late."

"Didn't think so. It's time to leave. We won't have long once they begin their slaughter."

"We've got to warn—"

She let loose the arrow and then another through the door, the mark confirmed by a brief squeal of pain and the rapid succession of three men slipping through the door, their faces blackened and their armour thin.

"Assassins!" Ricard snarled and launched himself at the closest two whilst Aika finished the third with a perfectly placed headshot. "Can't say they're worth their coin, mind you." He spat at the heap on the floor. "Come. I need to warn the captains to scatter their men," he said, donning his kit.

Ricard re-emerged from the nearest command tent with a Flint captain in tow and prompted him to awaken the next captain not of Ingleton or its assumed allies. And so he set in motion a chain reaction of movement and silent alarm that aroused those on the verge of an unescapable sleepy death, a chain reaction that continued unimpeded until one of Zyphyr's advanced party of bloodied assassins discovered the scheme midway down the field of pitched tents and raised the alarm.

The subsequent melee was bloody but brief, with an abundance of confusion on both sides, for not only were a large number of M. K.'s men still oblivious to the plot but a large portion of Acro's men had never been made privy to it, and so, assuming the assault came from a breach in the gate, the ignorant on both sides focused their collective defence in said direction.

It didn't take long, however, for the whisper of betrayal to spread like wildfire through the gathered ranks, and though some refused to fight their perceived brethren, the majority joined the skirmish, and it was only with a determined effort from M. K.'s captains that Ricard was able to salvage the remnants of the army by withdrawing south under the blanket of night.

CHAPTER 53

Marx 11, 485; Zyphyr, Zylencia—"So Evia slips away undetected, and the Mountain King's ragtag militia moves south with the Ox of Borealis at the helm." Erzse smirked. "How romantic. And Acro—has he rejoined his men?"

Aiden nodded.

"Have him march south and engage Brutus's men. Make an example of them…but bring me Ricard alive. I want to punish him publicly, along with Brutus."

"I'll make preparations for the garrison—"

"Not the garrison, just Acro's men!" she hissed. "Let them wear each other out. No, we can't afford to part with the regulars, not now."

"And Evia's girl?"

"She's none of your concern," she said as she peered to the man in the silver mask standing at the door.

CHAPTER 54

The night before; inside Xander's head, Zyphyr, Zylencia—"What is this?"

"What is this?" a distorted voice echoed back.

"Where…"

"Where…"

"Where am I?"

"Where am I?"

Xander turned around, looked up to the sky and then down to the spotless ground that was absent of even the slightest groove or bump, and in disbelief, she took in the whiteness that stretched across the perpetual horizon. A milky vacantness not much dissimilar to a cumulus cloud, it bore into every nook and cranny of the nothingness that enveloped the landscape.

"Hello!" she screamed.

"Hello!" the voice screamed back.

"Is anybody out there?"

"Is anybody out there?"

She clenched her fists and sprinted desperately into the void without thought of her destination, running until the light thump of each footstep cascaded into an overwhelming echo of pitter-patters, and the fatigue of her muscles and the burn of her lungs dragged her to a halt in a spot no different from the first. A world devoid of matter, no people, no trees, no animals, no rivers or streams or mountains or anything.

"It can't be."

"It can't be."

She clambered again through the mist of nothingness and through the agony that traversed her body and again ground to a halt.

"What is this?"

"What is this?"

She quivered at the claustrophobic sensation instigated by her entrapment.

"Xander."

She turned abruptly to the familiar voice, and relief enveloped her at sight of the shadow from the steppe. Her silhouette.

"Where am I?" she asked.

"You're still under the city."

"What—how can that be? What is this place?"

"Your mind. Erzse's attempt to weaken your will and, well, take control."

"Control! I need to get out. But how?"

"I haven't figured that part out yet, but you're not where you're meant to be."

"Don't you think I know that?"

"I don't mean in here. I mean out there. Never mind. Look, Xander, *he* knows you're here. Whatever you—we think to do, we need to do it soon. He won't show mercy to the daughter of Carolus when he arrives…"

She wished to respond, to ask about his priviness to Erzse's dealings, and who *he* was, but all that remained of the encounter was the echo of those last mysterious words filling the air.

CHAPTER 55

Marx 16, 485; Zyphyr, Zylencia—Xander gasped desperately for air as the invisible lead weight atop her lungs evaporated. It was only after several terrifying, bleary-eyed moments of shuffling her hands over the rotten mattress and the slimy brick wall to confirm she was in fact free of the paralysis in her mind and body that she realised she was not alone in the dank, grotty cell under the city.

The tormented gems of green that glared through the silver mask of the man sitting on a stool just outside the metal bars of the cell unnerved her to the core. Illuminated by the flickering torch on the nearest wall, his eyes glowed like those of a beast stalking its prey in the dead of night.

"Who are you?" she managed in a raspy voice, her tongue and lips deprived of moisture and unused to speech.

He didn't respond and only stared at her curiously, as a cat might a mouse. Slowly, she sat up, and an immediate rush of dizziness hit her, followed by an intense throbbing pain in her head.

"I need water. I'm dehydrated."

He didn't budge, only continued to stare.

"Please, I'm thirsty. My mouth's as dry as a desert."

"Empty words coming from one who knows not what it feels like to drink sand." The man spoke in a worn voice, his demeanour seemingly agitated by her remark.

"And yet I am thirsty. Please."

Though he stared without sympathy, he relented under the onslaught of her silent plea and chucked a small bag onto the bed. Xander reached in cautiously and withdrew a small water bottle and a cloth with bread in it.

"Use them sparingly. You'll receive no more," he said and stood to leave.

"Wait—who are you? Where am I?" she said, hoping for a clue, but he left the cell silently.

She uncorked the partially filled bottle and took a sip. It wasn't fresh, but it did the job, and despite her hunger, she avoided the dry, stale bread altogether. The air of the cellar was heavy and unforgiving on the tightness of her chest, and it took many a moment for her legs to adjust to the exertion of simply standing up and completing a circuit of the tiny, dimly lit cell. She peered through the bars of the cell door and noted that the torch on the wall was the only light source in what appeared to be a long corridor of identical rooms.

"Hello!" she whispered to no response. "Hello!" she called slightly louder, but there was nothing, no voices, no footsteps, not even the drip of water or the white noise of a distant street or the rats in the sewer. Nothing. "Not sure what's worse, this or the prison in my mind," she muttered and walked another round of the cell before collapsing on the bed in exhaustion.

▲ ▲ ▲

Xander couldn't tell if it was morning or evening when the hallway door creaked open. All she knew was that she was grateful for the modest inflow of fresh air introduced by the disturbance. Sitting in the corner of her cell on the cool bricks, she gazed through the bars into the hall as the man in the silver mask and Erzse's horrid scowl emerged from the shadows. He strode up to the edge of her cell and leaned against the wall just outside it whilst Erzse continued to stand in the centre of the hall, staring.

An uncomfortable silence abounded as Erzse looked the girl up and down, and a chuffed grin soon flickered into being on the woman's decrepit face.

"Something catch your eye?" Xander said defiantly, suddenly uncaring of her aunt's cruel reputation.

"I trust the place is to your liking?"

"What do you think?"

"I think you'll get used to it with time. It's not like you have much choice."

"What do you want with me, Erzse?" she asked, standing up and stepping into the centre of the tight cell.

"What, no 'Aunty'?"

"You're undeserving."

"Ha! Can't say I disagree." Erzse disappeared into the shadow and re-emerged with a stool. As she sat down, she let out a sigh of relief, as if she had been busy on her feet all day. "I must admit, when I found out you had been under the tutelage of the famed witch, I thought you might be stronger. But nearly a week in that blank canvas of a head and no attempt to escape—"

"A week!"

"A week. Like I was saying, I'm disappointed. No worries, though. It'll make it easier for me."

"What—to take control? You vile thing."

Erzse glanced curiously at the man in the silver mask and then back to Xander.

"What could you possibly want or need from me?" Xander continued.

"With time, little pea, with time. For now, I'd like to regale you with a little history lesson. Oh yes, a tale about your diluted blood. First that of your weakling father, and then that of your farm rat mother—"

"Your words are like venom," Xander responded with a calmness that barely checked the rage in her words.

"And I suppose you think I'm what—evil?"

"It wouldn't be a stretch."

"Ha! There's no such thing as evil, my whimpering little niece. At least not in the truest sense. Every damn insect on this planet struggles for its own petty interests. And if that interest requires subservience to a collective according to certain designated social constructs that define good and evil, then the insect's definition of what is good and evil has been defined by society. But what if it works in the insect's interest to deviate from the collective and redefine what is good and evil? I think you'll find, more often than not, that the insect breaks society's rules according to its own self-justified definitions. Point is, my dear, good and evil are entirely subjective."

"Only a warped mind would try to justify self-serving actions taken against another to that person's detriment. Not everybody is a monster, Erzse. Not everybody is absent a moral compass."

"Is that so? In your short, pathetic life, how much villainy have you witnessed against yourself and others? Lots, I bet…yes, your silence says it all. And how many of those deviating little insects do you think defined their own rules of what is right and wrong to justify the actions they took to benefit themselves? How many of them feigned ignorance when caught by the society they wronged, knowing full well the line they crossed? Here's the thing, you little worm, the ability of so many people to break the rules to benefit themselves shows there is no true right and wrong, only what is construed to be socially undesirable when on the receiving end of the deed. There is no internal moral compass, for it surely would not be the case that so many insects choose selfishness over selflessness in defiance of the compass, assuming there was such a thing."

Xander didn't respond, just observed in silent curiosity at the abundant antipathy exuding from the woman in front of her. Then she grinned.

"Something funny, little one?" Erzse asked.

"I just find it strange that we share the same blood."

"Back to the point, I see. Very well, let me begin. But first, an observation: I didn't think our people so prone to weakness and naivety. I would put it down to your mongrel blood, but then our mother wasn't exactly whole."

"My grandmother?"

"Who else?" Erzse said with amusement.

"My father only mentioned her in passing and only that she was from Anemoi, nothing about a mixed background."

"Well, you could argue that everybody in Anemoi is a mongrel to some extent, given all the migration and mixing of the different races and cultures over the millennia, but in this instance, how very strange that you know nothing of your grandmother's family from beyond Anemoi…And what of your grandfather's origins?"

"Just that he was a fisherman from somewhere north of Anemoi," Xander said.

A bizarre blend of curiosity and pity took Erzse.

"How odd that I must be the first to detail one of several reasons why it is that you're so valuable to me."

Xander's ears perked.

"Your great-grandmother was from a well-off merchant family in Anemoi and your great-grandfather, the aristocracy of Flameria. In fact, he was an heir to the Flamerian throne before it was abolished. And from them, your grandmother—my mother, Isabel—was born into a decent household in Borealis, though she held citizenship of both nations."

"Flameria?"

"Small kingdom in the north. Once very rich and powerful in its own right but now a vassal state of the much larger Cresedi Empire. Don't be ashamed you don't know these places. They tussle in a land beyond the school curriculum in Anemoi, and your father, the fool, failed to fill the gaps."

"I know who the Cresedi are," Xander said, irritated.

"Well, that's a start."

"And my grandfather came from Flameria also?"

A proud grin took Erzse's expression. "This is where it gets really exciting. Your grandfather, Sabien, was one of three concurrent emperors that ruled over the Cresedi Empire, an empire too vast to be ruled by any one man—"

Xander stumbled backwards against the wall as the colour drained from her skin and her mouth dropped in shock.

Erzse chortled. "Hard to believe, I know!"

"But then, that means—" Xander vomited the remnants of her stale bread onto the damp floor. "I'm…I'm descended from the monsters that destroyed Borealis."

"So, you've figured out that much. Funny, I don't recall anyone of note having determined that it was the Cresedi. Nonetheless—"

"But why? Why would they do it?" Xander stammered.

"We'll get to that."

"But—"

Erzse slammed her foot against the brick floor. "Listen when I speak! Understood?"

Xander nodded, though her mind still rocked from the ripples of the revelation.

"Sabien," Erzse continued, "ruled over the smallest of the three boundaries to the south and is also credited with absorbing Flameria into the empire after a series of viciously brutal wars. That's when he met your grandmother, and together they had Carolus and me. Of course, as is usual in the Cresedi Empire, our father had already fathered other children before he met our mother, and so we entered a family with four older brothers."

"Why would my father not tell me this?" Xander whispered.

"The risk of you talking. It's no secret in Anemoi that Carolus and I are only partially descended from the 'great' people of this nation, with our mother passing us citizenship. For a nation that brags of equality and openness and disconnection of the state from superstitious rabble, there's an awful lot of deceit and hypocrisy, especially when one considers the mix of people that make up Anemoi. Nevertheless, some would still consider us outsiders, and this presents a liability. However, with all that being said, we're still passable. Two siblings with a humble lineage on our father's side. Imagine the intrigue, the rumours, if it came to light that we were descended from royalty. It would call into question the strength of our loyalty to Anemoi and her principles."

"That didn't stop you from dragging my father's name through the muck—a foreigner looting the riches of Anemoi."

"A means to an end. It's no different to you being down here. The offspring of Carolus, of all the sorry souls, certainly can't be afforded any respite. You and your brother both with your parts to play."

"Lawrence?" Xander averted Erzse's gaze as her mind grappled for his memory, but like the faces of her parents, his features were a blur warped by time. "I was young when he left."

"Not so long that you shouldn't remember his face. And to think he came back for you, to search for you after your parents died, and this is how you repay his memory."

"He came back for me…I thought he must've drowned with the rest of the northern fleet," she said, aghast, and then confusion took her. "What do you mean, 'memory'? How do you know all this…What did you do, Erzse?" she said with growing apprehension and anger in response to the wicked expression spreading across the witch's face, any hint of maternal pity and sympathy evaporated.

"Why, I killed him." She laughed wickedly.

Xander lunged at the cell door and reached her hand through the bars in an effort to grab Erzse's throat, but she fell short. "I'll kill you, bitch!"

"Before you do that," Erzse retorted calmly, "would you not rather find out why than attack me in your feeble state?"

"Why does it matter, Erzse? You killed him, your nephew, my brother. How could you?" she seethed, her fists balled and ready, but her limbs were still weak and heavy.

"You squirm over a boy you barely knew. Yes, I killed him, but I killed him out of necessity. Your brother made the mistake of being your father's child. He was a threat and had to be taken care of."

"A threat—what do you mean?"

"Think about what I've told you, you little weakling. Your grandfather was an emperor—he had five boys, your father being one of them. That's five claims to one throne. Custom dictates only the strongest should survive to rule. Your father fled, as only a weakling does, and so both him and his brat child of the male line had to be disposed of."

"You killed my father…" the girl said in utter disbelief, and the weakness of her limbs and stubborn grogginess of her mind swiftly parted way for a surge in anger-induced strength and clarity of mind. "You organised the attack on Borealis?"

Erzse stared with intrigue at the rapid rebound in the girl's strength.

"Not me," she responded. "I have no right to command such a vast army. That's not to say I wasn't—"

"Complicit," Xander seethed.

"Little girl, there are forces at work far greater than you or me. Your father was a threat, and he was removed for it."

"Who removed him?" she spat between clenched teeth.

"Your uncle, the oldest of the five brothers and current emperor of the South Cresedi Empire. Gorzan."

"Gorzan!" Xander muttered with vicious hatred. "Is it him that comes for me?"

Again, Erzse glanced at the man in the silver mask before turning back to the girl.

"You don't miss much, do you?" she said to Xander.

"Why does he want me? And why destroy an entire city to murder one man? Or was it all part of your grab for power in Anemoi?"

"Grab? Little worm, I have Anemoi in my hand."

"But why? Was being a senior minister not enough? Why help destroy your mother's birthplace and so many innocents along with it? Was your brother's assassination worth all that?"

"Anemoi's wealth and her manpower," Erzse said matter-of-factly.

"That doesn't make any sense. You exterminated tens of thousands when you destroyed Borealis."

"Anemoi is more than Borealis. Sacking that city was a necessary move to take power without committing the whole army and without destroying the resources we need. Though the threats to the empire are pressing, we can afford to wait out a decade for the results. It's not just the ore in the ground but Anemoi's location on a peninsula that connects north to south and east to west. Anemoi is the crossroad of the world and is a highly valuable prospect."

"And her manpower?"

"Delivered the moment Aiden made me commander of all her armies."

"They'll not fight for the Cresedi, if that's what you think."

"At some point it'll become clear to the masses that they have no choice."

Xander's eyes widened. "You're going to make Anemoi into a vassal state like Flameria?"

"Like I said, the people will see little choice once the time comes. I'll make sure of it."

"Then that's your prize? That's what you get out of all this? Total control of Anemoi as a vassal state of the Cresedi Empire."

Erzse shrugged. "That, amongst other things."

"That's not enough for your liking?" Xander jibed angrily. "Let me guess, the thousands of young Borlencian girls that you can maim and kill? Is that the rest of your prize?"

Erzse's expression hardened.

"I've touched a nerve," Xander said with growing defiance.

Erzse stared dangerously at Xander for several moments before a wry smile took her. "Another reason, I just recalled. Let's not forget that control of Anemoi gives me access to the magical gifts born from her waters and the people that can get me said gifts."

Dread seized Xander's muscles and lungs. She dared not utter another word for fear of accidentally revealing an item Erzse may not actually be after.

"Say it," Erzse said tauntingly.

"I don't know what you mean."

"Of course you do. Say it. What is it that you, of all the people on this wretched strip of land, can get me? Will you really withhold such wonderful words from my ears? So be it. The Rose. You can, and you will, get me the Rose."

"I'll do no such thing."

"You'll have little choice once I'm done with you," Erzse said, standing up. "You know, I think it's about time for one of those naps of yours. Oh! Don't worry. I'll see to it you're fed whilst out cold."

"Try it! Come inside and try it."

"I don't need to. The moment you fall asleep, you'll be locked back inside."

"I'll—"

"You can't fight it. Sleep will come, whether you want it or not. So just let it," Erzse said, turning her back to the cell. "And be sure to eat and get your exercise. It won't do any of us any good if we have to resort to force-feeding your wasted flesh."

At that, she disappeared down the hallway with the man in the silver mask immediately behind her.

Anger and nerves surged through Xander as the door clicked shut a moment later, leaving her alone in a stupor over the revelations. She felt revulsion at the thought of Cresedi blood streaming through her veins and was utterly distraught by Erzse's knowledge of her mother's lineage and the gift it carried. Overwhelmed by panic, she sat on the bed and rested her forehead on the palms of her hands. It was her mother's blood, that of the bearer, that had driven the evil woman to seek her out. And despite her determination to fight it, she knew it was probably just a matter of time before Erzse succeeded in acquiring an item that could turn the tide of any failing war. She slammed her fists into the bed.

"I'll not let her get it," she said inwardly. "I'll train my mind and body to repel her. The hell with that woman."

CHAPTER 56

Marx 29, 485; Crowton, Borlencia—Evia looked on as the stuffy room filled with known faces and their trusted confidants. Already sitting beside her were Joseph and Dogner. Next in, and taking the empty seats opposite, were Wiston and Robyn with the captain of their guard. Next, Ronal and Aiden's messenger, slowly shuffling to the left of the room as they exchanged words. Then, in a flurry and taking all available chairs or spots wide enough to stand, Fredrick, Santos, and the leaders of Borlencia's resistance.

But just when she thought the room was full and ready to begin, Grendal entered. Evia couldn't help herself and quickly approached him as the rest of the gathering got settled.

"Grendal," she uttered and hugged the man whose skin still carried the black-and-blue blemishes of multiple undeserved beatings. She pulled away and took in his fatigued features. "How…I don't understand."

"Aiden realises the gravity of the situation he's created. I'm here for the same reason you see *him*." He nodded his head in the direction of Ronal. "May I?" he asked, pointing to the ground next to Evia's chair.

"Nonsense, lad," Dogner said, having inferred the request. He stood up and moved to the side. "Take my chair. I need to stretch my legs anyhow."

"Thank you," Grendal said, and he walked over and slumped onto it whilst Evia took her own.

With the room filled and the atmosphere keenly intent, Evia leaned forward, ready to start. She had already scanned Ronal's mind for deceit, and though she still doubted her abilities, she was confident of his sincerity. It was Ronal, after all, that had offered her shelter in the aftermath of the vote. He had no love for Erzse, and though fiercely loyal to Aiden, he was still fond of Evia and the others. Already weeks had passed under his care, and still no harm had come to them. Strangely enough, she still trusted him.

"Thank you for coming. All of you," she began. "Even with Ronal's assurances, I know how dangerous it is for you to be here given what's transpired in the past three weeks. Erzse's appointment to commander of Anemoi's armies the day of the vote has already resulted in the replacement of much of the military leadership in the west and the beginnings of a national military that answers to her. And then there's the political subterfuge. As was somewhat expected, she's cracked down on all those Zylencians, and some Borlencians, that opposed her and her own in the past and since. Her ascension has come about at a frightening pace, and it's beyond apparent at this point that Aiden is prime minister in name only."

"Can't blame him," Ronal muttered. "I'd have given her the reins the moment she asked if she had my little ones locked up."

"I think most would have," Evia admitted. "But as it is, she's not held up her end of the bargain. His daughter's not been released, and now Erzse threatens execution if Aiden doesn't step down as prime minister entirely."

"That was fast," Santos commented. "The vote's hardly cold, and she's already pushing him out."

"It's that or she has him murdered," Evia said. "One is slightly less palatable than the other."

"Has a date been set?" Ronal asked.

Aiden's messenger spoke. "Two weeks from now, his daughter and M. K. will be executed for the crime of treason."

There were inaudible mutterings across the different groups.

"What will Aiden do?" asked one of the merchants that had been instrumental in building the resistance in the Borlencian north, a middle-aged man with a swollen nose.

"His battalion is still loyal to him—" Evia began when another from Crowton interrupted.

"He threatens civil war? The man's gone mad!"

"You can't storm Zyphyr with five thousand men and not expect some kind of repercussion," Robyn said sternly, having not been made privy to the information beforehand.

"It's probably as good as standing down and handing her the chair," Ronal pondered, also surprised by the revelation. "She'll use the illegality to have him removed."

"His conscience won't allow him to step down," the messenger said. "It'd be making it too easy for Erzse. But then it means he'll be condemning his girl."

"So risk civil war?" the man with the bulbous nose asked.

"Let's face the facts—she's going to get the chair regardless of whether he fights or not," Evia said. "And all attempts to free his daughter by way of his position have fallen flat. At least this way, whilst he's still got the means, he can rescue his daughter and, if he's lucky, hurt Erzse in the process."

"When and how?" Wiston asked, eager for details.

"The day of the vote, when she and M. K. are being marched to the forum to be executed," the messenger answered. "It's worth mentioning, though, he's not committing the full battalion to rescue his daughter. Erzse has political prisoners stashed all over Zylencia and Borlencia. The battalion's been broken up and will launch targeted assaults against a handful of strongholds. Those that aren't in the initial strikes will be given other orders."

"How many will commit to Zyphyr?"

"Six, maybe seven hundred."

Wiston swore. "Six hundred! Will that be enough?"

"Commander Ricard's war in the south has drawn down the last of the Zylencian battalions not already committed elsewhere. There's a couple thousand of Erzse's men left in the city, and they're spread all over the metropolis. It should be enough."

"Then why call us here?" Fredrick asked.

"We need you to expand the network," Evia said. "We're expecting a heavy stream of political refugees—"

"All Zylencian?" asked a woman in the crowd.

"Most, but loyal to M. K. and Aiden. Politicians, merchants, soldiers, and their families. Those risking it all in the targeted assaults. Those to be freed. Those affiliated. It'll be too dangerous for them to remain in Zylencia."

There was quiet as the ensemble digested the news.

Joseph cleared his throat and looked to Santos. "We also need you and people like you to take positions in the Borlencian battalions that will be formed from the militia. Experienced men and women that can get into positions of leadership. At some point, when the time is right, we're going to need to cleanse the top ranks of Erzse's loyalists."

Santos eyed the man, unsure what to make of such a dangerous ask. "I know a few that might be up to it, but it'll be a difficult conversation. Nonetheless, I'll see what I can do."

"Thank you, Santos," Evia said. "And Ronal—"

"Let me guess—keep Erzse in check?" Ronal spoke.

"It'll be a dangerous game, but you and the other Borlencian ministers are loyal to Aiden, not her. Even with him removed, he's asked that you present a front against Erzse when the situation calls for it."

Ronal shifted in his chair awkwardly and turned to the messenger. "He couldn't tell me himself?"

The messenger shrugged. "This is him telling you."

"It's true then?"

"Just don't get yourself killed trying."

"His words or yours?"

"His," the messenger retorted.

"Anything else?"

"No," Evia interrupted before addressing the whole room. "We're about to enter a period of uncertainty not too dissimilar to what we've already been through. Please don't forget you're not alone." Several of the Borlencians glanced at the Eurencians. "Joseph and Dogner will fill you in on the details of where we need you focused."

Dogner marched to the corner and manoeuvred a foldable table into the centre. "Gather around and we'll get going," he said as Joseph sauntered over and laid down several maps.

As the Borlencians pulled up around the table, the Eurencians walked up to Evia and Grendal, while the messenger remained seated.

"And what of us?" Wiston asked Evia.

"Aiden's assault will present an opportunity for us."

"Xander?" Robyn said.

She nodded. "If it's not too much to ask, can I please commandeer some of your men? We've already got the nondescript clothes and armour we use to hide the identities of men operating within the network—"

Wiston waved his hand. "You've got our support. Though, I must admit, part of me would almost rather Erzse knew there was Eurencian involvement—"

"But that would be reckless and premature," Robyn added, eyebrow raised quizzically.

"Of course, of course. You know, what's happened since they elected *Aiden* into power is going to come as a bit of a shock to Varela and the others. I doubt any of them will take kindly to the knowledge that their electee is Erzse's puppet. But no point instigating a war on two fronts until we can call a session." Wiston looked at Robyn. "We need to send a messenger letting Varela know what's happened."

"I'll see to it once we're done here."

"Alright." Wiston peered to Aiden's messenger, who now lingered on the outskirts of the group gathered around the table. He turned back to Evia and the others. "What about Aiden? Where will he go? That's five thousand men we could use in the eventuality of war with Erzse."

"He and a good chunk of his men will travel west," Evia said.

"They're leaving Anemoi?" Robyn said, surprised.

"The ones not burdened by family. Believe it or not, it'll be less risky for them than staying in Anemoi. At least until the dust settles."

"A waste," Wiston said, shaking his head. "And what about you, Grendal? Why did he let you go?"

"As part of his redemption, he's given me the means to liberate several ministers and persons of note that were sold off by Nala to the Buto."

"Senior Minister Nala?" Robyn asked, aghast.

"None other."

"But sold as slaves?"

"They're not the first and won't be the last as long as she's in power," Grendal said.

Evia recalled the woman and her ability to irk Erzse, as well as her praise for Aiden. "What is the woman's relationship to Aiden?"

"They go a long way back. A decade—maybe more. I don't know the ins and outs of their relationship, but they've helped each other consolidate power."

"And he knew of the slave trade?"

"There's not much Aiden didn't know of." Grendal withdrew a parchment. "A sealed letter from Aiden giving me authority to act on his behalf. He wants me to put an end to the trade and do what's necessary to stop the flow of narcotics. Unfinished business he'll no longer have the opportunity to put right, or so he says."

"And Nala?" Evia asked.

"He wants me to arrest her."

"Thought they were allies?" Wiston said, confused.

"More like a means to an end that's outlived its purpose," Grendal replied. "It's no bother to me. The woman's a termite that needs to find the bottom of a boot. Even without the letter, the merchant navy is on my side and ready to assist in cleaning up the province."

"When will you leave?"

"I'm headed for Bulgar tonight, but I'll not leave for Notencia immediately. I need to gather as many ships as I can, which will take several weeks. I'll likely still be there once you get Xander—I assume Eurencia is your destination once you have the girl?"

"It's safe for them there," Wiston said.

"Then I'll make sure we all sail together. There's safety in numbers." Grendal glanced to Aiden's messenger, who had returned to his seat and now stared at them. "What's next for him?"

"He says Aiden travels south to find an audience with Ricard," Evia said. "I assume once he's done here, he'll return to his commander."

"You trust him?"

"Not particularly, but what's there to tell? Aiden has no need of us beyond what was presented today. He knows his action to save his daughter will give us an opening, and he's left it at our discretion if we want to risk an attempt to rescue Xander or not."

"And do you know where she is?" Grendal asked.

"We have an idea but sadly no confirmed location."

"Not even Aiden knows?"

"No." Evia's expression lifted as an idea struck. "It pains me that I didn't consider this before, but I think we could use a hand from two brothers and a stag."

CHAPTER 57

Marx 30, 485; Zyphyr, Zylencia—Xander sat upright and, as had become customary, sucked in a mouthful of air as she woke from the white abyss within her mind. Her head pounded, and her eyes throbbed from the prolonged slumber. Teeth gritted and fists balled, she cursed through pursed lips.

Every several days it was the same. Unable to keep her eyes open any longer, she would drift to sleep and find herself locked in the endless prison Erzse had constructed in her mind. Though never more than two days at a time, as far as she could tell, each stretch still felt like much, much longer. To the point where hallucinations had become a common occurrence, and she had begun to think in months and years instead of days.

And though she tried to keep her mind and body strong during the periods she was awake, she could feel her mental strength waning and Erzse's grip tightening. She balked inwardly at the implication.

About to get up and do some exercises, she glanced into the hallway, drawn by an exceedingly rare flicker of movement.

"Hello," she called, discomforted by the unusual interruption.

She tensed as the man in the silver mask emerged from the shadows. She hadn't seen him, or anybody for that matter, since Erzse had visited on that lone occasion a lifetime ago. Every time she awoke, there were three buckets. One with drinking water, one with bland food, and another for her waste. There were no voices emanating from the surrounding empty cells, and there was no noise except for the scurry of the odd rodent and the drip of water from the rotten ceiling. In truth, all that separated her waking moments from those in her sleep was the slimy brick underfoot and the horrid taste of her sustenance.

"What do you want?" she asked.

He didn't respond as he walked up to the cell and tossed a small parcel wrapped in greasy newspaper onto the bed. She picked it up and turned it over in her hands. It was warm. "What is it?" He didn't respond, just stared. "I'll open it if you tell me who you are." Nothing. "Whatever," she muttered dismissively and pulled off the newspaper to reveal a soggy cardboard box. She opened it.

Her nostrils flared as the salty aroma of the breaded fish pierced the musty odour of the prison. Not wanting to show weakness in front of the man, she held her urge to rip a chunk off with her teeth and calmly placed the parcel on the bed.

"Why?" she asked.

"Something to keep you going," he grunted.

"Erzse worried about my strength?"

"Something like that," he said and then turned around and began down the hall towards the exit.

She stood up. "Wait—who are you? Where's Erzse?"

No response except for the soft pad of his shoes against the floor.

"Please, just answer me." Nothing. Irritated by the slight and utterly frustrated by her predicament, she reached her mind out to his without any regard for subtlety.

The man stopped in his tracks just as Xander jolted her head back and swore under her breath.

"You're...you're not just you. There's two of you in there. But how's that possible?"

The man hesitated for a moment and then continued to the exit and left, letting the door slam shut.

"What in the bloody hell is going on?" she uttered as she sat on the edge of the bed, brow creased with bafflement. "He's…the same man from the square, the one dressed as a dog." Her eyes widened with horror. "But then, that means…"

In shock, she slumped onto her hard pillow. Her gaze was intent on a lone drop of water clinging to the grotty ceiling, but her thoughts dwelled on the man tormented by internal conflict. The man from the steppe, the same man in her dreams that was wholly human, also inhabited a tiny sliver of that empty vessel of a creature that was her captor's servant. The servant that just so happened to be a street performer whose character of choice was a dog. She suddenly had to stop herself from laughing at the sheer ridiculousness of the idea. But as bizarre as it seemed, she knew what she had seen.

"That's why he only comes to me as a vision. He's trapped inside his own mind. And that's how he knows what Erzse is doing to me. It must also be how he knew where the prisoners were being held."

Caught in the barrage of thoughts on what it all meant, it was some time before her attention returned to the fish wedged to the side of the mattress.

"It won't do me any good to starve," she admitted, tearing off a chunk of the flaky white flesh and throwing it into her mouth.

CHAPTER 58

Aprix 1, 485; 120 kilometres south of Zyphyr, Zylencia—From the thicket at the base of the hillside and through the morning's heavy drizzle, Aika motioned to Ratin a simple but effective array of gestures easily determined by the keen sight of the forest folk, and he responded in kind from his vantage point atop the opposite hill.

Ricard watched the interaction with fascination and again inwardly praised Aika's decision in the aftermath of the vote to travel south and gather a group of her best to assist with the war. The elite archers had joined only a handful of days prior after making the trek north at a blistering pace, and already their presence had been a massively useful addition to an army predominantly on foot. Bolstered by the thought, he peered back down to the valley bottom with a determined eye.

"Makes you wonder what they're drinking to line themselves up so obvious," he muttered as they observed the column of five horsemen and twenty spearmen march the length of the valley depths.

"Perhaps death is a better alternative than living under Erzse's witchdom," Aika remarked.

"You just make up that word?"

"Will it stick?"

"I think you should pay attention, Princess. Ratin's men ready?"

She nodded.

"Good," he said. "When they reach the mark, start with the front and make your way backwards. I want them to panic and backtrack into the second ambush whilst we rush them from the sides."

"You mean, as we discussed?" she jibed.

"Just making sure we're all up to speed."

"Twenty metres…fifteen…wait!" She quickly gestured to Ratin to hold the volley.

"What you doing?" Ricard nearly roared.

"It's Aiden, head of the column."

"Aiden? As in, Anemoi's freshly minted prime minister?"

"Yes!"

"Unlikely, Princess, not on the front like this. Tell Ratin to proceed."

"No, it's him. He's not wearing his colours, but that's him."

"And he chose his lot. Proceed, Princess!"

But as Ricard spoke, the column stopped, and the man beside Aiden rose the flag of the neutrals.

Ricard instinctively gripped Aika's arm as she readied to reveal herself. "Wait!"

There had been a moment's silence before Aiden removed his helmet and bellowed, "We're not your enemies, Commander Ricard. No, we are allies with a common cause."

"We should hear him out," Aika urged.

"You mad?"

"Are you?" she said sternly.

Aiden's features had worn considerably in the weeks since Aika had last seen him, and despite the heat of the tent, his skin and eyes were grey, weary, and cold and his old age very apparent. Even his arrogant demeanour seemed weak and diminished as he stood before the collective judgment of Aika, Ricard, and Ratin.

"How can we trust you, spymaster?" Ricard said. "You betrayed all those who voted for you by throwing your lot in with Erzse. You had it within your power to prevent her rise, but it was your own selfish desire for the seat that allowed her success."

The weathered man didn't flinch, only stared back with some semblance of tired cunning. "I wouldn't trust me either, at least not after what you say, but then, my circumstances aren't what they were."

"Your daughter?" Aika interjected, having heard the rumours. And though she couldn't verify it, she had concluded that the disfigured girl she had spied from the shadow of the tunnel shortly after Xander's capture was none other than the prime minister's child.

Aiden nodded with a profound sadness.

"And we can help each other how?" Ricard said, still unmoved by the man's apparent sincerity.

"I know how to rescue M. K. I can get him out along with my daughter, but I'll need his militia."

"That's quite the ask. Wouldn't do us any good to diminish our forces here in the south."

"Of course," Aiden began. "That's why I refer to the ones already in the city." Ricard didn't react. "I know you've already got a sizable force across the city. What is it, a thousand? Maybe more? Don't worry, old boy. Your secret's quite safe with me, regardless of your response. But I do think it's worth both our whiles if you let me use them."

"What makes you think they'd follow you?"

"Absolutely nothing. But they'll follow you. And failing that, I'm sure they'd do it for him, with or without your blessings," Aiden said with a hint of the arrogance Aika knew.

"I'm sure, but what good does it do to lay down lives to free M. K. when

Erzse will still hold authority?" Ricard said. "All M. K. can do is strengthen the resolve of the militia as Acro hunts their families, and if he does defeat Acro and the other Zylencian battalions in battle, well, I'm willing to bet Erzse will just send in the combined regulars of the provinces to finish the district off. So what does his freedom achieve, besides to give me a break? No, at this point, I'd rather keep as many alive as I can."

"And the daughter of Carolus?" Aiden asked.

Neither Ricard nor Aika flinched as those words escaped the man's mouth, but both were equally shocked that he knew of Xander's identity.

"Her life also holds value, does it not?" Aiden continued.

"Same as M. K.'s," Ricard said with forced indifference, though his feelings were anything but unbiased.

"And yet Evia seemed to think the girl capable of changing the tide against Erzse, even if I can only wonder as to how, and this would suggest her strategic value far dwarfs that of the Mountain King's. Surely that alone is worth the attempt?"

Ricard knew the man baited him, but it was also the case that he would do anything to get the girl out of the witch's grip, including risking the lives of the militia. And so he relented. "You know where Erzse holds her?"

"I have an idea, but her rescue is not so simple."

"This only works if you make it simple."

"Erzse has the girl in some sort of trance, deep under the city," Aiden said. "There are moments where she's allowed to wake, but there's no telling if it'll be the case on the day of the rescue. It means, even when we find her, the girl may be as good as a vegetable. It'll take more than a morning brew to wake her up."

"Then we need Evia," Aika remarked.

"I've already sent my messenger to her."

"And?"

"It'll be some days before I hear back, I imagine. But I know where she is, and I do not doubt that she'll help."

Aika looked at Ricard and then back to Aiden.

"Our help is reliant on you filling us in on everything," she said to the latter.

"Naturally."

"Look at how he watches you, Aika," Ratin said abruptly, his gaze lethal and fixated on Aiden. "Even now he plays you. You cannot trust this man. For all we know, he leads us down this path because Erzse tells him to."

"Well, that's certainly plausible but highly improbable," Aiden retorted. "Yes, as long as she holds my daughter, I am her plaything, but my daughter's also as good as disposable if I'm dead, and it's just a matter of time before Erzse places a knife in my back. And if I must be honest, I'd rather be proactive than tempt fate…that and I'm also bloody tired of being her puppet. I hope you can understand."

"I do understand. I understand that as long as it serves you to serve her, you will do her bidding," Ratin said and then muttered to Aika in a language of the Great Forest familiar to only them and Ricard. Her retort was enough to spark a heated argument between the two cousins, and it was only after several minutes of back-and-forth that Ratin reluctantly nodded to her.

"Erzse knows you travel?" she asked Aiden.

"Of course, but not where. Her men likely follow my decoy to Bulgar where I'm expected to arrest Evia based on deliberately incorrect information supplied by one of my spies."

"And what is it, exactly, that you require of the militia?" Ricard asked with as much curiosity as suspicion.

"Distraction."

CHAPTER 59

Aprix 10, 485; Zyphyr, Zylencia—To Xander, the white abyss in her mind had come to resemble the interior of a coffin. Not due to its lack of room—for as far as she could tell, the nothingness seemed to stretch for eternity—but because the expanse was where she assumed she would, in all likelihood, remain trapped until her last breath and then some. A forever resting place where she wasn't quite alive and not quite dead. Akin to the tomb that confined the enchantress, Bronte, for her last centuries of dying slumber.

Sitting cross-legged on the cool white floor, because in her opinion the white canvas should resemble the comfortable cool of marble, Xander breathed out through pursed lips before gently inhaling the fresh air of her dreams through her mouth. In. Out. Mind calm. Heartbeat regular. A daily ritual designed to keep her sane through the seeming multitude of months and years that would pass during each day of her confinement.

Part of the process to ensure sanity was to recall the characters of the reality waiting for her outside her head. A string of sentences and images that she had likely repeated a thousand times, and would, she figured, likely repeat several thousand times more. Names, features, roles in her life.

"Evia—sky-whisperer, energy manipulator, aunt, guardian. Dogner— soldier, farmer, friend, guardian. Joseph—spy, trader, friend, guardian.

Aika—princess, soldier, friend. Ricard—soldier, friend. M. K.—soldier, friend—"

"Trying to keep your wits?"

She jumped from shock and let out a little yelp as she pounced to her feet and swivelled around to identify her frightener. She tensed as she took in the sight of the man behind the silhouette. He was wearing the now-familiar canine mask, and unlike previous occasions, there was no obscurity or shadow, just the crisp visual of him with his face covered.

"It's you," she said.

"The one and only."

"This isn't like last time. You're not blurry. I can make out the marks on your clothes. But the mask is new. Even before, I could tell you weren't wearing it."

"Correct."

"Then what's changed? I assume you're wearing the mask because you're not ready to reveal your identity, but why not just appear like you did before?"

"I figured you could use the reality check. Something that sets me apart from the hallucinations."

"Given I've not seen you like this before, it makes me even more inclined to think of you as a hallucination. Especially as you ran out on me one of the last times before admitting that you're the man wearing the canine mask, which means I have only my own thoughts for confirmation. So, assuming you are real, is this your alter ego?"

"Of sorts."

"And when you wear the silver mask?"

She sensed a flash of shame streak through him. He hesitated before speaking. "They're both one and the same person."

"But both are you?"

"I have no control over *his* actions."

"But he lives in the same body?"

"Yes."

"And Erzse put him there?"

He nodded.

"So she's using your body as her weapon?" Xander asked.

He shifted uncomfortably on his feet. "Assassin, spy, messenger. The canine mask is one my alter ego wears when on the streets, taking on the role of an inconspicuous street performer. Someone that can really just linger anywhere and everywhere without much interference. But the silver mask is the one he dons when—"

"He kills?" she said with more anger than she had originally intended.

He stared at her through the slits in his mask, carefully measuring what he could tell her. "Do you know how I know she traps you in your mind as a means of taking control?"

"Because she did the same to you."

He nodded. "She had help on that occasion, but that was some time ago, and she's much stronger now. Either way, it's why I only come to you like this. I'm trapped in that body that's wreaking havoc on Erzse's behalf."

"How do I stop it from happening to me?"

"I'm not really the person to ask, am I?"

"No, I guess not. But does that mean she's going to win? Take control and get the shard?"

"I don't know yet."

A sombre quiet filled the air as they both contemplated the situation.

Then, remembering the last encounter she'd had with the man's other presence in the cell, she spoke. "Can I reason with your alter ego?"

"Unlikely. He wouldn't hesitate to kill you if given the order. He's Erzse's minion, her creation, moulded and commanded to perform different tasks. He is not me and cannot be trusted."

Sadness took her. "She turned you into a killer. I'm so sorry. It must be awful. To see it all and not be able to stop it."

He shook his head. "It's like peering through a sandy hourglass most of the time. Except when I'm about to commit something vile. Then it clears up. Like Erzse wants me to witness all the horror she's performing through me. Every single time I've wanted to stop it. To wrest control, even for a smidgen of a second." There was a pause. "Only twice have I succeeded."

"But I thought you said—"

"I said I'm not the person to ask. I'm still trapped. A slave to Erzse's whims."

"But if you got back control before, you could do it again?"

"No, I'm not strong enough. Both times I bought myself only a couple of minutes. And the first time was not without severe repercussions when Erzse found out."

"What about the second?"

"We'll soon find out."

Her brow creased. "What do you mean?"

"I mean, it's time."

"Time? Time for what?"

Xander jumped as a frigid stream of water wrapped around her feet. She quickly turned around to find the source, and her mouth gaped. Her gaze followed the waterfall descending from the sky of nothingness right up to the farthest reach of the heavens and then back down to the floor, where the abyss was rapidly filling up like a bathtub. Already, in those mere moments, the cold liquid had risen level with her knees. She turned back to where the silhouette had stood, but he was no longer there.

"What in Anemoi is going on?" she said and began to wade in no particular direction as the water reached her waist. And then her breasts.

Panic started to ensue as her every attempt to swim faltered, as if she were gripping and flapping through nothing but air. And before she knew it, her head was fully submerged. Again and again, she tried to jump up and clear her mouth of the water. Even a fraction would've been enough to relieve the involuntary gasp building in her chest. But her strength was sapped and the physics off. With frantic desperation, she tried and tried until, suddenly, it was too late.

Unable to hold it back anymore, she opened her mouth and sucked in a stream of water into her lungs, forcing her into a violent fit of coughs and chokes. Stars began to invade her peripheral, slowly at first and then at a shocking pace—spreading and consuming until her entire vision was blacked out.

▲ ▲ ▲

Xander jolted out of bed and gasped for air. She was in her cell, but not all was fine. Whilst she had been trapped in her own mind, water from some unknown source had entered the hallway and cell and now stood level with her bed.

Carrying the same desperate panic from her slumber, she waded to the cell door and screamed for help. Unlike her mental prison, however, there was a response. Not a moment later, voices filled the far end of the hallway, and another thirty seconds later, two guards splashed up to the door. Both appeared tired and altogether uninterested in being down there.

"Turn around and hands against the wall!" one of them yelled.

Xander quickly obliged. By now the water was level with her waist, and she figured there must have been a deliberate breach in one of the sewers or maybe a river. She listened intently as the duo opened the cell door and began towards her, and it suddenly occurred to her that she could, in all likelihood, take them out. Dispatch the first, using the confines of the cell to prevent the other from joining. And then use the first's weapon to kill the second. But as she geared up to do it, a thought struck.

There was a reason she was down there. The man behind the mask had planned it. He had told her to come to where the prisoners were. But not only that, he had, if she could recall correctly, told her, "You're not where you're meant to be." And now her cell was flooding just as the silhouette admitted he had, for the briefest of moments, managed to wrest control from his other self.

He had intended for her to be captured, and now he intended for her to be moved, which meant there was more to it. If she escaped, she might lose her only chance to find out. Against impulse, she relaxed and let the first guard grab her right wrist. He pulled it, along with her left wrist, behind her back. Together, the pair secured her arms and then turned her around and led her out of the cell and to the exit.

Two other prisons on that level had also been flooded, but as far as she could tell, they, too, were empty. Drenched in the smelly liquid, the three of them trekked through a series of partially submerged tunnels until they climbed a staircase. The next level was completely dry and the security presence far more significant. Even if she had taken out the two guards, she wouldn't have gotten very far, she admitted.

Led through a myriad of tunnels, some filled with prisoners, others filled with weapons or soldiers casually lying around or playing dice, she was finally checked into a prison not too dissimilar to the last. Except, unlike her previous one, there were only four identical cells in this tiny chamber, and only one of them was empty.

"M. K.!"

"Xander!"

The man's face and body were cut up and bruised and his eyes swollen. Still, he was quick to his feet from his bed, eager for a better look at her friendly face.

"What've they done to you?" she said as the two guards threw her into the cell opposite him. They closed the door behind her with a loud clang and exited the room.

"Everything but slit my throat." He peered to the door to make sure the guards were truly gone. "Where did they find you just now? Were you with Ricard, or maybe your aunt? Are they okay? Are they in the city?"

"I don't know. I was alone," she said, taking a seat on her new bed. It wasn't nearly as comfortable as the last. "I've been locked up here since before the vote. I don't know how long ago that was, though."

"About four weeks ago."

"Four weeks," she murmured, dismayed by how much longer it had felt.

"So then you've no idea about the others?"

"Sorry."

"That's okay," he said, sitting back down.

She could sense a heavy cloud of angst hanging over him. "What's wrong?"

He looked at her for a moment and then got up and approached the bars. He peered to the next cell over. "Gloria?"

Xander got up and moved to the cell door. Looking in the same direction as M. K., sadness took her as the soft-featured girl from the procession emerged from the shadows. Her fair skin had been torn and disfigured, and her stark blond hair ripped out in chunks. The remaining strands of her golden locks were matted with filth and blood. And her piercing grey eyes were reduced to just a single functioning one, the other having been scratched up with some cruel instrument. Though Xander couldn't see the girl's mutilated hand, she knew her to be the same one she had tried to rescue all those weeks prior.

M. K. introduced the girl. "Xander, this is Gloria—Aiden's daughter."

"Aiden's daughter!" Xander blurted.

"I am," the girl responded quietly. "I recognise ya, Xander. From the day me and me brother attacked Erzse. I'm sorry she got ya too."

"I'm sorry for what she's done to you."

"Why? Not like ya could've done anything about it."

Despite the girl's barbaric ordeal, she seemed to carry a positivity about her that Xander couldn't quite understand given what had happened.

"Have you been down here since then?" Xander asked, though she immediately regretted the silly question.

"Unfortunately. And ya say she got ya four weeks ago?"

"According to M. K. How do you know, by the way?" Xander asked him.

"What do you mean?" M. K. said.

"How do you know what day it is? I can't see any windows. It's about as open as the cell they had me in."

He sighed. "Two days from now they're going to—"

"Execute us," Gloria answered for the big man.

"What?" Xander blurted in shock. "How—how can she get away with it?"

"Erzse is a persuasive woman," M. K. said with a shrug. "She's had everything planned out for longer than any of us were in the game. And now she's won. Don't worry. It'll be a quick one, I'm sure. She may be a mass murderer, but she knows it won't go down well if she lets it drag on too long."

Xander glanced at Gloria and frowned. The girl wished for death more than anything, but the girl also knew it unlikely that Erzse would let it be a speedy one. Gloria caught Xander staring, and she smiled softly.

"It'll be fine," the girl said. "Nothing to be done about it anyhow." At that, she retreated into the recess of her cell, humming gently as she did.

The rest of the day was subdued, with the odd word or sentence exchanged between M. K. and Xander. Though Xander craved conversation, she could tell both M. K. and the girl were exhausted and keen to embrace the silence in their final moments. Resigned back to the painful solitude, she lay on her bed and began to run through all she had learned in the prior weeks and why her silhouette might want her in this new cell.

CHAPTER 60

Aprix 12, 485; inside Xander's head, Zyphyr, Zylencia—"Well, Malum, isn't this an intriguing place."

"Indeed, Gemin. Very intriguing."

"And who would've thought you could fit so much space into so little an object."

"Well now, let's not be too hasty to judge. You know as well as I do that the limits of one's mind don't necessarily conform to the limits of one's reality."

"And whose reality do we refer to—hers or ours?" Gemin asked.

"One and the same, don't you think?"

"Now, now, no need to sell yourself short. You certainly haven't found yourself confined to the recesses of your mind because of some rudimentary mental interference."

"Indeed I haven't, silly me," Malum said. "Oh! Look, she's awake."

Xander stared at the duo with a powerful doubt that questioned the reliability of her mind and sight, and on impulse, she viciously rubbed her eyes of the suspected deceptions. But even once the self-inflicted fogginess faded into clarity, the grinning twins stood before her.

"Malum…Gemin…this can't be. My eyes trick me. You aren't here. No, you can't be," she said, though her voice carried no fear, just curiosity.

"Is that so?" Malum grinned. "Then perhaps we really aren't here, and this is simply a trick on *our* minds."

"Indeed, must be the case," Gemin retorted. "In any case, I must ask you, Xander, did you learn nothing from your short time in our company?"

"I…this isn't real," she said, doubtful.

"Of course it is. How many visitors could you possibly have had in here?"

"Are we counting hallucinations?"

Malum glanced worriedly at Gemin.

"How long do you think you've been in here, child?"

"In here," she said, looking around at the expanse. "Many years. Out there—maybe four weeks. Though I can't say how long this current stint has been. There's no way to keep track, no day or night or urge to sleep or eat. Just nothing. Absolutely nothing." Again, she spoke without frustration or alarm, simply calm acceptance.

"You're not far off," Malum said.

"Time has different meanings in different realities," Gemin added.

"That's right. We should know."

"Relativity," they said in unison.

"Why are you here?" she asked.

"We're here because your aunt asked us to be here," Malum responded.

"Evia." Her memory of Evia's features, tendencies, and voice had been warped by the inconsistent projections of her subconscious over a period she knew not how to fathom, but she grasped on to what she thought to be the truest form nonetheless.

"The one and only," Gemin said.

"But why not before? Why's it taken her so long?" she said, confused.

"It's taken the combined strength of your aunt, us, and the stag to locate you and penetrate this world."

"Aes. You're not hallucinations, are you?"

"No, we're not," Malum said reassuringly.

"Then you're really here to get me out?"

"Before your mind descends any further into lunacy."

"And what if I told you there's no way out? Look around you. The nothingness stretches as far as the eye can see, and I've tried everything. I'm trapped for as long as she needs me trapped."

"Ah, so you've imagined the exit before you and still nothing?" Gemin asked, eyebrow raised.

"Huh?"

"Well, what good does it do you to physically search for the exit if you can't trust your eyes?" Malum interjected.

Confusion took her. "I…don't understand."

"This cloud of nothingness was designed by another to trap and deceive you, but it's your mind, and ultimately, you have the power to build your exit however you so please."

"Exactly! Now ask yourself this: How did we get in?" Gemin queried. She stuttered.

"A way in means there's a way out," Gemin said. "Simply imagine the door in front of you."

"Indeed, very simple when you consider it," Malum said matter-of-factly.

They smiled softly without intent to provoke, but the obviousness and nonchalance of their collective statement infuriated the girl who thought she had tried all to escape her own mind. Still, what good would it do her to whine and resist their efforts? So she breathed deep and long and then released her clenched everything.

"Good, clear your mind, like we taught you," Malum said.

"A horizon of nothingness isn't clear enough?" she jibed.

Her quip triggered no response, so she shook her head and closed her eyes and, with some difficulty, cleansed her mind of distraction by sweeping beyond consciousness the thoughts and feelings and illusions that sometimes tended to plague her unmeasurable confinement.

"Now," Malum continued, "imagine the door in front of you. It can be any door—blue, black, green, red, stout, wide, tall, wood, metal, crystal—as long as it's an exit from this place."

She knelt down, closed her eyes, steadied herself on the blank canvas, and put all her energy into conjuring up the image of a door in her mind, one of familiarity and comfort, the front door of the cottage in Nhata. She opened her eyes and smiled warmly at the oak door standing before her, the carved insignia and natural markings of the wood therapeutic to her nerves. She walked to it and placed her hand on the cold knob, but before she could open it, Gemin cleared his throat.

"Xander, before you walk through that door, we must warn you."

"Yes, we must," Malum chimed in.

"A lot has changed in the time you've been…asleep."

"The executions?" she queried.

Gemin continued, "Erzse's retribution has been swift and bloody against those who opposed her rise. The Anemoi you know is very quickly descending into ruin."

"Indeed," Malum spoke. "And as for you, daughter of Carolus, word carried by the winds says riders from the desert query your well-being with curious intent."

"Gorzan," she murmured.

The twins glanced at each other and then back to the girl.

"It's time, Xander," Malum said.

"Your friends come for you," Gemin added. "It's time for you to leave this place."

Xander's heart raced as she put her hand to the cool knob of the door. Hardly able to calm her breath, she peered at the twins and their warm expressions. Ecstatic, she turned back to the conjured door leading from her mind, and she opened it.

CHAPTER 61

"Took you longer to escape than I expected," cooed a cruel voice from the corridor.

Erzse was sitting in a chair directly outside the cell. The man in the silver mask wasn't there, and Xander couldn't sense Gloria or M. K. in the adjacent cells. Xander wiped the sleep from her eyes and stood up as Erzse continued to look on curiously.

"What day is it?" she asked, concealing her dread for the fate of the other two.

"The date is nothing for you to concern yourself over."

Xander could feel a horrid blend of glee and anticipation emanating from the woman. "Then today is the day," she uttered.

"You're getting quite good at that, aren't you?" Erzse said.

"Why are you here and not out there watching the execution? Thought you wouldn't want to miss it."

Erzse grinned, unbothered by Xander's jibe. "The show will come soon enough. Until then, I thought I'd come and greet you after your little feat."

"You were watching?"

"I was nearby and felt your try."

"Now what? I've figured out how to escape your prison. You'll not be able to complete the job."

Erzse looked on curiously and then shrugged. "I have other means. Though those means might have to wait a day or two. A special guest arrives today. Someone with a keen interest in our progress."

"Gorzan?"

"It doesn't matter who. All that matters is the time has come. The next stage of the plan. A stage in which you'll be playing quite the part."

"I already told you, Erzse. I'll not let you use me."

"And like I said already, it's just a matter of time."

"Even if I fail, the others won't. They'll not let you use something so powerful."

"Then I'll just have to kill them, won't I?"

Xander could feel Erzse probing her mind. She was about to try to repel the woman when a desire to poke her wicked aunt arose.

"I know it was you that killed all those Borlencian girls and dumped their bodies under the city," Xander said, her grin mischievous.

Erzse eyed the girl. "Whatever could you mean?"

"You're not just in the business of torturing and maiming. You killed all those girls, and I know why." Though Erzse showed no visible reaction, Xander could sense a flinch in the flow of the woman's thoughts. "It was an exchange. You sacrificed them to the underworld—"

"Only someone rotten to the core—a despicable, such as yourself— could conjure such an abhorrent thought."

"Maybe so, but you're not denying it."

"It's implied," Erzse retorted.

"Implied or not, it doesn't matter. As we speak, the Eurencians have probably already delivered the results of their investigation to their own." Erzse's left eye twinged. "They know the girls were sacrificed by a practitioner of the Zora." And now a twitch of the woman's wrinkled hand. "They've got witnesses testifying that it was you. And you want to know the best part? They've tied that cursed religion to the invaders, which means your game's up. You're caught, Erzse. And you're as good as hanged, like the treacherous cow that you are."

There was quiet as an intense hatred pierced through the woman's gaze. And then she smirked. "There are no witnesses. I killed them all. And if what you're saying about the Eurencians is true, they'd have had me arrested already under the crimes of treason. And as for your delivery, it's incredibly obvious that you've used however long you've been trapped in that little head of yours to build this rebuke. What a waste of what little time you've got left. Really. What a pity," she said, standing up. "No matter. It's nothing to fret over. Once I've got what I need, you'll not remember the half of it anyway."

Erzse turned to the door but only made it a metre before Xander called out, "Does Gorzan know?" Erzse stopped. "Does he know that you sacrificed those girls to the underworld in some sort of exchange? Last time I checked, the Zorforiat, and by extension, the Zora, are outlawed in the Cresedi Empire."

Erzse swivelled on her heel and strode right up to the bars with a smug smirk. "Little girl, who do you think sanctioned it?"

"But why? No energy, no matter what it does, can be worth the killing of so many innocents."

"It depends on who you ask." The woman lifted her hand as a green sheen began to envelop it, and then she closed her fist, causing a small area of bricks on the cell floor to crack. "A power even your aunt couldn't fathom." The green sheen vanished. "Well, that's not entirely true. She will know soon enough."

Erzse turned to the door, but in all her arrogance failed to sense the hand reaching through the bars to grab her neck. Xander violently pulled Erzse towards her and smashed the back of the woman's head into one of the metal poles. Again and again. But as she reached her other hand through the cell to try to choke her aunt, she was thrown to the ground by an unseen force.

Once again enveloped by the green aura, Erzse turned around with an angry scowl etched into her decaying features. "Like I said: power you couldn't even fathom."

Xander peered up from her daze, her eyes filled with horror, her lips quivering. Confusion took Erzse, for she knew the girl was no stranger to the unordinary. Not so gently, she reached out her mind into Xander's. Xander didn't stop her.

"Ah. So now you know," Erzse said. "It doesn't matter. You're not going anywhere. And I know your friends intend to rescue you today. They'll be mine before the day is up, and with them, you'll give me the shards. *Oh, such a beautiful day, now cometh the Rose to play,*" she sang with no real beauty as she sauntered into the darkness, her green glow evaporating as she did.

"It wasn't just…" Xander managed through heavy breaths. "But why?"

"An army created for the underworld."

Xander jerked around to see the man in the canine mask standing there, his projection clear and unobscured.

He continued, "That was born from the living. Borealis wasn't just the key to Anemoi. It was also the down payment on a power practically unmatched in our reality. She sold all those tens of thousands of men to the underworld in exchange for it. Her and Gorzan have, and will, use it to devastating effect."

"And the girls?"

"The new asking price from an individual just as unreasonable as Erzse."

"And my parents?" The man seemed taken aback by the question. "Are they also trapped in the underworld?" she asked, though, in truth, she didn't expect him to know. And yet the silence said otherwise. "You know, don't you?"

"They are truly dead." There was sadness in his voice.

"Why would someone in the underworld need an army of our kind?"

"Why does anybody need an army?"

"Do you know who made the deal with Erzse?" she asked, standing up, anger rising.

"I do, but we've no time to discuss it right now. As you may've already gathered, Erzse knows your friends are coming for you, and she fully intends to use their capture to force you to do her bidding. Which means we've got only a few minutes to get you out of here." He pointed to the ground where the bricks had cracked.

Xander looked down and glimpsed a discoloured tile underneath the brick flooring. Instinctively, she grabbed one of the broken bricks and pulled it from the floor, and then the next and the next, until she had removed more than half of the bricks in the cell floor. She took a step back and her face lit up at the ancient, faded mosaic still partially hidden underneath.

"The broadleaf!" she whispered and continued removing as many of the bricks as she could with the mattress and stool in the way, until most of the original flooring had been lifted and thrown through the cell bars into the corridor outside.

Her eyes fell on a mosaic tile at the edge of the room where the centre of the design disappeared under the wall. Unlike the others, this tile had its own miniature broadleaf carved into it.

"It's loose," she said and removed it to reveal a small crease similar to the one that marked the very centre of the Great Tree.

She placed her ring on the crease and then jumped back as a small tunnel opened in the wall and filled the cell with an orange glow and an uncomfortable warmth. She peered inside, and about to enter, she hesitated.

"Why do you stop?" the voice returned.

"The others. They're coming for me. I can't leave."

"They'll not find this cell, Xander. Erzse let your friends into your head, but she didn't reveal your true location. Just what she needed to lure them in. The only way you can help them now is through there."

She swore, and unwilling to tempt fate, she retrieved the ring and bent down to enter the tunnel but stopped short. She turned to him. "Will you tell me your name?"

"It'd only distract you."

"Then something else. Where you're from. What were you before—you know? Anything."

"Xander," he said, his voice filled with pain. "I'm sorry, but I won't tell you. Not today."

"I know you block me from making a connection," she said angrily. "But you can't interfere forever. At some point, I will figure it out."

"And when you do, we can spend all the time in the world discussing it. Now please, hurry."

Expression stern, she nodded and then crawled through the tunnel into the cave system at the heart of the mountain. A cave system that was so hot it seared all but the toughest of living tissue. Of course, unbeknownst to her, the ring on her finger provided for the most exceptional of circumstances.

CHAPTER 62

The cramped tunnel was long and monotonous, and the rock on which she crawled sharp and black and warm to the touch. A powerful orange glow akin to a recently heated coal beckoned in the distance, and loyal to its call, she continued forward with a conflicted blend of inquisitiveness, eagerness, and nerves.

"This feels like an eternity." She groaned, her body unaccustomed to the exertion and heat. "Well, I take that back—being trapped in my mind was close to an eternity. This is more like an unwelcome visit to the doctor's cottage in the pouring rain. Except this is a tad more exciting than the doctor's cottage, so maybe this is more like a stroll to Etlinga to visit Joseph after one of his adventures. Yes, I like that thought more," she muttered un-enthusiastically. A sudden wave of dread hit her at what awaited her friends. Awaited Anemoi. "No, there's too much riding on this…on me…I can't fail, whatever it is I entered here to do. The others need me." She pushed on harder and faster with a steadfast determination that honed her distraction and fuelled her impetus.

The tunnel opened up into a grand, brightly lit chamber larger than any hall she had seen, and though the floor immediately underfoot was bricked, the walls and dome-shaped ceiling consisted of the same jagged rock as the tunnel. It was an eerie sight made all the stranger by the gigantic metal door on the far end of the chamber and the much smaller metal door beside the tunnel she had just crawled out of. Both were connected by a long, metallic beam bridge traversing a sea of bright-orange light dividing the room. She inched towards the edge and gaped at the pool of breathing magma and the heat it radiated.

"This must be the underworld of the old religions, so deep in Camana as it is…nothing good ever came of those stories." She shuddered, wishing she had even the bluntest of knives on her. She looked to the door at the opposite end of the bridge. "I bet if I had the map on me, it'd be telling me to go in there."

Her first steps were unsure and awkward under the sway of the bridge, and the rising heat of the magma was potent enough to singe her protected skin. Her hands didn't leave the railings until she reached the sure footing of the opposite side, and even then, she strode to the door with an overly cautious gait. The door was larger than she imagined, at least ten metres in height and three in width, and a strange, unfamiliar insignia was etched into the material. She put her hand to the sleek metal and abruptly withdrew it.

"Careful, Xander," a familiar voice whispered into her mind. "The Guardian of the Mountain knows why you've come but has little patience for the issues of man."

"Evia! You're safe?"

"I am. Listen, Xander, the Guardian is not your enemy, but neither is the Guardian your friend. You should seek not to defeat the Guardian with strength, but neither should you seek to defeat the Guardian with cunning. For the Guardian to reveal the shard, you must brave the impossible and reach into the fiery abyss. Only then can you proceed. As the old saying goes, an eye for a hand, and a hand for an eye."

Xander's brow creased. She had heard those words before. Where? She couldn't recall. But the logic that made no sense then still made no sense now. "You mean an eye for an eye?"

"I said what I meant."

"I don't understand."

"I suspect you won't until the time comes," Evia replied.

"And I have no weapons."

"Again, strength is not the way."

"And you, where are you?" Xander asked. "Erzse says she waits for you and the others. She tricked the twins and set a trap. She means to use you against me."

There was a pause.

"Evia?"

"Noted, Xander. Now please concentrate. I cannot pass with you through that door. Good luck, and I'll see you on the other side."

"Guardian of the Mountain…" Xander said once alone and took in the size of the door. "Doesn't sound promising."

She placed both palms against the heavy door, drove forward with all her weight, and slid through the gap into the cooler arid air.

"What in Anemoi?" She gasped at the city that couldn't possibly fit inside of the mountain.

But there it was in the distance, row upon row of blackened houses and stalls and buildings, populated by people seemingly unbothered by the fact that they lived inside a mountain. A city lit by the natural light of the outside world that passed unimpeded through the transparent skin of the cavern roof.

"What is this place?" she said in awe and began forward along the stone path that wound down to the cityscape through a jagged sea of black rock. A few metres along, she glanced behind her to the entrance knocked into the cavern wall and panicked. "Where's the door?" she cried, feeling for the crease, but all that remained was the faint outline of the massive doorframe and, above it, these words crudely etched into the rock:

An eye for a hand

A hand for an eye

The dead man's hand may see
But only the living man's eye may proceed

"This is the underworld…how foolish of me to enter!" She trembled in bewilderment and fright, and again she frantically felt for the absent crease before crumpling in defeat. "And now what choice do I have but to go into the city?"

It took several moments to gather courage and continue along the path, and though her initial amazement at the settlement had been dampened by her predicament, she soon enough found herself intrigued by the architecture of the first outlying buildings that dotted the black fields on the city outskirts.

The uniform design of the buildings was unique and altogether beautifully strange. But what she soon found most bizarre was the people who wore only grey and manned the fields of black rock. Though she could not see their faces and could only guess at what it was they farmed, for there appeared to be very little by the way of vegetation, she found that for every field or building she passed, she had several more curious onlookers content to follow along the path. And it was only in the narrow streets of the city where the crowds had gathered in silent observation that she tensed up.

"They have no eyes…"

Her gaze fell onto a little girl in a simple grey dress partially hidden behind a woman—the only child she had seen. The girl, as if sensing Xander's curiosity, walked up to her and held out her pale hand, and though initially hesitant, Xander took it and brought a joyful smile to the girl's otherwise vacant face. Hand in hand, the girl pulled her along the rows of strange buildings and through the throng of silent observers into a market square not too dissimilar to those in Borealis. In the exact centre was a small pond of fiery light. Curious, Xander let go of the girl's hand and approached the pool of magma.

"An eye for a hand, a hand for an eye." She read the sign and looked into the molten rock that seared the air. "An eye!" she said, horrified by the eyeball at the bottom of the pool. "I don't understand. What is this?"

"An eye for a hand, a hand for an eye," the crowd said in unison.

"It's the only way," the girl called and held out an object concealed by cloth.

"The shard!" Xander instinctively moved towards the girl but froze as the crowd that now fully packed the square and blocked all exits reverberated aggressively.

They called in alarm, "An eye for a hand, a hand for an eye. It's the only way!"

"It's the only way," the girl said and pointed to the eyeball at the bottom of the pool.

"And reach into the fiery abyss," Xander repeated Evia's words.

She placed a hand over the magma and flinched. Even with the ring, the heat was enough to scald.

"I'll lose my hand. No, there must be another way," she said, gaze intent on the cloth and the shard it hid.

"There's no other way," the girl said. "An eye for a hand, a hand for an eye. That, or you may spend the remainder of your days under the mountain, for there is no way out but for what is down."

"An eye for a hand, a hand for an eye. It's the only way!" the faceless crowd chanted.

"Deeper into the underworld." Xander frowned. "No thanks!"

She hovered her hand over the magma and then abruptly retracted it from the pain.

"Think about it," she said to herself. "Why permanently cripple the bearer? It doesn't make sense. It's got to be a test. And what are your choices, anyway? The way out is shut, so even if I were to wrest the shard from the girl, I can't get out unless I go deeper. An eye for a hand, a hand for an eye… oh, heck! Let's get this over with," she growled. She removed her gauntlet and jacket before impulsively dunking her sword hand into the molten rock.

The sharp, searing pain was immediate and whole as it enveloped her arm from the elbow down, the dissolution of the skin and flesh and the charring penetration of the bone all instantaneous in their agonising onslaught, but still she pushed on and gripped the squishy eyeball between her rapidly dissolving fingers and yanked it out.

She cried and cursed in horror and agony at the scarred, bloodied, fleshy remnants of her right forearm, and she let go of the eyeball as she dropped to her knees on the verge of unconsciousness. The onlookers were emotionless and almost judgmental in their vacant stares, and the girl was nonchalant as she stood over Xander with her hand held out.

"That's your damn concern, the damn eyeball!" Xander cried and reached down with her unblemished arm, but the slimy ball of tissue refused retrieval and persistently hopped and slipped out of her every attempt. In her anger, she thrust forward her damaged hand and gripped the eyeball without resistance. She placed the eyeball in the girl's hand.

"An eye for a hand," the girl said softly, passing the clothed shard into Xander's disfigured hand.

Her pain partially forgotten, she removed the cloth and smiled weakly. "The third. It's shaped like an eye…The Rose of Anemoi is a mask!"

"And a hand for an eye," the girl said.

Xander looked up and did a double take. Her audience of tedious, eyeless plebs were no longer blind to the world. Instead of a wall of creepy, vacant eye sockets, she was greeted by a sea of colourful, abnormally large eyes like none she had seen before. Jewels almost, in purple and yellow and green and red and blue and orange and more colours than she knew. But that wasn't all that had transformed into the brightest and most extravagant of rainbows. Their clothes were no longer grey and dull, and the houses and streets no longer bare and black but all adorned in a whole array of mesmerising colours. Even in the distance beyond the urban build, she could see the hills and fields lush with green and yellow and brown.

"What is this?" she uttered.

"Look at your hand," the girl said, her large golden eyes irresistibly captivating and a perfect match for her bright-yellow dress.

"I don't understand. It looks almost normal."

"To you, yes. You've been gifted the sight of the dead. But how your arm appears to you isn't how it'll appear to the living. They'll still see the decayed, withered hand you witnessed when you first withdrew it."

Xander balled her hand, wiggled her fingers, and flexed her forearm.

"I can still move it, though it hurts a lot. How can that be?"

"What good would it do to cripple the bearer?" The girl winked.

"And what do you mean, 'sight of the dead'?"

"Putting your hand in the fire as you did scarred your flesh and also your soul…You now carry the mark of the dead. Because of this, you can see dead people for what they really are. But in your reality, in the world above, the rule holds true only if the dead want to be seen, which in most cases is unlikely."

"My soul?"

"A requisite of the Rose, for you must represent all, and we are picky in who we accept."

"And the way out?"

"The dead man's hand may see, but only the living man's eye may proceed."

Xander frowned. "Is it really a gift to have my soul marked?"

The girl smiled. "You must return to the surface now. The way out is revealed to you. Good luck, Bearer. You will need it!"

CHAPTER 63

Meanwhile, back in Zyphyr, Zylencia—"Wait!" Aika called down the dank brick hall to Ricard.

The hall was poorly lit by drain holes connecting to the street above, and the strong whiff of damp carried on the air. Donned in light armour concealed under a cloak, she had stopped immediately outside one of a handful of armouries under Zyphyr's streets, lured by a flash of gold through the wooden door's barred window.

"There's no time!" Ricard yelled back, frustration written into his posture and brow, his cloaked armour less discreet given his bulk. "We have to keep moving."

"Give me your axe!" She pointed through the locked armoury gate to a pile of kit on the nearest wooden table. "It's Xander's blade."

He backtracked to where Aika stood and peered through the gate. "It's a trap, Aika. A ruse designed to slow us down. Xander's cell, the guards, the damn maze down here—none of it's as the twins said it would be," he said, waving the crudely drawn map in her face. "We've been played!"

"And her stuff? You think it's deliberate?"

"Yes!"

The dull clang of armour echoed through the space and brought them on edge.

"Come on, Princess!" he urged with growing impatience, but she ignored his plea, grabbed his axe, and noisily broke the lock with a strength that belied her slim build.

"All of two seconds, old man," she said and ran into the armoury and grabbed the blade.

"What about that shield of hers?" he asked as she reached the door.

"I think you're getting slow in your old age—I told you Xander didn't have the shield on her when she was captured. It's with Evia."

"Listen here, Your Highness—"

Aika swiftly released an arrow past his ear and into a lone guard standing at the end of the hall in the direction they had been running. And though the thud of the arrow and subsequent gurgle of death were relatively quiet, the clang of metal on stone as the guard hit the ground was not. Cries of alert instantly rang out from the way they had come.

"Time to leave," Ricard murmured, and they dashed down the corridor to where the guard lay in a heap. Standing over the strewn body, the pair glanced down the two tunnels veering off in opposite directions. "I can't see a bloody thing down that left one," he said uneasily.

"Then I think that answers which one to take."

Together they swivelled into the tunnel on the right but had barely made it a dozen metres when the passage ahead of them caved in in a torrent of stone and dust, and shouts and screams cascaded from the now visible but still unreachable street above.

"That must have been the courthouse." Aika coughed, scraping away the film of dust that had plastered onto her face.

"Brace yourself!" Ricard said, teeth clenched, and another series of explosions erupted in the distance with enough strength to shake the foundations of the city and throw them to the ground. "And that the city barracks—means we haven't much time before the—"

"Oi! What you doing—" a soldier managed before Aika's arrow took him in the throat, felling him atop the other grunt already lying lifeless on the floor of the intersection.

The pair rushed back to the junction, ready to head back the way they had come rather than brave the black fog of the second tunnel, but the sight of men pooling immediately outside the armoury door stopped them still.

Ricard glanced at the only route not visibly impeded by armed foes or rubble. "Damn it, we'll have to—" he began when the ground underfoot shifted in multiple directions and knocked the lot of them over in a scene mirrored across the city.

"What was that?" Aika muttered from her knees, eyes still intent on the gathering of faltering soldiers. "Felt like the whole mountain moved."

"Can't be the palace. It's too soon—"

Again, the floor shifted and caused disarray, and in the mayhem, Ricard clumsily swung his axe into the chest of a lone soldier who had stumbled too close. As Ricard struggled to ready himself for the next, Aika grabbed him by the cuff and threw him into the eerily dark corridor, and then she pounced in after him as the roof of the junction collapsed behind her.

"I think that blast was the palace." She coughed, righting herself.

"Was certainly violent enough." He scowled through the dark as he stood up. "Can't see a damn thing!"

"You'll be fine, old man. You can hold my pack," she teased and started forward with him close behind.

Fifty metres in, she stopped abruptly and nearly knocked him into the wet muck of the ground.

"What is it?" he asked.

"Movement."

"And?"

She turned around. "Why don't you take a breath and give me a chance to find out?"

"Right!"

"It's gone," she whispered after several moments. Again the ground shook under a fresh barrage of distant explosions.

"That must be the gate," Ricard spat, wary of another cave-in. "It means we need to get a move on—"

She put her hand to his mouth, and they listened, their breathing all that cut the unnerving echo of the tunnel. A terrifying, animalistic cry emanated from ahead, followed by frantic screams and shuffling and the flash of an inhuman shadow across the width of the tunnel.

"What the heck was that?" Ricard blurted.

"I don't know…but I think the tunnel exits into a room," she said and crept to the opening for a peek.

She quickly pulled back.

"What is it?" Ricard said.

"Something in there," she said nervously.

"What does it do?"

"It eats."

"Eats what?"

"What do you think?" she hissed under her breath.

"Well, can you get a shot?"

She looked at him and mockingly offered up her bow.

"You've got this," he retorted.

She edged her head around the corner but flinched back and dropped to her knee as a thick claw grabbed for her head. Swift to react, she pulled Xander's blade in a flash of bright gold and swung at the beastly arm exposed in the air, cutting through flesh and bone and forcing the attacker to yank the remnants of the severed limb back into the shadow under a shower of painful cries.

The calls of agony were immediately joined by a chorus of angry howls and growls, and the two stepped back in nervous anticipation, weapons at the ready.

"Bears?" Ricard whispered, sneaking a peek at the barely visible arm on the floor.

"I don't know. Looked bigger and uglier and more vicious than any bear I've seen. And what would they be doing down here, anyway?"

Movement in the dark ahead had taken his eye when he abruptly shoved Aika into the wall and swung his axe into the same creature's neck as it rushed them. The blow was lethal and instantly immobilised the beast in a jittery mess on the ground, but the reprieve was short-lived, for it simply emboldened the chorus of hysteric threats in the room ahead.

He swore. "I still can't see a damn thing! If those creatures rush us, I'll be lucky to land another like that."

"I count three more."

"And what the heck are they? Definitely too ugly for a bear."

"There's four…now five."

"Damn it! No way out but through them. I'm not kidding, Princess. I'm as good as useless without some light."

She let loose an arrow into the dark, and it met with a cry. "Their hide is strong. I'll need several to the neck and head to bring one down." She fired two more. "They move closer but don't give me a clear shot."

Suddenly the pair were thrown to their knees by the force of an explosion overhead, and they clumsily clambered into the dark room as the roof of the tunnel cracked and then collapsed behind them under the weight of the target building. Along with the dirt and dust and noise of the collapse, a lone revealing ray of light pierced into the dark chamber.

"We're done!" Ricard muttered of the eight now-visible creatures staring back, their fur thick and black and bloodied, their eyes yellow and snouts boar-like, and their extraordinarily large bodies a bizarre blend of wolf and bear.

He backed up against the wall with Aika to his left.

"Well, what you waiting for, Princess—an invitation?" he growled, and she fired at the closest, provoking it to charge.

Two more arrows and its momentum slowed enough for Ricard to place his axe between its brows, but hardly had they dispatched the first when the others pelted forward in tandem, greedy and eager to tear into their new victims. It was only on the precipice of assured death did the beasts halt mid-flight, their grotesque expressions stolen by confusion and internal conflict.

Equally confounded, the duo stared silently at the odd scene, unable to determine what exactly they witnessed, and then they gawked in relief and shock at the man who emerged from the shroud.

"Joseph!" Aika whispered in disbelief, her mind and body still braced for the imminent attack.

"Well, are you coming?" he asked cheekily.

"Sensible suggestion, but should we not finish the critters off before they snap out of whatever it is that currently binds them?" Ricard said and raised his axe to snorts of anger and fright from the paralysed beasts.

"Don't be so cruel," came a voice from the shroud.

"Evia!" Aika called in delight.

"Who else? Now, as Joseph mentioned, can we please get moving? These creatures are strong-willed and can't be held long."

Wary of the crazed eyes and laboured breaths that tracked their movements, they edged between the beasts and over the bloodied remains on the floor towards Evia and together vacated the chamber into a maze of abandoned corridors, staircases, and rooms, each more brightly lit and more elaborately decorated than the last.

"What is this place?" Aika asked as they entered a room adorned with large, moss-covered windows on the walls and roof and where overgrown flower beds swallowed a line of elegant couches and stone fountains long ago dried up.

"It's a green room and the outer reaches of the palace," Joseph responded.

"The palace?" Ricard interjected.

"Yes, the east wing of the grounds. Don't worry, though. This wing was long ago abandoned, and we're a ways away from the explosions."

"I lost the connection!" Evia interrupted as they breached a glass door into an open-air courtyard.

"I was wondering when you lot would get out," Dogner greeted. "Good to see you found the little one in one piece and the lad, though he's a bit softer than I remember."

"Dogner?" Ricard grinned at the big man with his war hammer and shield in hand. "What a pleasure it is to see the old marine general in the flesh."

"Sight for sore eyes, I know." He laughed and embraced Ricard.

Faint growls emanated from deep inside the building and put them on edge.

"It won't be long before they track us," Evia muttered, winded from the rush. "Did you find us another way out, Dogner?"

"I did, but it doesn't take us from the thick of the action. There's too much happening on the streets."

"The East Gate will be our only sure way out at this point," Ricard added. "The other gates will soon be locked down, if not already."

"East is where we want," Evia said.

Aika spoke up as they readied to leave. "And Xander?"

"We can't help her."

"What do you mean? We're here for her, the city's in turmoil, and now you're joined with us. We can still find her and get her out, if you give it a try and locate her."

"No, we can't help her where she's gone," Evia said. "She's on her own until she returns to us."

"Wait—what? Then why coordinate with the twins to locate her?" Aika said with growing frustration. "Why have them direct me and Ricard down here to pull her out if we're not going to follow through? Why are you in the city, if not for her?"

"To help find her and rescue her, but as it turns out, she's found what she's been searching for all this time."

"How could you know this?" Aika asked with more anger than intended.

"Moments ago, and only by pure chance, I felt her presence deep under the city at a crossroad. We can't follow her down this path. She must go it alone and overcome the test that protects the shard."

"But—"

"Our ability to interfere with this particular journey of hers, beyond what I've done already, is severely limited. You must trust me on this."

Aika didn't budge.

"I'm sorry, Aika. We really haven't the time to discuss this further. You will have to take my word for it."

The girl nodded, but her sadness and loyalty to Xander was unwaveringly clear.

CHAPTER 64

Moments earlier—The cold air stung M. K.'s skin and burned his lungs, and his wasted legs stumbled and dragged as he attempted to walk the main street with some semblance of dignity and pride, but weeks confined to the humid rot of the cell, wearing the same clothes and with minimal nutrition, had left him weak and vulnerable and putrid. In the face of his accusers and the lined masses of brainwashed insects subservient to their new tyrant, he felt everything but his former self.

He glanced behind to Aiden's daughter, Gloria, and sadness and pity took him at the disfigured face of the once-beautiful girl. So young and righteous, and to be punished as such for standing up to tyranny. How he seethed at the injustice, but how helpless he was to right the wrong. He balled his fists in a weak grip before dizziness crept up from the overexertion.

The short distance to the forum in his deteriorated state drained him like the endurance races of his childhood, and he found himself unexpectantly longing for the destination. In fact, it was with some relief that he spotted the stage in the centre of the square, all prepped and awaiting their arrival.

A foolish grin took him. It was the grin of a man that had not only come to terms with his less-than-stellar fate but one that almost rejoiced in its proximity. "Who would've thought?" he murmured.

The square and adjoining roads were saturated with soldiers and civilians, their collective gaze intent on the prisoners as they were marched onto the stage for all to see. About to struggle up the stairs, M. K. was shoved to his knees.

"Couldn't let me go in peace, I see," he muttered over the roar of the thirsty crowd.

"No, that would be too good for you, you little cretin," Erzse said. "No, I want my face to be the last thing you see."

He stared at the witch and the man in the silver mask standing beside her.

"Seems you're getting everything you wanted, Erzse, including my life."

"Nearly. Still a couple of loose ends that need addressing."

"Will you address them also through breach of the law, or will you for once try to use a bit of honesty in your dealings?" he jibed.

She laughed. "What could you possibly mean?"

"The farce of my trial, for one."

"There was a trial, and you were found guilty of plotting to assassinate a government official."

"Always the liar," he said with pity. "And since when did capital punishment become a means of enforcing Anemoi's laws?"

"Since you committed treason against your prime minister."

"Last time I checked, Aiden's prime minister."

"Not for long."

"Venom, Erzse, that's all you spit every time you open that withered crap hole of yours."

Anger took her expression, but she held calm.

"Good luck on the other side to you and your little friends," she whispered into his ear and then nodded to the guards to proceed.

M. K. didn't flinch under the judgment of the blurred masses as the coarse rope tightened around his neck. No, he would deny the ignorant plebs the satisfaction and amusement of watching a beggar's lynching. He would stand proud and strong, knowing he did right. An accuser to his left retched on the floor, the stench of bile quick to take to the wind. M. K. forced his head to the right in search of reprieve, and there he saw Gloria, her face broken but somewhat calm, her gaze unflinching as it bore into the crowd.

Footsteps brought him back to, and he eyed the grim executioner making the rounds.

"All's in place," the executioner grunted to the mediator.

The mediator's sneer appeared all the more menacing due to his scarring. "Citizens of Zyphyr, the prisoners you see before you have been found guilty of attempted murder and treason against none other than Anemoi's deputy prime minister and this great city's senior minister, Lady Erzse, and as such, all shall be put to death as defined by our laws," he crowed to the excited delight of the crowd, their ignorant screams and shouts and curses deafening to the accused.

The mediator signalled the executioner to grip the lever that would open the boards and sentence the accused to death by suffocation, if they were unlucky, or death by broken neck, if they were lucky, and several of the accused started to plea and cry.

"Hush, have some honour!" M. K. roared, but their fear rendered them deaf. "Fools!"

He closed his eyes and tensed in silent anticipation, waiting for the board underneath to give way, but instead found himself abruptly roused by explosions from the direction of the courthouse. The mass of people stirred in confusion and then panic as the barracks also exploded in a cloud of rock and fire.

Cries rang out from the soldiers, and he spotted Erzse and her bodyguards moving along the road to the palace, her captains yelling orders to protect the ministers. Hope took hold in his stomach, and he saw the same light shine in the others. And the disfigured girl, she stared into the crowd, but it wasn't despair or hopelessness that had taken her. No, she stared at one man in particular.

M. K. flinched as a series of explosions hit the palace with such force that the flimsy trapdoor vibrated worryingly underfoot. More soldiers flocked out of the square towards the mayhem, leaving a thin guard and a rapidly dispersing mob of panicked spectators. He had shifted his head in search of a better view when a dozen arrows flew from the sparse crowd and instantly felled the remaining guards and executioner.

"Get them down!" the man from the audience shouted, and five men wearing concealed cavalry armour ascended the stage and cut the prisoners loose whilst another two hundred or so formed a precautionary barrier on the north and west flanks.

With much of the square evacuated, M. K. noticed that the two dozen archers dressed in the most recent fad plaguing Zyphyr's streets closely resembled Aika in facial appearance. Of course, squeezed amongst the masses of a renowned trading centre and within a square that held thousands, their presence wouldn't have been suspicious.

"Aiden." M. K. smiled excitedly at the emotional man embracing his daughter, but before the spymaster could respond in kind, another explosion erupted from the East Gate. "You attack the city?"

"I have another five hundred men securing us a way out in the east, not including your militia that bomb and attack multiple targets north and west of here, creating chaos and diversion. Erzse will have her—"

"Her what? Hands full?" M. K. laughed, but Aiden didn't laugh. Instead, seriousness and disbelief gripped his features, and he suddenly fumbled for speech.

"Pull back!" he bellowed. "Pull back to the East Gate!"

M. K. looked around and tensed.

"How's that possible? She must've known," M. K. said, shocked by the organised mass of soldiers converging on the square from the roads north and west.

But Aiden no longer listened, barking orders to pull back and hold the road east. "And get my daughter out of here," he called to the nearest captain.

The man nodded, and he and two others carried the weakened girl to the road and climbed the only mounts in sight.

"No more horses?" M. K. questioned, though he suspected the reason: Aiden had committed too many soldiers to make concealment of the mounts within the city a feasible option; securing his daughter's safety with an overwhelming first strike against an unprepared party was his first priority. Commanding his men throughout the withdrawal was his second.

"Archers, form up behind the line," Aiden yelled, and he gripped M. K.'s underarm. "Despite our differences, old boy, I won't let them take you without a fight. You can count on it."

"Thanks, brother," M. K. said sternly. "But you shouldn't be here. You're the prime minister. If she catches or kills you, she will have free rein. At the least, command away from the line."

"Prime minister in name only, old boy, and it's only a matter of time before a knife finds my back. Besides, can't let you lot have all the fun," he said with a smirk, though his unease was clear.

They had made it only two blocks when Erzse's army engaged, and with the momentum of so many soldiers largely unaffected by the volleys of the archers, the retreating group's primary advantage showed to be the confined width of the street, which forced Erzse's line to match Aiden's man for man.

"She'll send men down the roads running parallel and try and cut us off at the crossroad junctions between here and the East Gate." M. K. gasped, already seriously winded from the exertion.

"I factored in the possibility of a fighting retreat. The bulk of my men are in the roads to the north and south of this one. They'll fight to prevent her outflanking us."

M. K. nodded, but he felt doubt against such overwhelming odds and desperately wished he had his weapons and fighting strength.

Every block brought with it fierce clashes on the line and in the wings, and even with Erzse's unusual lack of cavalry, and the defenders' frequent use of explosives and archers against her tight infantry formation, the defenders' numbers bled out hard and fast.

"We won't hold much longer," M. K. said. "We're down to forty, and the archers won't last if dragged into the melee."

Aiden glanced ahead to the East Gate and cursed. "We'll hold the seven blocks. There's no alternative." He motioned to his captain. "If they're ready, split the horsemen at the gate and bring them to the line. And, Captain, make sure my daughter is clear of the wall and on the road to Bulgar."

The arrival of fifty horsemen three blocks from the gate was all that saved the small group of survivors from complete annihilation, driving the attacking infantry back and shoring up the diminished line that now consisted primarily of the archers and a trickle of reinforcements from the wings.

"Sir! The northern wing has collapsed!" shouted an officer as they reached the crossroad junction of the third- and second-to-last block. "They'll try and cut us off at the next crossroad."

"Damn it!" Aiden cursed. "That's two hundred men gone."

"You can dwell later. Break the line and let us run the last two blocks," M. K. said.

"You'll not make it in your state!" Aiden looked to the second row of horsemen and called.

A young soldier, already bloodied, trotted to their moving position.

"Take the minister and the other prisoners to the gate and bring up the remaining horsemen to the last crossroad junction," Aiden ordered. "Do whatever you can to secure it."

The beckoned horsemen yanked M. K. and the prisoners up and sped towards the gate, leaving Aiden to sound a running retreat.

The square of the East Gate was littered with torn bodies and the mangled remnants of the gate's metal door. The soldier quickly relayed Aiden's order to the fifty waiting horsemen, and they rode off west towards the last junction, leaving in the square thirty archers and their captain, all of whom resembled Aika—men and women whose bodies were long and slender, their skin pale and hair dark, and their features sharp and angular. Unlike the ones in the forum, this group wore the garments of the forest people. And unbeknownst to M. K., the captain was Aika's kin, her cousin—Ratin—and the accompanying contingent was his elite guard.

A lone watchman stood beside a dozen men attending barrels under the gate's stone arch, and just outside waited hundreds of riderless mounts, all prepped to go. M. K. nodded in admiration for Aiden's planning but turned worriedly to the growing commotion from the west.

"They won't hold it," Ratin called with alarm as Erzse's forces entered the last crossroad junction from the street to the north and engaged the horsemen still awaiting Aiden's arrival.

"Can you cover the crossroad from this distance?" M. K. asked.

"Not without risk to Aiden's men."

"Cavalry comes from the north!" the lone watchman shouted to their immediate dismay. He pointed down the road running north along the inside of the city's wall.

"How many?" M. K. called and scavenged a spear, sword, and shield from one of the fallen guards, unwilling to pass without a fight, however futile.

"Fifty, three blocks down," the watchman responded. "They'll breach the square within two minutes."

"Damn it! Archers, form your line!"

Ratin nodded, and he and his men jogged to the edge of the square and formed across the mouth of the road north, but no sooner had they drawn their bows than the horsemen holding the last crossroad junction to the west faltered and then melted under a violent hit from the street to the south.

"The south wing's collapsed. He's cut off!" M. K. managed just as Aiden and his men, exhausted and on the back foot, reached the turmoil of the last junction.

With only a handful of horsemen still mounted, the rest either dead or fighting on foot, and a small number of arrowless archers brandishing knives, the final gasp for life was violent but brief. And though the tenacity with which Aiden and his men pushed east sparked hope, the eventual sea of Erzse's colours rapidly pouring down the road from the junction towards the East Gate told a tale of defeat.

"Get outside the gate!" M. K. bellowed to the men finalising the barrels and the archers awaiting a still-too-distant cavalry charge from the north. "Aiden is dead. The battle is lost. Get out now!"

Ratin cursed, and indecision took him even as M. K. and the others started for the exit.

"What are you doing? Hurry!" M. K. shouted.

Ratin pulled his elite guard out of formation, but rather than retreat through the gate, he led them to the centre of the square and ordered them to draw their bows against the swarm approaching from the west, firing volley after volley into the infantry charge.

"Fool!" M. K. spat, perplexed as to why the man chose to stand his ground rather than run, all whilst leaving his flank undefended against the cavalry approaching from the north.

M. K. tensed as Erzse's infantry smashed into the front line of archers, and the captain and his men launched themselves aggressively into the fray, a somewhat strange spectacle given thirty lightly armoured archers currently stood defiantly against the brunt of Zyphyr's garrison, and with what motive he knew not.

Brought to attention by the racket of the approaching cavalry from the north, M. K. cursed and clambered to the gate, glancing back as the horsemen approaching from the north breached the square and veered towards the archer captain and his withered contingent. But rather than hit the archers from the rear with an almighty crash, the cavalry engaged Erzse's infantry, breathing life into the archers' withdrawal.

"Aika!" M. K. exclaimed, shocked by the presence of the girl on the lead horse and beside her, Ricard, Dogner, and Wiston. Behind them a wedge of elite Eurencian horsemen.

The four of them shot and trampled and skewered any man unlucky to enter their sphere, expertly directing the retreat whilst keeping the attackers at bay. Meanwhile, Joseph and Evia broke from the unit and pulled up to his position. About to greet the exhausted man, they turned abruptly to animalistic cries emanating from the way they had come.

"They've caught up," Joseph said and then turned to M. K. and Evia. "You two, get through the gate. I'll urge the others." He looked to the barrels and the soldier prepping the fuse. "Make sure he blows the gate once we're through."

M. K. nodded and jogged clumsily behind Evia, motioning to the soldier to wait for the survivors to pass before lighting the fuse. He instinctively directed the soldiers previously attending the barrels to stand ready to support and ordered the weary prisoners to mount the nearest horses. Together, they watched the ensuing melee with apprehension and dread, ready to flee at a moment's notice.

The near collapse of the retreating line's right flank was not immediately clear to those standing outside the gate, but it quickly became apparent when a wave of fear and desperation erupted across both sides under the indiscriminate slaughter by the creatures from the palace wing. Even the horses outside the gate jittered uncomfortably at the grotesque smell accompanying the arrival.

"Aika!" Ratin roared as a beast knocked the princess to the ground.

He threw himself over her and swiftly downed the creature with a single swipe of his blade expertly directed at the jugular whilst his archers pelted the next with the remainder of their arrows. His action bought time for Aika to rise, and she drew Xander's golden blade and felled two infantrymen on her flank, but she was then unwillingly absorbed into the funnel of retreating horsemen and pushed from her brethren towards the outer side of the gate.

"Ratin, fall back!" she yelled over the messy ruckus, but he was knocked to the ground by one of Wiston's retreating horsemen and, in his attempt to right himself, slashed in the chest by a beast.

The remnants of the unit drove towards their fallen captain, but try as she might to join them, Aika found herself gripped by three Eurencian soldiers at Evia's beckoning.

"We need to blow the barrels!" Wiston called to M. K. before impaling another attacker with his spear. "Before they overrun the fuse!"

"You can't blow it!" Aika screamed to M. K.'s dismay, but with Wiston's men on the back foot, cut off from the small island of rapidly dying archers and the weight of Erzse's infantry concentrated on that point, it was simply a matter of time.

"Sorry, Aika," M. K. whispered under his breath. "Soldier, blow the arch!"

The man gladly obeyed, touching torch to gunpowder and giving them only ten seconds to struggle clear of the arch. The explosion was brutal, and the force knocked the majority of them to the ground. Those still under the stone arch, a mixture of friendlies and foes, died instantly under the crush. And those of Erzse's men who had followed outside the gate, and who were now cut off, were unsympathetically cut down.

"We could've saved him!" Aika screamed at M. K.

She charged at him but was held in check by Wiston and Ricard.

"He did what he needed to, Princess. We couldn't have reached your cousin if we tried," Ricard said sternly.

"Cousin?" M. K. said, stunned by the revelation. "I'm sorry, Aika. I truly—"

"You bastard!" she screamed again.

"Aika!" Evia scolded.

"Cavalry, to the south!" Dogner called, pointing to the shadow growing from the southeast corner of the city's walls.

"Erzse rides at the front," Joseph observed.

"She's come to hunt us down," Ricard muttered.

"Then we must ride to Bulgar. We cannot linger," Evia said.

Wiston turned to the thirty survivors of his unit. "We ride for Bulgar. Gather fresh mounts. We will not stop until we're on the boat." He turned to the prisoners and the remnants of Aiden's men. "I suggest you do the same. You're more than welcome on my ship. But hurry. Time is precious."

"And how fortunate we are that Aiden left us an army of fresh mounts," Ricard said as he tied two to his own.

"One for every man who died inside those walls," M. K. said sadly, struggling atop one that could hold his bulk. "I only hope the men of my militia made it out safe." Though he suspected otherwise.

"Riders from the east!" one of the soldiers called.

"I count a hundred," Ricard added.

"I don't recognise the banners," Dogner called.

"I do," Ricard murmured, surprise and fear etched into his expression.

"The shadow warriors," Wiston said, astonished.

"They've come for Xander. We must engage them!" Evia called with alarm and drew her blade.

"You lot!" Wiston called to Aiden's men. "Take the spare mounts and ride behind us. Everybody else, form on me!"

CHAPTER 65

That evening; Zyphyr, Zylencia—Xander stared at the impasse in front of her—a frozen waterfall of mud and roots and rocks born from the roof of the cave, the culmination of her hurried trek back across the magma bridge and through the heart of the mountain with its ancient, rudimentarily built paths and cottages and markets and temples and walls. Villages and hamlets under the crypts, cellars, and dungeons of Zyphyr, all long ago abandoned and destined to the recesses of forgotten history, cut off from time by the blockade she now frustratingly faced.

"I can't go back, not now. Besides, the only other way out I know takes me back into that cell…or through the underworld," she said and slumped to the ground in an exhausted heap. In her daze, she removed her gauntlet and looked at her hand. "Minimal scarring, but the truth is anything but… What will the others think when they see it?"

She closed her eyes, desiring to see their reality, and she shuddered when she reopened them to a decayed hand, the weathered bone partially visible through the web of rotted flesh.

"At least the ring still fits," she said sarcastically and put on the gauntlet. "I only want to see their reality, lest I forget what I am. I shan't reimagine it as the hand it once was."

A noise drew her gaze to the top of the natural blockade. Wearily, she climbed the nearly vertical wall to the very top, and careful not to fall, she grabbed the boulder that had caught her eye and heaved it from the soft mud that encapsulated it, letting it fall to the cave bottom with a loud thud.

"A way forward and another tight fit," she said of the pothole that housed a faint light and the wisps of the cool, fresh air more common above ground than under.

The struggle of the crawl sapped the last of her energy reserves, and it was with sheer will alone that she was able to pull herself through the cramped quarters and emerge from a small opening at the base of Zyphyr's defensive wall onto the cold, windswept field of the city's eastern flank. Long and hard did she bask in the dissolution of the shackles that had bound her mind and the weight of the mountain that had confined her being, staring across the grass into the dark sky of the setting sun. Suddenly, she beamed joyfully.

"Aes…you found me." She laughed warmly and let him nuzzle her neck as she stroked his. "To Bulgar, you say? Okay!"

The chilly wind stung her paled skin as they rode east along the meadow before veering towards the road once a safe distance from the city's watch. The soggy mud of the throughfare had been torn by a vast number of fresh hoofprints in both directions, and the once-picturesque view of the black city had been tainted by the destruction wrought on the East Gate and the fires that still ravaged the city's interior.

A distant flicker of gold from the slush of the ground caught her attention, but it was the countless dead men and horses strewn around and beyond it that made her gasp. All had been stripped of their armour and cloth, their fair, naked bodies left to the devices of nature.

"What these people must've done to be undeserving of burial…"

She climbed down from Aes, and the two of them slowly meandered through the bodies, eyes intent for any clue as to who the victims or assailants were. But they could find none, bar the fractured remains of a sword not unlike a butcher's knife and a silver coin with a hole in the centre.

"The coin's Cresedi," she said, holding it up close. "But does that mean Gorzan and his soldiers were here, looking for me?"

She took in the lifeless bodies, forever exposed.

"And them—these men, are they being punished?"

Again, the gold flicker beckoned, drawing her from immediate thought. She edged towards it, increasingly keen to see what pulled her in. Standing over it, she gasped.

"It's my blade."

Submerged in the mud, only the smallest sliver of its tip was exposed. Confused as to how it got there, and no less eager to grasp it in her hand once more, she excitedly heaved it from the muck. But like a vicious gash to the chest, the respite was ripped from her bosom as waves of black abruptly tarnished the gold weapon in her dead grip.

Heart heavy, eyes glistening, and unable to look away from her decrepit hand, sadness carried in her voice. "It's truly a curse to have stained something so pure and so beautiful." She wiped her cheeks and looked at Aes. "What's it doing out here?"

He didn't know.

Angst wormed its way into her. "Could it have been Evia or maybe the others?"

He couldn't be sure.

Dread tore into her. Frantically, she examined every cold, lifeless face for familiarity, until her back ached and her head pounded. She recognised none of the slain. And still, it wasn't enough to calm the unbearable unknown weighing on her. Desperate for an answer, she reached out and tried to locate the whispers of her aunt's mind or any other she might know or recognise, searching as far and wide as possible in her state. But still, nothing.

It was a suddenly very lonely world with just her and Aes, and it took the repetition of his soothing voice to pierce her despair. She nodded grudgingly, knowing it would do her no good to linger in so dangerous a place.

"Bulgar it is."

End of Book Two

Thank you for reading!
If you enjoyed *A Hand for an Eye*, please consider leaving a short review.
It makes a real difference and helps other readers discover the story.
Xander's journey continues in the next book in *The Rose of Anemoi* series.

AUTHOR BIOGRAPHY

Born in the United Kingdom to a Guyanese mother and an English father, Haydn spent his formative years hopping between the Pacific Islands, Middle East, Central America, and the Caribbean to the tune of his father's job. Now based in New York City, Haydn has found the inspiration to write from his fascination with, and ability to become lost in, the worlds of fantasy and sci-fi. It is the perfect escape from his career in corporate finance.